THE PATH OF SAINTS

a novel by
Ross Inman

Sixth Ring Publishing Company, Inc. 2010

The Path of Saints
Published through Sixth Ring Publishing Company, Inc.

Interior Book Design and Layout by
www.integrativeink.com

ISBN 978-0-984-43580-7
Library of Congress Catalog Card Number: 2010901055

For my mom

THE PATH OF SAINTS

DAY 30

   Nish looked up to find a plane floating through the dark clouds over the graveyard. He remembered a story his mom had told him once about a man she knew who died because his heart exploded; he'd thought it sounded like a pretty good way to go. He imagined himself on the flight hanging above the cemetery as his heart burst out of his chest. There was enough love inside of him to rip the plane in half and drop it out of the sky.

   The killer cocked the hammer. Nish put his hand behind him to brace himself, his fingers sinking deep into the soil of the freshly filled grave. He looked again for the plane and heard a split second of the explosion before everything went black.

DAY 1

The lights in the whorehouse were so low that Nish couldn't tell if the thing sitting across from him was alive. It looked like a wax statue of an old Mexican witch doctor that had melted over the arms of a ratty brown chair until it was impossible to tell where her loose folds of skin ended and the seat began. Nish lifted his hand and snapped his fingers to get a reaction. A noise came from the statue like it had swallowed something and didn't like its taste. The young man frowned, checking his cell phone to see how much longer he had to wait for his friend.

"I'm sure you're having a great chat in there," Nish yelled at the nearest door, "but you need to wrap it up in five minutes." He always got bored sitting around after he'd finished. When his coworkers would come out of their rooms to find him halfway through a magazine, he would explain that he wasn't unusually fast, just that he always chose the youngest of the new arrivals to avoid disease. So you feel that more, he'd nod his head, hoping the movement would become infectious.

"You know this guy in here," he tried to get the attention of the ancient curer across from him. "This guy doesn't even do anything. Not that I have a problem with that, it's only right for a family man. But he takes the whole hour just to talk," he stared at the old woman, digging his fingernail deep into the discolored cuticle of his thumb.

"He used to not even want to come in. Now, I'm stuck waiting on his ass. Only reason I put up with him is because he scares the shit out of me. Oversized motherfucker looks like he should be wearing a horned helmet and attacking some medieval town," Nish tore a piece of dead skin from his finger. "Plus, he's my ride."

"I can hear you out there," a voice came from behind the door.

"I know," Nish gave his thumb a rest, jabbing his nail into the cuticle of his pointer finger.

-Come here,- the old woman in the chair croaked in Spanish, flicking a twisted finger towards her face. Nish lowered his head like a pit bull about to attack.

-No English?- he asked in her language.

-No.-

4

Pushing himself up from the deep chair, he made his way across the dark room towards the crone. As he neared, he could make out the milkiness of her blind eyes.

"Fucking nasty," he commented like there was a friend of his in the room and the old woman was deaf. She motioned him closer. As he hesitantly neared the curer, the smell of rotten teeth grew stronger.

-Over there,- she pointed to a table that looked barely strong enough to hold the dim lamp lighting its surface. On it sat a metal box with a Day of the Dead scene etched into the top. A tree blossomed from the desert, its trunk made of bones and its leaves made of skulls. The skeleton of a bird perched on a human branch with musical notes coming from its mouth.

-What is this?- Nish asked in Spanish, keeping his eyes on the top.

-Inside.-

He opened the box to find an empty metal interior. "What the fuck?"

-From the other side of the River Brave,- the woman motioned to him, -Is yours.-

Nish put the box down and stepped back from the table, picking his canine with his fingernail. "Fuck that," he stood in front of the woman again. "Voodoo shit doesn't work on me, lady. I'm Presbyterian," his cell phone cut him off. Checking the number, he turned his back on her. "I've got to take this."

"I only got a month to live? That's bullshit," Nish stepped off the curb, walking across the empty street towards the tank-sized truck. John followed in a daze, looking more dumbfounded than usual, Nish thought.

"You remember Heather, Chris Upton's girlfriend?" John asked. Nish walked to the passenger's side, "Yeah, what about her?"

"That lady in there told Chris that his girlfriend would gain a great fortune. You remember what happened last year?" he stared at his manager intently.

Nish inspected the gray sky above as he answered absentmindedly, "I don't know, what?"

"She won the lottery, man," John whispered barely loud enough to be heard. "The girl won the goddamn lottery." He waited for the gravity of this to hit home. Nish looked back at him like he was just realizing the giant had been speaking.

"The lottery, man!" John pleaded with him.

The dark sky seemed to be waiting, gathering strength. "First, Heather didn't win the lottery. She won a few thousand bucks on a scratch-off. Just because she was able to keep herself in cigarettes and wine coolers for a week or two without having to go to work at the restaurant doesn't make her rich. And secondly, some old lady making money off superstitious dumbasses isn't reading the future, it's just taking advantage of weak-minded motherfuckers," he made sure his polo shirt was tucked into the front of his jeans. He loved the way clothes hung off him after sex, he guessed because they had been worn already that day. "That's why I didn't pay. She tells someone they're going to learn a great lesson or some shit and then the guy goes around looking for it until he tricks himself into believing the universe has taught him something. It's ridiculous."

Shaking his head, the giant unlocked the doors to easily climb in. Nish opened his door and was about to lift himself up into the cab when something hit him. A drop of water sat perfectly on the back of his hand like a tiny crystal dome. He looked up at the heavy clouds hanging low over the city but didn't see any others follow.

"I don't know, man," John started the truck. "The lottery."

The water fell from the back of his hand as Nish hoisted himself in.

They drove through a maze of streets that only the locals and a few like them were able to navigate. The houses all looked basically the same to Nish, broken windows covered with plastic, Christmas lights turned on to take attention away from spots where the paint was coming off in chunks, even a -Happy New Year 2005- sign in Spanish no one had bothered to take down after four months. Nish had begun to think it was normal for people to paint the Virgin of Guadalupe on the sides of their cars next to their last names. He and his coworker might know their way around, he thought, but they couldn't look more out of place. Teenagers hanging out on the sidewalk would notice them, then quickly avert their eyes. Young mothers would push their strollers further from the street and keep their babies out of view. A popular country song came on the radio, prompting John to let out a holler.

"I tell you my sister went to school with this guy?" John smiled like he'd totally forgotten the witch doctor's prediction just minutes earlier.

"We need to hurry up, it sounded serious."

"Always worrying about business," the giant grinned.

"Better to worry about that than supernatural bullshit." Nish's phone vibrated again. "And here we go."

"Rusty needs to calm his ass down. You, too, if you don't mind me saying. Give yourself a heart attack you keep up like this."

Sending the call to voicemail, Nish squinted out the window. Just a little bit longer, he thought, then back to the real world. A regular job where he worked at a desk with a computer. His boss would come around in the morning and comment on the headlines of that day's paper. He readjusted his weight in the seat and tapped his front teeth together. "Rusty needs to grow up and assume some responsibility. We can't keep holding his hand," he looked at John to nod his head in agreement but the giant just watched the road. Nish put the phone back in his pocket, "And if I have to hear one more time about how he was in a fight club, I swear to God I'll go crazy."

"He's a pretty big guy."

"He looks like a dinner roll with a face. Motherfucker is ninety percent body fat."

John was silent for a few seconds, then shrugged, "My wife was watching this show yesterday about the obese and how stress eating is a big problem."

"Unless the guy is an air traffic controller in his spare time, I seriously doubt that's the issue," Nish looked at his friend, who continued staring out the windshield. "Because that's a high stress job." Nish waited again.

"Uh huh," John turned up the radio.

"Tough crowd."

The car rolled to a stop at an intersection where a shirtless fat man covered in hair and tattoos sat on a crate, a cigar in his mouth and two little boys buzzing in orbit around him. The man looked up at Nish and smiled, removing two sparklers from the back of his pants. He handed them to the boys, who were jiggling with excitement, and raised his lighter to the tips of the fireworks. The lighter sparked and failed, then sparked and failed again. The boys moaned in agony at the downfall of their hero. The smile fell off the fat man's face as he threw the lighter onto a small pile of trash next to him on the sidewalk. He took the cigar out of his mouth to spray thick brown saliva onto the concrete; after staring at the juice for a second, the smile slowly returned. Grabbing the sparklers, he pressed the lit end of the cigar to their tips. The fireworks exploded and the children did the same, running circles around the man and shouting out their love for him. The fat man looked back at the truck and Nish remembered a time when he had gone hunting and shot a quail through the chest. Its feathers were matted with blood so he grabbed the bird with both hands to pull at the disfigured mass until the skin tore apart to reveal a flawless mound of smooth muscle. It looked so clean and beautiful that he wanted to bite into it right then.

The man on the crate kept his eyes fixed on Nish, spitting on the ground in front of the truck. Nish stared back and picked his teeth until the light changed.

"And why do fortune tellers always have to be blind?" he turned to the driver again. "If I were them, I'd check out what eye surgeries they have going on in the future. Bring back some technology and heal my blind ass."

John looked pensively out the window for a few seconds as if in deep thought, then nodded. Nish relaxed back into his seat.

The howling coming from inside the refrigeration unit was audible from the door of the warehouse. Rusty stood in hip waders, spitting tobacco juice into a nearly filled plastic bottle. When the two walked in, he quickly wiped the dribble from his mouth to greet them. "Nish, John," he nodded at each in turn.

"Hey Rusty," John shook his colleague's moist hand. Nish crossed his arms.

"Those necessary?" Nish looked at the hip waders. Rusty nodded to his manager, "Oh yeah." The young man pointed to a mound of bloody towels next to the unit. "Reckon y'all might want to throw some on. Save them pants."

If the situation were that bad, Nish thought, he'd be burning the pants anyway. "I'll stay dry and let you have all the fun. Throw down some plastic we can have them stand on." He looked to see if the unit could be turned on its back so they could climb out the top but determined it wouldn't work. "What the fuck happened?"

"Looks like one of them killed another," Rusty answered.

Nish rolled his eyes, "Well shit, I guess we can pack it up and go home. Fucking forensic team's on the case."

Rusty let out a quick laugh as he went to fetch the plastic to spread on the concrete floor. "Heard your truck pulling up," he said to John over his shoulder. "Running like a scalded ape, they fixed that shit up proper."

"Yep," the giant stared at the unit with Nish. When Rusty was done he turned to his manager. John did the same.

"Well," Nish motioned to the unit, "open it."

"Alright then," Rusty spat onto the covered floor as he neared the transporter. Putting both hands on the primary latch, he pulled to open the door the full six inches.

First came the blood, sliding over the plastic to form in dark pools. A single deep red arm shot out of the unit, squirming like a dying rattlesnake. Another followed and soon the door was filled with writhing bloody limbs grabbing frantically at the air in front of them.

Sidestepping the growing red lake, John got close enough to the unit to get a hand on the bar that prevented it from opening all the way.

"Get our pistols out," he warned. Nish did so while Rusty fished for his weapon in the hip waders. John banged on the side of the unit.

-I am opening the door. Nobody run, understand?- he spoke in twangy Spanish, causing the moans to get louder in response. He hit the bar and the door flew open in a burst of red soaked bodies clawing at each other to escape. The first on the ground was a middle-aged woman, crying and screaming at the top of her lungs for Jesus to save her. She ran two steps from the unit before she slipped on the wet plastic and fell flat on her face. The eighteen others behind her did the same, creating piles of half naked humanity trying to get away from whatever was in the unit. The woman got up, running a few feet only to fall and slide towards Rusty.

-Please, not myself do you hurt! Please!- she pleaded in Spanish, her hand reaching out to the young man.

"Get the fuck back!" Rusty answered in English, kicking her hard in the top of the head with his boot. He raised his pistol to address the group. "All of you, stay the fuck where you are!"

The woman collapsed to the plastic. Her hands ran through her matted hair down her body until they found her exposed breasts. She covered herself, sobbing as if she hadn't realized she was naked. Rusty spit brown juice on the woman, "Keep your spic ass on the ground."

"Shut the fuck up with that racist shit," Nish pointed at Rusty. The sight of so much blood brought saliva to his mouth. "And if I see you spit on anyone else, I'll knock your fucking teeth out."

The new worker's smile disintegrated. He nodded, turning quickly back to the group of people on the plastic to hide his red face from his manager.

When the unit was clear of the living, John poked his head in to find one man left, dead with his eye dangling from its socket and a chunk of his neck missing. "Looks almost like a coyote got hold of this one. Reckon one of them bit the other, ate at his neck."

A mound of crimson, slippery people had grown in the middle of the warehouse floor. As Nish counted them, he felt something touch his boot. He jumped back to find the hysterical woman Rusty had spat on reaching for his hand.

-Stay yourself,- he commanded in Spanish, pointing his pistol in her face. She crawled closer so he pushed her back with his boot. A yell rose from the mass of people. -Son of a bitch, I am going to kill you!- one of the bodies detached themselves. The man stood, much to Nish's surprise, and charged at him. The pistol grew heavier in Nish's hand. The man was ten feet away when the safety clicked off subconsciously. It clicked back on right before the man flew at him. Nish moved back and to the side to avoid the tackle but the Mexican was able to wrap him up and take him to the floor, covering his clothes in blood. Nish's head hit the ground, red satin needles exploding in his closed eyelids, the taste of pennies seeping into his mouth.

"Fuck!" Nish threw the man off of him. Before the Mexican had a chance to get up, Nish twisted around to kick him, catching him hard under the chin with the heel of his boot. The man's face went slack like a child staring at some breathtaking scene painted on the ceiling. Nish kicked him again in the chin and he fell limp.

"Look at this," Nish inspected himself as he scrambled to get to his feet. Rusty ran over, jumping on top of the unconscious man to slam the back of his head into the concrete floor. The woman screamed and tried to get up but fell again, this time causing her legs to splay open. She curled into a ball, crying for the man to stop beating her husband while the rest of the mass began to untangle itself and advance on Nish and Rusty. Out of the corner of his eye, Nish thought he saw something dart out the front door.

"You see that?" he yelled to John.

"Fuck this," the giant pointed his pistol at the ceiling and pulled the trigger. The group jumped at the sound, the screams dying down to a soft whimper as they stared at him. Nish's eyes immediately went to the door to see if anyone was outside.

-Stay yourselves. Understand?- John waited for the group to nod their heads. "Where are you going?" he asked Nish.

"I thought I saw one of them make a run for it," Nish picked up his pistol lying next to the wreckage of his attacker. Stepping over the halo of blood growing out of the unconscious man's skull, he headed towards the door.

"Paranoid son of a bitch," Rusty whispered under his breath. John leveled his pistol at the group, -Now, which of you did it?-

With the sun already melting onto the horizon, Nish knew he had to move quickly. He could have sworn he'd seen someone. A smaller person, maybe a woman, he thought. He scratched his head with a red arm before remembering he was covered in blood.

"Shit." The shirt was only a few months old but it would end up in the fireplace. With DNA testing, there wasn't a point in taking chances, he thought. Let the other guys make fun of him.

The buildings of downtown Dallas stood black against the orange sky, the last of the day's light illuminating the workplace where he'd spent most of his time over the past two years. In a month it's all over, he thought, reminding himself he should start working on his resume. He never had to put up with shit like this in the communications firm.

10

A noise rang out from behind one of the nearby storage facilities. His hand slid back to his pistol as he quietly ran to the building. Pressing his body against the wall, he gripped the firearm that he'd only used in target practice. He heard something coming closer to him. It seemed to move in an offbeat rhythm, like it was injured. He positioned his finger over the safety and exhaled, then swung around the corner.

"Goddamn!" the woman jumped back and raised her fists, trying to act like it was her natural reaction. "Shit, boy, you nearly gave me a heart attack!" She was wearing a promotional t-shirt from a charity race Nish was almost certain she didn't take part in; black spandex couldn't contain her disproportionate hips, causing cellulite to explode out of the top like lard-covered cauliflower. He noticed one of her sandals was broken so she had to squeeze her big toe and its neighbor together in order to keep it from falling off as she walked, giving her the appearance of a limp.

"What are you doing here, Liz?" he lowered the gun.

"Fixing to clean up these here storage facilities," she pointed to a dropped supplies bucket on the ground. Nish noticed a row of medical staples on the inside of her arm; the skin around the metal and scabs had turned an unnatural color.

"You know I take whatever hours Deaf will give me since I lost my job down at the supermarket," she looked at him like he was stupid.

He nodded, prompting a one-sided discussion in which she relayed her last bout with employment and her unfair termination. She was delving into the company's faulty policies regarding sex on the job when Nish thought he heard something move in a pile of scrap metal over her right shoulder.

"...So I told him, if you think that was the only guy I ever blew in the break room, you're about as stupid as you look! Yes, sir, I did tell him that. So then he started into this big speech about how he was my boss and I can't talk to him like that..." Liz continued as a small animal darted from the pile of metal. Nish eased his grip on the pistol.

"How old you think I am?" Liz cocked her head. Nish was suddenly snapped back into the conversation. She pulled the dyed hair back from her face, "Go on, take a shot in the dark."

"Thirty five," he guessed while he scanned the rest of the area. When he looked back at the woman, she had turned her face to the side and was playing with her bangs. Nish shrugged, "What...lower? Thirty." His comment was met with a sassy look that he figured was about as genuine as her boxing stance earlier.

"Fuck, Liz. Twenty-five, eleven, I have no fucking idea. Did you see someone run past here at all, like a woman?"

Her eyes fixed on his; he imagined he was supposed to feel bad for some reason. She picked up her bucket and walked off towards one of the storage facilities.

Nish took a step toward the scrap metal pile, allowing his finger to run over the safety of the weapon in his hand while he listened. He thought he heard a soft, rhythmic sound like a live body would make. He took a step closer.

"Nish!"

He spun around to see John coming out the front door, stretching casually like he had just woken up. The bottoms of his boots were covered in blood, leaving deep red footprints that got less pronounced as he neared his manager.

"Did one of them admit to killing the guy?" Nish took one last look at the pile of scrap metal.

"Nah. Tell you the truth, I don't reckon any of those people did it. They're all so scared. Usually, one of them does another in and the guy's bragging about it. But all of them just keep talking nonsense about some sort of animal or something. Maybe something climbed in through one of the ventilation holes, killed the guy, then climbed back out."

Nish shot him a look that made him rethink the possibility of this.

"Or not," John shrugged, embarrassed. "My wife says sometimes I overthink things."

"I'm sure that's the problem," Nish looked downtown at the red sky. "Let's get out of here."

"Sounds good to me. Queer's on his way over. He'll have his crew take care of that mess in there."

The two walked back to John's truck just as the last of the day's light was extinguished by the sparkling buildings eating at the sky. "Liz out here tonight?" John asked as he hopped in the cab.

Nish took off his bloody shirt and jeans, stuffing them in a trash bag. "Yeah, she's here."

"You going to burn those?"

"I'm burning all this shit. And if you were smart, you'd take my lead." He retrieved a pair of athletic shorts and a fresh t-shirt from his backpack to change into. As he pulled himself up into the cab, he thought he heard a noise come from under the tarp that covered the bed of the truck. "You hear that?"

"Nah, probably just that storm coming from over yonder," John looked behind them in the distance. "Supposed to be wet this next week."

The first drops of rain tap-danced on the windshield as if on cue. Closing the door, Nish was thankful he had a good excuse to use the fireplace that night so the neighbors wouldn't be suspicious.

DAY 2

Thunder shook the windows of the office building, causing the secretary to jump in her chair.

"Oh my Lord," she put a hand to her chest. Nish moved his mouth into a smile to make her laugh at herself, then went quickly back to gnawing at the dead skin around his thumbnail. He searched for reasons why the CEO would want to see him. Losing a piece of cargo had never been a big issue before. Besides, if they died in transit that was the Mexicans' problem, not theirs. The sky outside got dark enough for the streetlights to turn on. No reason at all, he thought, unless the old man had found out how much he'd been stealing. A little here and there was expected but he'd pushed the limits to retire early from the business. His mind recoiled at the thought of being retired even sooner.

"Saving up money for Holland," the secretary said. Nish realized he had been staring at a calendar with a windmill on it while thinking. The sky in the background of the picture was light blue with cotton ball clouds. He could move to the Netherlands, he figured. Nothing would follow him over the ocean. He could grow tulips and sit around all day under that beautiful sky.

The secretary put down her donut to wipe her hands, "My mom used to have a decorative plate from Holland. I want to take my little boy there." Nish raised the sides of his mouth again.

Rusty walked past the waiting area and saw him. "Working on a Saturday, huh?" he beamed from ear to ear.

"Yes."

"Alright," Rusty stood in front of his manager, placing his hands awkwardly in his pockets. Nish waited for him leave but the new employee became animated again.

"You see how I smacked that one son of a bitch yesterday? Just like when I was back in the fight club," Rusty reenacted the scene as the secretary suddenly became very involved in her work.

"Keep your voice down," Nish grabbed Rusty by his fat wrist to pull him into the closest chair. "You'll get us in trouble with that shit.

13

If you were unloading a box of oranges, would you just start smashing them open?"

Rusty shook his head like a little boy being scolded.

"I didn't think so. Because you'd want to protect your investment." Nish wondered how many redneck assholes in this line of work had let racist anger trump self-control throughout the years. He figured most of these people relished the ability to act out their aggression with no consequences.

"When NAFTA was developed, the idea was to have free trade on this continent, create a more equitably prosperous North America," he picked his cuticle with a vengeance. "It worked to some degree. Canada has a lot that America wants and America has shit everyone wants. But what does Mexico have?"

Rusty opened his mouth to guess but quickly closed it.

"Labor. Their chief export, what the United States has a strong demand for, is labor. And what do we do? We outlaw it. We'll sell them our goods and build our factories right inside the Mexican border and take advantage of them, but we make it illegal for them to really prosper as a nation the one way they can. Does that seem fair to you?"

"No, sir," Rusty frowned, shaking his head conscientiously.

"Democracy and capitalism, that's what makes America great. You let the people take the jobs they want to work for and pay them according to the free market," Nish bit down on the inside of his cheek, tearing some of the meat away to let the blood waft into his mouth.

The secretary cleared her throat, keeping her eyes on the computer screen. Nish sat back in his chair, embarrassed at the volume of his voice. "Remember that," he pointed one last time for emphasis, then dismissed his worker.

The rush of indignation slowly washed away, leaving only the anxiety of being called into the boss's office. Taking out his cell phone, he looked at the self-affirmations one of his books suggested he store there.

"Mr. Smith will see you now, Nish," the secretary smiled at him.

"Thanks," Nish winked at her jokingly. Important not to let people know what you're feeling, he thought.

"You're crazy," the girl laughed and took another bite of her donut. Nish thought it was a pity none of the women who worked for the real estate company were attractive but the old man's wife made sure of it. Unfortunately for her, word around the office was her husband didn't exactly have discriminating taste when it came to the ladies.

He opened the door to find Deaf facing the bulletproof window, reclined in his leather chair with his boots propped up on a file cabinet. The old man's wiry frame was deceiving; Nish had seen him pick up one side of an industrial lay-down freezer and move it around to drop it on a man's head. It busted the victim's skull like a nutcracker would a pecan, but juicier. Nish never looked at sliding door units the same way again.

"Nasty out," Deaf didn't bother turning around.

"Yes sir, it is," Nish walked to the desk. He stood next to the chair, not sure if he should sit down. A stuffed rattlesnake eyed him from the corner, waiting for the chance to jump back to life and strike. On the rear wall, the buttons of the serpent's brethren were mounted with dates and locations. Besides the trophies and a broken clock, the walls were empty.

"They say it's supposed to last for a week," Nish put himself out there again.

The old man just looked out the window, making Nish wonder if he shouldn't have said anything. After a few seconds, the boss rubbed his potbelly. Nish had always thought it looked odd on his frame, like a pregnant skinny woman.

"Have a seat."

"Thank you," Nish quickly obliged.

"What do you think about this new coffee place over yonder?" Deaf turned to face him, his finger pointing out the window.

"Oh, it's alright. I think they have some good lattes. Sometimes a little too much sugar, though," Nish scratched his neck nervously. "I mean, I like sugar as much as the next guy but sometimes if something's too sweet, the back of my teeth start to tingle a little."

The old man looked at him, expressionless.

"But that's just me," Nish wanted to gag himself. "What about you, sir? Do you like their coffee?"

After a few more seconds of staring, Deaf turned back to the window. Hatred for the old man clenched Nish's teeth shut.

"I haven't drank coffee since back in Korea," he reclined in his chair, kicking his boots up on the file cabinet again. "My daddy always said it was for queers, anyway. Real man doesn't need anything to wake him up in the morning except a good kick in the ass every now and again."

Nish sat frozen while Deaf reached to his desk and hit a button on his phone. The two sat in silence until the door opened.

Bill almost had to turn sideways to get through the doorway. He reminded Nish of a dog in his neighborhood growing up that looked so much like a wolf. With its size and the unhinged look of a wild predator, he wondered if the animal had escaped from the zoo. Bill was the same but more like a grizzly, he thought, shaved in certain areas to appear more human and left with only hair on top and a gray handlebar mustache. A short sleeve work shirt barely stretched over his gut, faded blue jeans hugged his tree trunk sized legs. He nodded at Nish as he took his position next to the young man's chair.

"What do you think of that new coffee place over yonder, Billy?" Deaf asked.

"Reckon it's doing pretty good. Seems to be getting a lot of traffic. Parking lot's always full, especially during the morning rush hour," Bill smoothed the hair around his mouth. "Commercial real estate how it is in this area, you can probably get twenty percent more when their lease is up."

"I was thinking twenty five," Deaf looked back at the director and smiled. Nish thought it might have been the first time he'd seen the man show happiness in his two years with the company.

"You're the boss."

The old man nodded as he turned back to the window. "Nish," Deaf said the name like it confounded his mouth, "That situation yesterday, you handled it alright. Except for that one."

"I'm sorry about that, sir. I figured since he died on the road, we wouldn't be liable."

The old man turned to Bill and the bear spoke up, "One was dead. Another was beaten to point he can't do much more than drool."

Nish felt blood rush to his head, making a mental note to hold Rusty accountable as soon he left the CEO's office. He decided to act like he knew about the man's serious injury so as not seem ignorant. "I'm sorry about that, sir. I'm dealing with Rusty."

"Boy's got a wild hair up his ass. Keep an eye on him," Deaf scratched his jaw. "But that's not why you're here." The old man contorted his face like he was sucking on his teeth, smiling broadly, then letting his leathery skin fall back into its permanent frown.

Nish felt the walls close in around him. He'd finally got caught, he realized, gripping the arms of the chair. He'd skimmed too much and now it was over; Billy was going to see to it personally. He felt like he was watching a movie screen with what his eyes broadcast, interested in what came next but able to walk out of the theater whenever he wanted.

"Need you to go down to the San Antonio office. Boy down there working for Junior may be acting up," Deaf looked up at Bill again and said flatly, "Drugs."

Nish closed his eyes in relief for a split second while the viewer in his brain laughed at how close the main character had gotten to being killed. He felt his muscles relax until he had to hold himself up straight in the chair.

"Cocaine," the old man aimed successfully for the spittoon next to his desk. Everyone in the office knew the boss hated drugs. Not for any moral reason but for the fact that narcotics resided far outside the gray area where Smith Realty lived. Rural land and mineral rights, warehousing and storage facilities, some residential, these interests and all the attachments that came with them were on a blurry line that even the state's politicians hesitated to clarify. Drugs also brought with them the armies amassed just south of the border and inevitably black Americans. You never wanted to find yourself in someone else's pocket or in a position where someone will sell you out, Bill had once told Nish.

"I need you to check on this boy, see if these rumors are true or not," Deaf continued. "If they are, take care of it. If not, report it back to us. Junior knows to act like you're just on a routine check, watching how things are going."

Deaf stared at the young man, who eventually realized he was supposed to speak. "Oh, yes, sir. No problem."

The boss nodded his headed so slightly Nish almost couldn't tell it was moving. He wondered if he had missed these subtle motions in the past.

"Alright. You've done a good job here. Been cautious," Deaf sucked on his teeth again. "I'm hoping you handle this right."

"Yes, sir, of course."

The old man looked to Bill, who gave the details of the trip. When he was finished, he put a hand gently on Nish's shoulder for him to get up. As they walked to the door, Bill leaned in to speak, "Things are different down there. You take care, now." Nish nodded and left the room. After Bill had closed the door, Deaf motioned him to the empty seat in front of his desk.

"Junior's going to have someone watching him," Deaf said quietly. "That boy down there's selling cocaine, no doubt about it. Nish turns him in, he ain't too far gone. He doesn't, then he's gotten too greedy. I don't take kindly to folk stealing from me," Deaf sucked on his teeth. "If that's the case, want you to do it. He won't see it coming."

No reaction came from Bill's face.

"That's not going to be a problem, is it?" Deaf wasn't really asking his underling.

Bill opened his mouth mechanically, "No, sir."

Even though it was a Saturday, the office was as full as at any given time during the week. Nish finally found Rusty at the water cooler on the far side of the room, reenacting the scene from yesterday at the warehouse. After he had ended the story, he walked back to his desk, covered in useless items that Nish figured he'd bought off TV or from airplane catalogs. Nish dug a nail deep in between his teeth as he started out for his new employee but was intercepted by John.

"Hey," the giant stood awkwardly, like he wasn't sure if it was okay to ask about what had just happened in the boss' office. Looking at Rusty one last time, Nish turned to his friend, "Pack your toothbrush. We head to San Antonio in three days."

He motioned for the giant to follow him to the kitchen. "We've got to keep an eye on this guy down there. They think he's buying coke from the Mexicans on their way up and selling it," Nish spoke quietly as they walked. "If he is, you handle it," he looked his worker in the eye and the giant nodded.

"If he isn't, then we got a paid vacation," Nish smoothed the hair behind his ear. John furrowed his brow, opening his mouth to speak. There was a clap of thunder so loud the coffee mugs in the kitchen shook against each other, then everything went dark.

When the lights came back on, Bill was standing next to the circuit breaker and everyone else was frozen where they had been.

"Goddamn," someone said loudly from the main room as a tree across the street cracked loudly and fell into an empty lane of traffic. The old man strolled out, a path clearing for him as he walked towards the window.

"Y'all get on home," he announced. "You'll get a call tomorrow if you're needed."

"Raining like a cow pissing on a flat rock," John shook his head. "You want to grab a drink?"

The desire swelled in Nish to follow his coworkers. It had taken the first six months of his working there for them to ask him to go anywhere but an Indian food restaurant for lunch. Since his promotion to manager, he'd gotten more invitations than he'd ever wanted, but he still had trouble turning down an opportunity to drink. He shook his head regretfully, "No thanks, I've got something I need to take care of."

Nish knocked on the hospital door. Knowing there would be no answer, he gently pushed it open with his free hand.

"Hi mom," he walked to the bed to kiss his mother's pale forehead. She lay there, eyes open. "I brought some more flowers."

The roses from the previous week were in the process of dying, their petals lying stiff and dry on the bedside table.

"I told those lazy ass nurses to change the water in these every day," he spit out a loose strand of his cheek that had been holding on. Cleaning the vase, he arranged the new flowers for his mother. One of the nurses passed by in the hall and, upon seeing the man with the patient, lowered her eyes and quickened her pace away from the room.

"There we go," he smiled. "Nice and new."

He pulled a chair next to the hospital bed to hold her pale hand. He had conditioned himself not to pull away when he felt how bony it had become in the past year. As a child, her stomach was the perfect cushion for him to bury his head in if he'd hurt himself and didn't want the other kids to see him cry. Now, he thought it looked like someone had deflated her.

"So what's going on, mom?" he moved his face in front of hers so she could see him. Her light blue eyes were locked ahead of her as if she were witnessing something horrible happen but couldn't look away. "They treating you alright in here?"

The machine that breathed for her made a noise like a tire going flat. The first time he'd heard it, he thought maybe she was trying to say something.

"What's on the menu today?" he smiled, tapping one of the tubes going into her arm. He always asked the same question but figured she thought it was funny. She would always laugh at his jokes when he was growing up, even when he said the same ones over and over again. "They give you hamburgers through this thing?"

She kept staring ahead so he laughed for her. He picked up the television remote with his free hand, flipping to the news channel. It was important for her to know what was going on in the outside world, he thought.

"You remember Philip Leon? He was in Latin with me for a few years in high school," he spoke casually. "I saw him the other day at the supermarket. Apparently he's some sort of scientist now."

The breathing machine went off just as he finished speaking and that same glimmer of hope sprung up in him to fall just as quickly.

"Anyway, I was thinking I could show him some of the inventions I used to work on," he rubbed the back of her hand with his thumb. He remembered his ideas from a couple years before, machines to help his newly diagnosed mother with housework, all having gone unrealized after an eye-opening trip to the patent office.

"I talked with the pool guy yesterday," he spoke to himself as much as to her. "He confirmed the start date and said they should be done in a few weeks, just before your surgery. I've already sent out invitations for the pool party to celebrate your coming home in a month. Even bought us a couple floating chairs so we can just hang out in the water."

He pulled the blanket up on her, revealing a pamphlet adorned with Hindu gods that had been lost in the folds.

"What the fuck is this shit?!" Nish threw it across the floor, taking his hand off his mother's to pick his teeth. He dug the nail deep until the gums tore and the copper taste seeped out just as the doctor appeared in the doorway.

"Mr. Patel," he dutifully smiled, keeping his mouth closed. "Visiting your mother, I see."

He was always doing that, Nish thought, stating the obvious in a way that made it seem like some deep observation. The young man stood and smiled back politely. "Just checking in."

"Good," the doctor entered the room. He looked like he had frail bones; Nish imagined putting his hands on both sides of the man's ribcage, feeling them collapse into themselves as he squeezed. The doctor picked up the chart at the end of the bed. "Let's see how things are going."

Nodding in agreement, Nish put his hands in his pockets. His fingers grazed the list of questions he'd stuck there earlier. "Oh, before I forget, I was watching this thing on the news a few days back about a new medication they have."

"Zyranal, yes," the doctor didn't look up from the chart. "It wouldn't work in a situation like your mother's."

"But I looked it up on the internet and they were saying it helped the muscles..." he began but the doctor held up a hand like he was physically stopping Nish from speaking.

"It wouldn't work, Mr. Patel. Not in your mother's case."

"Okay," Nish suddenly felt very aware of how he was standing and straightened up.

The doctor took a pen out of his pocket to scribble something on the chart that Nish couldn't make out. The television suddenly seemed intrusively loud so Nish turned it off. With the background noise gone, he spoke more softly, "Hey doc, did you check out that big round thing on my mom's arm?" During his visit the previous week, Nish had gotten particularly concerned when he found the odd shaped spot. After checking all the medical internet sites, he still hadn't come to a conclusion as to what it could be.

"Yes, the large sphere located on the tricep. We examined it."

"Did you have to take a piece of it to test?" Nish didn't like them cutting into his mom. He imagined her trying to cry or scream but being unable to.

"We removed a portion of it for further analysis."

"Just let me know what you find out, okay?"

"As soon as we know, we'll get back to you," the doctor set down the chart. Lowering his head, he looked at Nish out of the top of his eye sockets. "I actually have something to discuss with you."

The doctor motioned for the young man to follow him and Nish did so, moving his tongue over the spot where he'd bitten out the piece of cheek. It felt like a giant crater although he knew it was only a few millimeters in diameter. That's how big he was, he thought.

When they were outside in the hall, the doctor put his arm around him like they were sharing a secret. "The procedure I was telling you about, it appears it's going to be a little more costly than we had anticipated."

"Oh," Nish stopped playing with the bloody area in his mouth. "I've been saving up for this for two years now."

"I know, I'm sure it's disappointing for you. But it seems that due to certain complications, your mother is going to have to undergo several preparatory operations. They're outside of your coverage and could be quite expensive."

"What kind of complications?"

"There has been significantly worse degeneration of the spinal motor neurons than--"

"Alright, whatever," Nish waved away the mind cluttering details. That's what he paid the doctors for, he thought. "So how much more is it going to be?"

"Almost half what the actual procedure itself will cost."

"Fuck!" he turned away from the doctor, wandering a few steps down the hall with his head back. "How am I supposed to get that kind of money?"

"I don't know. You still have the number of our accounts receivable representative, right?"

"Yeah," Nish knew better than to speak with the doctor about payment. "I'll give her a call."

"Good," the doctor gave one last closed-mouth smile before turning to walk away.

"Oh, I almost forgot," Nish called after him. "The nurses need to change the water in my mom's vase every day."

"I'm not a nurse, Mr. Patel," the doctor joked over his shoulder in a way that made Nish feel like he should laugh with him, and walked away.

The wind blew the door shut before Nish had a chance to close it. He peered out the window to find trees disintegrating in the wind, their stripped branches turned into spears that stabbed roofs and lawns. The cars on the street bounced on their shocks with each thick wave of wind. Nish waited for one of them to hop down the street and take off into the clouds.

He peeled off his jacket and boots in the entryway to let them dry. In his bedroom, he removed the rest of his clothing while inspecting his two wall hangings, the Rice diploma and the picture of him and his mother after a football game, to ensure the thunder hadn't shook them from their ninety-degree angles. He walked nude to the kitchen to pour himself a glass of whiskey. As he sank his naked body into his couch to turn on the news channel, two bloody hands clawed at the top of the backyard fence, pulling the attached body over.

DAY 3

"The pigeon shoots in Monterrey always bring out the swinging Richards," Bill pointed at the well-dressed Mexican men conversing with their designated shooters, all donning European skeet vests and gloves. The Texan shooters huddled around Deaf and the other American executives. Nish searched his manager's face for any trace of indignation or sadness but couldn't find it. One of his new coworkers had explained the situation earlier that morning, admitting that Bill was the best shot of the Texans but "can't shoot down here in Mexico, on account of the queerness and all." The Mexicans wouldn't take losing to someone like him, Nish thought, not on their own soil. The subtle social rules he'd learned in his first couple weeks at the new job didn't exactly endear him to the management of the company, but he figured that's what happens when you give power to rednecks, American or Mexican.

"Here we go now," Bill pointed as the two groups walked out to the open area with their shotguns. Young men dressed in baseball uniforms waited next to a full pigeon coop. Nish figured Presidio had their outfits made especially for the event.

The first shooter stepped to his mark at the side of the coop as a uniformed teenager unlatched the tiny gate on the pen to grab a bird. The pitcher looked up at Presidio, who had made his way over to Deaf and the engaged couple. The Mexican boss nodded. The pitcher nodded back, kicking the dirt at his feet. He grabbed a handful of feathers from one of the wings and tore them out.

"Pull!" the shooter yelled. The pitcher went into his motion to hurl the bird in front of him. The pigeon opened its wings and swerved dramatically to the right, a surprise for the shooter and the bird itself. The 20 gauge fired, causing the pigeon to jump out of its remaining feathers and fall limp on its trajectory.

"They do a Calcutta," Bill pointed at the Smith executives and their Mexican counterparts. "Last time, at the pigeon shoot in Texas, old man knew about an up and comer and bought fifty percent of the

23

team. Course he did this through some sales agent so as not to raise suspicion," Bill drained his miniature beer.

A boy ran to a nearby cooler, pulling another tiny beer out of the ice. He touched the neck of the bottle to a plate of salt, then opened the beer to insert a lime wedge before bringing it over. Holding up his hand to the young waiter, Nish finished his beer and handed him the empty.

-Sorry,- Nish apologized in Spanish for having the boy make two trips but another waiter was already preparing his drink. Nish looked at his new manager, "Fucking customer service down here."

Bill raised his bottle to the statement. A breeze swept through Nish, cool in contrast to the oppressive Mexican heat. He tried not to smile but couldn't help himself, grinning for no reason other than the joy of being alive.

The next shooter took his spot at the side of the pitcher. Nish looked up at the old man, his faced creased into a permanent frown. "Why would he do that at the company shoot? He couldn't have won more than a few thousand."

"He made plenty more than that but you have your point."

It doesn't exactly engender loyalty, Nish thought. He took a drink of the ice cold beer, then raised the steaming bottle to his forehead. "He just wants to keep folks on their toes?"

Bill shook his head, "He did it for the same reason this all boils down to. It's not like you and I couldn't be working construction somewhere."

Speak for yourself, Nish thought.

"See that boy over there?" Bill pointed at a Texan so large the shotgun in his hand looked like a child's toy. Next to the other shooters in the group, he reminded Nish of an action figure he'd owned as a child. His father had given him one that was a different brand than what he usually collected and it stood out above the others. It wasn't abnormal in any way, just a perfectly proportioned other-species that was out of place in a world where everything was fit to a smaller scale.

"He joins the service to pay his way through truck driving school. War breaks out and he gets shipped off," Bill paused the story while he pulled out a pack of chewing tobacco from his pocket. "Chaw?"

Nish politely waved him off. Bill stuck a tight plug of the tobacco in the side of his mouth and resumed, "Loses hearing in his right ear and sees cotton out of the eye. And here he is, supporting his wife and children."

Nish saw where his manager was going, "But even though he can't drive a truck, he could still work on a construction site or an oil rig or in a mall."

Bill nodded, "You always have a choice."

24

Nish felt the breeze sweep up through him again and turned his eyes back to the shooters, not letting anything get him down. He'd learned there wasn't much of a point in arguing with someone more senior.

The buzz of the lights filled the warehouse. One of the men across from Nish cleared his throat, snapping him back to the present. He quickly picked up where he'd left off. "Manuel, I know you see the problem here."

The Mexican laughed, examining the brim of his cowboy hat on the table.

Behind Nish, Rusty shifted his large amount of weight. He always insisted on standing behind the table like in some mob movie, Nish thought. The only reason he let Rusty do it that morning was because he was too pissed off at him to look at his puffy face.

"You can't bring truckloads of people who look like something from a horror movie into Dallas, right onto our property. Next time, dump the body."

"What if the driver loses cargo? That's our money," Manuel's accent hid the fact he was from south of the border. Nish had often thought the upper class Mexicans he dealt with spoke better English than his coworkers. "The guy wouldn't know how to clean it. It just doesn't make sense." He gave Nish a look of feigned ignorance, putting out his hands as if the truck's general cleanliness was a matter of serious concern to him.

Next to Manuel, his cousin was struggling not to fall asleep. Both were clad in Western wear Nish figured a rancher might be able to afford if he saved up for the outfit his whole life. The man's eyelids slid downwards until they just closed, then jerked up as if the bottom lid had a spring in it. Rusty watched the cousin hide a yawn, then followed in suit. The yawn spread around the table with each man finding some excuse to put their hand in front of their mouth.

"Then he should drive to a safe house we rent to you and hold the cargo there until the truck's cleared. Only then does he drop it off," Nish scratched his nose as he breathed in deeply. "How you run your business is up to you, but we're going to have to start imposing a cleaning fee if something like this happens again. And it'll be steep."

Rusty watched as his manager and the Mexican haggled. His gaze drifted to the cracked door of the warehouse where the rain tap-danced on the concrete outside. The chairs scraping the floor jolted his eyes back to the table.

"You going to the cookout next weekend?" Manuel asked as he stood up.

"And lose more money to you on bean bags? I'd rather skip it," Nish responded. The Mexicans laughed and said their farewells, Manuel eyeing the man behind Nish once more before leaving.

When they were gone, Rusty sat in Manuel's chair, kicking his feet up on the table to examine his worn boots. "Can you believe these greedy sons of bitches?" He picked off a loose string of leather and flicked it to the ground. His manager walked to the refrigeration unit that had carried the bad batch.

"How do you mean?" Nish examined the transporter. Bill's guys had been thorough in their cleaning; he was glad there was at least one person he could always count on.

"These people trying not to pay us. Acting like they haven't done anything wrong and that it's all our fault," Rusty pulled his foot closer to get a better look at the sole of his boot. "Guess that shouldn't surprise us, though."

Pulling a handkerchief from his pocket, Nish covered his hand to open and close the door, checking for blood on its latches. "These people are businessmen, same as we are."

"Not exactly the same."

"Why not?" Nish couldn't find any evidence after a close inspection. He nodded to himself, putting the handkerchief in his front pocket to throw away later.

"You know these people, coming to America, taking advantage of the one thing they can, living off our needs," Rusty furrowed his brow. "It's like they think we owe them something and they're fine with sitting back and taking whatever they want while we work our asses off. No class motherfuckers."

"No class? Rusty, the ancestors of those men were probably Spanish nobility. Yours were most likely prisoners from England shipped here against their will," the disdain of Nish's father towards Southerners rang in his ears. The rejects of the Kingdom, he'd told Nish when the boy had come home from another day of his classmates comparing him to a store clerk.

"I've seen Spanish folk and, trust me, those half breed motherfuckers that were just sitting here ain't Spanish," Rusty ripped another loose shred from his boot. "And my ancestors weren't prisoners, they were immigrants fleeing prosecution."

"You mean persecution?" Nish asked, prompting Rusty to nod like that was what he'd said. Taking one last look at the unit, Nish walked back to the table. "The English shipped prisoners to the American South for twice as long as they did to Australia, yet Americans act holier than thou towards everyone else on the planet," he took a seat across from his subordinate to look him square in the eye. "Especially half breed motherfuckers."

"Oh shit," Rusty's eyes opened wide. He jerked his foot from the table to sit up straight, "I didn't mean it like that Nish. I mean I know you're half white and all and I'd never disrespect you like that."

"Your family's been in the South since the Civil War?" Nish interrupted.

"Yes, sir."

"Then there's a one in two chance you've got Native American in you. A one in four chance you've got black in you," Nish ran his tongue along his teeth. "The ideas about the world you formed in whatever covertly racist, good old boy town you come from are just one tiny view of what the world really is."

"I went to the same high school as you," Rusty mumbled to the table.

"What was that?"

"Nothing," he looked down at his boots. Nish eyed him closely.

"I'm going to try to nap for a little bit in the trailer. I wake up and see you passed out when you should be keeping guard out here, it's your ass."

"Yes, sir," another piece of leather caught Rusty's eye but he waited for his manager to leave before putting his boot back up on the table.

Nish wasn't able to sleep despite the earliness of the meeting. As soon as he'd scratched microscopic bugs out of his imagination, more would attack another part of his body. The storm outside turned into a steady background noise like waves on a beach. He tried to calm himself to their rhythm but shocks of electricity shot through the marrow of all the bones in his body, filling him with strength to use however he pleased. He felt the energy pulse through him like he was a live wire left unattended and waiting.

Giving up on sleep, he looked out the window of the trailer. The warehouse, the highway leading to downtown in the distance, a billboard advertising an eye surgeon giving discounts to the first ten people who called after the Boys sacked the opposing quarterback. Dallas. Nish picked his teeth, feeling the gum in between ache as it stretched.

The wind lifted a plastic bag, dancing it across the asphalt like tumbleweed. "Watch the road," Nish pointed at the piece of trash. Rusty hit the brakes much harder than necessary, causing the two of them to jerk forward against their seatbelts.

27

"Sorry," he apologized as the bag skipped down the street unharmed, then continued his story as if nothing had happened. "So anyway, this son of a bitch loses three thousand last weekend. On bean bags!"

"You know, there's more to life than just going to barbeques, getting drunk and playing bean bags," Nish's leg bounced with nervous energy. "You ever think of going to college? Reading something besides the sports page?"

"Shit, I already got a job. What do I need college for? Be some doctor or lawyer?" Rusty laughed at the idea.

Nish opened the glove compartment to take out the traveler of whiskey, "Looks like you've got it all figured out." He took a long drink. "Over there," he directed Rusty to the mall's entrance. Replacing the traveler, Nish grabbed his umbrella as the car came to a stop in front of the main doors. "I shouldn't be any longer than an hour."

"You mind if I run grab a drink?"

"Just be here in an hour."

"Thanks," Rusty pursed his mouth like a child apologizing. "And what I said about college…maybe it wouldn't hurt if I--"

Nish stepped out of the car and closed the door quickly behind him.

Rusty stared at his manager walking into the mall, sucking his teeth as Nish disappeared through the doors. Putting the car into gear, he stepped on the gas too hard and it shot up onto the sidewalk before he was able to bounce it back down into the street.

Exiting the mall's driveway, he pulled out onto the major road that led through the nearby residential neighborhood to the bar. Halfway through the glut of newly built condos, he reached down to change the radio; the car jolted unnaturally from the dog underneath its tires. He threw on the brakes, seeing the mangled animal in the rearview mirror lying motionless except for its chest pumping up and down to a frantic rhythm. Rusty pulled at his hair until the roots stretched and tore in parts, his eyes stayed glued to the dashboard but it didn't tell him what to do.

"Alright, then," he put the car into reverse and gunned the engine. A middle-aged woman in a sweatsuit ran into the street to throw her body in front of the animal. Rusty hit the brakes to skid to a stop only feet away from her. The woman yelled something at him, covering her dog like she could protect it from the ton of metal aimed at them. Rusty put the car into drive, hitting the gas and hydroplaning up onto the sidewalk. As the dying animal and its mother disappeared in his rearview mirror, he finally exhaled, the sides of his mouth creeping upwards.

The noise from the video game arcade blared across the ice skating rink, beckoning kids away from their parents with dollar bills ready to be exchanged for rolls of quarters. Teenagers from every social stratum challenged each other to the obnoxiously loud games, shooting fake guns at screens with an intensity that Nish figured could only be matched if the situation were real. In the back, his police contact sat with a soft drink, flipping through a pornographic magazine like it was a newspaper. Nish wasn't sure if the fact he met with corrupt DPD officers in plain sight should make him feel less at ease or more.

"Jordan," Nish reached out a hand.

"What's going on, man?" the policeman disregarded the extended hand and embraced his old friend. "How's shit?"

"Shit's alright," Nish laughed. Jordan hadn't changed much since the seventh grade, he thought. He may have bulked up and got a badge, but he was still the same guy that used to throw fries at the nerdy kids in the cafeteria. "Hope I didn't interrupt," Nish pointed at the magazine. Jordan took the question seriously, "I was pretty invested in it but I can pick back up where I left off."

"Good," Nish took a seat across from him.

"How's your mom doing?"

"She's doing well. Getting her surgery in a month, then she'll be good as new."

Jordan clapped his hands like he was trying to kill a fly in front of him, "Hell yeah! That's fucking awesome!"

"You get my invitation to her welcome home party?"

"Hell yeah, I did. Mister fancy ass with the pool," Jordan raised his soft drink. Nish scratched the side of his neck, "It's not done yet. But it will be by then."

"Hanging out in the pool, just like the old days," Jordan nodded.

Nish thought his friend was overly sentimental sometimes, saying things that people say in movies to make a dramatic point. Nish scraped his nails against the skin of his shoulder. "Yeah. So about the situation on Friday."

"Don't worry about it. You could have a goddamn UFO in plain sight on a Smith property and the authorities wouldn't touch it. It's all good."

The authorities, Nish jabbed at his cuticle. When cops are against the powers that be, the animals are running the zoo.

"Besides, I wouldn't expect there to be much to find in a few months," Jordan grinned. "Not after how we treated that."

A ring of moisture on the table left from the soft drink attracted Nish's eyes. When he started working with the company, he learned a lot about people. Murderers who would walk an old woman across the street and legitimate businessmen who would hit her with a car if someone paid them enough. He'd seen how things work with law enforcement, with publicly traded companies, with politicians. The idea of working with Smith Realty for a few years to pay off the surgery and then going on about his life as usual seemed more in question with every DPD payoff or campaign contribution he witnessed. Most people stepping out to get their paper in the morning wouldn't let certain things creep into their brains when they saw someone stumping for a local judge in the yard across from them. He'd become a strong believer that you can know too much.

The old friends spoke about other issues, professional and personal. Jordan's test for gonorrhea had come back negative, which Nish heartily congratulated him on. Nish told him he'd be going to San Antonio for a few days and Jordan told him to look up an old flame from high school who had moved there. After agreeing this was definitely the year for a Dallas Super Bowl, the two shook hands and Nish left his friend to resume his Sunday afternoon reading.

Walking past the ice skating rink to the escalators, Nish headed towards the pet store on the second floor. As he approached, the puppies wrestling with each other in the window put a smile on his face. "Hey there," he said through the glass. One of the puppies ran clumsily to the window to put both paws up on it. "Cute little dog," Nish felt the concerns from downstairs melt off his shoulders.

As he entered, the two sales clerks smiled, greeting him by name. He walked past the teenage girls and they exchanged glances, their smiles disappearing.

Walking to the back, he positioned himself in the middle of the tropical bird aisle to more easily imagine himself on some Caribbean island. A large aquarium of colorful saltwater fish, the store's main draw, called to him from the sidewall. Taking his place among the crowd of spectators, Nish watched the vibrant fish dance with each other. A teacher had told him once that by the time a fish swims from one end of the aquarium to the other, it's already forgotten where it came from. He watched them with envy. A warm feeling swept up through him, pushing moisture to the front of his eyes. Feigning a yawn, he rubbed them dry. The phrases in his cell phone called out to him but he shook his head vehemently, causing a few people to stare. He walked back to the store's entrance.

The puppies at the front barked as he moved past them. He turned to their open pen. One of them sat in the corner away from the rest; it looked out the window like it was waiting for something. An aggressive one ran over to jump on its back. The lying puppy didn't snap at its tormentor but rolled itself into a ball. The other dog took a step back, then pawed at its neck like it was trying to scratch through it. Nish snatched the attacker from the pen. Holding it up to his face with one hand, he used the other to feel its body. Running his fingers along its tiny backbone, he could feel the ribs encapsulating the organs. He remembered eating squirrel on a hunting trip with a friend's family in high school. The meat was tough but not without its unique flavor. The skull of the animal was tiny like the shell of a walnut. He knew its brain had the human pinkness and longed for just a glimpse. Pinching both sides of its jaws, the puppy's mouth opened involuntarily. It howled in pain as Nish mirrored what he saw, bearing his teeth at the young animal. Someone was calling his name from somewhere else. A finger jabbed at his shoulder.

"Sir," the store clerk was practically yelling. Nish jumped back like she had just rudely woken him up. She reached for the puppy, "I'll take that, sir." She looked sternly at the man. He handed the dog over and quickly left the shop.

Fighting the wind and his own intoxication, Nish stumbled up the walkway to his front door. Cursing himself for spending half his day at the bar, he took twice as long to find the right keys to let himself in. When he had opened the door, he turned back to wave at Rusty. His worker waved back and hit the gas, swerving to avoid a downed mailbox as he jetted away.

Inside, the Provencal garden air freshener plugged into the wall let Nish rise above the smell of alcohol and smoke that stuck to his damp clothes. After peeling off the moist layers, he walked nude to the TV to turn on the Italian news channel for ambience. It's the small things that separate people, he thought, pouring himself a glass of water and imagining a place where the soft drink brands and candy bars were totally different. He was about to chug down the water when he noticed the tarp in the backyard beating the ground madly.

In hip waders and a raincoat, he stepped out the backdoor to face the monstrous hole he'd dug for the coming pool. The pool installation workers had insisted on digging it themselves but the price seemed astronomical. Upon taking up the task, Nish realized how much he enjoyed destroying something people are supposed to spend so much time taking care of.

His boot stuck in the ground, causing him to fall. "Shit," he lifted himself up, thinking how the workers would bitch if there were mud in the hole when they came the next week to finish the job. The tarp was flapping so violently in the wind he was worried the metal ring on the side may catch him in the eye so he lifted his foot as high as he could, then brought it down quickly. An unnatural noise rose from the tarp.

"Fuck!" Nish jumped back, falling down again.

He watched in horror as two claws emerged from the hole. The mud-covered animal, almost human in certain respects, pulled itself out of the earth, bearing its teeth at Nish as it stalked him. Swaths of insects concealed the hideous form underneath, their thousands of crawling legs giving him the appearance of moving even when he stayed still, poised to strike. Nish tried to scramble to his feet to get the high ground but the thing rose with him, standing awkwardly on its hind legs. It lurched at him, letting out a dreadful howl that eclipsed the thunder and the trees snapping apart around them. Its claw reached out to Nish's face but he ducked, then kicked the monster in the chest to send it flying back through the rain. It hit the tarp and slid down into its black hole with a splash.

Carefully standing up, Nish easily found a fallen branch he could use to bludgeon the thing to death. "You came to the wrong motherfucker's house," he neared the tarp slowly, jabbing a few times with the branch to make sure it wasn't close enough to the edge to grab him. His heart raced as he reached down to tear the plastic cover back. "Fuck, fuck, fuck," he repeated the frantic mantra under his breath. He flung the tarp as far back as he could, exposing the gaping wound he'd administered upon the earth. Inside, a horribly misshapen boy clung to the side of the hole. Nish could see the naked child had been badly burned on his head, disfiguring a side of his face and leaving a waxy hairless patch on top that made him look like a balding man. The burn led down past his milky left eye to a melted ear. The lips and cheek on his right side had been cut away, permanently exposing his teeth. Parts of his body seemed to be missing, not arms or legs but the stuff in between. Nish lifted the branch above his head.

The boy moaned, exposing a stump of tongue that had been cut off at its base. By his size and lack of hair on areas that weren't burnt or scarred, Nish figured the kid couldn't be any older than seven or eight. The energy running through Nish nagged at him, forcing him to take a step towards the thing, the weapon still poised to attack. The frightened boy jumped back from the side, balling himself up and covering his head. Warmth swept through Nish from his feet to his head, the moisture coming again as he dropped the branch to the ground. The alcohol in his body surged to his brain to fill it with white gauze.

"Hey kid, I'm sorry," he walked to the edge. Lowering to his hands and knees, he extended a hand to the child. "Come on, you'll die out here. You want to get dry? Clean?" Nish motioned to his own body. The boy looked up at the night sky, the rain causing his eyes to close involuntarily.

"I won't hurt you, I promise," he motioned again. When the boy looked at him, the energy came surging back. Nish figured he could grab the kid's face and finish the job, tearing it off from that fucked up mouth to expose his whole skull. Nish spit into the mud, shaking his head and extending his arm further. "Come on, I promise."

The child shook his body like an animal, then put a hand on the side of the dirt wall.

"There you go, I'll get you some dinner. I'm too fucked up to drive anywhere tonight but something will get worked out tomorrow," Nish smiled to him. "It's fucked up the way things happen sometimes, you know? If you don't know how to do things a certain way, you can get discarded," the moisture escaped from his body to fall into the black hole beneath him. "But I'll take care of you."

The boy howled one last time into the night before he clumsily climbed the side of the hole to take his savior's hand.

DAY 4

A dead branch struck Nish's window so hard the glass almost broke. He jolted upwards, looking at his clock to discover it was the middle of the night. Something weighed down on his brain like a tiny blob had seeped into his body by way of his skull. Rolling over slowly so as not to upset the thing, he fished for the bottle of pain reliever in his nightstand. After finishing off the cup of water next to his bed, he carried it to the bathroom for a refill. He was turning off the faucet when a noise came from the living room.

Quickly looking around the bathroom, his head not thanking him for it, he found the closest thing to a weapon was a towel rod. He slid it out of its holder as quietly as possible, then turned the bathroom light off to give his attacker the same disadvantage of blindness. Lowering his head, he peeked out. There was no one to be seen either way so he gingerly stepped into the living room. Something rustled near the couch. He instinctively jumped towards it, raising the rod above his head. The mutilated boy rolled over to put his thumb back in his mouth.

"Goddamnit, kid," Nish exhaled, letting his hand fall to his side. "You nearly gave me a heart attack."

The intruder tackled Nish from behind, sending the rod flying out of his hand and into the television screen as the two fell to the ground. The assailant tried to work his arm around his victim's neck but Nish overpowered him, throwing him to the floor and pinning him face up. In the dark, Nish could make out the man's lighter skin. Maybe Deaf was finally done with him, he felt electricity run through him at the thought. With his arms holding the intruder's hands above his head and his legs positioned so that the man couldn't move, Nish reared back his head, preparing to bring it down on his attacker's face as hard as he could.

"Wait!" the intruder yelled.

Nish slammed his forehead into the man's nose. A sound came from the cartilage like someone lightly tapping two pieces of wood together.

"Fuck!" the intruder struggled in vain. Despite his nose now being significantly flattened against his cheeks, it was able to pour forth a considerable amount of blood into his mouth and eyes. "Wait, Nish!"

Another headbutt to the broken nose caused the redness to fly upwards onto Nish. The warmth of it made him wish he could tear the man open to dive inside.

"Fuck! Nish, wait!" the intruder spit out the blood that had run into his mouth. "Wait! It's me Dhruv!"

Nish looked at the mangled face in the dark, the blood hiding its features. But the voice, the bony torso and lanky arms, he knew it was his brother. He reared back his head again.

"No! Wait, please!" his older sibling pleaded.

"Why? I don't know anyone named Dhruv."

"Dave!" the man closed his eyes so the blood wouldn't go in. He tried to turn his head to one side or the other but Nish had pinned his arms too close. "It's Dave, alright?"

Cautiously letting him go free, Nish jumped off his brother in case he tried to take a swing at him. Dave cupped his nose, careful not to touch it. "You fucking broke it!"

"You broke my TV," Nish went into the kitchen as his breathing slowed. He returned with paper towels. "Don't bleed on my carpet. You how much that cost to have put in?"

"You installed it yourself, dick."

Nish shrugged. The boy on the couch stirred as if he might wake up, then rolled over to drool on the other side of the pillow. "What the fuck are you doing sneaking around my house and jumping on me?" Nish sat down in his leather recliner. He slept in the nude and the cool leather of the chair sent a chill through his naked body. He'd bought it when his elderly neighbor died and her son had a garage sale. Every time he leaned back and the footrest swung out, he couldn't help but think what a steal it was.

Dave took the paper towels from his little brother, holding them under his nose to catch the blood steadily running out of it. "My apartment got flooded and I needed a place to stay, so I came over here. Excuse me for thinking my own flesh and blood would help me out."

This was what pissed him off the most, Nish thought, Dave putting himself in a situation where he's bound to fail, then blaming others when they won't pull him out of the hole he's dug for himself. Their mom used to put up with it but he wasn't about to.

"Maybe you shouldn't live in a basement, then. Maybe you should get a real job. Or better yet, go back and get your degree," Nish kicked the footrest down to lean forward. "And why did you attack me if you just needed a place to stay?"

"I didn't attack you. I just wanted to hold your arms down and explain the situation to you. I figured you'd swing that metal rod first and ask questions later."

Fair enough, Nish thought. "Regardless, you can't stay here."

"Are you fucking serious?"

"You're here less than five minutes and you've already done seven hundred dollars worth of damage," Nish pointed to the broken television. He would have been more upset if he hadn't been planning on replacing it soon for his mother's return. "Anyway, I already have one visitor." He pointed at the boy on the couch behind his brother. Dave turned casually, then jumped back like he'd been hit with a cattle prod. "Oh my God! What the fuck is that thing?"

The covers had slipped down, exposing half the boy's body. Dave covered his mouth, accidentally touching his nose. "Shit!"

"He's my new roommate. For the time being, at least. I guess the little guy can sleep through anything."

"What happened to him? It looks like a lawnmower chewed him up and spit him out."

"How do you think you look right now?" Nish got up again to get water from the kitchen. "Why don't you stay with one of your friends from your communist club? Isn't that what they're all about, helping out lazy motherfuckers who can't do for themselves?"

"It's not a communist club," David became suddenly impassioned. "It's a way for a better world. To let the underprivileged stand up to their oppressors. To stop the exploitation of immigrant laborers," Dave looked at Nish standing over the sink.

After filling his cup, Nish walked calmly back to his chair. He had seen a movie once in which one of the characters said you can't choose your family. He remembered how much he loved that saying.

"Listen to me, Dave. This identity crisis you've been having for as long as I've known you, it's holding you back," Nish spoke condescendingly. "But fortunately for you, all that matters is what you do next."

"You're going to start quoting dad now?"

"Dad was a smart man, a lot fucking smarter than you," Nish tightened his grip on the glass in his hand. "Since I went away to college, you've basically used the resources of this family, the money he made, to fulfill your dream of being an unemployed pothead following whatever anti-mainstream ideology is popular at the time."

"You think you're better than me? You turn migrants into slaves."

"'Slaves' is such a charged word," Nish scoffed. "And don't try to change the subject. Since mom's been sick, you haven't had her to run to so now you're trying to get me to be your parent. That's not going to happen."

36

Dave let the paper towels fall to the ground. "I go to see mom all the time!"

"But who pays the hospital bills? Do you really think I want to be doing what I do for a living? It's fucking horrible. You have no idea how embarrassing it is, someone with a college education doing work like that. Every day I wake up and wonder why I'm not going to some high paying office job like everyone else I graduated with. I wonder why the fuck I debase myself. But I do what I have to do."

"High paying office job? You were a history major, that doesn't exactly lend itself to making six figures. Besides, we both know you couldn't stand that sort of thing. You try to act like you're better than everyone else but you have the attention span of a gnat. You ask me, I think this current line of work is perfect for you." He looked at his younger brother in the chair about to break the glass in his hand. It wouldn't have been the first time he'd seen Nish draw his own blood.

"Get the fuck out of here. And stop leaving that Hindu bullshit with mom. I'm getting tired of having to throw it away every time I visit her."

"How could you throw away--"

"We're Presbyterian, Dave. Sorry to disappoint you. Now go," Nish pointed to the door.

Dave opened his mouth like he was going to say something, then closed it. Shaking his head, he walked silently to the door. Nish could tell what his older brother was finally feeling, the same thing he'd experienced the day he discovered Dave had tried to convince the doctor to turn off the machines. The remnants of mandatory love stretched to the point of breaking like a rope bridge dangling over a cliff, waiting to get snatched up by a strong wind to leave the two sides staring at each other. Pausing at the door, Dave turned to the side to look at Nish one last time.

"Keep it moving," Nish picked his teeth. Dave shook his head again and turned the doorknob. The wind flung the door open, hitting him in the face.

"Fuck!"

Nish chuckled until the door closed. With the intruder gone, he felt the adrenaline retreat, leaving a void that the blob gladly returned to fill.

"Alright, I've got to take care of this. Then I'll see if I can hook you up with something more long term than staying on my couch," Nish turned the windshield wipers up as fast as they would go. The boy, wrapped in a makeshift toga made from one of Nish's towels and a belt, sat next to his savior, sucking on an oversized novelty straw Nish had stuck in a gallon of whole milk. After the boy had spit out the soy based substitute that had been in the fridge, Nish discovered it was the only thing he would drink.

The car rolled to a stop in front of the loading docks of what had been a supermarket in Nish's youth and had since been converted to La Iglesia de la Natividad. The Catholic church was complete with a large marquis that pronounced -Jesus Saves- in Spanish where deals on canned goods were once displayed. Nish removed several stacks of cash from inside a backpack under the boy's seat.

"This shouldn't take too long," he checked his pistol one last time to make sure it was loaded. He hated doing these things alone but there was no other way, he thought. Even just dealing with these cockroaches, who kept their mouths shut since they stole the same as he did, flooded him with anxiety. He threw the stacks of money into another plastic bag and stuck it in the back of his jeans. "Just stay here alright?"

The boy extended his arms, offering his guardian the milk.

"Lactose intolerant," Nish shook his head, running his hand over the revolver in his holster the way a basketball player would cross himself before shooting a free throw. There was movement in the loading docks; a man standing like he was going to challenge the car to a fight. Nish opened his umbrella and got out.

The leader of the group watched the real estate agent approach. -Sit yourself,- he commanded in Spanish to the teenager. -Is the man from the House.- The leader went back to the cards in his hand. Throwing them face down on the folding table, one of the other teens smiled and swept the money to his side. The agent appeared from behind the curtain of water.

"Louie," Nish closed the umbrella, nodding at the leader. Louie rose slowly from the table until he reached his full height of five foot four, "Fucking rain," he motioned outside. Nish studied the teenagers at the table, the one who had been staring at the car was still standing. "Who's that?"

The teen puffed out his chest to give his best thug pose. He looked the same as all the others to Nish, littered with tattoos from his wrists up to his shaved head. The only telltale sign of his recently immigrated status was the skin tight t-shirt he was wearing.

Cops can get to anyone, Nish thought. And they start from the bottom. Although the DPD had almost as much to lose as Smith Realty, there were always small-minded assholes who could go on a crusade.

"New guy from Mexico. His name's Carlos," Louie answered, then addressed the teen in Spanish, -Boy, this is Nish.- The teen nodded ever so slightly, staring at the agent with a look of aggressive boredom. Nish studied the inked gangster. He had never understood the fascination with tattoos. The owl emblazoned on Nish's right bicep was only there because some other agents had got him drunk his first week on the job and convinced him it would look cool. He'd regretted it ever since he sobered up the next morning.

"What happened to the other kid?" Nish asked.

"Dead. Caught two in the chest by some niggers who were watching how he moved," the tiny leader crossed himself. "Left behind his girl, pregnant."

"There's a surprise," Nish picked his teeth. He turned to the new guy, asking in Spanish, -From where are you in Mexico?-

-Tamaulipas,- Carlos answered, swaying in his stance.

"No shit," Nish looked at Louie. The leader crossed his arms, keeping his mouth shut. Nish continued in Spanish, -Where in Tamaulipas?-

-A village small, Forest Green,- he answered, causing his interrogator to chuckle. Nish couldn't count the number of dried up desert towns he'd driven through in Mexico that were named after gardens or meadows or rivers. It was so common that he'd begun to think the conquistadors just loved sarcasm.

Looking back at Louie, he produced the plastic bag from his jeans and tossed it to the leader. "I'll be out of town for a little while, I don't know how long. If I'm not back in two weeks, I'll give you a call on the number."

Louie handed the bag to one of the teens at the table to count. People never just accepted money like in gangster movies, Nish thought, at least not the people he dealt with. Still eyeing the new guy, he walked over to an old lay down freezer unit from the '70's. "Latin Power, huh?" Nish motioned to the tattoo on Carlos's arm. The teen raised his chin slightly. The agent lifted his boot in front of him and swung it hard into the freezer. The noise that came from it reminded him of a dying fish slapping itself against the bottom of a boat. "How's that working out for you?" Nish looked out at the downpour, remembering his father talking about the rain in England he grew up with. He said it rained twice as much in India when he went there to visit his grandparents. "Put these people in an Indian drizzle and they think it's time to build an ark," he'd told his son. Nish spit on the ground.

"Who would you qualify as 'Latin', Charles?" Nish asked in English. "People from anywhere south of the border? In that case, are Jamaicans Latin, or do they not count because they don't speak Spanish? If so, that would mean the largest country in South America isn't Latin." His front teeth snagged a piece of the inside of his lip and bit down, causing electricity to shoot through him. "What about the millions of indigenous people in what's referred to as Latin America who can't speak Spanish and don't have a drop of European blood in them? Or the people who have no native blood in them, fresh off the plane or born in some Nazi expat town in Argentina or Brazil? Are they Latin?"

Louie looked up from the money being counted, "This motherfucker and his talking." The other teenagers laughed, except for Carlos who moved his hands behind him like a soldier standing at attention.

"But I guess that isn't the point of being 'Latin', is it?" Nish didn't let the interruption stop him. He continued testing the newcomer, "It's easier to throw labels on things that can't really be defined. That way you can create a stereotype to separate yourself from everyone else, then complain when others reference it." Nish caught the piece of lip in between his teeth again and tore it off, blinking hard so the tears wouldn't run down his face.

"What the fuck?" the tone of Louie's voice had changed. "You're short."

"You're throwing stones in glass houses there, Lou," Nish chuckled at his own joke. The others just stared at him. He shrugged, "It's the same as it always is."

"Exactly," the leader's body tightened up. "I told you last time we want that extra every week."

"We all want things, Lou," Nish wedged a fingernail between his teeth. "I want to live in a society where it's acceptable to walk around without the unnatural constraints of pants and undergarments. Carlos here wants to be able to afford a t-shirt that fits him properly. But my dick isn't hanging free and I'll be damned if Carlos didn't buy his wardrobe half priced from the kid's department. You see my point?"

With his hands still behind his back, Carlos slowly lifted his shirt, working his fingers around the pistol tucked into his jeans. Louie dropped his head, smiling like something on the ground was amusing him, "It's like you just don't learn. What do--" Something inside Nish's car exploded just as Carlos pulled out the pistol. Startled, the teen pulled the trigger, sending a shot flying into the concrete floor of the loading dock. Nish quickly reached behind his back to withdraw his own weapon.

"What the fuck?" Nish leveled his pistol at the teenager, his pointer finger trembling as it clicked off the safety. His right ear, closest to the teen's weapon when it discharged, was half full of cotton. Louie and the other gangsters looked just as disoriented and he felt a sudden likeness to them. Carlos stood frozen, his eyes open wide with the gun pointed at the ground.

-What are you doing?- Louie scolded the new member of his crew in Spanish. The leader recovered from the shock and leaned back in his thug pose, the rest of the group following suit. Carlos laid his weapon on the table, looking to Nish's car. The camaraderie having subsided,

Nish felt an urgent need to get as far away from the loading docks as possible.

"In a month, you'll get the extra," Nish inched backwards, the pistol still pointed at the teenager. "For this time and next."

"And interest," Louie bargained.

"No," Nish was worried his hand would start visibly shaking and moved faster. "I don't tend to give good deals to people who just shot at me."

"You don't bring it next month and I'll be the one taking a shot. And I'm not as clumsy as this motherfucker," the leader smiled, showing his teeth. Nish did the same and backed out into the wall of water.

As they drove down the highway, Nish's hands began shaking so badly he had to pull over. His body betraying him, he thought, you can't even trust yourself. A cool breeze touched down on his forehead, spreading his lips into a wide grin. "Goddamn!" he howled at the dark sky through the roof of his car. The boy let out an elated moan in accompaniment.

"No better feeling than getting shot at and missed," he pulled over and flipped on his hazards so his hands could work through their spasms and the tears that obscured his vision could fall onto his beaming face. "You did good back there, giving the warning about the gun. Quick thinking." He nodded at the boy, getting the same back.

He couldn't stop smiling until he mulled over the consequences of what the boy had seen. Mutes can point at a line up, he thought. He turned to look the boy squarely in the eye. "Now, what you just saw, it's something that's a secret, okay? You can't tell anyone about this," he waited until the boy nodded to continue.

"Some people consider what you just saw bad. That's why we have to keep it between us. But it's not really bad. All of this..." he deliberated on how to move forward, "You see, there really is no such thing as bad and good. They're just words, understand?" The boy didn't seem to, so Nish tried another approach. "Throughout time, those who have challenged unjust laws are seen as freedom fighters," he watched the boy pick his nose in confusion. A truck carrying a trailer barreled down the road past them.

"Okay, imagine someone wants to buy a house," he saw the boy's reaction change and stuck with the new scenario. "The problem is, you can't just go out one day and buy a house. There are certain things you have to deal with. You're not sure of the value so you hire an appraiser. Prices are too high to just pay for the whole thing outright, so you have to go to the bank and get a mortgage. You don't have the legal expertise to understand all the contracts, so you hire a lawyer. And after

41

the whole thing's done, you still have to make payments to the bank or it gets repossessed. You understand so far?"

The boy nodded slightly, taking off his towel so that he was sitting naked. "Put that back on, we're in public," Nish scolded. The boy sat frozen so Nish wrapped the towel around him and continued.

"Now think if the act of buying a house, one dream almost everyone shares, were illegal. Only when someone does break the law and does actually buy a house, they aren't the ones getting in trouble. The people who get in trouble are the banker, the lawyer, the appraiser, etcetera. Does that seem fair?" Nish shook his head, the boy did the same.

"That's right, it's not fair. Even if you say the bank technically bought the house, why screw the lawyer? Why screw any of the movers or plumbers or electricians who had to come in to make sure everything's working?" He leaned in closer, "Why should a carpenter go to prison for helping someone's dream come true?"

The boy stared at him with wide eyes.

"Do you understand?" Nish nodded his head, the boy mirrored him again.

"Good," Nish leaned back in his seat, satisfied with his ability to get a cogent point across; his attempts at doing this with the other real estate agents usually ended in yawns or confused stares. He turned on the engine. "You're a pretty smart kid. You may be useful to have around after all." As Nish pulled out into traffic, the boy took off his towel to play with himself.

DAY 5

The edges of the Texas plains were burnt to a crisp by the time Nish and Bill showed up at the construction site. The tattoo Nish had drunkenly gotten over the weekend, his college football number and the team mascot, had crusted over on his bicep. He tried not to scratch it in front of his grizzled new boss for fear of looking weak.

Allen had shown up early and was sitting in his truck, watching the site like it might get up and walk away if he blinked. Nish figured the other new guy was just as nervous as he was. Everyone wanted to be a field agent since the money was better but people had to prove themselves in their first month or they'd be sitting behind a desk for at least a year. The day hadn't started off well with Nish's car dying, forcing him to call Bill for a lift.

"Fifty years ago, only ranchers and farmers up here. Over yonder about a mile used to be the big Scurry ranch," Bill lifted a thick finger from the steering wheel without taking his eyes off the construction site. The wad of tobacco in his lower lip kept his mouth almost shut as he spoke. "Now, can't build fast enough."

Even though he hadn't been told directly, Nish had pieced together that the CEO of his new company had gotten his hands into the business at the right time. In some cases, he would use connections in local government to find out when a developer was planning on building a new neighborhood and buy ripe property from struggling farmers, then sell it a year later at an exorbitant profit. Other times, highways that were supposed to be built magically disappeared as quickly as they'd been planned. Things other investors couldn't predict, one of Nish's coworkers had told him, as if the old man were a real estate guru. Having only been with the agency a week, Nish didn't feel it was appropriate to shatter the old man's image.

Reaching into the glove compartment, he removed the 9mm automatic Bill had loaned him that morning. He figured this was the part in the movies where the two gangsters took out their guns, looked at each other and said something like "time to take care of business". Nish pulled back the action and looked over at Bill but he'd already stepped out of the truck to loudly pass gas. Unsure of where to put the pistol, Nish clicked on the safety before sticking it in the back of his pants.

Allen got out of his own truck to shake hands with his two new coworkers. Nish had heard the young man was the nephew of one of the agency's higher-level directors. The same good old boy shit he'd dealt with his whole life, he thought. The guy even looked the part, dressed like a cross between a frat boy and a ranch hand even though he'd probably never been to college or branded a steer in his life.

"Good to see you, Bill," Allen lowered his head slightly, shaking the man's hand. Nish got a kick out of how everyone kissed Bill's ass when they were face to face with him. No matter how homophobic most of the agents were, they held their tongues around the veteran director. Behind Bill's back, of course, Nish noticed that people had all the balls in the world.

"I have a cousin up around here," Allen said to Bill. "I used to come out here a lot. I know a great place we can grab some beers after--"

"I'm going to talk to the guy in charge," the boss interrupted, spitting on the sandy ground. "Y'all don't say shit."

The two new employees nodded their heads as Bill started towards the trailer in front of the site. Allen turned to Nish with a less respectful look on his face, "Car broke down?" he laughed like there was a group of his friends there to hear him poking fun at his coworker. The young man's stubbly chin caught Nish's eye. God must be an anal motherfucker, he thought, spacing thousands of tiny hairs so evenly apart. He wanted to hold a lighter to spots on Allen's face to break the perfect pattern. You can beat nature if you really try, he nodded to himself.

As they followed their boss, Nish noticed that Bill walked like a dog he'd owned as a child that was hit by a car, jolting forward like he was being carried by his momentum, then having to work twice as hard with his other leg to keep going.

"Got shot five times in Vietnam," Allen whispered. "He was in the Navy, one of those river boats."

Nish looked at him like he should shut up before their boss turned around.

When they reached the trailer, Bill knocked on the door. The sudden urge to piss rose in Nish, reminding him of the anxiety that had always preceded football games when he was younger. His eyes darted across the site as he ran his hand over the pistol in the back of his jeans. No workers, he noticed, which seemed right.

A red face popped out the door, so waxy that Nish thought its owner kept it out of the sun for fear of it melting down onto his neck. "Hold your horses," it said abruptly. Nish was surprised the guy wasn't more polite, especially considering why the real estate agents were there.

44

He looked over at Allen standing with both hands behind his back; he did the same to make his weapon more quickly accessible.

There was a noise from inside the trailer like the man was moving stuff around. Bill looked at the two assistants and motioned for them to move back. Nish's heart dropped into his stomach, almost pushing the piss out of him as he and Allen moved away as fast as they could. When they saw Bill step around the side of the trailer, they each ducked behind two large bundles of steel cable spaced a few feet apart.

The door flung open. The waxy man emerged with a 12-gauge pump action shotgun, "Come on you sons of bitches!" and took the first shot.

"Fuck!" Nish yelled out, pressing himself to the ground. "That motherfucker's shooting at us!" His voice cracked like a pubescent teenager's as he said the most obvious thing in the world. A shot hit the bundle of cable Allen was hiding behind, producing a metallic hollow noise. He looked over at Nish with a smile on his face like he'd just seen a naked woman for the first time.

"Fuck, fuck, fuck." Nish repeated as fast as he could. He saw Allen grab his pistol; he immediately tried to do the same but the weapon flew out of his hand and into the clearing between the two bundles. "You've got to be fucking kidding me." Without giving himself time to think, he dove into the middle of the clearing, grabbing the gun and rolling behind Allen's cover.

"What the fuck was that?" his coworker stared at him. Shot peppered the area where Nish's foot had just been. He tried to click the safety off his weapon but hit the clip release, sending the bullets sliding out of the pistol.

Another shot, this time closer as the man neared the two pinned down agents. Allen snaked his arm around the bundle to let three shots fly indiscriminately, deafening Nish's closest ear. With firearms exploding around him, Nish was almost paralyzed. It wouldn't have mattered if someone were watching cartoons at the same volume, he thought, the sheer noise jarred something inside him. The heaviness of the piss weighed down even more on his bladder, he was sure some of it would work its way out.

Allen pulled his arm back, the same stupid grin on his face. There was another shot from the other side of the bundle, but this time the sharp crack of a pistol replaced the clumsy explosion of the 12 gauge. The waxy man mollowed in pain but the only noise Nish could make out through the pound of cotton jammed in his ears was a high-pitched monotone siren.

"Alright," Bill's voice came from the clearing in front of them. Allen peered cautiously over the top of the bundle before standing. Nish followed his lead, making sure the clip was back in his pistol before he stepped out from behind his cover. The scene that greeted him was pretty much what he'd expected, but with more blood. Bill had shot the man in the back, the bullet exiting through his stomach. The fresh wound had already begun forming a growing red halo around him. It looked like someone had shot open a container of red milk that still drooled lackadaisically from his intestinal cavity. His mouth was moving but Nish couldn't hear him until they got closer.

"Goddamn you, Bill, you fucking faggot," the dying man spit. The absence of blood in the saliva was almost as surprising to Nish as the absence of a wet spot on the front of his own pants. The man flung an arm towards his shotgun but Bill's foot landed on it first. The man looked up at him, waxier than ever, his body rushing to pour out its contents while it still could. "Listen to me you fucking queer, you better kill me, cause if you don't--"

Bill shot the man in the head, the back of his skull spitting out its insides onto the sandy ground; it was like a scum had been on Nish's soul his whole life and he'd only just realized now as it lifted. Everything else in the world was just practice, a secondary existence for moments like this, watching the contents of the cracked egg run free. Every nerve was fresh, waiting to be exposed to feeling. Every sight was sharp so that nothing went unnoticed. It suddenly felt like he hadn't had anything to drink all day.

The feeling passed as quickly as it had come. A deep dread fell onto him as he looked around the perimeter of the area. No one was there but he knew that didn't mean there couldn't be cops or federal agents watching them from afar.

"Let's throw him in the foundation," Nish proposed hurriedly. He pointed to the construction site, "I saw a cement mixer. We toss him in there, cover him up."

Bill looked at the site, then back at the dead man. "Alright."

Without waiting for help, Nish grabbed the corpse's arms to drag the body, happy he'd brought his portable hand cleanser. Bill motioned for Allen to grab the dead man's feet. The two new agents had gotten halfway to the building foundation when the door to the trailer swung open again, revealing a stocky Mexican laborer with a machete and a crazed look on his face. Nish dropped the corpse's arms but by the time he'd pulled out his pistol, the Mexican was wheezing on the ground.

"Check the goddamn trailer!" Bill ordered as he lowered his smoking weapon. "I ain't about to get caught with my pants down around my ankles. And let me know what you find, whether pig sticker or RPG."

Being closest, Allen hesitantly neared the trailer as Nish watched the Mexican die slowly. The laborer's heart pumped so much blood out of the hole in his ribs that Nish wondered how the man's body could have contained all of it in the first place.

"Goddamnit," Bill took out his cell phone. He looked to Nish, "Ask that one what he was doing in there, then throw them both in the foundation. I'm gone." Bill hit a key on his phone and walked backed to his truck.

Nish finished dragging the waxy man's corpse to an area that was ready to be filled with cement. He threw it in; when the man's body hit the ground ten feet below, it broke in places that would have elicited screams if he were still alive. Instead, the expression on his face stayed the same. By the time Nish had walked back, Allen was standing over the Mexican and a plume of dust had replaced Bill's truck in the distance.

"This son of a bitch keeps babbling about something," Allen gave the Mexican a kick. "You speak Spanish?"

Nish listened to the man but he was just praying and talking about his family.

-What were you doing here?- Nish asked in Spanish but the man didn't stop his mantra of prayers to the Virgin of Guadalupe to look after his wife and daughters.

"What's that mean?" Allen pointed at the Mexican's t-shirt. Nish read it out loud, "Oy vey, it's Zach's Bar Mitzvah." He stuck a fingernail between his teeth before remembering it had just been clutching the arm of a dead man. He pulled it out and spit on the ground. "Jewish. It's like saying, 'Hey, it's Zach's birthday'."

"So what should we do?" Allen stopped prodding the man.

"Well, unless you're a surgeon, we've got to get rid of this guy. Bill's already counted him for dead. No return on this."

"Alright," Allen took out his pistol. The Mexican looked at Nish, pleading for his life. Allen lined up the shot as the man rambled on about his family, how he was sending money back to them every two weeks. He owned a nightclub inTamaulipas and was building a second floor on it. It could be Nish's if he could just see his girls again.

"What's he saying now?" Allen stalled.

"He's mumbling, I can't make it out," Nish lied. He stared at the man's head, waiting for it to eject the brains and blood into the dirt. Thirst spread across his mouth. Allen's fingers regripped the gun, his eye drifted from the sight, forcing him to refocus. The Mexican sensed his hesitation and turned to him, going into his plea in broken English.

"Shit!" Allen lowered the gun. "I can't do it like this."

Nish studied his face, the same as his brother's when he refused to take the leap after the crane had taken him all the way to the top for the bungee jump on his birthday. Weakness. He remembered his own panic just minutes before behind the steel cables and smiled now that he and his coworker were even.

Nish kicked the Mexican hard in the jaw. It didn't knock him out so Nish removed the pistol from the back of his jeans. Ejecting the clip and the bullet in the chamber, he swung it down hard on top of the man's head. The Mexican yelled out in pain.

"What are you doing?" Allen stepped forward childishly like he was going to try to stop him.

"I'm trying to knock him out," Nish struck the man again. "In the movies it only takes one hit." After a few more blows, the man lost consciousness. Nish dragged him to the foundation and threw him in.

He went to the back of the cement mixer to turn the thing on and when he'd returned, the man's eyes were open, staring upwards in a way that caused Nish to wonder if he were already dead. The cement started flowing and the Mexican focused on his killer, pleading one last time for his life until Nish aimed the cement into his mouth. He figured if the man swallowed some, the foundation might be sturdier and less suspect, although it probably wouldn't make a difference. In the downtown slums that were being renovated, he'd heard they tarred the holdouts right into the upgraded roof. Dallas is a city built on blood and bones, he thought to himself. He considered sharing the idea with his coworker but figured he wouldn't get the metaphor. Instead, he told him how they needed to scoop up the areas of sand clotted with blood and pieces of shredded organs and throw it into the foundation before they turned off the mixer.

The diner looked like a weigh station for people rolling down the other side of the hill towards death. Old folks wearing old clothes, eating low sodium mashed potatoes and forcing down chicken with skin that was crispy in some areas and hung limp and fatty in others. Half of them wore cowboy hats, causing Nish to wonder what a younger version of one of them would say if they got lost on the way back to the ranch and stumbled across their aged counterpart, smoking and drinking coffee and talking endlessly about nothing but high school football and various ailments. He'd never get old, he thought, not like that. He'd be sitting in a café in Paris drinking wine or living a life like the characters in the Jimmy Buffet songs his mom used to listen to when she would drink rum on the back porch and stare at the fence.

"Table for two, sir?" a young waitress approached the two agents. Nish felt sorry for her, being stuck in the grim reaper's halfway house. She looked like she could have been a child actress when she was younger, lisping in commercials to seem cuter. But age had planted a crust of acne on her face that connected her eyebrows, spreading all the way down the side of her mouth. He looked away from her, suddenly having to hold back tears.

"No thanks, we're actually here to meet someone," John smiled politely.

The waitress registered confusion for a second, then gave the slightest hint of a frown before a larger, fake smile forced its way onto her blemished face.

"Of course, y'all just come this way," she picked up two menus, trying not to look at the men.

She led them to a table in the back of the restaurant where Deaf sat with two other elderly men. Nish had only been asked to the diner twice before but both times the same old men were sitting with his boss. He had no idea who they were or why they were with him but he figured Deaf didn't keep them around for the company since he'd never heard either of them speak more than a short sentence, always something like 'Things are changing' or 'Only the good Lord knows', like they were in a competition to see which old redneck could lay forth some all encompassing kernel of truth he'd acquired from his many years on the Earth.

Deaf didn't look at either of his workers as they sat down. "A little more sweet tea, ma'am?" he raised his glass to the waitress.

"Of course, Mr. Smith," the girl smiled like she had for Nish and John.

After she'd left with the empty glass, the table was totally silent. Deaf looked out the window of the restaurant at the concrete monstrosity of I-35 looming over the flat landscape. Nish had gotten used to the distant expression on Deaf's face, like the old man was looking deep into the past and seeing something that filled him with quiet hatred.

"You boys going to San Antone tomorrow," he spoke up.

"Yes, sir," Nish acknowledged the plainly spoken fact.

Something on the highway caught Deaf's eye. One of the other old men took out a handkerchief to cough a massive wad of mucus into. When the waitress returned with the boss' sweet tea, Nish realized she had never taken his drink order. By how fast she'd retrieved the old man's drink, he figured her nerves were getting to her. She was about to leave again without even acknowledging the two newcomers until one of the old men raised a finger.

"Miss," his voice was high like he was trying to impersonate a woman. "Do y'all have that fancy coffee?"

The waitress cocked her head, "What coffee would that be, sir?"

"You know, that fancy coffee they sell on the TV. From Columbia or Jamaica or some such place," he moved his mouth around like he was chewing his lips off.

"Oh, the Puerto Rican Dark Brew," she smiled genuinely.

"Yes ma'am, that's it," the man smiled back, exposing a toothless mouth.

"Yes sir, we do have it. Would you like a glass?"

"Nope. Only drink my wife's coffee."

The smile dissolved from the young woman's face; she nodded and walked away. Nish made it a point not to look at John.

"When I was a boy, we used to come up here to the stock yards," Deaf ran his finger along a deep rut in the table. "We consume this Earth, it's human nature. You show me a man who doesn't, and I'll show you one who's about to be conquered by another who does." The old men nodded, the high voiced one raising his finger like he was waiting for a teacher to call on him. Nish turned and the man spoke, "But then to chaos. The poorest breed the most, beget more poverty."

Nish looked at the other old man, his eyes focused on something at the next table. Deaf took a sip of his tea. "What happened yesterday?"

The blood froze in Nish's veins. There were always issues, but it was never good if the boss made it a point to talk to you in person about something.

"I just had to deal with an insect problem down at the church, sir," Nish lowered his voice. "I threatened them and they backed down."

Deaf scratched his temple, still looking at the highway, "I never threatened people. Never had to." The old man turned to his worker. His glasses didn't reflect any light so Nish could see him staring straight ahead as if his two employees had already left. John stood and Nish followed in suit.

"I'll call Bill when we get there," Nish said, immediately regretting opening his mouth. He was never sure what he was supposed to say in front of his boss. Deaf nodded and they left.

"Old man's going to kill you if you fuck up in San Antone," John warned as soon as they had reached the parking lot.

He's probably right, Nish thought. Why else would Deaf have called him there and confronted him like that. "That's ridiculous," he said out loud.

As they neared John's truck, the grunting and heavy breathing coming from inside became more audible. "Sounds like two pigs fucking," John took out his keys. The boy's ears perked up when he heard the sound of the men's boots getting closer. He jumped up on the back seat of the truck, moaning excitedly. Nish figured if the boy had a tail, he'd be wagging it. "I want to bring him."

"Who?"

Nish pointed at the disfigured child.

50

"What? What the hell are you talking about?"

"He has no place to go. Besides, he saved my ass yesterday. If it weren't for him, I could be lying dead on the floor of the loading docks right now."

"What did he do? Show his face and the guys went running?" John spit emphatically on the ground before unlocking the doors. "Or did he take off that weird toga you made for him and start pissing all over the place like he tried to earlier?"

"Warned me as a guy was pulling a gun. Because of him, that asshole didn't get the drop on me." The two climbed in the truck. The boy greeted his savior with a hug around the neck; Nish realized how long it had been since someone had done that. "Let me make this conversation a lot shorter. I'll pull rank if I have to, but this kid's coming with us."

John squinted like he was trying to read tiny writing on the dashboard. "How much sense does it make for you to start building pools and taking in strays when you're under the microscope? You got the old man bringing up situations to you in person," he shook his head.

Nish watched the giant as he started the truck. While John had never stolen a dime from the agency, Nish knew he could count on him to always have his back. Even though John would get control of their crew if something were to happen to his manager, Nish knew his friend wouldn't turn him in. "I hardly invited anyone from the office to the pool party."

"Word gets around. And even if it didn't, that old man would find out somehow."

If Deaf were going to kill him, Nish figured San Antonio would be a good place to do it. The old man was a lot of bad things but he wasn't stupid. "You're paranoid," Nish turned to look at the smiling child, his mutilated tongue wiggling in the back of his throat. "The boy's coming."

"You hear this motherfucker?" Nish cornered the restaurant owner. He studied the disgusting little man, bald with a brown mustache smeared above his upper lip, his face shiny with a mixture of grease and sweat. John leaned casually against the wall of the tiny office.

"Motherfucker's talking like those windows out front are brick-proof. They make brick-proof windows now, John?"

"Not that I heard."

"What about the inside of buildings?" Nish took another step towards the man, who bumped clumsily into the wall. "They make it so the inside of buildings can't catch on fire?"

"Reckon not."

The owner gritted his teeth like he'd had enough, puffing out his chest as he stepped to his aggressor. If the disgusting man had been a few inches taller, they would have been face to face. "You threatening me, you towelhead son of a bitch?"

For the most part, Nish didn't enjoy going to restaurants or small shops to get payment. It made him feel cheap. He'd rather deal with the other end of things, even if it meant scenes like the one the previous day. When he started with the agency, he used to think of himself like some robot, incapable of having feelings for the people whose lives he was about to ruin. But over time, he began to develop a hatred for them, eventually blaming the business owners for putting him in the shoes of the intimidator. You can't have all the positives of the free market without also having to deal with the negative shit, he thought. And sometimes, when the situation was just right, he relished his work.

"That's the question you ask?" Nish dug a fingernail deep enough into his scalp to hit the wetness underneath. Turning to John as if he were about to ask the giant another question, he pulled the revolver from where it was hidden in the back of his pants, then quickly spun around to point the pistol in the man's face.

"Hold on a second, now," John stood up straight.

"Firstly, even an ignorant hayseed fuck like yourself should realize I'm threatening you," Nish held the firearm an inch from the man's greasy forehead. "And secondly, my towel's at the cleaners today, so I assume you were making some sort of derogatory racist comment."

The owner opened his mouth like he was about to say something; Nish quickly pulled back the pistol, swinging it into the man's teeth. He could feel some of the tiny bones crack away from the skull.

"Fuck!" the man doubled over. He tried to say something but his mouth wouldn't move correctly with the blood coming out of it. Nish thought how stupid he sounded; he raised his boot, aiming it at the top of the hairless head. Screams from the front of the restaurant stopped him short.

John placed his hand over his own weapon as he opened the door and peeked around the corner to check out what was going on.

"You know about this?" Nish asked the owner, who garbled a denial.

"Goddamnit," John took his hand off his pistol. "Little boy's running naked through the restaurant."

The owner looked up at Nish, puzzled.

"Shit," Nish replaced the gun in his pants, turning to the man before leaving, "Three days, or I'm sending someone down here who doesn't have my pleasant disposition. Got it?"

The owner nodded.

"He's up on a table, drinking someone's milk," John narrated. "Looks like he's going to piss again…there he goes."

"What are you doing talking about this shit to me? Go grab him!"

"This is your mess," John threw his hands up. "You take care of it."

"Shit," Nish ran out of the office to grab the boy.

Wrapping the towel around the child, Nish carried him from the restaurant's dining area into the kitchen. The new Mexican workers were almost unrecognizable to Nish now that they had on clothes and weren't covered in blood. The cooks stopped their work to stare at the hideous creature, the ones that had been in the unit wilting into the background.

-Not do you see anything,- Nish yelled out in Spanish. The workers turned back to their cutting boards. Spotting a container of milk in the open fridge, the boy tugged at Nish's arm.

"No, we're leaving," his savior scolded but he tugged harder, breaking free from the man's grasp. He lurched towards the milk, falling into the shelves of the fridge. Food tumbled out around him onto the floor. The milk itself taunted him from a high shelf so the boy grabbed a side of the industrial sized refrigerator and pushed. The stainless steel unit slammed to the ground like a wrecking ball had just hit it.

As the real estate agents and cooks stared in disbelief, the boy reached into the sideways fridge to pull out the milk.

-Little Hercules,- a Mexican pointed at the child in the makeshift toga. The others nodded, chiming in. Nish slowly approached the boy, waiting until he'd finished pouring the gallon of milk down his face and body to pick him up like a baby and carry him to the truck as the Mexicans repeated the name to each other in amazement.

DAY 6

The rain stopped its assault on the truck an hour outside of Dallas. Nish turned around in his chair to see the black clouds hovering over North Texas; it didn't look like they were going anywhere anytime soon.

"Sun," John summed up the new weather. His manager grabbed a soft drink from the cooler.

"What do you think fire is made of?" John cocked his head.

"Fire isn't made of anything. It's a reaction, energy. If you hold a metal box over a fire and close it, you can't open it later and have a flame," Nish cracked the drink open and set it in a cup holder, then dug through the bag at his feet until he found the spicy pork rinds.

"That's what they say, but think of the sun," John waited until after Nish had taken a handful of fried pig fat to grab his own. "It obviously has mass and a shitload of it. A whole solar system revolves around it, so its gravitational pull has to be crazy."

Nish contemplated this as he chewed. "That's some deep shit," he nodded at the giant, who burped and nodded back. They both stared out the window. "The sun is made of gas," Nish worked through the idea, "Its mass is so much larger than the mass of the planets' solid surfaces. Even though they may be denser, it's just that much bigger."

"Why doesn't the gas just float away?"

"Damn," Nish was stumped. He checked the back seat to make sure Hercules wasn't awake to witness his ignorance. "I'll have to look that up on the internet when we're back in Dallas."

The giant beamed at the sun above them. They stared out the window and ate while Nish pondered.

The truck drove past the pumps into a parking space at the gas station.

"Almost forgot what it was like going on road trips with you," John grinned as his manager hopped out of the cab. While Nish headed for the restroom inside, the giant began cleaning the truck. Hercules

54

opened his eyes like he wasn't sure where he was, then found John's face and rested his head back on the seat.

Exiting the bathroom, Nish walked down the aisles full of junk food to find a pack of gum. An old man in a cowboy hat inched his way up to the counter as the young girl waiting to check him out waited patiently.

"Darling," the man rested both hands on the counter for support. He cleared his throat noisily, removing a used handkerchief to spit the mucus into. "Pack of cigarettes, the usual."

"Yes, sir," the girl replied in a thick accent. Nish examined her from the waist up, imagining her inexperienced and eager in the restroom.

"Sure you don't want two packs, save you a trip?" she tempted her customer.

"No thank you, ma'am. This is the only chance I have to get away from the wife," the old man opened his mouth in a dry, silent laugh, then turned to shuffle slowly to the door. Nish smiled at the girl and they chuckled quietly. Nish noticed the lottery tickets behind her. "Just this," he pushed forward the gum, stealing a glance at her breasts. "And can I have two of the scratch-offs?"

"Sure," she turned to get the tickets, causing Nish to bite his lip. She laid them on the counter with a wink.

"Thanks."

Once outside, Nish stretched his arms one last time as a police cruiser rolled up a few spots away from John's tank. He opened the truck door to lift himself into the cab. Looking for a place to put his pack of gum, he opened the glove compartment and his pistol slid into view.

"What you doing with that gun, boy?" one of the policemen neared the truck with his hand resting on his own sidearm. His partner got out of the cruiser.

Nish picked his teeth as they neared, "Exercising my right as an American." He flicked an imaginary food particle to the ground before the policeman, who unbuttoned the strap that held his gun in its holster.

"Would you like to see a permit, sir?" John let the officer know he was there, making sure to keep his hands casually on the hood.

The officer exhaled, taking his thumb off the safety. Nish thought how much more at ease the cop looked once he'd seen John.

"Yep," the policeman responded. Nish clenched his teeth while noisily fishing for the permit in the glove box.

"Fucking small town bullshit," he stared at the ranch land as they passed through it. He felt an itch on the top of his head and dug his fingernail deep into his scalp. He pulled the finger back with red wetness on it.

"Forget about it, man," John shrugged. The giant turned on the radio as Nish dug the bloody finger deep into his thumb's cuticle. He looked at the blonde giant; it probably really was easy for him to forget about it, he thought.

"How do you figure the moon can affect the tide?" John lowered the radio's volume. "If it's so powerful over water, what if a slow moving comet were to pass by? Like if it took a year?"

Nish knew the giant enjoyed having these discussions with him since he actually took John seriously, unlike the other agents who saw him as a stupid ogre talking nonsense. To be the ideal physical specimen of the group, John didn't really have any friends in the company, or all Dallas, as far as Nish knew, besides himself. "If one were to move that slow, it would probably cause floods all over the place," Nish pulled out his fingernail, relaxing into the seat. "But I figure we'd shoot it down somehow before it got to that point."

Cattle grazed behind barbwire fences on both sides of the road, taking their time to get meatier as the sun evaporated the water in the tanks they drank from. Nish figured they might want to hurry up. "You ever have anal sex?" he asked John.

"Once," the giant nodded. "My ass was killing me for the next week." He winked and Nish laughed.

"For real, though," Nish suddenly felt so loose and happy he almost propped a foot up on the dashboard but remembered his driver.

"For real, a few times," John shrugged. "It was alright. I mean, it's tighter. But you have to worry about," John paused like he was trying to move forward delicately. Nish interjected, "Got it." He stroked his chin and pictured the girl at the counter. "Kind of a double-edged sword, then."

"Yep."

The teenager unlocked the metal gate. The TEXAS tattoo on his dirt-covered leg, the X having been replaced with a swastika, drew Nish's attention. After they had driven through, John waited for the teen to lock it behind them and get on his four-wheeler to lead them up the road to the dilapidated house hiding under an unnatural cluster of trees. A motorcycle sat in front in stark contrast, reflecting light off its chrome like it was brand new. A heavy, bearded man wearing a sleeveless leather MC jacket with no shirt underneath had parked himself next to it on a removed back seat. Nish figured it had been taken from one of several dead cars that sat rusting nearby.

56

After parking under a tree, the real estate agents retrieved their weapons and stepped out to face the house. Their guide plopped down on the other side of the back seat to fish a beer from the nearby water-filled cooler. Cracking it open, he raised it to his acne-pocked face as if oblivious to the presence of the men he'd just let in.

"The Colonel," Nish stared at the teen.

"I know who you're here for."

"Then why the fuck are you sitting around with your thumb up your ass?" Nish stepped towards him. The teen jumped up.

"Watch your mouth there, son," the biker leaned forward. Nish wondered where his swastika tattoo was.

"I look like your fucking son? You must be getting me confused with that little bastard sucking on your ex-girlfriend's disease-ridden titty," Nish's hand floated to the fresh wound on his scalp. The biker stood, rising to John's height. Nish dug the nail into the bloody opening on his head.

The teenager sat the beer down, spitting on the ground in front of the agents. He bit his upper lip, raising his chin, then suddenly his face fell slack. The biker next to him took a tiny step back like he was bracing himself, his eyes looking past the agents to their truck.

Hercules' face pressed itself against the window, drool dribbling down onto the side panel. "Goddamnit," John whispered under his breath. The disfigured boy beat at the window, causing the teen and biker to move backwards slowly.

"I'll get him," Nish walked to the truck and opened the door, catching the boy as he tumbled out.

"What the fuck is that?" the teen pointed.

Using Hercules' towel, Nish wiped the drool from the child's face. "My boy," Nish answered, grabbing a bottle of milk from the cooler. The sound of locks being turned came from the door. Nish figured the boy would be safe enough in the bed of the truck. "You stay here while we talk inside, okay?" Hercules moaned approval.

"I told you he'd get us out of trouble," Nish said quietly to the giant. John shook his head as he followed his manager to the door of the house.

The Colonel was a wiry man who always wore the same clothing; like a cartoon character, Nish thought, if only the character was a Vietnam vet whose outfit consisted of an army vest and a pair of filthy jeans. The arms coming out of the vest looked like they belonged to someone else, interchangeable parts the man put on when he was having company over. The only flaw Nish could see in this idea was the Colonel didn't give a shit about anyone else enough to try to impress them. The vet led them into the main room, spotted with broken couches and chairs. Nish could smell the stink coming off the shag rug and tried not to imagine what had caused the huge stains on it.

"Sorry about them boys out there," the Colonel kept his teeth clenched when he spoke, only moving his lips. "They didn't know y'all was with the House."

Bullshit, Nish thought. "No problem," he crossed his arms. John stood next to him silently.

"Got a buddy here with me. He's alright," the Colonel led them through the main room to the kitchen, where a blonde man about Nish and John's age was assembling an assault rifle. He was tanned and wearing shorts and a sleeveless t-shirt. Nish thought he would look more at home waxing a surfboard than loading the clip into a machine gun.

"How's it going?" the young man smiled broadly, extending a hand. Nish took it and introduced himself. Before the blonde man could do the same, the Colonel interjected, "This is Buddy."

The blonde man's eyes darted quickly to the vet. The Colonel picked up a box of ammunition from the table, handing one of the bullets to Nish.

"Can't buy this at your local guns and ammo store," Nish winked at the Colonel, causing the vet to open his mouth for the first time in a smile.

"Head downstairs?" Buddy asked. The others nodded, following the Colonel to the bedroom closet.

Little Hercules finished his bottle, burping his satisfaction. The boy stood to examine the world beyond the bed of the truck.

"Look at that goddamn thing," the teen hit the biker on the leg and pointed at the child.

"Ugly as sin," the biker rested his hand on the gun in his pants.

"Get back down there, boy," the teen motioned for Hercules to sit. The disfigured boy stretched while letting out a moan that caused his spectators to contort their faces. There was a laugh in the far distance. The boy jumped from the bed of the truck; he landed on his legs but quickly fell to his face. The men jumped up, the biker with the gun in his hand. "Stay back, motherfucker."

Hercules got to his feet, pulling off his towel to expose his body. The sight backed the men against the house. The boy lurched towards the sound.

When he arrived, the two children stopped poking their stick at the fire ant hill. They turned to face him, the boy recoiling from the grotesque form while his sister stood her ground. Hercules opened his arms like a bat.

"Ewww," the little boy made a face. He threw the stick at the ugly newcomer. The disfigured boy lurched to the side and lowered his arms, letting out a low growl. He took a step towards the little boy.

"Don't be mean to him," the boy's sister stepped in the way.

"He's gross looking," the boy picked up another stick.

"Shut up. He's special," the girl scolded her brother. She walked towards the outcast with her arms wide open. The drool fell from Hercules' lips down onto the yellow ground. The brother shook his head, "He's naked. That's how people rape."

"He's not going to rape," she contested. "Everyone's different," she was a foot away from Hercules. He ground his teeth together as he opened his arms wide again.

The men ascended the metal staircase, exiting the closet to the sound of a child's scream. The agents looked at each other as their hosts produced weapons from their clothes that Nish thought were from the set of some futuristic movie.

The group ran out the front door to find the two lounging men and their vehicles gone. Following the high-pitched cry, they found Hercules rolling on the ground with the girl, clumsily tickling her while she shrieked in delight.

"What the fuck?" the Colonel raised his weapon. Nish motioned for him to wait, "He's mine, it's okay. They're just messing around."

The brother of the girl ran towards the men, "He was hurting her. Rape." The boy passed the two children on the ground and grabbed his sister's shoulder to pull her away. Hercules took both ends of the boy's arm in his hands and pushed them together so his wrist and elbow touched. The bone stabbed outwards through the boy's supple flesh, blood flecked the earth below. The young boy stared at it for a second, then howled in pain. Before the men had a chance to pull Hercules away, he slapped at the broken bone and smiled like he'd just invented a new toy.

"I'm starving," Nish discarded the empty bag of pork rinds. The hunger didn't help his stomach, queasy from driving through the hills. He looked at John staring angrily ahead.

"What?" Nish threw up his hands. "I'm not going to dump the kid. You saw how he saved our ass with Adolf back there."

"They weren't going to do shit to us," John still refused to look at him.

"We paid Buddy enough to buy his kid a bionic arm. Besides, any guy bringing their children to a place like that isn't exactly parent of the year."

"What if Colonel tells the old man, huh? How would that look?"

"Colonel isn't talking," Nish wondered if what he said was true. "Besides, it's done now. No need to dwell on the past." He turned to the backseat, "But you need to watch yourself, you understand? No hurting nice people."

Hercules moaned sheepishly.

The smell of smoked meat permeated the cab of the truck even before the barbeque joint was in sight. As they pulled into the parking lot, they were met by rows of grills in front of the restaurant. A line of people formed at one where a man in a cowboy hat stood with a butcher's knife.

John turned off the engine. "He's staying here," he looked sternly at Nish, making his manager laugh. Nish shrugged and looked back at the boy, "Hercules, if you stay here, I'll bring you back some food and all the milk you can drink. Okay?"

The boy made a sound like he was noisily hyperventilating, bouncing up and down in the seat.

"Good, you just stay here," Nish gave him a thumbs up, which the boy returned.

Taking their place in the line, the agents tried to peek at the meat inside the barrel grill. Nish watched the fat of the brisket, blackened and crunchy on the top, turn to liquid and slide down the freshly cut slices. Next to the chunks of meat were ribs so tender that when the cook touched the blade to the flesh it slid right through. The sausage about to burst, juicy turkey breast, cabrito ready to fall apart at first bite, Nish loosened his belt to save himself the time later.

After the server had piled their plates with various parts of cooked animals, they went inside to order fixings. They grabbed jalapenos and onions from the common area on one side of the restaurant then sat at one of the many long benches stocked with sauce, white bread and paper towels.

"We forgot beer," Nish looked at the feast before him. John shrugged, grabbing his fork. Nish cleared his throat until the giant realized what was expected of him.

"I'm fixing to hoss this down," John pleaded.

"Grab yourself one while you're at it," Nish laid money on the table. "On me."

"I'm driving."

"Don't be such a pussy," Nish picked up his knife and fork to cut into the steaming brisket. The giant let out a childish moan before taking the money to the drink counter.

Nish scanned the restaurant as he ate, seeing through the families and old folks to the men sitting in small groups. He felt the butt of his pistol against his back. John returned with two beers, placing them both in front of his manager.

"Good work," Nish raised a bottle to salute a job well done. "I'll buy you dessert."

John rolled his eyes, "It's all on per diem." The giant stabbed a plump sausage, juice oozing from the holes made by the fork. He put his teeth around half of it, the casing providing resistance until he bit down hard and the contents burst out. As he chewed, he poured sauce onto his plate to dip the white bread into. His eyes floated to the walls. Football teams, governors and the occasional president smiled at the tables. He pointed to a large photo, asking with a full mouth, "How you think the Horns'll do this year?"

Following the finger, Nish inspected the group. "Should do alright," he popped a pickled jalapeno into his mouth, waiting for another question. It didn't come but he continued anyway, "We had to play against them a few times, you know. Almost beat them my freshman year."

"You play in that game?"

Nish studied the giant's face for a hint of malice. Although Nish often spoke about his college football experiences, his actual playing time was limited and he knew John was aware of that. "No, I didn't play in that game," he watched his subordinate eating with his eyes down. "How many freshman you think get playing time at all, much less in the biggest game of the year."

John shook his head, "Just wondering." Nish lifted the beer to his lips again while still watching him. The giant put a slice of raw onion in his mouth noisily.

"You're louder than that boy in your truck," Nish swallowed, then replaced the bottle with a fingernail to pick his teeth. "Maybe I should get you a fucking diaper."

"I can't help it," John looked back at his manager with childlike hurt. Nish remembered the words on his mirror and rubbed his eyes wearily. After draining the first beer, he returned to his plate. Occasionally dipping bread into sauce, he finished the brisket and sausage. He was slicing into a chunk of venison when a loud, sharp pop came from behind him. His hand dropped the fork and was on its way to his weapon when John snatched it in midair.

"It's fine," the giant still had his eyes on the plate in front of him. Nish turned to find a metal bowl of fried okra dropped on the stainless steel serving counter. He lowered the hand casually to the table, "Thanks."

"No problem."

The sound of teeth gnashing against bone coming from the back seat made Nish put his finger up to his ear. "Sounds great, I'll see you then," he hung up quickly. "Shit, Herc. She probably figured I was at the zoo at feeding time."

The boy moaned loudly, clapping his greasy hands together. The plastic tarp that the agents had covered the backseat with was only somewhat effective. A stray piece of fat that had been clinging to the boy's hand hit John in the back of the head.

"Goddamnit," he picked it out of his hair.

Nish laughed, "I'm sorry, man, I'm getting this whole thing cleaned. I didn't know he'd get this excited about barbeque."

John rolled down the window to throw out the fat. "Well, I guess I can't blame a man for that."

"There you go," Nish patted him on the shoulder, smiling.

"So you meeting up with that girl in San Antone?" John seemed to have accepted the boy's overzealous reaction to hill country brisket and moved on.

"She's having some people over to her place tomorrow night," Nish nodded. "It'll be nice. After we graduated high school, I only saw her a couple times. She hooked me up with the job at the communications firm I had right after college, though," Nish rubbed his fingers together to show imaginary money, "Family's hooked up. And she's in banking now, I doubt she's hurting."

John smiled, "And the rich get richer."

"Hardest working motherfuckers I ever met were rich people," Nish sat up straight and turned to the driver. John hunkered down in his seat as if preparing himself for a lecture. Nish turned slightly so Hercules could also hear, "Average man works forty hours a week, bitches about their boss and how they don't make enough money. A rich man, he'll work twice that in a week. Goes on business trips without seeing his family for long stretches. Expects his kids not only to do well despite the fact he's not there, but to excel in school."

The yellow ranch land passing by suddenly seemed to be the most interesting thing in the world to John.

"And you get some country music asshole talking about how he's a hard working, blue collar man," Nish motioned to the radio. "If a redneck really did work so hard, why's he still working class? This isn't fucking Russia." Nish stared at John. The giant raised his eyebrows as if he didn't know the answer. Nish looked back at Hercules gnawing on a rib. The boy met his gaze to wail approval.

"Fucking smart kid," he reached out and patted the boy's head, causing the child to hyperventilate with joy.

The receptionist was a bird of man who Nish thought smiled like a child molester. Holding Hercules's shoulder, the agent gave the name for the room. The man behind the desk looked at them and pressed his lips together in a smile so half-assed that Nish felt almost insulted.

"Sorry about the key situation," the receptionist handed over a single metal key. "We can only give you one."

"Really?" Nish put it in his pocket.

"I told the night supervisor a month ago that we should change the policy, but does she listen to me?" the man looked at Nish like he was expecting an answer. "Of course not, she's too busy stealing from the vending machines."

The receptionist went back to typing on his computer.

"Oh, and your friend is already here in the adjoining room," the man kept typing. "He showed up earlier today."

Nish and John looked at each other. "He give a name?" Nish asked.

"Yes," the man typed, then stared at the screen for an agonizing five seconds. "Michael Hunt."

"Oh yeah, Mike," Nish tried to play it cool. The agents thanked him and walked back outside to the truck. The sky over San Antonio turned from orange to red as the sun fell below the cracked earth of the distant horizon.

"What the fuck?" Nish took the pistol out of the glove box. "The San Antonio office has someone waiting for us?" John gave a bewildered look as he took out his own weapon. Nish watched him. If the old man really had found out about how much Nish was stealing, this would be a great place to get rid of him, he thought. And John could have known this whole time. Nish dispelled the thought from his head and turned away from his friend as he checked his pistol. The rattle of the snake shot inside gave him a measure of comfort.

John pulled the truck into a parking spot on the other side of the two-story motel. After telling Hercules to stay put, the agents tucked their pistols into the front of their jeans. They walked through a corridor past the motel's ice machines, then into the open hallway facing the back parking lot. Cars dotted the lot, mostly sedans, Nish noted. Nothing for families, nothing too conspicuous for one or two people to be driving on their own. He looked at the door numbers on both sides of the hallway and pointed John to the right, nearest the exit.

The agents walked on their toes so the heels of their boots wouldn't make noise as the room numbers counted down to meet the one on Nish's key. A red Jeep sat in front of the door with its top off and its bottom covered in dried mud. Texas plates with a license plate holder from a town Nish had never heard of. Checking to make sure the room's curtains were closed, he looked inside the cab. An oversized plastic cup from a convenience store sweated in the cup holder. Next to it were two packs of dip. An empty fast food bag lay on the passenger's seat. One person, he figured. The guy had probably just finished the food as he showed up at the motel since the trash would have blown out otherwise. Nish held up one finger to John, whose hand floated away from the top of his pistol. They wouldn't send one guy for a job like that, Nish thought. He relaxed for a second before taking another look at John's face. The giant stood like a soldier at ease, waiting for orders. There's no way, Nish pushed the thought from his mind again.

Nish took the lead as they tiptoed to the door. He raised his hand to knock when he heard voices laughing inside and he quickly retracted it. A radio turned on, country music shaking its weak speakers and coming out fuzzy around the edges. A man let out an enthusiastic yell.

Pulling out his pistol, Nish turned to the giant, "Fuck it." He motioned for John to step to the side of the door, out of sight of the peephole. Nish knocked, his face too close to the hole for the person inside to see anything but a cheek and mouth.

"Who is it?" a man's voice yelled from inside, followed by childish giggling.

"Hotel security, sir. We had a noise complaint."

"Fuck that!" the voice yelled over the music. He said something else that was followed by more high-pitched laughing.

Just when Nish was about to knock again, the door unlocked. It opened a crack and Nish slammed into it, causing the body behind the door to fall backwards. He rushed in and tripped on something that sent him sprawling across the cheap carpet, his pistol flying from his hand. He found himself facedown in a Styrofoam container of leftovers. Grabbing the plastic fork right in front of him, he pushed himself up to face the barrel of a 9mm. Behind it was a tall young man with a half-smile on his face that an NBA player would give a high school kid for trying to dunk on him. His brown hair fell down to his eyes in wide, lazy curls and Nish figured his tall frame hid a strength. If he had been born into a different life, he would have been some college kid bragging to his frat brothers about how many coeds he'd slept with the night before, Nish guessed. Instead, he probably doled out cocaine to strippers and fucked them in the back of his jeep.

The man looked at Nish for a second like he was studying a movie poster to decide if the film was worth seeing or not. He lowered the gun and smiled.

"Well, sheeyut!" the man drew out the word like he wanted to prolong the pleasure of saying it. The clip slid out of the gun and the man jacked the bullet from the chamber, catching it mid-air like a quarter he'd flipped. "You must be that Indian boy they were telling me about."

Nish sprung to his feet, fork in hand.

"Uh-oh!" the young man smiled, holding up his hands in a mock surrender. "Guess it's a good thing I'm not a salad!"

He turned to let out a high-pitch laugh. Nish regained his bearings and realized there was a young, half-naked woman on the bed. She giggled in suit, although Nish doubted she spoke any English.

"Enough of this bullshit," Nish looked back at the stranger. "Who the fuck are you?"

"They didn't tell you, man?" he turned around nonchalantly to set the pistol on the desk behind him next to a small mountain of cocaine. "I'm y'all's envoy."

Nish looked back at John, his pistol still aimed at the man.

"Vernon," the man shoved his hand into Nish's face so quickly that Nish almost gave him a prong in the eye. "Vernon Harris. You can just call me Verne." He flashed a car salesman's smile, extending the hand even further.

"I wasn't told about any envoy."

"Not my fault, man. I don't deal with the administrative side of things," Verne looked suddenly pissed off and withdrew his hand.

"Where are you from?" Nish asked.

"Just outside San Antonio," Verne answered incredulously. "Where you from?"

"You tell me."

Verne's face brightened. "You're quick as a pistol, ain't you? Y'all from Dallas," Verne lost interest in the conversation. "I'm teaching these snuff queens here how to drink," he grabbed the bottle of whiskey from the table to pour a glass for Nish and John each.

"Who told you to come here?"

"Junior, man. Junior told me. Who the hell else?"

Nish dropped the fork, trying to be as casual about it as possible. It wasn't surprising that they'd have someone to show them around, he figured, but it was also a great way for the old man to keep an eye on him. Or for Junior to see why his dad was up in his business. Nish's fingernail subconsciously went for his teeth as he contemplated the chances of ending up floating facedown in the River Walk.

"Well come on, man!" Verne shoved the glass in Nish's face, breaking his concentration. He took it and nodded at John to lower his weapon. As Nish drained the whiskey, Verne smiled and let out a moan of satisfaction that Nish felt was slightly inappropriate, at best.

"Good, huh?" Verne winked at the Dallas agents.

John took a sip of his drink and closed the door, exposing a second young whore who had been hiding behind it. Nish had assumed that the body he'd knocked over rushing into the room had been Verne. She walked to the bed to sit next to her colleague. She didn't giggle like the other; instead, she stared down ahead of her like she was trying to look through the floor and teleport to the motel's basement below her.

"Why'd they send you?" Nish handed the glass back to Verne for a refill as he eyed the floor for his revolver.

Verne took the hotel tumbler to refill it from the half-finished bottle. "I know what y'all are here for. Arturo, he's my manager. Junior's had me keep an eye on him for a while and I reckon that boy's running a goddamn street pharmacy. I'm here to handle whatever needs handling."

"I was told that was our job."

"Just here to help," Verne flashed his smile again.

Recovering his pistol from the ground, Nish studied the young man. "But why you? You say he's your manager, which means you must be support level. So why does Junior trust you to be his envoy?"

"I'm kin to him, Junior's cousin." He handed the glass to Nish, not making eye contact. "Anyway, I reckon y'all are tired after your trip and could use some relaxing," his expression changed suddenly again, this time to a sly look.

Nish looked past the whores to the single bed. He'd specifically told the secretary at the office that they needed two beds.

"These girls are still clean, too. It was hard but I resisted. I have amazing willpower," Verne scooped some of the cocaine off the desk into a plastic bag. "Just don't kiss that one. Or shake hands with the other one." The agents drained their glasses without speaking. Verne stood looking at them until he jumped at his lack of propriety, "Shit, I'm sorry. Here I am going on about handjobs and y'all probably just want to get some trim. Just let me collect my things."

After gathering his drugs and booze, leaving a little of both for his new partners, he walked to the door. "Y'all need me, I'm right next door," he raised the whiskey bottle to them and left.

"John?" Nish pointed to the girls on the bed. The giant examined them, one hungrily eyeing the coke on the table, the other staring through the floor.

"You know me," he responded and went to turn off the music.

"Alright ladies, you don't have to go home but you can't stay here," Nish waved the women out of the room. One of them said something in a mix of Spanish and English he didn't understand. She frowned, pointing to the powder on the table.

-No, no cocaine for you,- Nish spoke to her in Spanish. -This is America, girl. You need to earn things here. Not did you do anything.-

The whore shot him a nasty look and said something else that he figured wasn't complimentary, then grabbed her clothes and stomped out. The other prostitute followed as if she had been caught in the wake of the first.

"Fucking kids these days," Nish shook his head. He swept the cocaine into his hand to wash down the sink.

Hercules quieted down as his savior tucked him into one side of the bed. Nish found an extra pillow and blanket in the closet, which he threw on the floor with a loud sigh. "Hope this doesn't screw up my back too much," he said loud enough for John to hear over the running water he was washing his face with. "Old football injuries," he continued. "Bet you have some of those."

The water shut off. John emerged from the bathroom wiping his face with a hand towel. "I'll sleep on the floor," he offered.

"No," Nish rubbed his lower back. "I couldn't ask you to give up the bed. Not after you drove us all the way here, that's not right."

"It's no problem, I'm serious," John stood at the foot of the bed, ready to lay down.

"I don't know," Nish shook his head doubtfully, surprised he had to put this much effort into to it.

"It's cool, really."

Nish threw his hands up, bested by John's argument. "Thanks a lot, man." John situated the blanket on the floor.

"You know I'd never ask you to do this," Nish climbed into the empty bed. "It's just this football injury."

"Believe me, I hear you," John lay down. "I tore up my back playing football, too. At one point, they told me I could have trouble running again."

"So you understand how serious injuries can be," Nish fluffed his pillow.

"Oh yeah, if it hadn't been for the Marines running my ass off during boot camp, I probably wouldn't have ever started exercising again for fear of hurting my back even worse," John explained.

"You were lucky," Nish pulled the covers over him.

"You take the bed for the whole trip. You don't want to aggravate something," John got up to turn off the light as Nish tried to study his face in the dark. Hercules threw a misshapen arm over his savior and Nish kissed the boy's scalded forehead goodnight.

DAY 7

Nish opened his eyes to the find the bedside clock staring him in the face. 7:59AM. One minute before the wake-up call. He wondered if it had just turned 7:59 or if he was only seconds away from the phone jumping off the hook like hotel phones do, disarmingly loud and with an unfamiliar ring that makes you feel strange answering it. He positioned his hand over it. The seconds ticked by in his mind until he just wanted it to be eight o'clock.

"Get up," Nish had located the gun in the room before shaking Verne. He was surprised it wasn't next to him but figured the whiskey and cocaine were the reason it was on top of his pants at the foot of the bed. Verne groaned, making a semi-conscious attempt to wipe the drool from his mouth before letting his head fall into the puddle on his pillow. His back had a large scar that ran up its side for almost a foot, like a millipede had imbedded itself under his skin and a waxy pink layer had grown over the top of it. On his shoulder blade was a cartoon character wearing a white and blue jersey urinating on the head of an eagle. A rattlesnake coiled next to a 'TX' was emblazoned on his bicep. If Nish had a quarter for every Texas flag, longhorn skull or other symbol of state pride he'd seen tattooed on his coworkers, he figured he wouldn't have to be stealing from a crime boss in order to pay for his mom's surgeries.

"Come on," Nish pulled off the sheets to reveal the man's nude body, then quickly threw them back on. "It's almost nine o'clock. Junior told us to meet him in half an hour, we've got to fucking run."

Verne gave a halfhearted wave to his nightstand, "Don't worry about that."

"What the fuck do you mean don't worry about it? I've got an important meeting with an executive, I can't be late to that shit."

"Executive," Verne chuckled before pulling his pillow closer.

Little Hercules tugged at Nish's jeans. "Time to bring in the big guns," he patted the boy on the head, setting him in motion. The

69

child climbed onto the bed curiously, sniffing the sheets like an animal scouring the ground for food. He naturally made his way up to Verne's head. The curly locks on top too much for him to resist, he roughly grabbed a clump to see how they felt. He yanked and Verne's eyes flew open. Disoriented, the first thing he saw was Hercules's face, a smile showing off his mutilated gums, rotting teeth and sawed off tongue.

"What the fuck?" Verne pushed the boy off him and leapt out from under the sheets. Nish and John laughed while Hercules bounced on the bed, wailing and clapping his hands. Quickly backing away, Verne looked for his weapon.

"Calm down and put some clothes on, he's with us," Nish threw the pair of jeans at their guide, leaving the pistol on the carpet.

"This a friend of yours?" Verne pointed at the child. "They won't take kindly to that thing at the office."

"I'm parking him in front of the TV today. We already grabbed him food at the store down the street," Nish waved the boy back to him and he obeyed. "Some people are up before nine o'clock."

"Fucking nasty," Verne said under his breath. Not bothering with the formality of underwear, he put on his jeans while staring at the child. Finally turning away, he went to the bathroom to wipe a dry toothbrush around his mouth. After gargling the entire time he put on his socks and boots, he announced he was ready and stood at the door impatiently like he'd been the one waiting to leave.

The office was located blocks from the River Walk in the touristy section of downtown. Nish figured it must have cost twice as much as the building he and John worked in. Deaf would never have based the company in a high profile neighborhood; he wasn't sure why his son would put his outpost in a location that thousands of people walked past everyday, considering its function. If Dallas was the general's headquarters, then San Antonio was the field office, a straight shot down I-35 to the front lines of Laredo. It was the first and last stop for the cargo coming from and going into Mexico.

Bill's words of warning flashed through Nish's mind when he saw the tinted windows of Smith Realty. "A little obvious, isn't it?" Nish pointed at the dark glass.

"Bulletproof," Verne winked before hitting the buzzer on the door. Nish figured their guide didn't understand the question.

A CCTV camera studied them for a few seconds before the door buzzed open. They entered an antechamber with a security desk against the far wall manned by a uniformed guard with a submachine gun. He nodded at Verne.

"Couple guys from the Dallas office," the agent pointed at his two guests. "Big dogs," he turned back and winked at them again. The guard buzzed the next door open.

The main room was twice the size of its Dallas counterpart with only a fraction of the staff present.

"Verne!" the few men who were there greeted their coworker. Verne raised his arms like he was a dictator on a balcony being greeted by a throng of people shouting his name.

"What's up, motherfuckers?" he smiled. "What are y'all doing here so early?"

"Had to work last night," a young man sitting at a desk close to the door answered. He wore a t-shirt and shorts, something Nish had never seen in the Dallas office. Nish soon realized that all the men were dressed the same. The one closest to him kicked his feet up as if to show off his flip-flops.

"Little situation, but it's alright now," the man continued. "We figured we'd come back and stick around until lunch. I'll be ready to tie one on, boy."

"We're up for that," Verne nodded at Nish and John. "Oh shit," he turned back to the seated man. "Let me introduce everyone. These boys are from Dallas, just here on a regular visit," Verne slapped Nish hard on the back, causing him to clench his teeth together.

"This is Nish and this is John," Verne smiled like he was showing them off.

The seated man took his feet off the desk to stand and shake hands. "James Ewell Brown Childress."

"Quite a mouthful, huh?" Verne smiled. "I told this son of a bitch that with all those names, he might as well open a landscaping business."

Nish took the man's hand, "It's Jeb. As in Jeb Stuart, right?"

The agent nodded proudly. "That's right," he looked a second time at the darker skinned agent in front of him. "I'm impressed."

"History major."

They all went around the room introducing themselves. Nish assumed Jeb was the manager of the crew so he didn't bother trying to remember the names of the others. When they were done, he addressed the group, "You know where Junior is?"

Jeb looked to Verne and was unable to hold back a grin. "Hell yeah, I know where he is, curled up in bed next to that Mexican piece of ass he married." The San Antonio agents broke out in laughter.

Nish looked back at John, conveying his disbelief at how the group was speaking about an executive. He turned back to them, "When does he usually get in?"

"Shit, we usually meet up with his ass at lunch unless we're having a decompression day," Verne sat down on a nearby desk. A stuffed miniature basketball next to the computer caught his attention; he picked it up to practice his free throw in the air.

"Decompression day?"

"Yeah, it's like a day where we all go out fishing or shooting skeet," Verne answered without any embarrassment, focusing on his miniature basketball shooting form.

"He read about it in some management magazine or some shit," Jeb explained. "Said it's supposed to decrease turnover."

Nish had never thought of organized crime as having a lot of retention problems but he let it go. The local agents may badmouth their superiors but he wasn't about to start that shit.

"He's always reading craziness," Verne interjected. "That's his seat right there," he pointed to a large desk in the middle of the room that had accumulated a department store's worth of staplers, pens and half-used packs of paper. "He read that a good manager stays in the middle of the action, doesn't hole himself up in his office. So he made us all rearrange our desks for him to sit there. Course after about a week, his ass was back in his office," Verne motioned down a hallway.

"You sure he's not there now?" Nish asked what he thought was a reasonable question. It was met with more laughter.

"Shit, man," Jeb picked at his toenails, clearing chunks of black crud from underneath them and getting them stuck under his fingernails. "Hundred dollars says he's sleeping it off until noon, at the earliest." After finishing his public hygiene ritual, he stood. "Speaking of which, I'm fixing to take a nap in the back. Wake me up when y'all grab lunch." He extended his hand to Nish one last time, "Pleased to meet y'all."

Clenching his teeth, Nish shook the filthy hand. The others followed their manager down the hallway until only Verne and the Dallas agents were left.

"Might as well have a seat," Verne shot the ball at a trashcan halfway across the room. It missed; he didn't bother picking it up. "Junior made our tech guy put controls on the computers so you can't look at any porn, but you can still check out sites that don't have anything too nasty on them. Type in 'bikini competitions', 'lingerie models', stuff like that." A cowboy hat on the desk next to him caught Verne's roving eyes. He reached for it, propping it on the front of his head so that it covered his face as he reclined in the chair to nap. Nish and John, still standing at the entrance, looked out over the office, empty except for a single sleeping employee.

"Rise and shine," Verne's face was the first thing Nish saw as he woke up. Stunned, he grabbed the arms of the chair like he had been on a rollercoaster in his dreams. John was gone and the office was filled with agents engaging in various forms of what Nish's high school football coach would have described as grabass. Some were playing office basketball with a small hoop, others simulated fistfights as they told stories. One group was staring at a computer, all with money in their hands.

"You're lucky you don't have a fake mustache drawn on you," Verne turned his back to Nish, revealing his pistol sticking out the back of his jeans. No reason not to have your weapon holstered while in the office, Nish thought. As he stood to examine the scene, he noticed Verne wasn't the only one with his pistol visible. One agent in a Confederate flag t-shirt had a chrome-plated .380 just sitting on the desk next to him as he scribbled something on a piece of paper.

"This a fucking rap video?" Nish looked at the silver automatic weapon. His guide turned, saying low, "That's your boy."

Arturo looked up as if he felt eyes on him. By the time he'd found their owners, Nish and Verne were greeting the giant Dallas agent coming from the hallway.

"Where the hell were you?" Nish asked.

John raised two fingers.

"Lovely."

Verne whistled to get the attention of the office. The agents slowly quieted down. "Most of y'all know we got some visitors from Big D here, Nish and John," Verne put the two on display. Nish tried to watch Arturo out of the corner of his eye; the .380 had disappeared from the desk. "Since they're down here on a routine check, I reckon we ought to show them our best side. We can start by taking them out to lunch for the finest fried chicken in all San Antonio."

The group of agents let out a holler at the idea. Without needing any more instruction, they began exiting the building and piling into trucks and SUV's parked in the lot outside. Nish watched Arturo slowly get up, slipping the piece of paper in his pocket before he left. Nish turned to their guide, "Where are we going?"

A smile crept across Verne's lips, "Titty buffet."

Nish was surprised at how packed the strip club was for noon on a weekday. By the time the Dallas agents had shown up with their guide, people were already being ushered to other tables so the realty company employees could sit together directly in front of the stage.

"Titty buffet has the best fried chicken I ever ate," Verne spoke seriously, as if giving an expert opinion. Another agent chimed in, "Sometimes I come to titty buffet just for the sweet tea." Verne nodded, "Good ass sweet tea here."

Nish tried to find Arturo in the crowd of over forty agents. Verne tugged on his sleeve, "We sit in crews. That way we can write it off as a business expense." He motioned the Dallas agents to the table where Arturo sat with another young man.

"Nish, John, this is Arturo and Smiley," Verne introduced them all.

"We met before," Arturo stared at them. Nish studied the man to spark any recollection: thin nose, sharp beady eyes and a dark pompadour. When he stood to shake hands with the Dallas agents, Nish figured he stood six feet tall but couldn't have weighed more than 140 lbs. Arturo interrupted his train of thought, "At Junior's wedding."

"Oh yeah," Nish feigned recognition. "Sorry about that, good to see you again."

"Don't worry about it," they shook hands. Smiley stood and extended a hand, his mouth not living up to his name. "Hey."

"Verne tell you about the sweet tea here?" Arturo sat back down. He stared at the Dallas agents with such intensity that Nish thought the tea might be poisoned. Arturo picked up the napkin in front of him, "Best in the city. These Mexicans out here don't know how to make sweet tea. But this place, it's fucking awesome."

"You're not from San Antonio?" Nish asked.

"Fuck no," Arturo looked offended. "I'm from outside Space City."

Verne motioned the waitress over. "This son of a bitch is always talking about surfing in the channel on the wakes of oil tankers. He's a swamp puppy."

The waitress introduced herself as Candy and asked the table what they wanted to drink. Nish figured the girl was the last call entertainment on weekdays, going onstage long after the big spenders had forked over their money to women who didn't yet look like they had birthed a few children. "Sweet tea with a double of whiskey on the side," Arturo jumped to order first.

"All around," Verne ordered for the table. Arturo looked sideways at his subordinate, then turned to the Dallas agents. "I remember both y'all from the pigeon shoot," he looked to John, "You shot left handed because of your eye."

The giant smiled, "Yep. How'd you remember?"

Arturo shrugged, quickly looking towards the empty stage. "I hope Amber's here today," he checked his cell phone for the time. Verne shook his head, "Every time we come to titty buffet, he's asking about

74

that girl," he turned to Nish. "He'd walk naked through a briar patch just to hear her fart into a walkie-talkie."

"She's just fucking sexy, alright?" Arturo snapped at his worker. Verne put up his hands, "Alright, man. Just saying."

Smiley, looking like he was about to fall asleep, stood silently to get his food. Verne followed and then the Dallas agents, leaving Arturo at the table alone with the napkin in his lap.

On his way to the line, Nish got a call on his cell phone. John watched him as he looked at the name.

"It's that girl, the one I grew up with who lives here now," Nish explained before answering. As he spoke with her, the deejay took to the microphone, announcing the first dancer to the hoots and cheers of the rowdy audience. Nish covered the receiver end of the phone when he wasn't talking so the girl he'd taken to the tenth grade homecoming dance couldn't hear as 'Puss in Boots' took the stage in the background.

Upon returning from the strip club, their guide led the Dallas agents through the main room and down the hallway to Junior's office. Another uniformed guard with a submachine gun stood in front of the door. He knocked three times when Verne nodded to him.

"You ever met Junior?" Verne asked.

"Only seen him from afar at his wedding a couple years back," Nish answered. John kept his mouth shut.

"Let him in," a voice yelled from inside. The guard stepped aside so the agents could walk into the office.

"Where the hell y'all been?" Junior was walking towards them with a smile on his puffy, unshaven face. During lunch, Verne had told Nish about the time Junior had burned his urethra from going on a bender. Couldn't piss without pain for weeks, Verne had said. Nish hadn't believed this was physically possible but seeing Junior made him think that if anyone could put himself in that situation, it would be him. An alcoholic's gut strained against khaki shorts and a tight pink polo. He had a look in his eye that made Nish think his mind was always cloudy with being drunk or hung over, never fully lucid. The kind of guy who'd spend thousands of dollars on filet mignon for a barbeque, then eat the leftovers the next day on the toilet.

"We were out grabbing lunch," Verne embraced his cousin. "They got a taste of some real fried chicken and sweet tea."

"Titty buffet?" Junior had a sly look on his face.

"You know it."

Junior slapped his cousin on the back, then shook hands with Nish and John before leading them to the chairs in front of his desk. "When

I was at school in Austin, I used to take his underage ass to titty buffet whenever I came to visit," Junior pointed at Verne.

"For years, I thought strip clubs were only open for lunch," Verne nodded seriously.

"A lot of assholes will tell you they know where the best fried chicken in town is. But it's right there at titty buffet, I swear to God," Junior motioned for the agents to sit. He walked to a cart stocked with alcohol at the side of his desk, "Toddy?"

"We'll all take a whiskey," their envoy answered for Nish and John. After the executive had poured drinks for everyone, he sat across from them with one leg propped over the arm of his chair. He had the old man's nose, Nish thought upon further inspection, except with busted capillaries that made it red.

"Y'all know why you're here," he looked at the Dallas agents. "You met Arturo?"

"We sat with him at lunch," Nish answered.

"Good, then you saw he plays it close to the chest," Junior took a long drink and put his glass down, half empty. "But he's greedy, so that can outweigh caution."

Nish felt the tiny hairs on the back of his neck stand on end.

"Y'all witness the transaction his crew's handling. Try to burrow under the surface. My daddy said you're smart, so you should be able to dig deep, get confirmation on this stuff," Junior looked at Nish. "Tell you the truth, I would have let Verne handle this as soon as he brought it to my attention but my daddy wants to be a hundred percent sure before something gets dealt with in that fashion. He figures y'all will be able give him that peace of mind."

The Dallas agents nodded silently. It became apparent after a few seconds that Junior, unlike his father, expected people to speak when at his desk. "We'll do our best, sir," Nish broke the silence.

"Good. You'll have Verne to give you a hand, just go to him if you have any questions," Junior stood, prompting the others to do the same. "And in the meantime, enjoy the town. It's a fun ass place."

"I already gave them a little taste of the local flavor last night," Verne grinned. Junior caught his drift and turned to the Dallas agents, "Fucked some whores?"

Nish and John looked at each other, Nish spoke up, "Not exactly, sir."

"Oh, I get it," Junior winked at him. "More of a boxed lunch man," he smiled, then wagged his tongue out of his mouth and shook his head from side to side. Verne cracked up, "Hell Nish, if I knew that was your preference, I would've told them to wash up downstairs before y'all came."

Not wanting to interrupt the fun that the two were having, Nish played along until he and John had backed out of the office. The guard closed the door behind them. Once they were halfway down the hall, Nish opened his eyes wide at John, silently communicating the craziness of the scene they had just left. John nodded.

"I was thinking about it," Nish broke the silence, "And I'll just take a cab tonight."

"You mean to your ex-girlfriend's party?"

"She's not really an ex-girlfriend, we just went out a few times because she had a fake ID. But I still think it could be weird if you came along. You know, since she and I went to high school together and you could feel out of place." Nish tried to save his friend's feelings. Rebecca was a banker now, and he didn't see the giant being able to mingle well with the sort of people that would be at her house that evening. People with college degrees and real world experience, like himself. "And I don't want you to have to drive me and drop me off, so I'll just get a cab."

"Alright," John shrugged as the two emerged from the hall back into the main room where the agents' grabassing had resumed in full swing.

When the door had closed behind the Dallas agents, the cousins exhaled the last of their laughter. Junior finished his drink with a quick gulp, then refilled his glass while speaking more seriously. "Like I said before, keep an eye on the Indian, and try to see if that big motherfucker knows anything. I reckon he would but he looks dumb as a brick, so who knows." He took another drink. "Arturo's done for, so this could be a chance to get two in one."

"I'm on it," Verne finished his whiskey, letting the alcohol burn in his mouth for a few seconds before finally swallowing.

The woman who answered the door looked nothing like the Rebecca Coleman that Nish remembered. He'd almost been expecting her to show up still wearing some all-black outfit with piercings in her nose. Instead, she looked like she belonged on a yacht in a New England bay. The few extra pounds had melted away, due to either liposuction or years of kickboxing and pilates, Nish figured. Underneath was a body that made him hope she found him as attractive now as she did back when they were sophomores.

"Nish?" she raised an eyebrow at the man on her porch. The sound of music and people talking and laughing wafted through the door, making Nish more anxious to get inside.

"Rebecca," he smiled. The other eyebrow raised and the sides of her mouth lifted higher than he thought possible.

"Oh my God!" she took a step backwards into the house, opening her arms as wide as they would go. "Nish! How long has it been?"

"It's been a while," he focused on the feeling of her breasts as he hugged her. "It's great to see you," he looked at her body, not minding that she noticed. His tongue ran against the inside of his teeth.

"Come on in!" she ushered him out of the entryway and into a dark, great hall that looked like it was made to shelter people from storms that never took place in San Antonio, complete with a fireplace large enough to roast a pig. People stood in casual patches, almost all Nish's age, talking over the music. They passed two men, "Inflation rises and they spend more on social services. I guess they think the people won't notice how much more expensive necessities are if they're subsidized." The other man shook his head, "Hell, you have some countries raising export taxes on products, forcing producers to sell domestically at lower prices, basically creating an artificial scarcity." The first agreed, "Controlling prices is like shooting the messenger." Nish checked to make sure his dress shirt was tucked in properly.

Rebecca walked her guest over to a group assembled on the couches in front of the dormant fireplace. A stick woman on the couch whipped her head around, causing hair to fly in her face.

"You've killed someone right?" dirty blonde strands stuck to the lipstick on her open mouth. Nish felt the molecules in his blood shift to cold. "What?"

The group laughed. The bony woman leaned forward, pushing out her flat chest for Nish to get a better view. "We're judging people's innocence."

"Some stupid quiz from the internet," Rebecca explained.

"How do you like your sex?" the woman asked again.

"Quick and inexpensive." The group laughed again and Nish thought he might as well act like that was the response he'd been going for. Rebecca introduced him to everyone on the couches, all either friends from college or colleagues from the bank where she worked as an analyst. By the way they were talking to each other, Nish could tell the group was pretty drunk.

After they all shook hands, they cleared a space for him on the couch between the skinny blonde and another of Rebecca's coworkers, a curvy young woman whose teeth looked like they needed to be knocked out and put back in, starting from scratch. The two girlfriends weren't the most attractive women in the world but Nish had drunkenly had sex with worse. When Rebecca offered him a cocktail, he asked for a tall glass of whiskey.

"So what do you do?" one of the men on the couch asked Nish.

"I'm in real estate."

The man looked impressed. "A lot of money to be made in that nowadays."

"It's doing alright."

The curvy woman next to Nish laid her arm behind him on the couch, "Jenny got the best score on the quiz," she pointed to the stick woman, "She's practically evil."

"No such thing," Nish smiled.

"What are your three hidden talents?" Jenny asked. The others laughed like they had been talking about this before and gotten some interesting responses. Nish leaned back into the couch, noticing the curvy woman didn't bother to move her arm.

"Well, I guess first off, I have an amazing sense of smell. And you know when you bunch up a piece of paper and there's not a trashcan close to you? I'm able to throw the paper into the trashcan every time. I've never missed in my whole life." He stared at Jenny like she should be very impressed. "And I'd have to say lastly, I'm amazing at giving oral sex."

"Oh my God!" the curvy woman covered her mouth as the group laughed. Nish looked at her like he didn't know what was controversial about the statement. A hand with a glass of whiskey reached over his shoulder. He took the drink and turned to find Rebecca standing there with a look of fake shock on her face. "Are we already at this point in the night?" She motioned for Jenny to make room on the couch, taking her time as she bent over to sit next to her high school flame.

Grabbing a handful of her muscular ass, Nish reached further to find her wet opening with his middle finger. Rebecca's moan, amplified by the tile of bathroom, was all the approval Nish needed to retract the hand and quickly lift off her dress. She was suddenly standing there in only her bra and a thong; Nish felt like a performer who had whipped a tablecloth out from under plates and glasses without moving a single one. Her breasts bulged over the top of her bra, begging to be set free. He figured that no woman would wear something that uncomfortable unless they were planning on it not staying on that long. People are always manipulating one another, he thought. It's usually not a bad thing.

He undid the clasp in the back to expose perfectly shaped breasts with pink nipples pointing slightly upwards. He took them in his mouth one at a time until the nipples had shrunk half their size and stood hard, staring at the corner of the ceiling. Rebecca undid his khakis to slide her hand inside. She gave him the most genuine look he'd seen all night and dropped to her knees. After a few minutes, Nish lifted her up to reciprocate, tearing off her panties to expose her bikini wax. He'd finished and was getting a condom out of his wallet when there was a knock on the bathroom door.

"What are y'all two doing in there?" a female voice playfully asked. Rebecca laughed; Nish ignored it, opening the condom wrapper.

"I want to have some fun, too," the voice pouted. This time Nish stopped in his tracks. He glanced up at Rebecca to gauge her interest in the proposal.

"Find your own man, you can use my bedroom," Rebecca drunkenly yelled at the door. As Nish took the condom out of its packaging, she pinched his nipples hard, "You're in luck, I've been to yoga every day this week."

He paused again, this time for a different reason. He felt the dried clump of blood on the top of his head. He picked the area as Rebecca smiled seductively. "You need a hand with that?" she asked and took the condom. As she rolled it onto him, Nish watched her bent over in the mirror. Pulling her up, he kissed her one last time before she slapped him, then turned her back to him and bent over again. He wondered how many young bankers or oilmen or lawyers she'd lured into the bathroom while one of her cocktail parties staggered on outside. He'd have to make it memorable, he thought, grabbing the back of her hair with one hand and picking at the bloody clump with the other.

DAY 8

Nish looked out at the empty sky over the hills of Monterrey. Nothing but the dusty Mexican earth below him and thin air above, he thought a breeze could lift him away like a piece of paper. He turned back to the two Mexicans standing on either side of the doorway with their arms crossed over their chests, eyeing the parking lot with a wandering vigilance like someone trying to swat a fly. Nish walked past them with a nod, through the door of the old structure.

Inside, a great hall filled with tables jumped to the live mariachi band. People moved between the tables and up to the two-inch stage where the guests of honor sat. On one side, the two sets of parents shook hands with their invitees. On the other sat a government official wearing a sash with his title on it like an American beauty queen. The other rooms of the historic restaurant had been closed off for the night but weren't left unattended. Men with submachine guns in plain view stood at their sides; Nish thought he recognized the make of their weapons. He took one last swig as a waiter came over with a tray of fresh beer, so cold in contrast to the warm air that steam rose off the ice particles clinging to the bottles.

People were seated at the tables by association and importance: tables at the front were occupied by family or close friends of Deaf or Mr. Presidio, further from the stage were business associates of a less important nature, and in the back sat the real estate agents and their Mexican counterparts. Nish excused himself in Spanish through the crowd until he reached his seat next to John, the giant he'd watched shoot pigeons earlier in the day.

Iron griddles with melted cheese and plates of beef, some chargrilled and juicy and some salted and dried, were heaped on the table next to plates of soft corn tortillas. Either a beer bottle or a glass occupied every other inch of the table. Nish pulled a tortilla from the plate and used it like a glove to pick up cheese from the griddle, then forked meat on top.

"He's working offshore now, rig manager," one of the agents across from him addressed the table. "Making over two hundred grand a year in the North Sea."

"Off Maine?" another asked. Nish noticed the puddles of grease forming around the cheese and meat.

"Scotland," John interjected. "I can't believe Matt Starr has his own rig. Seems like just yesterday he was director level."

"What are you talking about 'has his own rig', he's just running it," the geographically challenged agent laughed. "You hear this son of a bitch?" he looked around the table and others started chuckling. "Acting like Matt owns an oil rig! Goddamn!"

"I didn't say he owned it, I just said he had it," John defended himself a bit too quickly. Nish drank from his beer until they had finished laughing at the giant's expense.

He looked at Deaf's son, drunkenly belting out the mariachi song the band was playing with his arm around the guitar player. His Mexican bride made it a point to publicly smile at her new soul mate's antics.

"Who's he related to?" Nish asked.

"Matt? Ain't kin to no one, just a smart son of a bitch," the first agent answered. He slurped down a greasy wad of cheese that had been dripping from the end of his tortilla. "Let's hit the Old Neighborhood tonight. I talked with some of Presidio's boys and they said they can get us into the best clubs in town."

"Initiate the new guy," another tipped his beer at Nish, who raised the corners of his mouth and took a swig. Voices died out in the background until everyone was looking silently at the stage as the politician rose from his seat.

The boats drifted lazily down the manmade lake, occasionally getting close enough that the agents on one would cast their lines into another's territory. Fully stocked coolers sat in the bottom of each, easily accessible to the fishermen enjoying their decompression day. Nish reapplied his sunscreen while Arturo and the other agents in Junior's boat cast off the side.

"Only drinking vodka sodas today, trying to lose weight," Junior inserted a plastic cup into a camouflage drink koozi to pour himself a cocktail. "From my daughter's first birthday party last year," he held up the commemorative drink holder for Nish to read.

"It was crazy," one of the agents in the front of the boat turned back to them. "How many kegs you have there, Junior?"

"Sheeyut," the executive drew out the word as if to buy him time while he tried to remember. "Reckon about four or five."

"That was fucking awesome," Arturo nodded his head quickly. From the look of it, Nish figured Arturo didn't care much for decompression days as the act of fishing visibly tried his very limited patience. He spit into the water, reeling in an empty hook. "You remember Bobby doing those keg stands?"

"Hell yeah I do," Junior grinned. "Son of a bitch was shit-housed before the sun even went down, running around the yard half naked telling people he was a superhero."

"He was a good guy," the agent in the front said. Junior's grin dissolved. Sitting down next to the cooler, he watched the lake pass silently under the boat.

Nish squirmed in his seat. Growing up, he'd gone hunting with his friends and their parents out in West Texas but had never spent much time fishing. He hated the idea of catching something and throwing it back like he'd seen others do in the boats around him. Only the larger fish got kept, punishing the ones who excel and giving a free pass to the weak. His fingernail found its way to his teeth. He remembered talking about how new situations could be hard for him and was glad he'd brought his prescription for refills down just in case he was in San Antonio longer than expected.

"I'm fixing to leave for a few days, wife and I are heading down to Monterrey," the executive announced suddenly. "Her momma's in the hospital sick. Anyway, need for one of y'all to water the plants in my office."

The agents stared at their lines in the water.

"No volunteers?" Junior said with a desperate chuckle but the men didn't respond. "Andy, what about you?"

"I would, boss, you know me," one of the agents in the front answered. "But I'm bowed up like a cut worm, working overtime in the field next week."

Junior looked to the other employee in the front, who shrugged helplessly, "Bowed up."

"I could do it," Nish offered. "I have time on my hands down here."

"I ain't having a guest do that shit," Junior snapped at him, his voice rising to sound effeminate. The agents in the front giggled. One of them faked a woman's voice to mock their boss, adding a lisp for good measure, which caused the boat to erupt in laughter. Nish watched silently as Junior cracked a smile. "Son of a bitch," he pointed at the agent in front and laughed along.

John kept his distance as they followed Arturo's SUV into the slums of San Antonio. While the giant's truck didn't exactly blend in, Verne had thought it would be better than using his jeep, which the agent would surely recognize. The SUV turned a corner, stopping at one of the first houses on the block.

"So where's Junior going?" Verne asked while waiting for the pair of binoculars the three agents were passing around.

"Monterrey, he said his mother-in-law's sick."

"Oh yeah," Verne nodded. Nish kept watching him out of the corner of his eye until John handed over the binoculars. When Nish raised them to his face, the fresh scabs on his back from the night before ached; he clenched his jaw and felt himself stir.

A thuggish young man walked out of the house accompanied by a blonde woman with tattoos staining her exposed arms and legs. "There's the driver," Nish commented as he saw the blonde. Drug runners usually had white women drive to reduce the chances of getting stopped, he'd learned. However, he felt this cautionary measure was outweighed by the sticker of the traveler saint on the back window of the runner's car in the driveway.

"Dumbass Mexican shit," he handed to binoculars to Verne. "Might as well have a sign saying 'Please arrest me' in Spanish."

"Fucking spic runners, what do you expect?" Verne studied the magnified scene.

"Keep that racist shit to yourself," the crusted blood on top of Nish's head itched at him. Verne turned to him with a surprised look, "What the fuck? You were talking about it first."

"I was talking about the characteristics of a nation's people, not about someone's ethnicity. There's a difference. It's like if I say something about Somalians and you say something about them being black."

"Whatever. I'm part Mexican anyway, so I can say whatever I want."

"You are?"

"I'm from South Texas, aren't I?"

After a minute, Nish motioned for him to give the binoculars back to John. When he had, the giant read the license plate number of the runner's car out loud as Nish wrote it down.

"You Catholic?" the traveler saint caught Nish's eye again. Verne made a face, "Only my grandma was Mexican. I'm still Anglo."

"There are white Catholics."

"Sheeyut," Verne grinned. "White man praying to the Virgin of Guadalupe? I'd like to see that."

The SUV's engine started as the runners walked back into the house. Arturo looked around to make sure no one was coming, then pulled out. The agents kept their heads down as he drove within twenty yards of the back of the truck.

"He'll be heading back to the office. Drop me off there," Nish instructed John. "I'm going to talk to him, try to dig deeper. You take the boy out to eat. I'll meet you back at the motel."

"I'll go with you," Verne offered to John. "I'm starving."

The office was only a quarter full when Nish returned. Arturo sat at his desk with a piece of paper and a calculator, his leg jumping frantically as he scribbled. Nish felt the butt of the pistol in his back. "Fuck it," he said under her breath, approaching his target.

"How's it going?" Nish leaned casually on the desk next to Arturo's. The agent jolted up, flipping over his piece of paper.

"You have a second?" Nish motioned outside. Arturo's leg stopped dead. "Sure."

Neither of them wanting to be positioned behind the other, they walked practically side by side out of the office. Caught up in the flow of tourists outside the parking lot, they naturally made their way to the River Walk. Nish began to think that maybe the office's location did have strategic purpose as the noise of the people and music around them made it impossible for others to eavesdrop.

While studying abroad for a semester in London, Nish had spent many hours walking along the Thames. Sprawling buildings from centuries ago that channeled the river through the city, turning its natural contours into straight lines and right angles. Having it bend to human will, surrounding it with civilization; it was breathtaking, he thought. The River Walk, on the other hand, didn't exactly fill Nish with awe. It was the American version of the great European rivers in the most unfortunate sense of the word. The stores and restaurants that crowded every inch of the waterfront were larger than the actual river and the buildings and trees blocked much of the light from above, giving him the feeling he had walked into a crowded mall with a manmade stream running through it.

Arturo sat down at one of the many eateries' tables. Nish looked around like he wasn't sure it was okay to just claim the space without speaking with a hostess or waiter, then eventually did the same. Arturo clenched his teeth as if his mouth may try to betray him if he didn't clamp it shut.

"I'm just going to come out and say this," Nish looked him in the eye like they had been friends for years and he was about to divulge something Arturo had never known. "They sent me to spy on you. They think you've been dealing coke."

"What the fuck do you think?" Arturo spit out the words, barely moving his face.

"I don't think shit. I know you're dealing," Nish looked out around at the tourists corralling children or pointing at buildings. "I want in."

Arturo's eyes lowered to the table in front of him as if the answer to his problems were hidden in its surface. He looked back at the agent, "I have no idea what you're talking about."

"Fuck that, I followed you to that cockroach's house today. I saw what you have going on."

Arturo breathed in heavily like he was in physical pain but trying not to show it. "No idea what you're talking about."

"Think of the position you're in," Nish picked his teeth while he let the man stew. "Say you're not dealing. You're obviously under suspicion. All I have to do is say you're guilty and that's it. There's no fucking trial in this business."

The muscles in Arturo's clenched jaw were visible. A burst of air from a pedestrian's portable fan hit the back of Nish's sweaty neck and a hundred icy centipedes crawled from his spine up his head to the valve of crusted blood on the top of his skull. The tickling brought joy to the front of his eyeballs. He blinked to keep the moisture back.

"My mom is sick. If I don't get her these surgeries, she dies. And these motherfuckers are expensive," the joy escaped from his body in a breath. "So I tell them you're clean and you let me in on this."

Saliva built in his mouth until Arturo spit onto the restaurant floor. He removed his wallet to take out a piece of paper with something scribbled on it. "An hour before the truck comes onto Smith property," he slid the paper to Nish. "I hope you're as smart as you fucking act," he got up from the table and stepped out of the restaurant's invisible border. After he'd disappeared into the tide of tourists, Nish opened the paper.

After shaking longer than what's generally considered acceptable, Verne zipped up his jeans and turned to the sink to wash his hands. The mirror in the bar's bathroom was covered with writing, threats scratched over a reflection to some invisible enemy. Verne was too busy reading them to realize the steam coming off the water he'd turned on.

"Fuck!" his hands recoiled from the heat.

A man leading his young son into the bathroom frowned at Verne, covering his boy's ears.

"Shouldn't bring your kid to a fucking bar then," the agent muttered as they entered one of the stalls. The child whined about how badly he had to go while his father tried to help him out of his shorts as quickly as possible; Verne looked back up at the mirror as he slowly replaced his hands under the water.

After drying off, he went back to his seat next to the Dallas agent taking up half a table. "So y'all been working together long?"

"I don't know," the giant shrugged. "About a year."

John took another drink of his beer, his eyes wandering back to the basketball game on the television as Verne kept watching him. Hercules let out a guttural growl at the San Antonio agent, causing the other men in the bar to wave the smoke away from their faces to get a better view of the feral looking child.

"What the hell you want, boy?" Verne broke his stare to throw a fry from his Styrofoam plate onto the ground. The boy looked at it, then back at his own empty plate and drained glass of milk. He jumped from his chair to grab the food off the filthy floor and eat it. The agent smiled to himself.

"Big son of a bitch like you," Verne continued to John, "Ugly little motherfucker like this human scab right here, some Indian. Y'all look like a fucking carnival coming to town."

"I've always been big. My mom said having me was like pushing out a baby elephant." He laughed, looking to Verne to do the same but the man just kept staring. The giant went back to the game.

"How long you been with the company, man?"

"Started after I got discharged in '02. I was hardly overseas at all before I got wounded."

"And the Indian's only been with the House for two years, right? That's got to make you awful pissed they have him running this thing here."

This time, John turned away from the screen. He looked at the floor in front of him for a second, then answered. "I'm not pissed. But I would like to be in charge. Just once, prove myself, you know?" he played with the napkin on the table in front of him. "Everyone thinks I'm too stupid to do anything. They think all I'm good for is muscle work."

Verne shook his head in sympathy.

"But I graduated from high school with a 3.5 GPA. How many stupid people could say that?" he finally looked up.

"Shit, man, none that I know. Most big ass sons of bitches aren't the sharpest tools in the shed, but a 3.5?" Verne opened his eyes wide to show surprise. "You ask me, it's about time you were making a white man's salary, none of this support level bullshit."

A look of gratitude came over John's face. Hercules looked from one man to the other. The growl formed in the back of his throat again.

"Stop that, boy! You're like a goddamn dog or some shit," Verne scolded him. He took out his wallet to retrieve a bill. "You want some more milk?"

Hercules looked up at the money that Verne was dangling just out of his reach. He shifted his weight uneasily, then nodded his head.

"Alright, but you got to let the grownups talk, you hear me, boy?" Verne held the bill a little lower.

Hercules let out a moan of confirmation. Verne let go of the bill so that it fell between the boy's grasping hands. Hercules picked it up from the floor and hobbled over to the bar where the patrons got up from their seats to clear a way for him. As he jumped onto a stool to point out his order, Verne leaned in to speak with John.

The candles on the tables barely cut through the darkness, creating islands of people in business attire totally disconnected from one another. Nish held the cocktail menu up to the flickering light. Something was walking out of the black towards him; he assumed it was a waitress so he decided on a whiskey.

"How's it going," he pointed at the menu, "I'll have the twelve year--"

"Nish!" Rebecca's voice preceded her image. When she appeared, Nish felt himself stir again as thoughts from the previous night flashed through his mind. The light danced in her blue eyes in a way that made it hard for him to remember to get up to hug her; the scenes racing through his brain also doing their part to prevent him from standing.

"Hey," he pushed out his chair. When she pulled him in, he felt the thin body and full breasts through her little black dress. "Thanks for meeting me here."

"No problem." He was glad they'd made the plans to have dinner together prior to having sex the night before. He'd said he was only in town for the weekend and Friday was the only night she was available, so it worked out well. Any sense of embarrassment in keeping the plans despite the possible awkwardness was pushed out of Nish's mind by the necessity of a cover. There could be times in the next few days when he needed to be 'spending the night' at Rebecca's, he thought.

"I'm glad you didn't want to eat on the River Walk," she was apparently unphased by the potentially awkward situation; Nish figured it may not be an uncommon one for her. He respected that in a woman.

"I've already seen it. Besides, this place sounded good when you talked about it."

"It is. And I'm in the mood for a steak," she waved her hand in the air, flagging down an invisible waitress. "Work was hell this week. They have us visiting local branches, trying to give analysts a look at what it's like in the field or something stupid like that. It's gotten to the point anyone with a pulse is buying a home. It's great for business but I spent half my time dealing with people who can't speak a word of English. I have to hire translators just to be able to give people money."

A waiter passed in front of one of the orbs of light coming from another table. Rebecca saw this and snapped her fingers at him, something Nish had seen in movies but never in real life. When the waiter turned, she ordered wine and food for both of them.

"Sorry, I'm starving," she explained. "So anyway, I couldn't wait for the week to be over," she made a face like this was a common topic of conversation for her. Nish remembered how she'd mentioned her father had gotten her the job after her stint in K-12 education had ended abruptly; he wondered if she ever bitched to him about it.

"Ever think about going back to teaching?" Nish asked. "That's all you ever talked about in high school."

Rebecca laughed like she was making a point of being as loud as possible. "I was young and idealistic, which is really just another word for stupid. There's no way in hell I'd go back to that, especially not down here."

"Why? Is the San Antonio school district too bureaucratic or something?"

"It's too full of anchor babies who care less about learning how to read and more about throwing gang signs," she tore a piece of bread in half. Nish scratched his jaw, Rebecca continued unprompted, "And the parents are even worse. They did the most important thing in their life when they snuck over the border and had a kid in America at the age of sixteen. After you've done that, the government checks just come rolling in. We'll even change the street signs to Spanish and give them driver's licenses."

"That's a little one-sided," Nish spoke up. "I mean, less than five percent of Americans don't speak English. You look at the U.S. a hundred years ago; you had whole communities of people in the Midwest who only spoke German. Towns printed their newspapers in other languages. But all that changed because of money. If you don't speak English, you'll stay broke. People aren't stupid."

Rebecca let out a quick laugh, "Tell that to the blacks. They speak English and they're still poor. They haven't bothered to integrate into American society."

Nish looked uneasily at the tables around him but the other islands were trapped in their own conversations. "That's different."

"It's the same lazy victim mentality as the Mexicans have, except blacks are cashing in on people's guilt." The waitress brought the wine to the table, presenting the bottle to Rebecca. She nodded but didn't stop talking, "Slavery ended over two hundred years ago. We've given them affirmative action, not just leveling the playing field but tipping it in their favor. We even gave them their own month." The waitress coated the bottom on Rebecca's glass with wine as her voice rose. "If an alien came to Earth during February, he'd think the invention of peanut butter was more important than putting a man on the moon."

She tossed the wine down the back of her throat without any of the swirling or smelling usually associated with the tasting of a bottle. The light danced on her face in a way that made it look to Nish like she was twitching. The dog that had snuck into their backyard, he remembered, like something coming alive in an old science fiction movie. The waitress poured Nish a glass. He spoke up, "We are where we are, and problems aren't going to just disappear. Education is the best way to solve them. The most effective way to run a capitalist society is to give everyone a fair shot," his fingers tapped the glass's stem.

"Then you go be a teacher." Rebecca turned to her own glass once the waitress was done pouring. The conversation had heightened her breathing and Nish watched her chest rise and fall more enthusiastically than before. He remembered the hardened pink nipples staring up at him, bouncing in small circular motions when Rebecca was propped on the edge of the marble counter. He took a long drink, almost finishing the glass. "You're right about that, I'm sure as hell not stepping foot into a school. It's amazing you did it so long. It shows real compassion."

Taking a measured sip, Rebecca evened out her breathing. "I just always wanted to help people." The last of the frustration drained from her face. Nish nodded, "You're a good person."

DAY 9

The doctor set the phone on his desk to open the stubborn packet of creamer. He muttered an occasional "uh-huh" as he peeled off the top and poured it into his coffee. Placing the phone between his shoulder and ear, he browsed his e-mail, scanning through advertisements for penis enlargement discounts and erection pills.

"Sure."

An e-mail forward from a colleague caught his eye. He clicked on the link to find a monkey in a zoo masturbating while a man just outside its cage laughed at the animal. Seemingly in response, the monkey ejaculated onto the side of the man's face. The doctor shot forward in his chair, only somewhat succeeding in clamping his mouth shut so he wouldn't laugh into the phone. He coughed loudly, "Yes, of course," then replayed the video, this time keeping his hand over the receiver.

He said one final "sure", hanging up as his colleague walked in.

"You son of a bitch! Where'd you find that?" They both cracked up.

The speakerphone went dead. "It's all real, I wasn't fucking with you," Nish turned to Arturo in the driver's seat. He was just glad the doctor had accepted the call to confirm his mother's illness instead of forwarding him straight to Accounts Receivable. The driver nodded, starting the SUV.

"Alright," Arturo motioned to a transport truck coming down the side street of the deserted industrial neighborhood. "These guys trust me so just keep your fucking mouth shut." He turned off the air conditioner and they got out to meet the Mexican. As they walked to the truck, a low rider with a painting of a woman on the side, nude except for a sombrero, crept up from the opposite direction. The agents watched as both vehicles converged upon them.

"I can't believe I let you come to this," Arturo's eyes didn't blink as they shifted from the truck to the low rider.

You didn't have a choice, Nish thought to himself. He realized his hands were slipping into his pockets and made sure to keep them in plain sight as the vehicles stopped. Several men in their late teens and early 20's emerged from the low rider dressed like extras from a low rent rap video. From the other vehicle, a single man got out of the passenger side. The Mexican moved like a rodeo cowboy who'd been thrown from a bull one too many times. He dressed the part as well, from his silver belt buckle to his black ostrich skin boots. As he approached, Nish noticed the thugs modify their stances in what he could only imagine was an attempt to look more intimidating.

The Mexican spit on the ground. "Arturo," he extended a hand to the agent. After they'd greeted each other, Arturo introduced the Dallas agent. Nish had learned that Arturo had been working with the drug dealers a long time, longer than what he'd expected it would take for management to notice. Regardless, the apathy of the Mexican surprised him. The man motioned to the driver, who hopped down from the cab of the truck carrying a submachine gun lazily like an employee having to go back to work after a long break. The driver patted Nish down, feeling the holstered pistol but not stopping, then nodded at his boss before walking sluggishly back to the truck. The Mexican pulled Arturo to the side to talk, leaving Nish and the thugs standing together on the side of the road. They looked awkwardly at the factories and warehouses that composed their crumbling surroundings until one of them finally spoke up, "So you with the House?"

"Yes," Nish let his hands slip back into his pockets. "How do you guys know Arturo?"

"Family of mine," another answered. "His sister's married to my cousin. He offered me the connection," the thug motioned at the man in Western wear talking with his relative.

"You buy straight from the source?"

The thug nodded, "We paid for the connect. Additionally, Arturo gets a cut of the profits."

The way the gangster said 'additionally' stuck out in Nish's mind, like he was trying to make himself seem smarter; he picked up on the fear in the young man. "Seems like the long way around," Nish feigned stupidity.

"I could have just bought direct from Arturo since he runs his own shit but the price would be the same. Now I take orders for others. We're standing here because he got us in on this," the thug justified himself. "Besides, I'm not about to cross family. Or the House."

Nish watched the young man. He'd seen the look in his face before; a thought that had nagged at the back of his mind was getting light shone on it for others to see. Hurt pride was the only thing more dangerous than greed. After checking the men talking in the distance,

Nish took out a small pad and pencil from his jeans and turned back to the thug.

Arturo dropped Nish off at a school playground a few blocks away from the warehouse. The truck would be arriving there in thirty minutes, he'd explained, and Nish would show up late to unload its more fragile merchandise. Nish climbed into a concrete tube covered in graffiti to lie down. Rebecca had kept him up half the night; not that he minded, but he wasn't used to sexual encounters lasting any longer than the previously negotiated sixty minutes. He'd said goodbye and offered to take her out the next time she came back to Dallas, a nice gesture and ultimately harmless as he knew she'd never take him up on it. Newness seemed to be the most attractive characteristic in a partner for her, second only to convenience; Nish figured two hook-ups put him past the expiration date. And since he didn't want to hear another dinner's worth of her alarmist political views, he was fine with that. At least he could brag to his friends about having sex with her when she showed up at the ten-year reunion. He rested his head on his arm to drift off to sleep.

"I'm tired of taking care of your goddamn pet," Verne jumped on Nish as soon as he walked through the door of the warehouse.

"Sorry I'm late," Nish hurried towards the truck. "Long night."

"I bet it was. You're off fucking all night and I've got to deal with your mutant boy," Verne turned his attention back to the illegal aliens being helped out of the transporter by Smiley. One of them tugged at his shirt, holding up a canteen.

"Get the fuck off me," he knocked the canteen to the ground.

"These are paid in full, Verne," Smiley shot his coworker a look. Verne furrowed his brow in frustration and pointed the alien to a faucet. "I was up all night, too, you know. Except I was listening to that boy howling at the fucking moon. And he nearly trashed the goddamn motel room. J had to bring him here cause he thought that little bastard might burn the place down while we were gone."

"What? Herc's here?" Nish looked around quickly.

"He's in the goddamn truck. J's making sure he's taken care of," Verne scratched his arm. "All this bullshit you're putting me through, you're lucky I'm not in a bad mood."

Sleeping on the bench had put a crick in Nish's neck. He placed his hand to the side of his head and jerked it, cracking the bones. It felt like blocked spinal fluid rushed to his brain so quickly he almost lost his balance.

"If we weren't getting fried chicken for lunch, I swear to God I'd be mad enough to spit," Verne crossed his arms like an angry child who just recently learned the gesture.

-I have much hunger,- the Mexican emerged from behind the truck, speaking in Spanish. -Let us go to this buffet of the tits.-

Arturo walked out behind the man, "Everything all good here?"

"Yep," Smiley pulled the last of the cargo out of the truck. "Just got to finish processing these and we're good to go."

"Alright then. Finish up and we can head out." Arturo removed a traveler of whiskey from his pocket to nip. Nish could see the man's nerves jumping through his skin. You do this kind of shit, he thought, you need to get better at hiding those things. Not that it made much of a difference soon, anyway.

The Mexican pulled the metal spoon out of the thready green mush, looking to his hosts in the buffet line for an explanation.

"Collards," Arturo answered. He made a face like he was trying to think of the word in Spanish. Nish butted in, -The collards,- he used the Spanish word and the Mexican nodded pensively like he still had no idea what they were but was trying to play it off.

-This is the food of the South,- Arturo quickly explained. -The steak fried like chicken, the sauce white so thick, all from the South.-

"Confederacy," Verne slopped a spoonful of sweet potatoes onto his plate alongside two battered and fried drumsticks. "Our culture."

-Like the flag,- the Mexican nodded to the battle flag on the wall.

"Hell yeah, Stars and Bars," Verne smiled at the others, "He knows."

-Why do you take so much pride in the side that lost?- the Mexican inquired with an expression showing neither curiosity nor intended offense.

Nish smiled at the question. -Because all the Americans want to act like they are underdogs,- he translated the last words directly, causing the Mexican to furrow his brow. Nish elaborated, -Here, the winners are those who have been oppressed more, not those who have succeeded.-

-Always those with power are seen as bad, and nobody wants to be bad,- the Mexican waved a fried drumstick as he gave the proclamation.

-Is weakness,- Nish said flatly. -Our poor eat food and have a roof over their heads. The average American is rich in comparison to people of other countries. But people are weak and want to blame others for what is bad in their lives. And they fly the flag of another country that was so bad they either left it, or it lost a war,- he pointed at the battle flag.

Arturo gripped a set of tongs so hard Nish thought they might break. Unable to understand the long speech, Verne grabbed rolls from the end of the buffet with his bare hands and went to sit at their table, humming along to the strip club's background music. The Mexican smiled, -You speak Spanish well. From where are you?-

-I am from Dallas. I learned it in school.-

The Mexican looked impressed. -I am from Nuevo Leon, a village called Wind of the Ocean.-

-Sounds beautiful.-

-Is a shithole in the middle of the desert,- he slapped Nish so hard on the back he nearly dropped his plate; it felt as if the man was wearing a metal gauntlet. -You speak better than most in my hometown.- The Mexican laughed and Nish decided he should, also.

The rest of the agents took their seats at the front of the stage as the first dancer, Roxy Loving, came on. She had a cheerleader theme going on that the Mexican seemed to be a fan of by the way he was gyrating along to the music, mirroring her with tiny movements of his own. Verne poured his double of whiskey into the plastic cup in front of him, "Sometimes I like to Tennessee up my sweet tea." He winked at Nish, who had just downed the alcohol in his glass before someone grabbed him by the throat from behind. Nish pushed himself away from the table, spitting up alcohol onto his shirt as he reached for his pistol. Hercules jumped on top of him, hugging his savior with all his might.

"Boy's been crying for you for over a day now," John pulled up a chair. "I'm sick of watching his ass."

Nish tried to push Hercules off as he gasped for air. The boy stepped away from his guardian to reach out for his sippy cup. John handed it to him like an annoyed but attentive mother.

"That's the goddamn thing I was telling y'all about," Verne jabbed his colleagues. He stared at the disfigured boy, the others joining him with looks of disgust. The Mexican's eyes took in the boy for a second before returning to the stage.

When Nish was done choking, he motioned for Hercules to sit in his lap. Covering the boy's ears, he turned to John, "You couldn't have left him in the truck?"

"He pissed all over the tarp we threw in the back. That son of a bitch is your problem," the giant's face was red.

"Alright man, sorry." Nish couldn't remember the last time he'd seen his friend so upset.

The boy's cheeks imploded as he feverishly sucked on the straw. The milk ran out just as the woman onstage freed her breasts from the stretched top she had on. They burst forth, milky white and adorned with cherry red nipples, to the hollers from the men in the audience. The boy also let out a moan, focusing on the oversized mammaries. Drool fell from his open cheek down onto his chest, his mutilated tongue lapping at the imaginary milk. He pushed himself off Nish's lap and staggered the few steps to the stage.

"Where you going, Herc?" Nish reached out to him but the boy hoisted himself easily onto the stage. He ran, arms open, towards the giant breasts. The woman screamed but the crowd erupted in laughter, drowning out any sounds of her horror or the DJ's pleas for security to get the animal out of the building. A large man tried to grab Hercules but the boy headbutted him in the knee to bring him down, then grabbed his ear so he could rip it off.

Nish flew onto the stage, "Hercules, stop that!" He grabbed the boy, careful not to yank him away too quickly while he still held the man's ear in his hand. The child let go of the security guard, all bones and pieces of cartilage in his head still intact. Another guard coming up the other side of the stage flicked his wrist to extend a hollow metal police baton.

"Fuck, sir, I'm sorry about that. He's just a kid," Nish pleaded.

"Put that shit down!" a man dressed in a suit pushed his way to the front of the tables, yelling at the guard. The guard looked quizzically at his boss, then noticed the table he was standing next to. Putting the baton away, he walked past Nish to help his friend up.

"You do that again, you won't see the light of day," Nish scolded the boy as he pulled him from the stage. "You'll be stuck watching the historical channel in that motel with no milk." Hercules kept his head low as he jumped off the stage, tumbling to the ground. The Mexican grinned at Nish, -Not should you be too hard on him, he has good taste.- He produced a few one hundred dollar bills and waved them in the air at the traumatized dancer hiding behind the DJ booth. She slowly peeked her head out from behind the speakers like an animal not sure if it was safe to approach. She eventually made her way over to take the money. After confirming they were real, the fear vanished from her face. The Mexican pulled out a stack of hundred dollar bills, just like the movies, Nish thought. The dancer motioned for him to follow her offstage.

-Let us go,- the Mexican turned up his glass of whiskey, prompting the men to do the same before pursuing Roxy to the back area. Nish looked at John, then at the boy.

"Goddamnit," the giant flagged down the waitress to order his own drink as his manager disappeared behind the crimson curtain along with the others, leaving him stuck with the boy once again.

The agents sank into the velvet pillows while Roxy finished undressing. The Mexican took half an inch of hundred dollar bills and placed them on the ground in front her, then began disrobing. As he pulled off his undershirt, the tattoo of the death saint that covered his back came into view. She looked like the Virgin Mary, only she was a skeleton wearing what appeared to be a wedding dress. Verne poked Nish, "Been a while since you seen the white lady?"

Nish realized his mouth had dropped open and quickly closed it. The last time the death saint had stood in front of him, it was at an altar to the woman in the Mexican desert. The offerings had been gathered earlier by Presidio's men, the man's arms and legs plunged into boiling water until the skin hung loose and discolored from the bone and muscle. It had slid off easily to expose the bloody tissue underneath to the air for the first time. Laid next to each other in front of the money-laden statue, Nish thought the four pieces looked like human sleeves that you could zip onto shorts or a vest if you got cold. That next Thanksgiving, the fatty skin of the turkey that hadn't been properly cooked seemed to cover Nish's plate. He ate until he almost threw up.

The Mexican tossed his weapon onto the seat next to him. The extended clip made the 9mm look like a thick black boomerang.

-Want to watch?- the Mexican turned to the four agents. Arturo declined for the group, -We want more girls.-

The Mexican took Roxy by the hand and disappeared behind the curtain into the hallway of the private area. The agents heard him speaking in Spanish, an occasional confirmation coming from a female voice, then two women pushed the curtain aside to enter the private room. They began kissing each other on the lips and necks, working their way down to each other's breasts. Their tops came off, a pair of pink nipples and a pair of dark brown flirting with each other.

As the other agents leaned forward, Nish sank deeper into the cushion. He'd never cared much for strip clubs, much less lesbian shows. He didn't see the point of watching naked women you weren't going to have sex with. As for the scene going on in front of him, he could only imagine how much the Mexican had to shell out for the two strippers to sixty-nine. It wasn't only the price but also the fact they seemed to be enjoying it. He figured it was the same as if he charged people to watch him jack off.

"You not into this?" Verne narrowed his eyes.

"I'll take a whorehouse any day," Nish shrugged. Verne waved off the comment, his attention quickly refocusing on the girls.

When the Mexican returned with Roxy fifteen minutes later, Nish felt a renewed kinship with him. He shooed the bisexual strippers out of the room to make an announcement to the agents.

-I am taking her with me to Mexico,- he pulled Roxy close to him. She stood a few inches taller in her heels, looking down at her new lover with as much affection as Nish figured a whore could have. He noticed the rest of the Mexican's stack of money was in her hand. He'd learned that hundred dollar bills added up quickly; a suitcase full of them like he'd seen in movies would be ten times the amount the director would have you believe.

-Forever?- Verne cocked his head.

-Until Wednesday.-

Nish figured he must have promised her much more cash that what he'd given her so far. He also guessed the Mexican hadn't told her about the strong possibility this was the last time she'd be on American soil.

"I just got to talk to my manager," Roxy beamed, leaving the Mexican with a passionate kiss. Nish hoped the owner of the strip club would talk some sense into her.

Roxy held onto the Mexican's hand as she stepped down from the SUV into the warehouse. A group of filthy men in MC jackets next to the refrigeration truck stopped talking to stare at the dancer, wearing just enough clothes not to be arrested. Nish noticed Jeb standing with the men while his agents buzzed around the warehouse across the property.

"Hey man, they were at the gate so I let them in," Jeb explained as Arturo neared the group.

"You're early," Arturo crossed his arms. The crusty looking men didn't bother with a response. The Mexican walked to the leader of the crew, Roxy still at his side.

"What's up?" the Mexican asked in English, shaking the leader's hand. The biker greeted him with a smile and responded in broken Spanish, -All good, all good.-

-My new woman,- the Mexican put his thick hand around her hips. The MC members stared unabashedly at the scantily clad whore. The Mexican looked at the amount of cargo in their open van, then at the truck. -We will need to make room for her in the back.-

As the bikers began loading their cargo into the transporter under the Mexican's watchful eye, Nish pulled Verne to the side. "I'm going to head back to Arturo's place after this. I think I'm gaining ground."

Verne nodded. When Nish had walked away, Verne relayed the message to John. The giant glared at his manager.

"I don't know if she's going to fit back here," Smiley watched the crates fill the truck. "May have to pack her into a box and lay it on top of the others, secure it down."

"I don't want to see the fucking, just show me the baby," Arturo patted his jeans like he was drumming a frantic beat.

After some soothing words in broken English from the Mexican, Roxy agreed to be boxed up and hoisted into the truck. Once the door had been closed, Jeb brought out beers from the office and the Mexican cracked one with the bikers.

"That crew we met up with earlier today, I sell mostly to them. It started off that they'd buy a certain amount from the Mexican and with the profits from that, they'd buy up whatever I hadn't sold yet," Arturo threw his keys on the table standing in the entryway of his home. The living room struck Nish as very different from his own in that it was twice the size and decorated with hanging art instead of laminated posters. His eyes scanned the room quickly while Arturo continued, "But now they're buying up almost everything I get over the course of a month. If they don't, I got a guy back on the bay."

"So you're the reason I always hear people complaining about shortages in Houston," Nish smiled.

"No." Arturo walked to a well stocked bar. "Whiskey?"

"Sure," Nish followed, intrigued by a framed set of military medals hanging above the bottles of alcohol. Arturo saw him staring, "Ancestor of mine in the 26th North Carolina Infantry, a colonel. These have been handed down in my family to the first born son for over a hundred years." He looked at the medals like they were saying something only he could hear, then poured the first glass of whiskey for his guest. "My family came out to Texas during Reconstruction like most everyone else, when the Yankees starved folks from their homes."

Nish felt the itch from the crusty crown of his head; he drank to keep from reopening the wound onto the fleecy white carpet. After Arturo had poured himself a drink, he took the backpack with the cocaine into his bedroom. He removed an old map of Texas from the wall to expose a hidden safe. After looking at Nish to make sure he'd turned around, Arturo turned the dial to open it.

"I know that crew's working on something big. He said there's a chance they may call me tomorrow night," Arturo put the narcotics into the wall. "If that's the case, we drop a quarter of this off tomorrow."

"Why don't they just come here?" Nish looked over the agent's shoulder at the self-wrapped stacks of cash in the safe. He figured it held at least a few hundred thousand dollars.

"You don't think a fucking ghetto sled with a naked woman painted on the side coming up to my front door would be a little suspicious?" Arturo snapped. "You got to be fucking smart, fucking careful doing this shit."

Nish wanted to blurt out the irony of this statement since Arturo had just gotten caught 'doing this shit' but he decided on another direction, "That's a good point, I wasn't thinking."

Sucking his teeth, Arturo closed the safe. Nish made another peace offering, "I know you didn't have much of a choice but I really do appreciate all this. It's just that, with my mom sick and all, I've been scrambling to get money for the last two years," he finished his whiskey. "How about we go to that Cajun place we passed on the way here. I'm buying."

Arturo's expression changed drastically, "Fuck yeah. That's awful white of you," he stopped short as soon as he'd said the phrase, looking at Nish as if for the first time. "Well, you know what I mean."

Nish waved off the statement. After covering the safe, Arturo threw back his glass. "I got some shine an uncle of mine makes, we can have a little after dinner," he nodded his head quickly like it was a broken machine stuck in a limited range of movement. Leading the way out of the room, he didn't see Nish rip off the scab on the top of his skull to allow the red moisture underneath to ooze out.

DAY 10

The smell of the leather boots reminded Nish of his childhood baseball glove. He remembered his father teaching him to stop a ball with his body in Fretz Park; he wondered how much his dad had intentionally thrown the ball so it would bounce to catch him under the chin or in the chest. He doubted the bonding time other kids shared with their fathers resulted in so many bruises. It seemed fitting the bat his dad used to hit the balls to him was the same he grabbed on the way out of his room when he heard his parents yelling and stomping around the living room in unison as if they were doing some violent waltz. The look on his dad's face, he thought, pulling on the boots with a smile.

Hercules whimpered as he held up his glass for more milk.

"I'm coming," Nish quickly smeared anti-bacterial cream where Rebecca had raked her nails deep into his back, then carried the carton to the tarp the boy sat on.

"Remember what I told you, only clean boys get more milk," Nish held the new carton back until Hercules had wiped his face where the liquid and saliva had escaped from his missing cheek. Nish helped him clean the scaly areas of his neck and body that the boy's malformed limbs weren't able to reach. Hercules looked back at his caretaker with love in his one good eye as Nish smoothed out his hair. Kids mimic what they see, the man in the chair had said to take away blame from his client, show them love and they'll give love in return.

"Sorry I haven't been spending much time with you but I'm close to having enough money for my mom's surgery. This should all be over soon," Nish filled the boy's glass halfway with milk. "If this is how much I had when we came," he explained using the visual aide, "then this is what I have now," he filled the glass to the top. The boy's hands shook in anticipation. Nish lifted the newly opened carton in his hand, "And this is what I'll have when we're done here." He handed the glass to Hercules, who did his best to tilt his head so the milk would go past his tongue stump and down his throat as opposed to out of the gaping whole in the side of his face.

101

Nish had applied his extra strength sunscreen by the time Verne and John returned from breakfast. The giant stepped over the tarp while the San Antonio agent shook his head at the boy like it was the first time he'd seen him, "Goddamn."

"What's your problem with Little Hercules?" Nish tried to act upset but was in too good of a mood to be very convincing.

"You fucking blind?" Verne tiptoed around the tarp, the child staring at him. "Don't you wonder why he's so messed up? What he did for someone to chop him up and burn him like that?"

Lying back on the bed with his boots hanging off the end, Nish stretched his arms behind his head and yawned. He felt the air expand his rib cage; bones were soft, he knew from experience. John sat on the bed next to him and turned on the TV.

"Put on the historical channel, Herc needs to be learning while we're out," Nish didn't bother looking at his subordinate as he gave the instructions.

Verne let out an indignant laugh, "That thing isn't learning shit. And I don't think we should be leaving him here alone. He might burn the place down."

"Everything will be fine. You show love, you'll get love back."

"Listen to this hippie shit," Verne sat in the desk chair he'd pulled away from the boy's area. He paused before getting to the point, "You any closer to figuring out this thing with Arturo?"

"I'm closer but I still don't know for sure," Nish shrugged. "I just need a couple days."

"Well that's about all you got. Junior should be back before too long."

"When?"

"No telling," Verne watched the television. "Sometimes he's down there a while and others, he's hardly gone. But I reckon this should be a short trip."

The phone in Nish's pocket vibrated loudly, spurring him to rise from the bed. "Rebecca," Nish pointed at his cell as he opened the door. "I'll be back in a second."

Verne adjusted his crotch like he was digging for a thorn stuck deep in his groin. "Rebecca, huh?"

John lifted a corner of his mouth, changing the channel. The boy growled low, watching the two and picking his teeth.

The yard behind the expansive house was overflowing with Smith employees and associates by the time Nish's group arrived. Various members of the crowd lifted their koozi-wrapped plastic cups as they entered the side gate. The backyard was packed with people, leaving only an open area for the beanbag game surrounded by cheering onlookers waving twenty and hundred dollar bills. A large meat smoker close to the glass doors of the home poured mesquite smoke onto a Mexican barbeque of cabrito, hotel ribs, chorizo, the whole head of a cow, and blood sausage. Water shot from the glands under Nish's tongue at the site of the thick black links.

The man tending to the smoker saw him eyeing the sausage. -Will be cooked in ten minutes,- he said in Spanish, tapping the plump links with his tongs.

Verne pulled Nish away from the grill, "Don't even fuck around with that bullshit, this is a fancy party." He pointed to a table against the fence where two Asian men prepared rolls of sushi and sashimi. "Flown in fresh from Washington state," he paused for a second, "The fish, not the dudes."

"I figured. People in our line of work aren't exactly big on springing for airfare for humans," Nish watched as the red flesh of the fish was deftly cut and placed on a tightly packed bed of rice. The rawness of the animal drew him in. Fighting his way politely through the crowd of men in polos and women in bikini tops, he made it to the table, somehow accumulating a drink on the way. With his free hand, he removed a piece of salmon from its rice podium. One of the Asian men said something he didn't understand but the other quieted him. Nish put half of the chunk of meat into his mouth, tearing it apart with his teeth. He remembered when he'd eaten it warm, straight from the ocean on the fishing trip off Padre with Bill and a couple other directors. The fish was still twitching as he placed its flesh into his mouth; its eye staring upwards, Nish bent over in the hopes it was watching.

"This is the only way to eat it," Bill didn't bother dipping the meat into the soy sauce in front of them. The fish beat itself hopelessly against the bottom of the boat. The two men looked at each other, smiling.

"I tell you one time I knew this guy, worked with the company a while back," Bill put his foot on the head of the fish as he carved it alive. "He was in love something awful with this girl round the office. So he asks her out a few times and she finally says yes." He handed a slice to the other directors who had come to scavenge on Bill's catch.

"You talking about Tom Green?" one of them asked. The man looked like a preppie fisherman in his polo and sunglasses dangling by a line around his neck.

"Yep," Bill didn't look up at him. "So as sure as they get married, he's cheating on her with another woman from the office within the year. As you'd reckon, the wife finds out and they get into a hell of a row. She kicks him out of the house and he goes speeding off into the night. Until he gets t-boned by an eighteen wheeler."

"Shit," Nish shook his head. The other men focused on the chunks their colleague was cutting from the fish. Bill continued, "Old boy goes into a coma, all hooked up with wires and all that shit. Hospital calls his wife and she runs in tears to see him, screaming how she loves him with all her heart and how she doesn't want him to die."

"Talk about luck," the preppie director shot Nish a grin. Nish smiled back politely, "Did he die?"

"Nope, he woke up after a few months," Bill answered.

"No shit?"

"Except when folks wake up in real life it ain't like in some soap opera," the director spoke while chewing the warm flesh. "You're all fucked up. Can't talk, can't walk, just like a retard or some shit."

"Yep," Bill nodded. Nish reached for another piece of fish but the sushi chef pulled it away from him. The other chef pulled back his partner's hand as he scolded him in a foreign language.

"Fuck," Nish tried to remember back to the last time he'd taken his pill. Fucking booze, he thought. That and the stress getting to him, making him forget and only compounding the problem. He looked at the alien drink in his hand, full and clear with a lime stuck in the top. "Only thing that can help me until I get back to the motel."

He took a long drink of the vodka soda until it ran down the sides of his mouth.

"There we go, boy!" Verne appeared from behind him. "We're getting shit-housed today!" He turned his own drink up and let out a holler. Others in the immediate group echoed the yell. The phone in Nish's pocket vibrated, causing him to break away towards the side gate.

"Where you going?" Verne had a look on his face like he was being left on a deserted island.

"I've got to take this."

When Nish reentered the backyard, the blood sausage was gone. He looked at the pickings left on the grill, finally pointing at the cabrito. The grill master lifted the goat meat with his tongs, laying it gently on a plate as if it were a delicate treasure. -Sauce of blood?- he asked in Spanish. Nish nodded and the man poured on the chunky gravy before placing a small stack of tortillas on the side. After refilling his drink, Nish scanned the yard. The giant's head caught his eye; he followed the body down its trunk to find Verne, Arturo, Smiley and a few other agents standing in a group, watching the game of beanbags. He sat on a cooler and ate alone until he'd finished his meal.

"There that son of a bitch is," Verne pointed at Nish as he approached. "You're missing one of the best games of beanbags I seen in my life. Where you been?"

Arturo looked particularly interested in the question, one hand in his pocket while the other let his drink dangle from his fingertips like a crane's claw ready to drop its cargo on an unsuspecting passersby below. Nish took his spot in the group next to the giant, "Girl won't stop calling me. She wants to hang out tonight."

"Sheeyut, I got that problem all the time," Verne shrugged. "The problem is they get addicted to the dick. You've got to let her know she has to share, it's not all for her."

"Some kindergarten shit," Smiley agreed.

"Yep," Verne put his arm around his coworker. "This son of a bitch right here knows, his dick stays wetter than an eighteen year old snuff queen in a thunderstorm." Smiley raised his glass and Verne cheersed him, "I had the same situation a couple months ago with two girls at titty buffet. Mexican girl and a blonde, both hot as shit. I started off paying the Latina for a lap dance, but she gave me a lot more. And I mean all sorts of shit, rubbing on me, jacking my dick through my jeans, making me about to explode," Verne simulated the moves. "It got to be quitting time so I told her I had two grand in my pocket that was all hers if she came back to my place. When she goes to the dressing room to get her stuff, the blonde comes over to grind on me. Must have heard about my money. Well, the Mexican girl comes back and catches us, and she gets crazy pissed off."

Smiley and Jeb nodded knowingly at the scenario. Nish thought he might as well ask, "So what happened?"

"Oh, I fucked both of them. It cost a shit ton but I didn't want to seem racist."

Nish downed half his drink. A beanbag plunked down on the burnt orange board in front of them, causing the crowd to erupt. Jeb, standing across from them with a wad of dollars bills in his hand, threw the money onto the ground, followed quickly by his body. He cradled his head in his hands as some guy Nish didn't recognize stood over him with us arms held up victoriously.

"Eight hundred Jeb just lost on that," Verne explained to Nish with an amused smile on his face.

Money exchanged hands as people settled their bets and prepared for the next game. Arturo inconspicuously made his way next to Nish. "What's up?" he tried to read his face.

Nish raised his eyebrows innocently, "Nothing, just having a good time." Arturo didn't look convinced but Verne noticed the two and interrupted before they could talk any further. "Nish, I know you think you're a smart motherfucker. What's this mean?" he raised his drink, revealing a koozi from an Irish pub.

"It's Gaelic," Nish answered quickly, appreciating the interruption. Verne's face wrinkled in confusion.

"It's what the Irish used to speak."

Verne cocked his head to the side at first like he didn't believe Nish, then opened his mouth wide like he'd finally realized something. "You only know that shit because your family's from there," he turned to John, "I knew he wasn't really that smart."

"My family's from England."

"What's the difference?" Verne shrugged like he wasn't asking a question but rather stating he didn't care to hear any elaboration on the subject. Nish didn't take the hint, "England conquered more of the world than any other nation in history. There still hasn't been an empire to rival its size," Nish ran his hand through his hair, tickling the scab. "Ireland, on the other hand, has a proud history of terrorism and agricultural failure. It's like if I told you that America is the same as Mexico."

"Ireland isn't that bad," Verne waved him off. "My grandfather told us we had Irish in us."

"The Irish in the southern United States were the Protestants who were forced to leave because the Irish Catholics chased them out. They were enemies."

Verne burped, turning back to the game of beanbags.

"Who cares about all that? Last country my family was a part of was the Confederacy, and we don't get a fucking parade or any of that shit," Jeb pointed angrily like there was an invisible man in front of him responsible for this injustice.

"That's cause they're afraid we'll rise again," Arturo spat on the ground. This incited the group to raise their drinks and give praise to the defunct country. When others around the game heard the cheers, they joined in. Nish imagined the group drunkenly driving to DC to declare their secession; he wondered how many times they'd have to stop for piss breaks or to refill their coolers.

The phone vibrated again in his pocket. He tried to slip out of the group unnoticed but Arturo put his "C.S.A" chant on hold to inquire where he was going.

"I'm going back and forth with this girl," Nish lied. "We're not sure where we're going out to eat tonight."

Verne also stopped the chant, killing the group's momentum. "You ain't going anywhere tonight except the honkey tonk with the rest of us." He studied Nish, "She should come."

Nish acted appreciative of the invite, "Maybe she will." Verne raised his glass to the statement, watching as the Dallas agent dug his fingernail into his teeth as he walked away to take the call.

The honkey tonk's Western-garbed security didn't take their eyes off the men escorting the deformed boy across the parking lot. When the three reached the front door, Nish wished he'd taken the risk of having Hercules destroy the motel room in a fit of hunger instead of agreeing to meet up with the rest of the agents later. As he tried to step into the bar, one of the bouncers shoved a meaty arm in front of his face to block the entryway.

"Excuse me?" Nish felt the scab on the top of his head burn like someone had put out a cigarette on the spot. The doorman looked him up and down slowly, then did the same with the boy. Nish cracked his neck. "Something I can fucking help you with?"

"Yeah there is, boy," the bouncer stepped directly in front of him, his body doing a good job of obstructing the doorway. Bigger offensive linemen had been flattened on the practice field, Nish thought. The booze swished around in his body but he tried to hold himself up straight to look the man in the eye.

"They're good, Donny," Jeb yelled from inside, "Let them in." The bouncer turned quickly to nod, then stood aside.

"Yeah Donny, get the fuck out of the way," Nish deliberately planted his shoulder into the man as he passed. He tried to etch the name into his memory in case Donny ended up working in the San Antonio office one day, but the list of people he wanted to get back at was long and alcohol had blurred the letters over the years.

Nish had always thought the honkey tonk that the Smith employees in Dallas frequented was more of a redneck mega mall, complete with a dozen bars, separate areas for multiple pool tables and dart boards, Western wear vendors and a dance floor almost half the size of a football field. What the San Antonio honkey tonk lacked in size and attractions, it made up for in authentic grit. The country dancehall in Dallas had just about every walk of life but never so many filthy drunks glaring at newcomers from under the shady brims of cowboy hats. Men with overweight women or underage girls did their best to stay upright on the dance floor while those at the bar dipped their noses into the glasses of whiskey in front of them on the way to passing out.

"I know what you're thinking, it's a bad scene when the Mexicans are the best dressed dudes in the joint," Jeb motioned to a group of men in well-shined belt buckles and white hats. "It's a Sunday, so the place isn't exactly jumping. But usually, sheeyut, there are women five deep trying to get a beer. Hot ass band on the stage. Hell yeah!"

They followed Jeb to the tables the agents had pulled together. Arturo and Verne sat next to each other; Nish guessed it was the latter's doing. When they saw him arrive, Verne beat his manager to the question, "Where's your girl?"

"She told me she wouldn't be caught dead in this shithole," Nish winked, eliciting chuckles from most of the agents. Arturo and Verne stared at him as if some movement he made might give away an alternate truth. Nish helped the boy into a chair at the opposite end of the table from the two, then sat down next to him. "I need a drink. We go to the bar or a waitress comes around?"

"She'll come," Jeb scanned the large room until he found her. Nish wondered how long it would take for his pocket to fill with blood if he chopped his fingers off. Some of it would seep through, so it would be a matter of how much was produced versus how much was lost. He'd seen plenty of fingers turned into stumps, the red pumping out over the barely visible white columns hidden in the meat. He realized his toes were curled inside his boots and straightened his whole body as he expelled the thoughts from his mind. Clenching his teeth, he excused himself to go to the bathroom, bringing Hercules with him.

The feeling of revulsion subsided as they passed an etching of a skull and crossbones on the wall. "When I was a little boy, about your age, it was my dream to go up in a hot air balloon. So when I was nine, my mom let me do it for my birthday," Nish helped the boy into the bathroom. "While the guide was messing with the engine that sent the fire into the balloon, my brother took out his pocket knife and cut one of the ropes that held us down. At that point, the guide went ahead and cut the rest, I guess he figured he might as well. There were a bunch of other people there waiting for their balloons to go up but we floated on, high above them," he smiled as he let his stream fly against the back of the urinal. "I felt so free, watching the others fight against their ropes. It was like I was floating above all the fear, all the love and hate in the world. It's not that those things didn't exist or weren't something to believe in, they were just beneath me, for the people still tethered down."

The boy threw his robe to the ground, moaning his approval of the story.

Nish remembered taking the end of a metal baseball bat and knocking out a woman's teeth so one of the other agents had an easier time of cutting out her tongue. Everyone knew what they were getting into, he thought, and he didn't believe women should be treated any differently than men. "You go to some other country and see how they treat a rape victim," Nish swayed as he pissed, "If they do anything more than give her a pat on her head and send her on her way, they publish her name in the newspaper and no man touches her again. And I'm not just talking the obvious places like South America or Asia or Africa, I'm talking countries that should know better, places in Europe."

Nish finished up and flushed. "The point is that sexism is wrong. Treat everyone equally." The boy nodded and Nish gave him a thumbs up, which the boy returned along with a joyful howl. Nish spit into the urinal, "I've never once held the door for a woman." He flushed for the boy. After throwing water on his face in the hopes it would make him sharper at deflecting the probes of the San Antonio agents, he washed the boy's hands. He'd need to take twice the amount tomorrow morning, he reminded himself, especially considering the circumstances. You can't be constantly talking to yourself, he dried Hercules off and helped him back to the table.

DAY 11

The phone vibrated on the nightstand. Nish opened his eyes to read the clock, just after noon, and was thankful the San Antonio office considered it a holiday when Junior wasn't in town. Rubbing his head, he looked around the room to find it empty except for the boy lying on the plastic-covered floor below. He picked up the phone, "Yeah."

"We're in. You take Arturo out of the equation and hook us up direct with that connection and we'll pay," the voice of the thug on the other end of the line sounded strained. Greed takes over the weak, Bill had once told Nish. They hate themselves for it but they can't help it. Nish figured the thug's decision to have his own relative killed just to get a better discount on the Mexican's coke was eating at him.

"Good, you give him a call saying that you want to meet tonight to buy the leftover. When he and I show up, don't be rolling too deep, you don't want to scare him off." The boy made a noise and Nish studied him; drool leaked out of his open cheek onto the plastic. "I'll bring my guy and we'll take care of it, you just make sure we can get rid of the shell easily. However you do it down here."

"That's no problem." The voice hesitated, "And you're sure the House is alright with this?"

"I told you, this is why they sent me here. Consider it your lucky day," Nish rolled gently off the bed to fish for his pills in the travel bag.

"The way I see it, you're pretty fucking lucky too," the thug became defensive. "What with us paying you for some shit you were going to do anyway."

"But then you wouldn't have the connect. I've been on the phone with the Mexican all weekend. Next time he makes a run, you just meet him at the spot, no middle man to deal with."

There was silence from the other end while Nish dry-swallowed the pills. Finally, the thug spoke, "Alright. Tonight at two. You bring Arturo and we'll bring the money."

Nish hung up, thinking of the hot tub he was going to have added onto the side of his pool. His mom loved the hot tub in their old place. When he was growing up, she'd spend weekends in it with her head

110

against the stone side. A smile spread across his lips as he remembered their dogs going up to her and licking her face. The motel door opened just as Nish threw the pills into his bag. He turned to face Verne and John, "I think you may have been right. I think Arturo's dealing."

Verne stopped in mid-step, stubbing his foot into the carpet. "I fucking knew it," he swung his arm out in front of him. Nish watched his face for a real reaction.

"Don't get too excited, I'm not sure yet. We have a chance to catch him in the act tonight," Nish looked at the men earnestly. Hercules stirred, wiping the saliva from where it had pooled around his face. "I think he's meeting up with some roaches he sells to. If I'm right, we can put an end to it then."

Running his hand through his hair, Verne looked past the bed to the floor below. "Why wait until then?"

"Junior called me in to be one hundred percent certain. I know you're itching to be manager of that crew but you can wait a day."

The jab had the desired effect, causing Verne to snap out of his contemplation. "Fuck that, I'm here to do my job. We can wait."

"I'm going to his place this evening for a little bit, I'll find out the address and call you."

The men nodded as the boy on the floor shot up from his slumber. He stared at the motel door like the devil himself was on the other side.

Arturo opened the door to let Nish in, scanning the streets as his new partner entered his home. "Everything good with Verne and John?"

"I told them I was going to Rebecca's, they don't suspect anything," Nish stood in the entryway until the door was closed.

"Whiskey?" Arturo asked. His guest accepted and he went to the bar to pour them both a drink. "I got the call, they need us to meet with them tonight."

Nish raised his eyebrows, "That was quick."

"This shit's flying right now," Arturo handed him a glass. "I'm going to have to start upping my order from the Mexican."

The first sip of the whiskey burned its way down Nish's throat, dissolving the old lining and making way for the new cells underneath. Drinking when you're hungover is almost better than drinking after taking a long break, Nish thought to himself, although he was unable to remember the last time he'd gone more than two days without alcohol.

"You eat dinner yet?"

Nish shook his head, "I'm starving." His host went to the kitchen to retrieve half a bag of chips and a bottle of salsa that had plastic wrap for a lid. When he sat back down, he held the TV remote in his hand but didn't turn it on. "You got a lot of calls yesterday."

"I'm a popular guy."

"I doubt that," Arturo's fingers brushed the rubber buttons on the remote. "Who were you talking to?"

The stretched gums between Nish's teeth screamed out to him, begging to be ripped open. "That girl half the time," he shoved a fingernail deep in between the teeth, allowing it to work its way down from the front until it cut into the gums and let the copper fill his mouth. "The other times it was my mom's doctor. I told him I'd have the payment in time for her surgery. I didn't want the others to know because they'd get suspicious about where the money was coming from."

Arturo's fingers stopped their movement. He clicked on the TV, propping a boot off the end of the coffee table and sinking into the couch. "My dad died a few years back of prostate cancer. They said they could have caught it if he'd been tested regularly but I guess he didn't want the finger up his ass once a year."

"I can't blame him," Nish tried to act interested as he opened the bag of chips.

"The fucked up thing is, why'd they tell him that? I mean, it wasn't enough that the guy's dying, the doctor has to rub it in? Fuck that shit," Arturo flung a hand in the air as if he were slapping a miniature version of the doctor in front of him. "And they say what we do is illegal. Fucking vultures."

Nish felt the alcohol compounding in his system, working faster since it already had a solid base from the day before. He'd need to drink water when he went to the bathroom, stay as alert as possible.

"What do you carry?" Arturo interrupted his thoughts, reaching behind his back to pull out the chrome-plated .380. A smile crept onto Nish's face at the sight of the flashy weapon; he quickly lowered the sides of his mouth. "That's a nice pistol," he held his hand out but Arturo didn't pass it to him.

"I asked what you carry," Arturo motioned to his guest's belt. Nish reached behind him to pull the snub-nosed .44 revolver from its holster. "Half snake, half hollow."

Arturo smiled, "Like a little handheld shotgun." He reached for the weapon and Nish let him take it. He weighed both pistols in his hands, then checked the sites on each. "Only holds six, though," he finally handed over his own weapon to Nish for him to inspect. "This son of a bitch has a dozen in it."

Nish hit the clip release as if looking at the magazine would help him to confirm the number of bullets. "Guess I'm just a better shot than you."

"Sheeyut," Arturo chuckled, raising the revolver to take aim at a talking head on the TV. His attention jumped to the television personality in his sight, "You know this asshole?"

It took a second for Nish to recognize the political pundit on the screen. "I remember this guy, always talking about affirmative action." He nervously ran his thumb over his fingertips as he eyed his host with the revolver.

Finally handing the pistol back to Nish, Arturo reclaimed his own weapon. "I say give them all their forty acres and a mule, see how long it takes them to starve. Only we won't be giving handouts anymore when they come crawling back."

"No black person would get the full forty acres, though," Nish checked subtly to make sure no bullets had disappeared. "You can't find a black person who doesn't have white in them. Most of them would probably get about thirty acres, some with lighter skin may get half that. Then you'd have a shit load of embarrassed white people getting an acre or so."

Arturo laughed, "That's all most white folks want right now. I'd kill for an acre plot."

The choice of words caused Nish to grin.

Arturo relaxed back into the couch, looking satisfied at the outcome of his thought process. Nish grabbed another handful of chips and leaned back into the soft cushions of the sofa. Arturo pulled the bag away, "Fuck that. I need some more substantial shit."

"Sounds good."

Arturo stood, running a hand through his black pompadour as he retrieved the phonebook. Nish took a drink, the dark liquor swimming through his body, floating his head like a buoy bobbing up and down in the ocean. He smiled at the thought; no burning on the top of his head, no aching between his teeth, no flesh taunting him from under his cuticles. The air conditioner filled the room with a perfect atmosphere, man besting nature. He watched the sun begin its descent to the Texas horizon and relaxed.

"Wake up," Nish slapped Arturo again, the surgical glove sticking slightly to the man's skin. It had been hours since he finished wiping the place down; he knew from experience the pill he slipped into Arturo's beer was strong but he was getting restless. The booze in his own system had worn off, leaving Nish with a heat resting on his forehead that he couldn't shake.

"Come on, man, wake the fuck up."

Arturo's eyes opened slowly, focusing first on the duct tape holding his feet together. When he reached to undo the restraints, his hands wouldn't move from above his head. Looking up, he saw two holes had been made in the wall protruding into the kitchen and another wad of duct tape holding his arms behind the exposed beam. He's awake now, Nish thought to himself as he watched his victim struggle comically.

"What the fuck?" Arturo's eyes widened as he saw Nish in the plastic suit. "What's going on? What the fuck are you doing?"

"The combination to the safe," Nish dangled Arturo's own butcher's knife in front of him.

"You're robbing me? Are you fucking stupid?"

The ears were always a good place to start, Nish thought, people don't want to look like a freak; the weakness of vanity. Before Arturo could move, Nish kicked him in the face with the heel of his boot, then dropped to one knee. Forcing his victim's head to one side, he pulled the top part of Arturo's ear down to expose its root. Keeping the weight of his body on Arturo's head, he asked again, "The combination."

"The House is going to kill you, you know that? You're a fucking dead man," Arturo tried to lift his head but Nish's elbow made his attempts useless.

"The House isn't going to do shit to me. I'll tell them you were onto me sniffing around so you took the money and left town. And if I were you, I'd be thinking that scenario sounds pretty good right now."

Nish felt the muscles in Arturo's neck loosen before he muttered out his surrender, "Fuck it then."

Nish lifted his body weight from the man's head.

"This is some blackmail shit," Arturo tried to spit but didn't have the saliva. The red area of his face where he'd been kicked began to inflate. "You're not scared of the Russians in Houston coming after your ass?"

"Any Russian that has to buy drugs piecemeal from you isn't worth being scared of. Same with any Vietnamese, so don't bother threatening me," Nish cracked his neck. "At this point, this is your only way out of Texas alive. I'm actually doing you a favor," Nish smiled. Arturo didn't return the gesture so Nish lifted the knife again. "The combination."

"Fuck!" Arturo yelled like he just realized the situation for the first time.

"Keep it down," Nish raised his foot again.

"Wait, wait. Alright," Arturo licked his lips. "Can I have some water?"

"You fucking serious?"

"I'm dying of thirst."

"You don't tell me how to get into that safe, I promise thirst won't be what kills you," Nish kicked him in the chest, knocking the wind out of him and setting off a coughing bout that didn't seem to end until Nish reluctantly brought over a glass of water to hold over his captive's mouth.

"The combination."

Arturo's coughing seemed to magically stop while he recited the numbers. Nish tipped the glass so that water poured onto the man's partially discolored, puffy face. "If you're lying to me, I'll just come back and cut you up," Nish sat the glass in the kitchen sink after the man had finished drinking.

"Don't fucking insult me."

Leaving the knife on the kitchen counter, Nish walked past the bound man to the bedroom. He took down the old map to expose the hidden wall safe. The combination worked. Inside was the money, a few hundred thousand by his estimation, and the cocaine. He unfolded a trash bag from his pocket to drop the stacks of bills and half the allotments of coke inside, leaving the rest of the narcotics to be found later. Turning to the bed, he took the Confederate medals he'd laid there earlier and placed them carefully into the safe before closing it and returning the map to its place on the wall. Halfway down the hall back to the kitchen, he realized he hadn't heard a noise since he'd left Arturo. He reached behind him to pull his pistol. As he slowly neared the corner, he listened for any sound at all but was met with only the loud hum of the refrigerator. Lowering his body to the floor to avoid being shot in the face, he peeked around the corner. Arturo sat with his head down and his eyes open wide like he was deep in thought. Nish got up from off the floor, "Glad you decided to stick around."

The man didn't bother to look at him, "Just let me have my pistol. Take the fucking bullets but let me have the gun."

"Why?" Nish replaced his revolver in its holster before walking past his victim to the kitchen.

"I go to Mexico, I might as well stay in Texas. I'll need to protect myself. They'll hunt me down there just like they would here," Arturo spit, his mouth agreeing with him this time. "And I don't want the Mexicans getting a hold of me."

Nish picked up the butcher's knife from the counter, "I wouldn't worry about that." Arturo looked up as Nish walked over to him. "What the fuck?" his mouth stayed open. His captor kneeled in front of him.

"This shouldn't come as much of a shock considering today's events, but I lied to you. I can't let you go."

"What?" Arturo made a face like a confused child and Nish wanted to disfigure it right then, before he'd even forced the cloth into his mouth.

"I can't take any chances," he explained. "If you're picked up, you'll start singing about everything that's happening right now. And the last thing I need is to give the old man an excuse to kill me."

"Hold on a second, just wait a second," Arturo acted like he wanted to talk rationally as Nish retrieved a gag that had been resting on the sofa cushions. Arturo shook his head calmly, "Wait, just wait. Now, listen to me. There's no--" Nish kicked him in the nose. Arturo cried out as the waterfall of blood gushed forth and Nish shoved the cloth into his mouth. He tried to spit it out and bite at the hand but Nish pressed his thumb onto the flattened cartilage, causing his mouth to open involuntarily. Once the gag was secured, Nish rested his weight on one side of Arturo's head to bring the ear into view again. The ear was a great place, he thought, just a little tricky. It reminded him of an artichoke, with the top separate and flimsy and the bottom compact. He knew from experience to stay close to the skull; he pressed the blade at a fifteen-degree angle into the bone and sawed downwards. If you try to go straight down, you risk cutting through the weaker cartilage and then you have a hell of a time trying to get started again, since you don't have the top part of the ear to hold anymore. The red juice ran down his victim's neck, the gag partially absorbing the screams; Nish felt himself stir like an electric jolt had touched him. The blood obscured the white of the cartilage so he tried to cut faster to see it in all its purity. As he got to the bottom, he grabbed the earlobe. He'd found out this was actually easier with people who had earlobes that were naturally separated from their face. You could always cut the bottom anyway but this made it cleaner. The OCD in him, he thought, a blessing and a curse.

"Sorry to carve you up Mexican-style but I've got to make this look like your thug ass relative and his boys fucked you up, pin this on them," Nish cut from the bottom to finish the ear and the knife sprung free. A tiny bit of cartilage jutted away from the skull; Nish tapped his teeth together, he wouldn't fuck up on the other side. "But don't worry, they'll get their's tonight. You know how these roaches do one another, it's like gangland warfare out there," Nish forced the man's head the opposite direction to expose the other ear. "It's enough to make a decent taxpayer like myself donate more money to my local police department."

After Nish was finished with the other ear, he dropped them on either side of Arturo. The man had tears running down his face; his body betraying him, Nish thought, taking the last of his dignity. Then he remembered. "You know, I could kill you right now," he peeled off the plastic suit and removed a lighter from his pocket. "I mean, that would be awful white of me."

116

Walking to the closed curtains, he held the flame up to the cloth until it caught hold, crawling quickly up to the ceiling. Arturo tried to yell something through the gag. He struggled wildly against the duct tape to no avail. Nish watched him floundering on the floor and shook his head before stuffing the money-filled trash bag into a backpack and heading for the backdoor. He had just enough time to get to the bus station before he had to meet with John and Verne, he thought.

DAY 12

"Where you been?" Verne whispered, his white knuckles clutching his gun.

"Fucking bus," Nish ducked behind the dumpster. "They all here yet?"

John nodded as if his manager had just asked if he'd like to go out for something to eat after the bloodshed had finished. Nish had always admired the way the giant handled tense situations. He figured John had taken cover with a weapon in his hand plenty of times in his life.

"A couple cars, folks talking and smoking but I can't see faces," Verne bounced his knee nervously. "Reckon that's all of them. We need to act quick."

"Listen, we don't need to get into a firefight with these fucking insects. We go up with our guns on Arturo only, tell the rest of them this is some in-house shit and let them leave with the drugs they're buying and they get to keep their money. They shouldn't argue with that," Nish looked to John, who nodded casually again. Verne's knee kept bouncing, "I don't know."

"We've handled shit like this before, it'll work out," Nish spoke calmly. "Just follow me." He poked his head cautiously from behind the dumpster. A small group of men stood in the parking lot catty-cornered to the agents' hiding place, their faces illuminated by the tiny glowing buds inches in front of their mouths. Only three, Nish thought, glad Arturo's relative had been foolish enough to take his advice. Nish holstered his pistol, looking at the others to do the same, then stood to walk towards the group.

The thugs heard the noise of the boots approaching before they could see anyone but their leader motioned for them to act normal. "Don't tip our fucking hand," he said low as the men came within ten yards. He bristled upon making out their faces, "Where's Arturo?"

"What the fuck?" Verne turned to Nish, his hand naturally gravitating towards the pistol tucked into the back of his pants. The leader of the thugs saw this and lifted his shirt to expose his own weapon, "I said where the fuck is Arturo?" he yelled this time. His fingers shook slightly as they hovered over the handgun in his khakis. "Someone was supposed to die here tonight," he lifted his chin.

"I wouldn't worry about that," Nish pulled his pistol. Verne did the same, swinging it upwards at Nish. Before Verne had a chance to raise it to Nish's face, John kicked the San Antonio agent in the back of his knee, forcing him to the ground and causing the gun to fall from his hand.

The thugs didn't have a chance to squeeze off a round before John had dropped to the asphalt and put a bullet into the base of the leader's neck. The two others let loose a hail of lead; Nish hugged the parking lot, his tongue wagging out of his mouth.

As Verne reached for his gun on the asphalt in front of him, one of the thug's bullets caught him in the side, tearing through his organs and exiting through a larger hole. John shot again, missing to the back and upwards of a thug running for his car. He shot a third time, catching the teenager in the shoulder and causing him to fall. When his friend ran back to pull him to safety, John trained his sight on him and pulled the trigger, ejecting the young man's brains from the back of his head. He then did the same with the downed teen.

"Fuck yeah!" Adrenaline flooded Nish's bloodstream. His tongue darted manically on the tips of his teeth. "Nice shooting, Tex," he smiled at the giant. John raised himself up, keeping his pistol aimed at the thugs. He walked over to make sure the job was finished as Nish put his own cool weapon back into its holster.

Stepping around the widening pool of blood gliding across the parking lot, Nish kicked Verne's gun away before kneeling down in front of his head. The red juice pumping out of the dying man made saliva drip from Nish's open mouth. He felt himself drooling but didn't bother to stop. John reported back, "They're dead."

"Guess we don't have to worry about them making a rap song about this, blowing up our spot," Nish smiled as the spit made its way past his chin to form a long drop yearning to connect with the blood below. "Can't trust kids these days, you know?" he turned back to Verne. "Well, of course you do. That's why you ended up taking them out with that unregistered nine over in John's hand."

Nish unzipped his pants to remove the cocaine he'd taken from Arturo's safe as the giant walked back to his manager, wiping the pistol clean of his prints. A backpack swung from his shoulder. Nish dropped the narcotics just out of Verne's reach and rubbed his face like he was just waking up, "But that's what those cockroaches get for not bringing money for the coke you're trying to sell them. You're not going to let them rob your ass, not a bad motherfucker like you who can take out three men at once."

John tossed the backpack to his manager, who opened it to find hundred dollar bills formed into stacks inside of plastic bags. "Two weeks from now, this whole thing will seem like it was just a nightmare." Nish still had dreams about his mom walking around and talking like she used to; it's tough when things get all backwards, he thought. Verne suddenly began shaking like someone being electrocuted in a movie.

"Look on the bright side," Nish put his face in front of the dying man. "At least you won't be alive when Junior comes to get you. It was hard to convince him you were in on it with Arturo, took all weekend to talk him into it, but eventually the evidence just added up." Nish closed the bag and swung it over his shoulder as Verne's spasm passed, leaving him sucking in his own pale lips as he wheezed. John slid the clip out of the 9mm and jacked the bullet out of the chamber before placing it in Verne's hand. Once his hand had left its mark on the weapon, the giant pulled it away to reload and place a few feet from the dying man.

"See John, never such a thing as being too cautious."

"You're right about that," a voice shouted from behind them. Nish's heart dropped, pressing on his bowels. He felt a tickle in the back of his throat like the pizza he'd eaten earlier was trying to escape before the feeble body it had inhabited was turned off. The man behind them spoke again, "Both of y'all put your hands in the air."

They did as they were told, turning to find Jeb pointing a fully automatic assault rifle at them. "He figured y'all might try some shit like this."

"I guess it's a good thing he had you as backup then, huh?" Nish swallowed down the first taste of vomit as he motioned to the man's friend shaking violently in his own blood.

"Fuck you," Jeb walked closer. He saw John inch towards Verne's pistol on the ground, "Don't even think about it, you fucking ogre." As he neared, Nish could see his eyes were red.

"I'd kill both of y'all right now if I didn't know what Junior and the old man are going to do once they find out about all this," Jeb sniffled. Tapping his teeth together, Nish watched the man alternate between looking at his dying friend and aiming the rifle at the killers' heads. Nish slowly let the backpack slip from his shoulder, catching it in the nook of his arm.

"I understand you're upset, Jeb. I'd be, too," Nish spoke calmly. "But you've got to know, my mom's dying. And John here, he's just a loyal friend who doesn't want to see me get hurt. Now I know you of all people can understand that."

"Stop fucking moving," Jeb's voice was higher than usual. He looked frustrated at how the words had come out and took aim at Nish's chest.

"Wait, Jeb," John kept his hands up. Jeb turned to the giant and Nish threw the backpack at him. He instinctively raised a hand to keep it from hitting him, taking the men out of the rifle's sight. Nish pulled the pistol from his holster as Jeb swatted the bag away. The revolver fired its snake shot, shredding the man's knee until only a few stragglers of muscle and cartilage held it loosely together. Jeb collapsed to the ground, his hand tightening around the weapon and spraying rounds into a cement wall in the distance. By the time he'd swung the gun up, Nish had leveled the pistol at his head. Nish pulled the trigger and Jeb's face was smeared along the asphalt. His body fell limp, no spasms or convulsions, just dead.

"Fuck!" Nish clicked the revolver back on safety. They'd been careful to ensure the bodies had slugs in them matching guns the police would find on the scene, guns that obviously couldn't be traced back to himself or John. They'd done a good job, Nish thought, until Jeb ended up with his head missing its front half. He turned to the giant, "We've got to get rid of this body."

John had gathered Verne's pistol so that only the planted weapon was near his body, hiccupping out the last of its life. Grabbing the backpack, he strapped it on so he could help Nish carry Jeb's corpse. "Any place we could do that easily is going to be run by Smith," he said the obvious.

"I know that shit," Nish raced through the possibilities. "Mountain lions will eat him whole as long as he's warm. Just as good as pigs but you don't need a farm."

"We're driving out of town, we could always clean him up and bury him."

This also seemed like a good idea to Nish since only the far left side of Jeb's mouth still existed. He quickly looked up into the dark, realizing that while a couple of Jeb's teeth may have turned to powder, the rest could have been scattered over the parking lot. The neighborhood was isolated but anxiety crept into the back of his mind. "How long do you think it takes the cops to arrive on the scene here?"

"San Antonio?" John shook his head, unworried.

"Alright," Nish nodded quickly, then put his hands up as if a panicking crowd had gathered around him and he just wanted everyone to calm down. John stuck his hands in his pockets.

"Alright, so here's what we do. You bring your truck around so we can throw this asshole in the back. When you pull up, park a little bit away at first so we can clean up all this shit," Nish pointed to the pieces of skull and leg being eclipsed by the growing lake of blood. "We do this shit quick, then we clean him up and dump him in a hole we dig out on the prairie. Got it?"

121

John nodded and ran off to get the truck, leaving Nish surrounded by the five corpses, their blood reaching out to him in a last attempt to mark him with his guilt. He easily stepped out of the way.

On the way back into town, they listened for any mention of the crime scene on the radio but it didn't come. After dropping the money off in the bus station locker, they grabbed breakfast at a greasy spoon on the highway. Neither opened their mouth to do anything but yawn and eat until Nish decided to verbalize a game plan. "We'll hit the motel, clean ourselves up," he looked at the dirt under his fingernails. Despite all his caution, he wouldn't be surprised if there were drops of blood visible on him. "Last thing we want to do is show up in front of Junior dirty."

"You don't reckon we should stop by the office first? It's getting close to nine. We wouldn't want to show up late, not today."

Nish looked at John, his eyes red, the muscles of his face too tired to hold themselves up. Golden stubble on his chin caught the light as if in energetic defiance of the man it was attached to.

"You're a good friend, John. Sorry if I haven't said that enough."

"I've never had too many buddies, so I guess I've been saving up my friendship," the giant gave an exhausted smile.

"You're right, we'll just wash up in the bathroom here and head straight to the office. It's not like anyone saw what we were wearing yesterday." No one still alive, anyway, he thought.

They kept the radio tuned to the local news on the way to the office, still listening for the shootout. As they took their spot in traffic waiting for a light to change, a half naked man outside the window caught Nish's eye. He didn't have any business going shirtless, Nish thought, but it didn't stop him from displaying his gelatinous torso covered in ink and stretch marks. He held a cigar in his mouth, his lips peeled back like he was showing his teeth to an invisible dentist. The crate he sat on swayed under his weight; Nish waited for it to collapse, trying to imagine the man crashing to the ground, the cigar falling out of his mouth and scalding his jiggling fat. He imagined plunging his hand deep into the man to pull out some vital organ hidden under the soft mountain of lard. The man didn't fall but instead took the cigar out of his mouth to exhale. Nish's eyes followed the ribbon of smoke as it floated lightly upwards, adhering to the will of the fickle wind. Behind it in the distance, someone stared at him, someone he knew.

"Fuck," Nish's fingers dug into his leg. Bill stared at him from Junior's truck across the intersection no more than twenty yards away; Nish read his mind. "We're not going to the office."

122

"What?"

"Bill's here," Nish stayed frozen.

"And you think…" John let his words trail off as he searched for the man.

"Yes. Take a right and we'll go to the motel." And then what? Nish wondered. They'd have to get the fuck out of Texas, that was for sure.

"I guess Junior didn't believe you after all," John said matter-of-factly.

"How'd you fucking figure that out?" Nish spit. Maybe there was a way. Maybe after they learned of the scene at the warehouse they'd think he'd been telling the truth all along. He quickly dismissed the idea; Junior had probably known about the warehouse as soon as he'd woken up that morning. And if he was the first person the cops called when a couple of good old boys showed up dead, he might have enough pull to tell them to arrest the suspects on sight. "Let's just grab Hercules and our shit and we'll figure out what to do."

Two of Junior's agents guarded the door to the motel room. Nish and John crept up to the back driveway of the motel, making sure to stay behind the fence line of bushes. If Smith owned the property then it was covered in cameras, Nish had warned his partner.

"We can't go in there shooting. There's still a chance we can talk our way out of this," Nish spoke to himself as much as the giant. "We kill a couple of Junior's guys in broad daylight and going back isn't an option."

"Then how do we get the boy out?"

Nish picked his teeth as he studied the entrances and floors of the motel. "You still have Verne's pistol?"

"Yep."

One of Junior's agents pulled a can of dip from his back pocket, offering it to his partner.

"Nah, trying to stay away from it," the young man refused. The other agent packed it before sticking a wad in his mouth.

"My dad's been dipping his whole life and he's healthy as an ox," the agent's words were slightly distorted from the bulge in his lip.

"You seen that video, though? The one with the baseball player with half his face missing?"

The agent waved the comment away. "That's one guy out of millions who dip. And it didn't even kill him," he spit on the concrete. "And that was olden times, back in the early '90's. They got all sorts of medicine and treatments now that'll keep you good. Science has gotten a lot more advanced in the last decade."

The other agent raised his eyebrows in consideration of the facts, "I didn't think about science." He motioned for his partner to pass him the tobacco. A gunshot from around the side of the motel caused the can to fall to the ground in the middle of the handoff.

"Goddamnit," the agent hooked his finger into his mouth to pull out the wad. They both unholstered their weapons and ran to the noise. When they had rounded the corner of the motel, Nish sprinted for the front door of the room. As soon as he'd opened it, the boy jumped on him, moaning loud enough with joy to take the hearing from his right ear.

"Shhh," Nish put his finger to his mouth but the boy was too relieved to quiet down. The room had been turned upside down with the contents of the Dallas agents' bags strewn onto the floor. Nish gently pulled the boy off him to check the bathroom. The bottle was nowhere to be found. "Fuck!" He turned to find a pistol in his face.

The guy behind it couldn't have been more than eighteen, Nish figured. A single strap of metal across his upper row of teeth shone in the light as he grinned at his catch. Nish remembered when he first had braces; biting down as hard as he could until every inch of his mouth screamed out in pain and that taste came out. The kid spoke up, "Now why the hell would we just leave two guys outside the door?"

Hercules jumped onto his back as Nish ducked to get out of the gun's sight. He pushed the kid over, pinning his shooting hand with his boot. Hercules crawled out from under the kid to plunge his teeth into his neck. He gnashed at the veins and tendons, clipping them like piano strings with his teeth until his nose was buried in the flesh.

"What the fuck are you doing?" Nish's voice cracked. The boy removed his blood-covered face, roaring as he stood on his hind legs and beat his chest with his fist.

"Fuck!" Suddenly panic-stricken, Nish grabbed Hercules to carry him out of the motel room. He could feel the boy's strength and knew the child could have easily gotten out of his arms if he wanted. Halfway across the parking lot, tiny explosions came from the side of the motel as lead zipped past them, sounding like something from a cartoon. John pulled up to the back entrance, pushing the passenger's side door open. Nish threw the boy in first, then jumped in close behind as a bullet hit the side of the truck. The noise of metal on metal made Nish's heart skip a beat. As John turned the corner, a smile spread across Nish's face. He looked at the boy, whose red mouth mirrored his own.

The sun had reached its peak by the time the truck pulled into the dusty border town. Nish had forgotten John was from Harlingen until he suggested meeting up with a relative there who could get them across the border under the radar. They pulled into the parking lot of a motel as Nish hung up with his brother.

"Everything good?" John asked.

"I hope so, I left a voicemail," Nish would usually never leave such sensitive information as the bus station locker number and the location where he'd hidden the key on a recording but this was an emergency. "I told him he needs to get down to S.A. in the next few days to get the money for the doctors," Nish stuck a finger in between his teeth, "He should be fine."

They got a room nearest the exit of the parking lot on the ground floor. With no change of clothes or toiletries, Nish washed his face with the motel's complimentary soap, helping the boy do the same, and lay down on one of the double beds next to Hercules. He was worried the events of the day would bring out the electricity but exhaustion sunk him into a deep slumber before John had even finished securing the room. Within ten minutes, all three were asleep with the sun still high in sky.

DAY 13

"Best burgers in the Valley," the giant pointed to a restaurant in a strip mall.

"I'm hungry, too, but we need to see your guy," Nish was amazed they'd overslept. "It's almost noon."

John shook his head, "We'll need to eat now."

After grabbing the food to go, they drove on to the government building. John picked at his fries with his free hand while Nish and his boy ate greedily.

"A truck leaves every few days taking the corpses of the illegals back home," John explained. "Each truck is assigned a different route and follows it on a bimonthly schedule. No real hassle since both sides figure they've got nothing in them but dead bodies."

"What about the way back in?" Nish asked with his mouth full.

"The coffins are state-owned so they're only used to drop off the corpses, then they come back to the U.S. for the next batch."

Nish was still surprised when he heard the big man speak so intelligently. "But there's no such thing as an empty truck," Nish slurped his soft drink.

"Nope."

The government building looked like it belonged in a Southwestern themed strip mall, complete with an Alamo-style decoration on the roof. John circled around to the back where his relative was waiting impatiently. By the time he'd parked, his contact had jogged up to the truck. "Goddamn, I thought you were going to be here an hour ago."

"Sorry about that, we got held up," John apologized as Nish helped the boy out.

"I've told the driver about the stop. It's way the hell out, someplace no one else is going," the man wiped the sweat from his forehead, his eyes darting back and forth. "One more thing, I'm going to need your guns."

"What?" Nish stepped back from him.

"Yep, can't risk having you get caught with firearms crossing the border," he nodded quickly. "Folks is one thing but weapons is a whole 'nother set of federal laws."

126

The reasoning behind this was alien to Nish but John nodded slightly. Nish removed the pistol from the holster at his back and handed it to the nervous man. He watched John's relative, he'd forgotten exactly how they were related, stick it quickly in his pants. Nish didn't have time to process it further as they were rushed to the back of the truck. Inside were the two worst looking wooden coffins he'd seen in his life. "These look like something I would have made in Shop class in the seventh grade."

"Probably as old, too," the relative kicked one of the boxes but it was sturdy.

"We need one more."

"No we don't," the giant stood with his hands in his pockets. He motioned for the relative to leave the area and the man ran his hands through his hair, "You got one minute."

When he'd gone, John laid his enormous hand on Nish's shoulder. "We both run and there's no way either of us will make it to see the end of the month."

Nish squinted, pissed off he was having to go over the plan again at such a late hour. "Look, we lay low in Mexico for a little bit until things have cooled down. Junior's being a hothead but the evidence is on our side. Deaf will see that and realize we ran because we were scared, not because we're guilty."

John didn't budge. "Old man always liked me. That can go a ways with him. As for you, he was just looking for an excuse," the giant helped the boy into a coffin, handing him one of the large bottles of water sitting at the edge of the truck. "I go down with you and I sever that tie. I stay here and plead our case, and we both have a shot. Otherwise, next time you get into a coffin you won't be getting out."

"Misunderstandings have happened before. Friends get killed and people want blood. It just takes a little time for calm heads to prevail."

"Verne was kin to that old man," John crossed his arms. With his elbows jutting out to the side he was almost twice the width of Nish. "Deaf doesn't need time, he needs an explanation from someone he trusts."

Nish spat onto the floor of the truck. Looking up at the giant one last time, he embraced his friend. "I'll be back on the next truck up. Make sure everything's good with my mom, alright?"

John nodded, handing a large bottle of water to Nish as he climbed in. "Everything will be fine," the giant reassured him before closing the coffin. Less than a minute later, there were voices outside in Spanish and the boxes were nailed shut.

The light from Nish's cell phone died, causing the tight space to get even smaller. The blanket John's relative had laid in the coffin was balled up at the foot of the box within a few hours, soaked with urine as Nish quickly realized he didn't have many options. He hoped the boy used his blanket in the same manner so the piss wouldn't leak out of his box, possibly tipping off checkpoint guards, but he seriously doubted it. The truck stopped. It jerked forwards slowly, then jolted to a stop again. After repeating this cycle a dozen times, it sped off like it was trying to outrun something.

He tired of imagining himself freezing, coming out of the cold to lie in the bed of heat voluntarily. Everything is relative, he thought. In the winters, his father would scold Nish and his brother for asking him to turn on the heat. They wouldn't last a day in an English winter, he'd laugh, dismissing the request so as not to raise the gas bill. Nish got used to huddling around their home's large fireplace with Dave. They'd play a game to see who could sit closest to it for the longest amount of time. It was unbelievable how hot it could get; he imagined his skin crisping and he'd grab the hardened edges and tear it off as it crunched and cracked under his fingers. The whole outer layer of his body would be peeled off, leaving untouched pink flesh underneath. A fresh start, he thought.

The truck took a hard turn, sending the coffins smashing into one another. The irregular movements were starting to have an effect on Nish's stomach. He tried breathing in through his nose and out through his mouth but the stifling air was so thick it grew hands that wrapped themselves around his neck. He awkwardly lashed out at the thing trying to strangle him, throwing tiny punches from where his arms were trapped near his waist and scraping his knuckles against the inside of the coffin lid. He made a noise that came out as an effeminate sound of desperation; he thought back to the shootout at the construction site two years earlier and shuddered, trying to breathe calmly again. He should look at this like a test, he thought. He wished the cell phone could turn back on so he could recite the texts he'd sent to himself. Even better, he tried to force himself to smile, like a final exam. The truck took another hard turn, propelling the contents of Nish's stomach up through his mouth to coat his neck.

The heat worsened. He shouted as loud as he could to the driver or anyone else in the front or back of the truck; he knew it was useless but continued, anyway, like a passenger in an airplane hurtling towards the earth. He let them know there was a boy with him and asked if he was still alive but answers never came. He thought how sorry they would be when they realized Hercules wasn't just some stray running from the law; how stupid they'd feel when they found out who Nish was. The violent thoughts comforted him and he explored them in gory detail long after his throat had gone raw. The movements of the truck caused the saliva to rise in his mouth again. He wasn't going to rest his head in solid vomit for hours. Readying himself to swallow it back down, he stared upwards and waited miserably.

The truck's stops became more frequent, followed by turns. Nish had lost the battle against his stomach and was trying to throw up to his right side but a good portion of it ended up drooling down his face and neck. When older vomit had crusted over, he tried to pick it off in chunks. He imagined it seeping into the fresh scabs on his back, infecting the area. The truck stopped again, this time for longer. The respite in motion brought a relief that was quickly replaced by a desire to cause serious pain to whoever was driving. The back of the cargo hold opened. Voices spoke to each other in Spanish as coffins were moved around and unloaded. He yelled for them to let him out, first angry and then pleading. The door shut. A few minutes later, the truck's engine started up again.

After several stops, the noise of the boots finally neared Nish's coffin. It suddenly slid across the floor of the truck. He braced himself against the sides of the box as it floated unsteadily up into the air, then downwards until it hit rock and sand. The boots walked away.

Nish struggled against the lid of the coffin but it didn't budge. He wasn't able to kick his feet up so he tried to push with his knees to no avail. He yelled out to the men in Spanish, saying first he was going to kill them, then offering them more money than they'd seen in their whole lives. The boots came back. A coffin fell next to his with a thud. Nish yelled for the boy, threatening the drivers if Hercules was hurt in any way. After what seemed like forever to him, a crowbar struck the wood inches from his face, wedging itself between the lid and base of the coffin. When half the nails had been removed, Nish burst from the box, breathing in the warm air deeply.

"What the fuck?" he turned to find the man with the crowbar next to another, leaning on a poorly maintained antique shotgun like it was a cane. He was looking at the portion of the coffin covered in dried vomit. -This one it dirtied,- he commented to the other. Nish tried to stand but fell over the side of the box into the rocky sand. Pushing himself up, his legs did their best to slip out from underneath him but he grabbed the coffin to steady himself. The man with the crowbar worked the lid off the boy's coffin. Little Hercules stood up, stretching like he'd just enjoyed a good night's sleep. He saw his savior and ran to him, embracing Nish's lame lower half.

-Fucking idiots,- Nish yelled in Spanish at the men loading the empty boxes back onto the truck. -We could have died in those things.-

The transporters looked at him like he was a cow mooing its discontent. Nish turned to the boy, "I swear to God, I'll never let something like that happen to you again," he turned away to dry heave. When he was done, a thirst swelled from deep inside of his stomach. "When you make a promise, you hold yourself to it."

The truck drove off down the dirt road, creating a plume of dust that seemed to be the only real landmark in the barren Mexican wasteland. When it was gone, there was nothing. Nish scanned the land for electrical lines or fences that would lead to civilization but all he could see from the high road was cracked, yellow earth spotted with islands of cactus-infested brush. To his right, a range of mountains shot out of the desert, looming over the badlands at their feet. Hercules tugged on his hand, pointing to something in the distance.

"What is it?" Nish followed the boy's finger to a wisp of smoke about a mile away. He patted him on the back and they stumbled and lurched towards the possible source of water.

When they first saw the village from afar, it looked like it was made of paper mache that had hardened and flaked away next to the dry riverbed. As they drew closer, the picture became clearer: cracks became gashes in the stone, rough edges were chunks of buildings that had let go of their base. The two followed the smoke to a bleached house down one of the few side streets off the main square. A woman sat knitting a quilt that covered her legs. There was no noise or movement in the surrounding buildings, no signs of life whatsoever that Nish could see.

-Good day, ancient one,- he spoke in Spanish. The old woman didn't look up, -Good day.-

Nish felt the dried vomit prick his neck, his mouth craved the saliva that had filled it when he was nauseous. -What is this place?-

-Tierra Mojada.- She continued laboring on the scene in her lap without glancing upwards.

-Where are the others?-

-They left.-

Nish turned to Hercules, "Not exactly the fucking visitors center, huh?" Sticking a fingernail between his teeth, he stepped closer. -To where did they go?-

The lines in the woman's face deepened, -The United States.- Her fingers deftly caught the needle, then replaced it back in the quilt. Sewing didn't look that hard, Nish thought as he watched the crone.

Maybe he'd take it up for the next couple weeks, bring back a souvenir for his mom. -We need water.-

-There,- the woman pointed to the steeple of the church poking above the nearest row of abandoned homes and shops.

-Many thanks,- Nish patted the boy on the shoulder and they left her to the scene slowly unfolding stitch by stitch on the fabric.

The church did its best to stand at the head of an old Spanish style square, surrounded by the decrepit one-story structures that blended into the yellow and brown landscape. Weeds and short cactus had taken root in the square itself, making it hard to distinguish where the wild ended and the town began. At the side of the church, a baby mule mollowed its last. Its killer rattled its buttons, touching something primal inside of Nish, a fear he knew someone had felt a thousand years before him. "Everything in this country wants to either stick you or bite you," Nish warned the boy, pulling him closer. He backed towards the front door of the church, feeling the sudden need to piss as a tarantula scuttled away from the holy place and towards the Americans. Nish lifted his foot to stomp on the giant spider and when he did, it exploded underneath his boot into hundreds of tiny spiders that shot out of their pregnant mother and across the entryway of the church.

"Fucking Mexico!" Nish danced on the stone as some of the babies crawled their way up his boot into his jeans. The boy slapped at the ground wildly and laughed.

After he'd killed what he could and the rest had dispersed, Nish turned his attention back to the door of the church. It looked as if it might collapse under its own weight but it proved solid when he knocked on it. The dryness in his mouth spread to his brain and intestines; he felt if he didn't get water inside him soon, his organs would grind against each other and tear themselves apart. He knocked again. No answer.

"Fuck it," he pushed the door inwards at the same time the frightened young woman on the other side pulled it open.

The nun kept her eyes on the boy while her new guests gorged themselves on corn tortillas filled with beans. Nish poured water into his mouth until it overflowed, running down his face to splatter on the stone floor of the church. It gave him a satisfaction better than any sex or food and more fleeting than the pieces of metal that had flown through the air inches from his head the day before. He looked at the boy, who kept his eyes fixed on the nun like he was staring into the coffin of someone he hated. Nish recognized the look from windows and sides of downtown buildings.

-You want more?- she asked timidly in Spanish.

-Yes.- Nish studied her as she placed more corn tortillas on an unglazed ceramic plate. He figured she couldn't have been any older than twenty. Her exposed hands and neck hinted at a gaunt frame hidden beneath her habit, a contrast to her round face. After setting down the plate, she went back to refill her cup at the end of the table. Nish recognized the opaque liquid as agave beer. He poked the boy in the sides as the nun took a long drink, "Boozehound." The boy let out his hideous laugh for it to echo off the church walls.

-You are alone here?- Nish asked the woman.

-There are the ladies who help me,- she answered, keeping her eyes on her cup.

Nish dipped another tortilla into the bowl of beans as he looked around the church. Some of the pews had been rearranged to line both sides of the rough wooden table they sat at; he figured it had room for about fifty. The stained glass crucifixion scene cut the last of the day's light into a thousand colorful shards on the ancient floor. He squinted in a fruitless attempt to see into the far corners of the church where neither the painted glow of the window nor the flickering of the saints' candles could reach.

-We are very tired,- Nish finished his tortilla, standing to remove his shirt. He poured water from the pitcher onto the area where the vomit had dried. It splashed onto the floor and the nun shifted in her seat before standing; she had to steady herself by holding onto the table. Nish smiled to the boy at the nun's inebriation. -Where can we sleep?-

Not responding, she walked up to the altar to cross herself before kneeling. She turned back to the boy, who tried to raise his hand to his forehead before Nish caught it.

"We don't do that voodoo bullshit," he patted Hercules on the back as the woman fixed her eyes on him. Nish pointed to the candles under the statues of the saints lining the walls with bowls of money in front of them. "I guess that's why everyone's Catholic in Mexico," he said to the woman in English. "It's probably more expensive than getting the power company to run some lines out here but at least you know you're going to heaven, right?" he smirked. The young woman began praying.

After finishing her ritual, she led them behind the altar to a hidden stairwell. The flickering light from her candle illuminated only part of an expansive basement that Nish figured had held food and valuables back when the church still had both.

-There are rats here?- he asked. She shook her head. He looked into the dark around them doubtfully, then turned to the nun, -Bring us more, please.- He took the candle from her to outline a perimeter on the basement floor.

She went to retrieve extra candles as Nish sat on the ground. "Two weeks is going to be a while," he said out loud. His thoughts drifted back to the motel room earlier in the day, all the places he didn't look for the bottle, the extra time he could have used to find it. "No pills for me, no milk for you. They say Omega 3's help but I don't see many fish around here."

The boy moaned as he shook his head.

"We'll just have to make it a point to exercise," Nish realized his fingernail was in his teeth and pulled it out. "Exercise and rest, that's all we need. We'll be just fine."

The boy hugged him in agreement.

"Of course, we'll have to do something about the sun, too, but that can wait," Nish yawned. He thought back to the motel bathroom; if he'd just stayed for two seconds longer, hadn't screamed like a woman at Hercules. He shook the thought from his head. "Trouble can wait, isn't that right, Herc?" The boy nodded his head into his savior's chest.

"It's important to get a good night's rest. It may be a little uncomfortable tonight but we won't spend our two weeks down here. We can pick out a nice house tomorrow after we go for a run."

The boy squeezed tighter. Nish felt as if his bones were going to give in so he pushed the child away gently.

When the nun returned, he lit the candles, placing them around the perimeter of their sleeping area where the woman had laid their bedding. When he finally lay down, Hercules did the same, pulling the sheet over to make sure it was smooth, just like Nish had.

DAY 14

Nish was awoken by an urge to piss. He felt like he'd slept an eternity, dormant energy having settled into his veins. The candles guarding their sleeping area had gone out; things in the dark scurried away as he rose to his knees. He imagined an army of rats and roaches retreating after daring each other to see how close they could get to the invading giants. He stood, his legs taking a second to regain their composure, and stretched his arms high over his head in a satisfying yawn. Little Hercules stirred at his feet.

"You can go back to sleep," he pulled the covers up on the boy just as something made a noise in front of him. It wasn't the sharp clicking of rats' claws or the sound a mass of roaches make crawling over each other, like a breeze through a small tree. It was a heavy sound. Every molecule inside Nish screamed as he froze. To his side, another noise like two soft things brushing against each other. As his vision adjusted to the tiny amount of light coming from upstairs, he was met with a stomach-level wall of eyes staring up at him. He remembered the tarantula guarding the door of the church. Something long and sharp extended slowly towards him, the light glinting off the protrusion. The eyes blinked at different times, the noise of breathing quickened from the thing. Nish felt the boy graze his leg below him and knew Hercules was crouched to attack.

Lifting his hands like he was surrendering, Nish quickly reached out to grab the protrusion. It retracted, drawing a line of pain on his hand. "Fuck," he winced and the eyes rushed towards him like the word was their mark. Hercules flew forward to hit a torso and legs that crumpled to the ground. Nish grabbed the protrusion again, this time pulling the hot thing free. There was a pain in his chin and he was arcing backwards through the air to crash to the ground. He regained his senses and grabbed the sword as the eyes descended upon him. Thrusting upwards blindly, the blade's progress was slowed to the point he knew he'd hit something deep in the softness above him. The thing shrieked. A body struck Nish from behind; he turned on his knees to swing the sword and it hit something hard that it stuck to. A heel came

134

down on his head before Hercules pounced on the attacker. A light from the top of the stairs grew brighter until it illuminated the nun, her face trapped in an expression of disgust; Nish thought how stupid she looked. He pulled the sword back as the light fell on the group of bleeding, disfigured boys that surrounded Hercules and himself.

The first sounds of the church bell caused several broken windows around the square to fill with faces. As it continued, more of the buildings revealed their inhabitants. Boys emerged from one door, lurching towards the top of the square. Their bodies were similar to the boys in the basement: scarred and burned, some missing limbs or other chunks of body like they'd been run through a factory machine and gotten spit out. More came from another house, then more from other buildings until the plaza was filled with them moving slowly towards the church like zombies. Nish cracked his neck to the side, the sharp crunches bringing him a base satisfaction.

With the boys lined up in front of the church, Nish counted a little less than a hundred, half of which were in good enough shape to walk without help. The sick and the ones missing legs had been brought out and laid next to the two boys he'd wounded. One had a red piece of cloth tied to his head that wouldn't accept any more blood and leaked onto the dry sand. His head had been turned to the side so his drool would trickle out of him during the long process of dying. The nun attended to the other child with the help of a boy who Nish figured was the injured one's brother due to his looks and loyalty. The brother looked healthier than the rest of the children with less scars and all major pieces of his body intact. The nun dabbed at where the American had gored the boy. Nish thought that if someone brought fresh gauze, the sight of the pure whiteness alone would make the people want to frame it. "Everything covered in this fucking sand," he stuck the sword in the ground to rest his hands on it, then motioned for the nun to come to him.

-Who are they?- he asked.

-Orphans. They have been hiding from the killers,- she looked down at the blade piercing the earth.

Nish ran his tongue along his teeth, -Not do you need to wear all your clothes. There is much heat.-

The young woman looked at her feet. When no response came, Nish asked, -Who are the killers?-

-Men very bad from the town to the north. When the government changed the course of the river, the towns like this suffered. The people left, many were hoping to send back money but everything died. The land, the systems,- she looked up at the boys. -The killers come once a week to prey on the towns dying. If not can we give them enough money or valuables, they kill one of the boys.-

-Not are there police? The army?-

The young woman looked at Nish like she didn't understand what the words meant. He picked his teeth, -The girls, they took living?- The nun crossed herself and nodded.

"Sick motherfuckers turning little girls into whores," he looked at Hercules. The boy shook his head along with his savior.

-I am going to kill these men,- Nish passed gas, then waved it away with his hand. -You and your bastards will be free. Like in America.-

The nun didn't react except to turn away from Nish and the lingering smell.

The older bastards filled the long table inside the church, staring silently at the American and his boy while their little brothers buzzed around the church. When the nun and her group of old women brought out the food, Nish readied his fork.

"I'm starving," he winked at Hercules. He'd noticed most of the bastards only had spoons and some didn't bother with silverware at all. -Not do you teach them manners?- he asked the nun. She didn't answer but sat plates of tortillas with soupy beans in front of the diners. She delivered Nish's plate herself; he noticed tiny chunks of meat swimming in his beans that were absent from the bastards' lunches. Earthenware jugs were placed on the table. Nish reached for one, noticing his arm. He grabbed the hand of a decrepit waitress, -Have you lotion for the sun?-

Her single brow pushed closer to her sunken eyes. -Wait yourself,- she shuffled off.

Nish poured the contents of the nearest jug into his cup. It surprised him by coming out milky with the rounded bitter smell of agave-based alcohol, the same as the nun had drunk the day before. Looking around the table, he noticed the bastards pouring the simple beer into their own cups. He sniffed his bowl of beans.

-Not is there water now,- an old woman explained. -Some of the boys go to the dam tomorrow for more.-

Nish took a sip, letting the mildly carbonated liquid wash around his mouth. It was light and surprisingly refreshing, unlike the bottled variety he'd had in Texas. No fruit had been added along the way so the taste was pure. He drained the glass down his throat.

Hercules watched, then mimicked the action. Nish thought to stop him but decided against it. "We can't forget to exercise," he hoped that by saying it out loud, the chances of it happening would be increased. "I'm good when I'm drinking but the days after are the hardest," he remembered holding onto the sheets like he might be thrown from the bed at any second, unable to shake the painful tickle. If he'd only had a little longer to look around the motel room. "Maybe we'll go for a jog this afternoon," he raised the sides of his mouth. The boy let out a wail of approval.

Halfway through the silent meal, the old woman returned with a bowl filled with thick ointment. -For the sun,- she motioned to her skin. The American dabbed a finger into the grayish-white paste and thanked her. The bastards whispered amongst themselves, attracting Nish's attention. One stood out among them, fat like a tick and without a blemish on his skin.

-Fatty,- Nish refilled his cup with the agave beer. The bastards stared wide-eyed at the foreigner as he spoke. -How did you get so fat?-

The obese child dropped his tortilla into his bowl of beans, -Just is my body.-

-You are a liar, Fatty,- Nish took a drink, the alcohol smoothing out the rough edges of his brain. He turned to the boy who had been nursing the injured brother earlier, -You, how did the fat one become so fat?-

The boy froze until another turned to him, -Guillermo, tell him quickly.-

Guillermo looked past Nish, -The men come and from us they take our things. If not do we have anything for them, one of us they take.- He pointed at the round child across the table from him, -The fat one decides who goes to die.-

-Why Fatty?- Nish leaned forward.

-I do not know,- Guillermo took a modest drink of his beer before going back to his meal. The boy next to him looked like he was going to explode until he finally did, -The killers think that the fat one is funny. They give him candies and breads. They joke one day they will eat him.-

Nish pressed his lips together but couldn't hold back the laughter. Hercules joined in, moaning at the girth and situation of the fat child. The bastards looked at each other, only a few laughing at first, and then they all were.

-Not can I help it,- Fatty hid his hands in his face. -Not do I want to be the person who decides nothing.-

A tortilla struck him in the side of the face, -Eat up, fucking fat son of a bitch,- a boy yelled to the approval of his peers. The nun raced to Fatty's side to shield him from the onslaught of food. She begged the boys to stop and the hail of tortillas reluctantly died down.

-Not do you treat another child like this,- she scolded them as harshly as she could, which sounded to Nish more like a weak suggestion. He watched as some of the boys dropped their heads with shame, others went back to smacking on their food or talking. The nun patted the fat one on the head before returning to the kitchen.

-Do you bastards go to school?- he asked the table. The group quieted down again, responding this time by shaking their heads. Nish made a face like he was surprised, -Why not? School is very important. Not does the nun teach you to read?-

-I know how to read,- one boy raised his hand. Some of the younger did the same, as if they were playing a game of who could reach the highest. Nish dabbed at the ointment on the table again, spreading the oily cream on his arm. It lay heavy like a skin-tight shirt trying to suffocate the life from him. -You will be my army of bastards,- he addressed the table. -Together, we will kill the men of whom you speak.- He raised his glass but the boys didn't do the same.

A younger one spoke out, -Not can you kill those men. Are the serpents of the devil.- He nodded his head up and down quickly, others joining in.

-My mother they took,- a boy of about seven without a right forearm said. -When she tried to jump out of the truck, they tied her and dragged her behind them as they drove away.-

-Is the truth,- others nodded.

-They had my father beat my sister in front of the town,- another blurted out like a schoolboy shouting the answer to a problem on the blackboard. -She was pregnant and they did not let him stop until she lost her child.-

Nish raised a hand to silence the flood of stories. -These men will die like others.-

-The leader is the devil,- one bastard yelled out. -He put my brother in a bag of tarantulas.-

-He threw gasoline on me,- another dropped his pants to reveal flesh that had melted and hardened again in a different position. -He is evil.-

Quieting the children, Nish rose from the table. -I have seen the devil, not is it this man. Now there is a chance to be free,- he swayed from lack of water and the cups of agave beer. -If you follow me, we will kill these men and create a new society. A place where the weak can grow strong, the strong can grow great. Where people are judged on where they want to go, not from where they came.-

-But how can we do that?- a bastard held up the thin shirt that hid his emaciated frame.

-When do the men return?- Nish asked Fatty.

-Two days-.

Nish picked his canine, pointed from years of sharpening with his fingernail. Hercules rose from his seat to assume his place next to the savior; Nish removed the finger from his mouth to put an arm around the boy. -Then we start now. Find everything that can be used as a weapon,- he turned to the nun, watching from the kitchen door. -Bring me a map of the area. Not can we do nothing without water.-

The bastards looked to one another, the younger watching their seniors for a sign. Nish slammed both hands on the table, -Go!- The boys jumped up, running out the front door to begin building their arsenal.

"Don't listen to what those bastards were saying," Nish comforted Little Hercules as he poured over the map. "Truth is, there's no such thing as good and evil. At least not like those bastards think. Someone says killing is evil and makes a law against it, then men are drafted by the hundreds of thousands to kill other clueless teenagers and they're called heroes. Someone says extortion is bad and makes it illegal, but banks run people into bankruptcy with the interest they charge. What interest rate is evil? At what percentage does God say someone is going to hell?"

There was a good chance many of the bastards would die, Nish projected. He needed to question them, get a better feel for the usual number of gangsters, their weapons, if they carried phones to call for reinforcements and, if so, how long it would take for more of them to come. He figured the thugs ran a pretty low rent operation if they were killing children; the Mexican gangsters he'd worked with through Smith Realty wouldn't let a potential labor source go untapped, much less kill it off. He thought of the money he could take from the thugs after he'd done away with them, no need to get back into those fucking coffins in two weeks.

"Someone who rapes a child, you think of them as evil. But he has no choice in the matter. He was born with certain DNA, and into a certain situation in life. His DNA doesn't change and every situation he gets into is a result of how his genes caused him to react in the preceding set of circumstances," Nish leaned back next to the boy. He pictured the town square painted a red so consuming that even the gnarled cactus and animal feces would be blotted out by its depth. "There's no free will, no good or bad options that we have a choice between. We're born to satisfy needs that reside deep in our marrow."

He looked at the boy, who grunted his agreement. Nish ran his finger along the old riverbed up to its source at the dam. He could save the lives of these boys, he thought, and probably countless others. Water and freedom. He nodded, tapping the dam with his finger. "Sorry Herc, but it looks like we'll have to postpone our afternoon jog. Round up those bastards and grab me some more beer, we've got an army to get ready."

Jacobo squinted up at the mountains looming in the distance. The last of the orange light slipped under their peaks; he leaned forward as if it would help his view. Getting up from the rock, he stared at the ground for a second then ran to the town's square.

Several of the local boys were standing watch over the growing piles of machetes. Others were swallowed up by the deserted shells of homes then spit back out with kitchen knives and hoes. Jacobo navigated his way through the frenzy up to the church. One of the guards smiled, -Jacobo, what passes?-

-Where is the American?-

-For there,- the boy pointed at a hastily constructed pen the American had ordered built to house the town's stray dogs. Jacobo's eyes rested on the rusted machetes. -No guns hidden?-

-The killers have taken them all. The shotguns, the pistols, everything,- the guard shrugged. -Not did they work anyway.- His eyes turned to another group with armfuls of forks and various farming equipment. Jacobo left for the dog pens.

A group of boys surrounded the American as he spoke to them in Spanish, occasionally turning to his partner with words no one else understood. The large man had taken off his shirt to cover his body in the greasy ointment, causing the nearby fire to dance on his skin. Jacobo approached him, wincing as he noticed the thick red claw marks on his back.

-Pardon,- Jacobo raised his voice. The American turned around so quickly Jacobo jumped back. The man made odd motions with his head, his hands moved constantly like a fly's. He said something Jacobo didn't understand.

"Only little English," Jacobo said in the foreigner's language.

-You are smart. The one who could read, yes?- the American asked in Spanish.

-Yes, sir. Pardon but there is a light in the hills,- Jacobo pointed. The American moved his neck to the side, producing a disgusting noise.

-Not can I see it.-

-Continue to watch,- Jacobo studied the hills until he saw the eyes of the man's partner on him. The child spit on the ground, staring at

Jacobo until he looked back up at the American, who had started crying without moving his mouth. His partner patted him.

-Why does this dog have no friends?- the American frowned through his tears, pointing at a stray.

Jacobo shrugged, -Not do I know.-

The American dropped to meet Jacobo's eyes, pointing a grimy finger in his face like it was a knife he was brandishing before an enemy. -Does anyone own these dogs?-

-You do.-

The American stuck the finger in his mouth before rising to shout for all to hear, -No. This not is my town. Is yours. If no one owns these dogs, they are of the town. Dogs to guard. Dogs for the violence.-

The crowd erupted at the word. Boys thrust forks and metal rods in the air, swearing allegiance to their new leader. The noise was so loud, Jacobo's pleas for the American to look at the reappearing light in the mountains was drowned out.

DAY 15

The flickering lights of the building made it sparkle in the night sky. Nish looked through the binoculars to make out shadows moving behind drawn curtains in the penthouse.

"Call it 'New York style', stores on bottom and folks living up above," the driver held a lighter up to his cigarette. "Reckon it's for all the Yankees moving down."

Energy buzzed from Nish's backbone throughout his body until he wanted to take a sledgehammer to his arms to get it out of him. He handed the binoculars back to the driver.

"Used to be Dallas was ranch houses and strip malls done up adobe style. Cowboys in windows selling you things, like a Texas theme park to make folks remember where they'd come from. Or at least what they chose to remember of it," the driver continued. Nish had noticed how the veteran agents loved to talk to newcomers like they were experts on whatever subject they'd decided to bring up while dipping or chewing or smoking. Nish figured he was older than the guy but wasn't about to point that out.

"Reckon Dallas still is that way to some extent, it's these new suburbs spreading like a goddamn virus," the driver exhaled, sending another cloud of smoke to bounce off the windshield and dissipate. "Used to be Plano was a place for running cattle or farming. Now, you can't throw a rock without hitting a Yankee."

"You from Plano?" Nish asked. In the darkness of the car, the driver's baseball cap hid his eyes. Nish could only make out the light bouncing off the goatee and the silver chain around this neck. He rubbed his eyes from the smoke.

"Nope, Dallas. Hamilton Park."

"No shit?" Nish suddenly forgot the situation at hand. "I used to play ball with some kids from there. We're practically neighbors."

The man let out what Nish considered the unhappiest smile he'd ever seen. "Spring Valley league?"

"Yep." The two laughed.

"I know what you're thinking," the driver paused to inhale. "I'm a little pale for the HP. But there are some besides niggers there."

Nish turned back to the tall building.

"Alright," the man turned to the giant curled up in the seats behind them. Nish couldn't imagine himself getting to the point where he could sleep before a job. The driver nudged John, "Y'all know what to do, go do it."

The giant got out of the car, stretching like a lion kept in a cage too small. Nish gathered his bathrobe at his feet to follow him towards the building.

The noise of the alarm sounded loud even around the side of the building where Nish hid. The urge to piss crept into his mind; he contemplated opening his robe and dropping his shorts right there but figured he wouldn't have the time.

Young couples with babies and middle-aged loners came out in t-shirts and shorts and pajamas to make jokes or complain in front of the building. He scanned the crowd but couldn't find who he was looking for. He drifted from the side of the building into the growing group to search more closely, wondering if the device John had shown him earlier hadn't worked.

"Someone probably left something in the toaster making a midnight snack," a man holding his daughter grinned at Nish. The agent felt his face drop with the pressure of the tears forming behind his eyes. "Probably," he laughed. Acting like he saw someone he knew, he distanced himself from the father.

The exasperated murmur of the crowd turned to shock as the first sheets of black smoke escaped from the top of the building. Nish watched the front door, this time wondering if the other exits hadn't been blocked well enough or if the fire engines would show up too soon. What started as an idea turned to hope; he wished the lights of the fire trucks would appear around the corner at any second. He squinted to find them and when he turned back to the door, the men were there. Two taller, lighter skinned Mexicans in bathrobes who would have been identical from a distance stood surrounded by several shorter guards. Nish examined the faces of the taller men, searching for the mole. One stood in front of the other so Nish moved to the side as inconspicuously as possible. After spying the mark, he tapped the person closest to him, raising an arm towards the building.

"Can you believe this?" he lifted the hand as high as it would go.

The resident shook his head, "And of course I didn't get renter's insurance. Hope my place doesn't go up in flames." A scream spread through the crowd. Nish turned to find the body on the ground with blood on the pavement behind it like someone had flicked a red paintbrush. He'd learned most silencers weren't like in the movies, letting only a pinch of air out of the barrel and muffling the explosion. During one of their weekly outings to the shooting range, John had explained how the action on a pistol slides back to eject the bullet and load another into the chamber, letting the noise escape from the side of the weapon. But on a rifle, the noise had nowhere to go; you pulled the trigger and somewhere else a man was dead like part of his body had spontaneously exploded.

The pool growing around the man's head made the weight in Nish's stomach disappear. He felt a breeze that could pick him up and take him wherever he wanted, ecstatic and full of love for all of God's creation.

"Fuck!" the man next to him yelled out. The weight returned so quickly Nish thought he might soil his bathrobe. Taking advantage of the people scattering, he walked unnoticed around the side of the building to the car where the other agents waited.

The need for water permeated Nish's brain and body; he felt it in every particle of his being and couldn't believe that just days before he'd been in a place where it flowed from faucets and showerheads, unlimited and free. "Fucking Mexico," the baking heat evaporated the spit in the far corners of his mouth. A boy with a long kitchen knife ran ahead of the small army, skipping and kicking stones out of the sandy road leading to the dam.

-The Killer was shot three times by the police when they were still here, but the bullets not did they enter his body,- the boy danced as he spoke. The older bastards passed a pig's bladder full of pulque amongst themselves. Nish had been forced to leave a few able bodies behind staring at the filth of the square, the flowers of the agave tucked behind their ears. The thirst had been too much to get through without the aid of the hallucinogen.

He felt a bubbling at the top of his head, something trying to burrow out of his skull to freedom. He scratched the thick crust of dried blood.

-Not can you kill him with pistols or shotguns,- another young boy dragged his machete on the ground behind him. -You need to cut off his head and burn his body.-

Nish tried to wet his mouth as he pulled the conquistador's sword from his belt. The boys stopped to stare at the shiny, half naked American. -My bastards, do you know from where this sword comes?- he held it out for the children to admire.

-The church,- one blurted out.

144

-Spain,- Jacobo took the opportunity to sit while the marching had paused.

-Very good, this is from Spain. In the century fifteen, Spain was controlled by the Moors, Muslims from Africa. They had been there for seven centuries, occupying the land, taking from the Spanish. The Moors brought the war constant, raiding towns to the north, persecuting the Christians for their beliefs. They were the civilization most advanced in the world and they spit on the Europeans like dogs. If the Spanish did not convert to Islam, they had to leave their lands or die,- Nish unplugged his agave gourd to take a sip. He knew it wouldn't satiate him but he needed the liquid on his tongue to continue. The boys that had gathered around him did they same.

-At the end of the century fifteen, the Spanish finally took back their land, freeing the Christians in the south of the country. They took Muslims and tortured them in public, hung them from cathedrals until all were gone from Spain. Then, they did the same with the Jews and the Protestants. The same year that Spain defeated the Moors, they sent Columbus to find America. His soldiers carried this sword,- he held the blade higher. -This sword defeated the tyrants of the Old World and conquered the inhabitants of the New World.- He lowered it so the boys could touch it. His eyes floated over the army of children, imagining their ancestors hacking indigenous people to death and being hacked to death; Deaf's eyes on the highway in his silent disdain of what he saw. As long as he got some water, he'd be alright, he thought. Every day that passed, no matter how horrible, was a day closer to being back in America. He wondered if John was in Dallas already, talking to the old man. He'd probably smoothed the whole thing over by now and was kicking back with a margarita in one hand and his wife in the other. All Nish had to do was just stay alive for a couple weeks, he thought, then he could reclaim the prize waiting for him in the locker of the San Antonio bus station.

Hercules hid behind a rock, looking up at the guard's post. He turned back to the group further down the incline and saw Nish nod. The boy picked up a stone to throw at the tiny wooden shed.

After half a minute with no response, Nish figured the post was abandoned and motioned for the boys to follow him. As they neared the top of the dam, his thirst peaked. He'd been pissed off they had taken an extra half hour maneuvering so that they weren't in view of any guards but the annoyance evaporated when he saw the water. Then he wasn't able to think at all, just run. The boys did the same, sweeping across the sandy earth until the guard squeezed off the first round. The shot stopped the human tidal wave in its tracks, sending boys sprawling to the earth all around Nish. The guard, a pudgy man wearing a uniform that might have fit in his slimmer days, stepped from his post to shoot again in the air and shout something Nish couldn't make out. Looking up from his position on the ground, Nish saw Hercules creeping up behind the man, the butcher's knife he'd taken as a weapon in his hand. The guard shouted something again, this time pointing his pistol at the biggest target in the sand. Hercules tapped the man on the back. He turned, startled as the child buried the knife deep into his side. The boy grabbed the arm holding the gun as the guard fired its contents into the air, then fell to the ground. The bastards rose with a battle cry, wielding their makeshift weapons over their heads to hack the man to pieces.

-Stop yourselves!- Nish commanded. The boys quieted, their hands falling by their sides.

-Not are you animals,- the American stuck his own sword in his belt. He pointed at the water, -Now it is ours.-

Another cry grew from the army as the boys threw down their weapons to run faster towards the dammed river.

Drying himself in the sun, Nish sauntered over to the guard post to find the dying man belching his own liquid onto the sand. He was laying the way a body does when the police make a chalk imprint of it in TV shows, Nish laughed to himself. He bent down to reach into the man's pocket, pulling out his wallet. Stuffing the money into his own pants, Nish went through the rest of the billfold to find the ordinary: identification, pictures of the guard's wife and children, some sort of government supplies card. "Folks everywhere are the same," John had told him of the Middle East. He smiled, patting the man on the shoulder. "Would have been nice if you'd had some extra ammo, though."

When he rose, the dam stood directly in front of him, cutting the land in two. He imagined a pair of fish swimming down the stream just before a switch was thrown, stopping the flow of water and trapping one inside the dam while the other was spit out into the dying river. They'd never be together again, he felt his body get heavier. He sat cross-legged next to the dying man, letting moisture fall freely from his rehydrated body.

Light ribbons of smoke curled around the head of the Killer. He brought the beer to his mouth, not taking his eyes off the flat screen television on the other side of the small living room. His son ran in front of the picture, chased by his daughter. The boy tripped on a snag in the carpet and flew into the wall, causing a Virgin of Guadalupe figurine on the shelf above to fall to the floor.

-What are you doing?- the daughter pointed at the mess her brother made. Tears welled up in his eyes, his mouth contorting. The Killer laughed and motioned his son over as he began crying.

-Not should you cry,- the Killer lifted the boy onto his knee. He turned to his girl, -My daughter, get your mother to clean that.- She did as she was told as her brother buried his face into his dad's chest. The Killer patted the boy's head, taking another drag of his cigarette as he fixed his eyes on the television again.

There was a knock on the door; the Killer listened for his wife's footsteps until they were audible. She appeared in the entryway to open it.

-Roberto, what passes?- the Killer lifted his son from his lap. -A beer?- he raised his own bottle.

Roberto shook his head, stepping into the house. -Is the dam. A group was seen there earlier,- he put his hands in his pockets, then removed them to press his palms awkwardly against his jeans. -The river runs itself in the way of old. When we arrived, not was there no one but a dead guard.-

The Killer looked away, his wife closing the door behind their guest.

-It is downstream,- Roberto looked at his boots. -Not is it important to us.-

The Killer flicked his hand to dismiss the comment, -No one changes nothing but me.-

The Killer stepped out his front door to survey the land as he walked to the well. The sun had set, the sky was black except for the stars twinkling above him. He noticed one especially close to the horizon.

Uncovering the pit, he pulled the rope to bring the bucket towards him. There was a crash from inside the house, followed a second later by his wife yelling at the children. Setting the bucket on the side of the stone well, he rested while its water calmed. The stars were so bright he was able to see his own face looking back; he pushed it from the ledge and covered the hole in the earth. His son was crying again, he scratched a raw spot on his arm.

DAY 16

"Land," the director swirled his glass of single barrel whiskey, prompting a chorus line of agents standing at his side to do the same. "I've seen more goddamn legal battles over mineral rights than I can remember: oil's found and all of a sudden everyone's great granddaddy claimed that plot after the Civil War. But whenever there are complications, there are opportunities to hasten a resolution. And just one well can change everything."

Even the night sky in Highland Park looked fancier, Nish thought, with the stars sparkling a little brighter over the two story houses. He drank from the glass of brown liquor in his hand and puffed on the Cuban cigar the home's owner had given the managers. He had no idea his recent promotion brought with it such perks.

"You don't have to break the law in Texas, you just get the right folk on board and make a new one. How it's always been," the director put a finger to his nostril, expelling a string of mucus that barely cleared the cuff of his dress shirt. "A few decades ago, Dallas was built to be what it is now. It became a haven for commerce because of the planning of a small group of men who controlled the city, taking turns in high public offices. Benefactors from here who wanted to see their hometown turn into a thriving metropolis. Houston had already let the monkeys start running the zoo, so there was a need for a strong Texas city."

The director's eyes glided along the managers' faces and bounced off Nish. He took another puff, the young men following in suit. Nish thought the man waited for him to press the cigar to his lips to continue. "Of course, nowadays if you're not a black lesbian in a wheelchair, you can't get elected to find your ass on a sweaty day. Fortunately, those men had planned the city so well it took until now for it to get fucked up."

Nish remembered his father coming home late at night from work, pouring himself glasses of the straight, warm gin he'd allowed his homemade spice mixture to steep into. Depending on what had previously been said in conversation or on the news, he would talk at length about the superiority of the British Empire or the oppression his Indian ancestors suffered at the hands of the greedy imperialists. By the time Nish and his brother were teenagers, they'd chosen their sides opposite one another. Nish took another drink of the single barrel whiskey in his hand; he'd never touched his father's gin after he'd found the bourbon that had been forgotten in the back of the liquor cabinet.

"Don't forget who started this country," the director's words snapped Nish back into the real world. "Our ancestors, good Protestant folk from England, Scotland, Northern Ireland. Folks chased out of Europe only to have the Catholics want a piece of their country once they saw what we had created."

Nish held back his laughter at the last statement, thinking the man looked surprisingly good to be a few centuries old.

"You boys think about that the next time you're unloading a truck, helping some Mexican woman off who's working on her fifteenth baby," a chunk of ash fell from the director's cigar. "We could always use good men in Mineral Rights Acquisitions."

The purpose of the dinner suddenly became clear to Nish: to recruit up-and-comers away from urban real estate to work in the director's department, hauling their asses all over West Texas to secure property with oil to lease out. He figured the man must be pretty desperate to get good staff if he was resorting to this kind of a speech. In Nish's year and a half working with the agents, he'd learned they could get easily riled up about 'how things used to be', but their bank accounts had the final say in any business decision.

"Just think about it, boys," the director looked back out to the yard. "What we got going on here is economically unsustainable. We keep on like this, it's only a matter of time."

The crow of the rooster awoke the Killer to the first dusty shafts of sunlight entering his room. He looked for his wife on the other side of the bed but found only a swirl of covers. Lying back, he saw a crack in the ceiling inching its way towards the wall.

He sat down at the plastic table, cuing his wife to bring over the pan of eggs scrambled with dried and shredded donkey meat. After she'd spooned out the contents onto the plates of her husband and softly arguing children, she brought over a stack of tortillas and sat.

"Thank you, beautiful," her husband pulled her down for a kiss before she sat in her chair for the morning prayer.

After the silent meal, the Killer smoked in front of the TV with his children buzzing around him until there was a knock on the door. He extinguished the last of his cigarette while his wife opened it. He rose to meet Roberto outside.

-To where first this morning?- Roberto asked as they walked towards the group of trucks waiting at the other end of the sandy lawn.

-To Tierra Mojada,- the Killer answered, nodding to his men in the vehicles. They all nodded back respectfully.

-Not to the dam?-

-I have thought on this, the dam will stay as it is. There will be war amongst the villages for the water. Those who have had, not will they any longer. And they will want,- the Killer waited for Roberto to unlock the passenger door. -When everyone else is weaker, we are stronger by comparison.-

He climbed into the truck, closing the door to hang an elbow out the window as the others in the convoy started their engines. -This land,- he waved his finger in a circle, - My family has lived on it for more than a century. My father farmed it, and his father before. Every morning I pray that I have something to pass on to my son, that I can protect my family, that my ancestors who fought for this land against foreigners and communists have pride in me for holding on to what is ours.-

Roberto started the engine. The Killer sniffed at the clean air of the morning blowing across the parched land. He looked back at his home once more before closing his eyes, relaxing his head against the glass of the back window.

-They come!- the lookout yelled. The boys of the village, fortified by the small stream of water trickling down the old riverbed, tensed up like an electric current had run through them. They collectively looked to the top of the square to find the American standing in the doorway of the church with the sword in his hand. He turned to close the door behind him, signaling for the bastards to hide their weapons on their bodies and line up in front of the aged cathedral.

Through a window, Nish watched the cloud of dust near until he could make out four white pick-ups at its source. "Those small trucks usually only carry two in the cab," he turned to Hercules. The boy looked up from sharpening his butcher's knife on the back of a ceramic plate to listen. Nish squinted, "It could make for a rough time if they got pissed about the dam and brought people in the beds. Otherwise, we can handle less than a dozen."

He pressed his fingers into the blade of the old Spanish sword in the hopes it would produce the burning sensation. Instead, it left only an indention on his skin. He checked the poled weapons behind him on reserve: shovels, hoes, pitchforks. A 'Mexican arsenal' he'd told the boys the previous night but none of them seemed to get the joke. All the weapons were in a pile for quick access if the bastards were pushed back into the church. He'd also thought about using the dogs to attack the gangsters but learned they would need more training before being used in battle.

The sun reflected off a piece of chrome on a truck, hitting Nish directly in the eyes. The light mixing with the heaviness in his stomach reminded him of his first time his work with the agency had taken him south of the border to a small village just outside Matamoros. The downtown area, consisting of a few rows of tiny houses, a currency exchange building and a taco shack, barely stood out from its desolate surroundings in color and raggedness. There was a black hole in the center of the town that Bill explained had come from a gas tanker being t-boned in the intersection a few weeks before. It had spun like a firecracker with flames shooting out of one end, burning a dozen alive in their homes and leaving a perfect circle in the sand. Darkness radiated from the center where the truck itself had been. When they drove through the middle of the blackness, Nish half-expected to fall into the earth and out the other side, the four-door cab swimming in stars. He thought about how the pills may have slipped behind the toilet; if he'd only had time to check.

The greasiness of his hand pushed the steel unwillingly through his palm as he tightened his grip on the sword. He wiped his right hand on one of the spots on his jeans that hadn't been darkened by the suntan lotion residue. The noise of the trucks' engines grew louder until he could hear the rocks being spit up into their undercarriages. The weight in his bowels grew heavier; he wondered if there was time to relieve himself but quickly dispelled the thought.

The trucks rounded the final bend to the village, then disappeared behind the buildings. He felt like he wasn't in his body anymore but controlling it from inside his brain: looking out through the eyes, hearing noises coming in through the ears, listening for alarms to announce pulse or breathing were off and moving arms and legs by lever. The trucks reappeared, driving through the wrecked center of the square and finally coming to a stop in front of the boys.

The Killer climbed down, his men doing the same with machetes in hand. His eyes scanned the line to land on Guillermo. -Where is your leader?-

Guillermo shifted his weight from one foot to the other, then back again. -My brother is injured. We were playing with the knives and he was stabbed.-

The Killer watched him redistribute his weight nervously. -You boys should not be doing such things.-

The bastards looked at the ground like a teacher had just scolded them. The Killer removed the handgun from his belt. He pulled the action back, loading a bullet into the chamber. The boys kept their eyes trained on the dirt immediately in front of them.

-Where is the fat one?-

The obese boy shuffled forward, his head still down.

-Disrobe, Fatty,- the Killer growled. The boy undressed hurriedly. The gangsters laughed at his girth, pinching their fingers together to mock the size of his young penis in comparison to his whale-like body.

-Roberto, bring me the candy,- the Killer ordered his second-in-command.

Nish kept his head low as he peeked out the church window. "Those motherfuckers can't be older than fifteen," he whispered to Hercules, who nodded next to him. He could understand having young thugs to act out violence but he'd figured the leader would be more than a lanky teen with a wispy, uneven mustache. The leader was saying something to Fatty but Nish couldn't hear. A bastard from the line up stood in front of the obese boy; the leader pulled a knife from a sheath on his leather belt. He said something that made the teenagers behind him laugh, then motioned to the church. A couple of the boys turned towards it. The leader pulled the nearest bastard to him and pressed the knife against the child's throat. The boys ran for the church.

"What the fuck are they doing?" Nish felt the tingling from the bottom of his torso shooting energy upwards as the boys neared his hiding spot.

The bastards opened the door, looking at Nish but walking in the opposite direction like they were on an invisible leash. They entered the room of the injured boy and the screaming began. The stab victim questioned what they were doing, pleaded for mercy, and cursed them as they carried him out of the room. He threw up from the pain but the bastards didn't put him down to wipe the vomit from their arms. Nish imagined what he looked like to the children as they passed him, squatting in front of the window; a squirrel poking its head out of a tree to witness a predator destroying its prey. Hercules sat with one hand on his butcher's knife and picked his teeth with the other.

The injured bastard cried out for Mary as his carriers laid him roughly down in front of the gangsters. -Was that so hard?- the Killer smiled. Suddenly, his face went slack like a puppeteer had dropped all the strings that controlled him, -There was a change in the course of the river yesterday, as you know. Now, it runs alongside your village. This will bring a change,- he paced in front of the group like a general addressing his troops. -People will come, people with the thirst and the hunger, and they will take your homes and everything you have. You will live on the streets like dogs.- He held out an open fist, closing it finger by finger as if to emphasize his point. -You need my protection now more than ever. For this, I will take more.-

Roberto walked up behind the Killer and whispered something to him. He nodded, -The sword.-

The boys looked at each other, the older ones moving their hands towards the back of their pants. Their eyes settled on Fatty.

The Killer walked to the stab victim to kick him in the side, sending blood and curses spewing out of him. -Not did you hear me? The sword. Now!-

The bastards waited for Fatty to pull his knife. He was within reach of the Killer and had a clean shot at his gut. They prepared to attack, silently urging the fat child to spark it off.

-We lost the sword,- Fatty cried out. The Killer didn't look at him but tucked the gun in the back of his pants. He threw the nearest bastard on the ground, holding his skull still as he stuck his pointer finger in the corner of his eye socket. He hooked the finger around the back of the eyeball and pulled outwards; the finger slipped out around the eye at the bottom of the socket. He quickly stuck two fingers as close as he could to the opening of the child's skull and pulled again. The boy took a moment from his anguish to watch his own eye being raised from his head.

-The sword!- the Killer ordered over the child's cries. The bastards stared at Fatty, their chests pounding out their breath in unison.

-I will get it,- Fatty blurted out. He ran towards the church, his stomach and breasts bouncing so that he appeared to be moving in slow motion.

Nish stayed low, staring at the door until Fatty stumbled in, exhausted. "What the fuck are you doing?" he pointed the sword at the boy, getting his point across despite the question being in English.

-I am sorry,- the boy panted. -It I will do, but I need the sword.-

-What?- Nish wanted to grab him by the throat but feared he'd make too much noise while struggling.

-I am sorry but I need it. If not do I bring it to him, he will take the other eye.-

The sword was only inches from the engorged body of the boy; Nish contemplated grabbing the back of the child's neck and running him through. The act would get the attention of the gangsters outside and their leader would send them to check out the noise. He and Hercules would be waiting for them. After finishing them off, they'd emerge from the church, signaling the boys to attack. It actually seemed to make the most sense. Nish looked at Hercules who was picking his teeth, waiting for any order. He turned back to Fatty.

-When you get there with this,- he handed the sword to the obese child, -Walk to the leader like it is an offering. Then you must stab him. Do you understand? You must kill him right then,- his eyes burned a hole into the child.

-Yes, I understand. I am sorry. I am sorry,- Fatty took the sword to begin the hard jog back to the line up.

The teenagers laughed at his body as he ran up. One made a joke about wanting to suck the boy's tits and the others roared. Fatty stopped a few feet from the Killer. The smiles on the teens' faces gradually went slack until none of them were smiling at all.

-What, boy?- the Killer spit. -Not do you think Luis is handsome?- The teens busted out laughing again, even their leader cracked a smile. He motioned the boy forward, -Give me it.-

Fatty stood frozen. The other boys leaned forward again in anticipation.

The Killer raised his voice, -Give me it!- Fatty looked at the boys, some of them nodding so lightly the teenagers didn't notice the movement. Fatty gripped the sword handle, his knuckles white, every muscle in his arm flexed like they never had before. His toes dug into the earth to get a better hold of it, something to push off of for a strike. His breath became one with the boys, panting with their necks craned forward like pit bulls moving in for a kill. He handed the sword to the Killer.

The gangster examined the blade, -It is old.-

Tears came to the boys' eyes from the adrenaline that hadn't fulfilled its purpose. Some shook while others ran their hands through their hair. The movement was too much for the teenagers not to notice.

-Stand still!- one of the Killer's crew ordered. He stood directly in front of two of the older boys. Guillermo and Jacobo couldn't control their breathing. Their necks stayed pointed towards their enemy, their teeth as close as possible to the teen with the machete.

-Has it been shined?- the Killer asked, still fixated on the sword. When no answer came, he looked down at the fat boy trying to pick up his dropped knife. The boys' panting doubled, some removed their weapons from their hiding spots before the Killer registered what was happening. -Fat one, what are you doing?-

Guillermo pulled his knife and punched it into the stomach of the gangster in front of him. The teen doubled over, his mouth in an O shape. Jacobo went behind him to slash his throat, causing the dying teen to drop the machete in his hand. Jacobo retrieved it, raising it in the air to signal the attack but the boys had already begun swarming on the gangsters.

Nish saw the group jump forward and, grabbing a pitchfork from the pile, ran towards the melee with Hercules behind him. He figured he would have to go straight to the Killer since Fatty hadn't stabbed him and he was the only teen with a firearm. No sooner had Nish thought of the boys being chopped down by pistol fire as the first explosion came from the weapon. He kept moving to get out of the open ground and into the middle of the fight.

The first gangster he encountered had been isolated by a group of boys away from the line of trucks. The children held their knives up to him like they were aggressively showing them off more than using them to fight. The teen slowly cocked his arm back like a toy being wound up, then quickly swung downwards to slice through the tissue that connected a boy's neck with his shoulder. Nish raised his pitchfork only to realize he'd grabbed a shovel. The teen saw him coming and stood upright, baffled by the grown man charging at him with old farming equipment. The American slowed, holding the shovel halfway down its handle with his left hand to guide it, his right hand gripping the end to punch it forward. The teen swung his machete; Nish skipped backwards, moving to his left. The thug did the same as the two entered into a dance that the circle of nearby boys observed while the battle raged on behind them. Nish didn't know why the pistol fire had stopped but figured he could be cut down by it any second. He punched the shovel forward, hitting the teen in the face. It drew an invisible line that became red, then leaked the color out. The thug hastily swung the machete at his attacker. Nish punched the shovel into his face again, then reared back the weapon to hit the gangster broadside. The teen fell to the ground slow and dramatic like a downed tree. Nish stood over him to take aim at his neck. He plunged the shovel down as hard as he could. It shot back up at him like the teen's neck was spring loaded.

"Fuck that," he rested the shovel carefully on the shocked gangster's throat like he was going to dig a hole, then kicked down on it with all his weight. He felt the stringy, flexible pieces that hid under the skin snap as the farming tool sunk deep into the flesh, partially severing it from the body. A sense of accomplishment went through Nish. Celebrate your accomplishments, he remembered from his mirror at home. He pulled the shovel from the teen's body with the feeling he'd just finished writing a paper in college or cooking a satisfying meal.

Since the pistol hadn't fired again, Nish figured the leader of the thugs had been taken down and the battle was soon to be theirs. Turning to the main group, he and Hercules neared the closest gangster as the boys pounced on the teen he'd just killed, sawing off ears and fingers as keepsakes or otherwise desecrating the body. The next thug had already been stabbed a few times in the leg but had sprinkled the ground around him with pieces of child. He saw the American nearing him, his eyes registering the large, half naked man with the bloody shovel marching closer to him. The pistol fired again; every nerve inside of Nish screamed at him as the cartoon bullet zipped past his head. He was a child again, his brother chasing him as he laughed hysterically. Nish scanned the melee to see where the bullet had come from and quickly found the leader standing in a clearing with dead children littering the earth around him.

Nish fell to his hands, still holding the shovel, and scuttled towards the truck closest to the leader. As he put his back up against a tire, he noticed none of the boys had ducked or ran for cover in anticipation of a second shot. He cautiously peeked his head around the tire to find the leader, now only about fifteen yards away, swinging his machete at a group of boys to keep them back. In his left hand, the action of the handgun was open, emptied of its bullets. Nish charged.

Upon seeing the American advancing on him, the Killer tucked the spent pistol into his belt and grabbed the closest boy by the hair. He pushed his machete against the child's neck.

-Stop or he dies!- he warned but the American didn't stop so he slit the boy's throat, throwing the fresh corpse in front of him in an attempt to slow down his attacker. Nish jumped to the side and heaved the shovel, hitting the teen squarely in the chest. As the Killer staggered backwards, Nish pulled the knife from the back of his jeans and pounced on the gangster before the teen could swing his machete. The two toppled to the ground.

-Hold his arms and legs!- Nish ordered the boys around him. They hesitated at first, then rushed to bite and claw at their oppressor's limbs as they held him immobile. Nish forced the back of the teen's head to the dirt. He knew dealing with body parts wasn't like handling a machine; things were slippery, every organ, tissue and appendage had a mind that worked independently from its master controller. He turned the Killer's head and poked his eyeball with a finger for retribution, letting it slide into the skull. He extracted it with a quick pop.

Removing the gun from the teen's belt, he stood to hold both trophies high in the air as he yelled out his victory. The army roared around him. In all the excitement, he squeezed the eyeball too hard, causing it to fly from his hand onto the hood of a nearby pickup. It rolled down until it sat on the front edge of the truck, looking out over corpses and hewed off limbs in front of the church. The boys who weren't finishing the last of the gangsters or cutting off trophies cheered their approval of the hood ornament.

Nish sat at the church's table that had been carried outside to the top of the square. It had taken most of the day to bury the bodies on the side of town away from the widening stream and he felt exhausted. The trucks had been parked at the side of the church, some of their gas siphoned into small barrels that hadn't been used to hold agave beer. The bounty from the trucks was a few coolers of beer and soda, random lunches, a few cartons of cigarettes that he figured had been given as tribute, as well as a small amount of money and jewelry that hadn't disappeared from the dead teenagers' bodies before Nish got to them. All was locked in the Treasury, an unused room in the church. He knew it wasn't much but it gave him an odd connection to the world outside the decayed ghost town; a connection that was disappearing with every day away from what he'd left in the bathroom of that motel. He wasn't sure what to do with any of the bounty but knew it would be squandered if it wasn't kept safe.

The burden of liberty hadn't settled over the bastards yet, who playfully threw shovelfuls of blood-soaked sand onto each other while freshening the earth. The injured were tended to by the nun and her women. Many of them had gashes across their fingers from stabbing their knives into hard tissue or bone and not having a hilt to stop their hand as it slid up the unmoving blade. Others had limbs missing, gashes in their flesh or chunks of body hanging from them that had to be lopped off. The nun's women put homemade poultices on the wounds, wrapping them in boiled cloth. Nish rolled his eyes at the remedy and slurped fresh water from his jug.

The bastards trickled into the open dining area as they finished their work. After bloating themselves with water, they began drinking the agave beer. One of them called out for the cigarettes and Nish motioned for the nun to remove them from the Treasury. She did so, her face a puffy mask of what it had been the day before. Nish wondered what she'd look like if she'd been born in a ritzy neighborhood of Mexico City or the suburbs of Monterrey. Sand had clung to his greased upper body so he wiped it off his nipples, making them erect. As the nun walked past with the cigarettes, he held out a hand to stop her, grazing her breasts.

-Know that these things cause the cancer,- Nish looked at the table that had become dead silent with his first syllable. -Not them do I smoke.-

The boys looked at each other, shaking their heads, then motioned the nun away. The American grabbed her arm to take one of the cartons, then let her go. He threw the cigarettes on the stone steps of the church for all to see. His troops watched the carton as if waiting for it to grow legs and run off.

A stray goat spat its juices into the roasting fire, signaling the women to begin slicing off pieces for the boys, serving the injured first. They brought out tortillas and beans to fill the children's stomachs after they'd all had their meager portion of meat. The bastards leaned back in the evening air as the sun shot its farewell into the sky like a peacock opening its plume for the final time. Nish remembered his final sunset in San Antonio with Arturo's air conditioning. He cracked his neck and relief washed over him.

The torches around the table were lit so the boys were able to continue drinking. They toasted the American and each other; their leader toasted them back until his front was covered with agave beer and the tops of his pants were soaked in the sour smelling liquid. They occasionally walked over to the captured Killer to urinate on him, laughing as he squinted his eyes so the piss wouldn't get into the hollowed socket. He tried in vain to overcome the ropes that attached him to the stakes in the ground, blowing air out in short bursts to keep the urine out of his mouth. One of the bastards kicked him in the crotch but was quickly scolded by another child. No one was to touch the Killer but the American, he was reminded, or the offender would share the teen's fate.

As the night wore on, the old women carried intoxicated children to their destroyed homes. Hercules gave his guardian a drunken hug with a loving wail loud enough to bring a few of the bastards out of their stupor. The boy stumbled into the church to go to sleep as Nish continued drinking. He propped his feet up, imagining packs of coyotes covering the hills watching the torches burn bright, too scared to approach the town. The bullet zipping past his head suddenly replayed in his mind; he felt every ounce of his body light up and smiled without meaning to.

After the last of the bastards had been carried to their shacks, the old women retired to their own beds. Only the nun stayed to wipe down the pews. When she'd cleaned her way down to Nish, he patted the wood next to him so she'd sit. As she did so, he noticed her red, swollen eyes and her shaky hands. He filled a clay cup with agave beer and handed it to her. She accepted without looking at him.

-How many years do you have?-

-Twenty,- the nun answered, still averting her eyes. He took one of her trembling hands in his own, leaving the other free to drink the agave, and held it gently on his leg.

-Nun,- Nish chewed the word. The young woman nodded slowly for a moment, then stopped as Nish stroked her hand. He leaned back, stretching his legs in front of him. -Why a nun?-

-God chose me,- she stared at her free hand.

Nish frowned, -You must think very lowly of God.- He felt her hand tense but she didn't move it. He scratched the top of his head with his free hand. The oversized scab had formed a crown of crusted blood at the peak of his skull.

-I am a bride of God, of Jesus,- she spoke slightly louder but faded at the end of her statement.

-What does Catholicism have to do with Jesus?- Nish laughed. -They preach about a carpenter poor, but do it from a city of gold.-

-Here not is there gold,- the nun looked at her free hand.

-Not do you understand my point,- he slid his body further under the nun's hand until her palm reached his groin. He was erect, straining against the jeans.

-It is a religion in which the women are inferior. Not can they lead a congregation. They can be more intelligent, more pious than any man, but not will they rise in the hierarchy of the church. For a religion that teaches the equality, not is this a problem for you?-

The nun stared ahead of her as Nish put more pressure on her hand. He moved his body up and down under it in a slight rocking motion but his face didn't register anything. -Not do you want?- he pointed at her cup. She shook her head so slightly that Nish wondered if a gnat had flown into her ear. He massaged her hand as he continued, -Of course you do not have an opinion of this. You were brought up in a country that treats women poorly. If a man in Mexico cheats on his wife with a woman younger and she says something, she is shamed, condemned. The man not does he need to take any responsibility for his actions, as long as they are masculine. The homosexuals are beaten to death and not are there consequences. A man beats his wife, the same. All that matters is masculinity perceived. This is the thinking of little men. This is why this country is nothing.- The pace of his rocking increased. -This is a country of people who believe in your god in Rome because it is all they know. You baptize children as soon as they are born because you know that if they were able to choose a religion, they would pick one that does not punish them with one hand and pick their pocket with the other.- His breath quickened, he closed his eyes. -For you, everything is shame from the second someone is born. For me, the world is beautiful. My heart is filled with love for everything that God has created.- He jolted upwards, pushing on the nun's hand forcefully. He picked the crusty crown on his head to let the blood leak out, then gritted his teeth. His breath halted for a second as he ground her hand into his groin, then he made a noise like he'd just dove into freezing cold water. Letting go of her, he shivered back into a reclining position. He sat with his eyes closed for half a minute.

-But we can debate this more tomorrow. Now I am sleepy,- he rose to walk to his makeshift bed on the church floor. The nun didn't move her hand from where it had fallen on the chair. She brought her other hand to it cautiously like it was a dead animal, then lifted and cradled it as she stood.

Almost tripping on an overlooked child passed out next to the creek, she dipped her hand in to bring water to her face. She did this again, letting it cool her ears and run down the back of her neck. Closing her eyes, she allowed her muscles to relax. When she was finished praying, she looked out in the distance. There was a blinking light, like a star in the void of black that was the mountains. She squinted; it blinked, then burned bright like a match that had just been lit. Forgetting about the intoxicated boy, she tripped over him a second time as she ran back into the church.

DAY 17

The warm air rushing into the antechamber of the church nudged Nish awake. He rolled over to put his other cheek on the cool stone floor. When the boy saw the sun nearing its peak in the sky, he headed in again to nudge his naked savior. He tapped one shoulder gently like a baker rounding the edges of biscuit dough. Nish responded with an angry moan. The boy cautiously moaned back. Nish moaned louder. The boy let out a moan of resignation, walking out of the church.

Outside, a group of older boys was waiting for him. He shook his head; they looked at each other and shrugged. Little Hercules pointed at the farming equipment they'd stockpiled in the shell of a nearby house, then pointed at the square. The boys nodded.

The sounds of children splashing in the water finally woke Nish. He lay so his back touched as much of the cool floor as possible. A clay pitcher sat next to a small box a few feet away. Rolling closer to inspect them, he found water in the pitcher warm to the touch and with a thick blanket of dust that had drifted down from the rafters. He took a long drink anyway, letting it fall from his mouth to the stone under his chin. Like a pig in shit, he remembered one of Bill's favorite sayings. He laughed until a knot in his stomach rose to his throat, then ran out the front door to vomit.

After he was done spitting up the remnants of half-digested tortillas and mushy beans, he looked up to find the bastards cleaning the square under Hercules' supervision while the younger ones played in the widening stream in the distance. As Hercules approached, Nish gave him a thumbs up, stepping back into the shade of the church. He raked his fingers over his skull to dislodge the sand that clung to his scalp, hitting the crusted mound of blood and puss. Upon further probing, he guessed it raised almost an inch off his head.

"Gather the boys in thirty minutes," he gently picked the mound. He imagined eating it like a piece of beef jerky; saliva wetted his tongue. The spaces in his teeth felt like giant holes that begged to be filled with

161

the dried blood and hair. "One of the most annoying things about the real estate business back in Dallas was dealing with the cockroaches directly," he began speaking to no one in particular. "They'd always say something like, 'You know who the fuck I am?' or some stupid shit, like there's a database of every piece of shit gangster in North Texas that I refer to before going into low income neighborhoods," the saliva filled his mouth and he spat onto the dusty stone floor.

"One time, I had John hold this guy down and I cut off his ears. I told him I wanted him to keep them in his pocket at all times. I told him if I ever saw him and he didn't have his ears on him, trying to act too gangster to be told what to do, I'd cut off his nose," Nish sat naked on the floor admiring the scab. He picked around the edges so blood would seep from his scalp and feed into it. "I was too smart for those motherfuckers," he nodded. "Everyone got my sense of humor at the communications firm."

The floor expanded in front of him, pointing at a wooden statue of Mary at the head of the stale cathedral. Nish figured the Killer had taken the original and this was the cheap replacement. "I should still have that goddamn job, I could be a fucking director by now."

Hercules made his way to the pitcher of water for his savior.

"You're walking better!" Nish beamed. When the boy handed him the water, he gave Hercules a high five. After he drank, his hand drifted back to his crown. "Cutting through an ear's like cutting through cartilage on a turkey," he burped. His brother would have picked up the money from San Antonio and given it to the doctor by now, he thought. This Thanksgiving, they'd all be eating together again.

The staccato yelling of Spanish outside froze them both. Nish grabbed the gun lying on his discarded pants. He wished he'd had a chance to repair it so the bullets fed from the clip into the chamber. Cursing his laziness, he loaded a single bullet into the weapon before stepping outside.

-Our crops, our land, all is dying,- the old farmer raised the machete so it was level with Guillermo's face. The boy just stared at the man and his family.

-What is this?- Nish marched towards the farmer, gun in hand. When the old man saw the large, naked American with the pistol, he nearly dropped his weapon. His wife covered their granddaughter's eyes.

-Who are you?- the man asked, baffled by the sight before him.

-I am the mayor,- Nish watched out of the corner of his eye for movement from the boys. -We will have elections but now I am the leader.- Jacobo leaned on his shovel and exhaled cigarette smoke that clouded his face from the American.

The farmer raised the blade again, this time at Nish, -Why have you our water?-

-No one owns water,- Nish answered. -Lower the machete or I will kill you in front of your wife and child.-

-We are dead anyway if we return to our home,- the man's jaw tightened enough for Nish to notice. He felt the heat of the hangover pressing in on all sides. Sand had managed to get into the crack of his ass; it hung in layers so thick where he'd applied the grease that he felt like he was wearing an itchy suit. He began urinating where he stood. The farmer jumped back, turning to the boys and then to his wife like he was trying to ask a question without saying any words. Jacobo eyed the granddaughter, just old enough for her breasts to push against the thin cotton shirt.

-You can make your home here,- Nish said plainly as he continued pissing in the direction of the farmer.

The man stepped out of the way of the growing puddle. -And pay you a rent that will starve my family?- he motioned to the pistol, shaking his head.

Nish ran his tongue over his front teeth, finally speaking when he'd made up his mind, -These bastards own this town. You can buy land from them in the borders of the city. Or you can buy land from the government of the town for to farm.-

-For how much?- the man spit out the words. The growing puddle of urine pushed him back another step.

-Is a town free, the boys can sell at whatever price they want,- Nish felt his stream coming to an end so he squeezed to keep it going. When he relaxed again, it arced to the ground. He clenched so it shot straight out in a final burst, then died. He shook his hips side to side to shake the last drops from the head of his penis, slapping it loudly against his upper legs. These violent distractions are good, he thought. A few days away from the pills and still holding up. The tingle returned at the top of his head but he put the thought in the back of his mind.

The bastards filed into the church to find the statuettes, crucifixes and candles gone, only the American sitting naked on the altar. He drank deep from a pitcher in his hand, water splashing on the stones around him. Some of the boys whispered to each other, the s's and t's amplified by the cathedral's walls no matter how quiet they tried to be. Thwarted in their attempt to go unnoticed, they shut their mouths and avoided the deranged stare of the American. Guillermo sat in the front pew to look out the window above where Jesus had hung; Jacobo stood in the back so the boys just walking in didn't know he was there. The door to a side room was open so the bastards staying in the makeshift infirmary could listen to what their leader had to say. When the last of the children were in the church, Nish began.

-As you can see, I have done some redecorating,- the sand in the crack of his ass itched inside him, he leaned forward to scratch it against the edge of the altar. -This is the building most strong in the town. For this, it will serve as the capitol building. The politics and the religion must be separated, so all symbols Christian have been removed. Them I have given to the nun, she can reestablish the church in a location more suitable for those of you who choose to attend.-

Holding up a finger to keep the questions at bay, Nish took another drink of the fresh water. It ran down the front of his body to find his groin, eliciting a pleasurable moan. Nish imagined someone stumbling into the ghost town to find a church full of disfigured children being led by a naked man with a gun rubbing his ass on the altar and making sex noises. Chuckling at the thought, he poured the cool liquid over his head. It ran over the crusted crown, he imagined it softening and bit down at his stupidity.

-The mayor will live in this building. I am the mayor until we have elections, which will be in one week. Anyone can run for office. I leave in just over a week, so it is in your best interest to have a government established by then.- He paused, expecting an outburst of shock or sadness at this announcement but the older ones scratched their bald chins and the young laughed and slapped at each other until they were quieted by their elders.

Turning to Hercules, Nish motioned for him to bring over a large scroll. He unrolled the piece of paper so all could see the crudely drawn map of the town. -Every one of you now is a landowner. You will tell me where your family lived and I will try to give you the same area. But know it is possible you will have more or less land than your family.- He pointed at the long skinny plots in the town with corresponding numbers. -Each bastard will have a house in the town and also land on the river. You can do with these as you want: to sell, to work, to rent to storeowners, that which you wish.-

The boys nodded. Jacobo's eyes scanned the unnumbered expanses around the plots. -And the other areas?- he spoke up, startling many of the boys who had been unaware of his presence. They looked back at the map, then at the American.

-Is the land of the government, to be worked by its employees. These will be jobs offered to you bastards so you can have money in your pockets.-

The audience applauded, except for Jacobo who continued studying the map.

-But I encourage you not to sell your land. It you should work, or when the others come, which they will, have them work it and pay rent to you. The same with the houses, can be stores to rent. Think of manners to capitalize from being the owners for the first time in your lives.- He'd rather die than get back into that coffin, he thought. And a pool cleaning service wouldn't hurt, either.

"Just because we're politicians in Mexico now doesn't mean we have to lose all sense of forethought," Nish turned to Hercules while the children found their plots. "It also doesn't mean we have to allow corruption to run rampant, letting the rich take advantage of the poor and the poor take advantage of themselves." Hercules motioned for the first boy to come up.

After the bastards had staked their land, they began clearing their respective plots of brush and their homes of trash, carrying these things to the designated area behind the church. Nish switched to celebratory agave beer as he watched the boys shaking hands and moving stakes. The alcohol washed over his brain like the tide on the beach, erasing the divots and footprints, then leaving it dry and in need of another wave.

Jacobo widened his plot on the waterfront, moving the gnarled piece of wood that served as his marker down the bank to signify his expansion. He looked at the next plot. Two younger boys splashed in the water while their brother, an older boy of about ten with a crippled leg and a fresh bandage on his forearm, breathed heavily from his walk from the church. Jacobo squatted as he looked out at the river, now fifteen yards wide and almost up to the edge of the dry bed. Upstream, the dam sat over the horizon. Nish followed his eyes, wondering how many ponds had formed, created from dead ends that appeared when the land dried up.

-Who will work your land?- Jacobo asked the older brother from his own land. Still panting, the boy answered, -Me.-

-You are injured,- Jacobo picked up a rock to toss in the water.

-Then those from the towns will work it, like he said the American,- the boy answered. His brothers jumped into the water. He turned to yell, -Stay near.-

-Not do we know when they will come. Or if they will,- Jacobo picked up another rock. He walked to the invisible line the stakes had sectioned off, separating his newly acquired land from the boy's.

-With permission,- he waited to step onto the injured bastard's territory. The boy nodded. Jacobo walked to where he reclined on the ground.

-I can buy this land from you,- he squatted next to him. -It I will work and give you half of all it yields. You and your brothers not do you need to come down here everyday, you are in no shape for that and they are too young. You stay in your home and rest, regain your strength so you can work in the future.-

-How will you be able to work this land and yours?-

-Not was I injured in the battle,- Jacobo held out his limbs to show no wounds. The crippled boy looked at him like he was checking the bill at a restaurant. Jacobo continued, -You can sit on this land and starve while you wait for others to come or you and your brothers can have food in your stomachs. This is what the American means by to capitalize. Both of us gain something.-

The boy watched his brothers as he scratched where the sand had stuck to his neck. After a minute, he extended his hand. Jacobo took it and they shook.

-Rest here while I clear the other plots. Enjoy the day,- Jacobo went to his stake to move it further down the bank. The American and his boy were waiting for him. He neared the two cautiously, his eyes moving over the firearm hanging from a thin rope the man had slung over his shoulder. His boy carried the shined Spanish blade.

-If the cripple were dead and just his brothers were left, would you have offered them toys for the land?- the corner of Nish's mouth rose slightly.

Jacobo walked to the shovel lying on the ground. -That land would have gone unworked, now it will yield food. The more food in the marketplace, the lower the prices, the less starving.-

Nish's grin widened. He looked at Hercules, eyeing the land. -I will be enacting a law that no one can buy land from boys younger than eight.- Hercules and Jacobo both frowned, averting their eyes.

-Is the same as when the others were here,- Jacobo muttered. Nish stared at the boy's head like he was trying to see through his skull. When he realized he wasn't able to, he walked to the small path that led back to the town. Hercules looked down at the tip of his sword scraping against a cactus plant. He watched the boys playing in the river, then turned to follow his guardian while Jacobo began the long job of clearing the land single-handedly.

"It would've been unfair to give you a piece of land," Nish put an arm around Hercules' shoulder as they walked back to the former church. "But you're the Vice Interim Mayor so you can use City Hall for anything you need," his voice brightened. "This might be a great chance for you to practice starting a business. I wish someone had done that with me at your age," he patted the boy's head.

The sound of crying swept over Nish like a cold breeze. Goose bumps sprung up all over his body, his toes wiggled childishly. These distractions were good for him, he reminded himself. It took his mind off the thoughts that settled at the bottom of his brain. The sound was coming from the infirmary off the side of the meeting hall. He walked to the door to watch the nun cry as she held the stab victim who was having the electrocution-like shakes. He touched the boy's feet to find them warm.

-Is fine,- he waved a dismissive hand. Surveying the stuffy room, he found a handful of boys on makeshift cots or blankets on the floor. On the far side, a door led out to the back of the church.

-Where did you get that food?- he pointed at a half eaten sandwich next to a dying boy.

-I took it from the room,- the nun motioned to the locked storage area. Nish realized he hadn't thought to take the extra keys from her when he'd founded City Hall. A piece of cheek wandered in between his sets of teeth; he noticed it like a tiny surprise. Biting down, he ripped it further away from its base to let the coppery taste waft into his mouth. -So this hospital is funded by the government,- he relaxed his teeth and brought the pitcher an inch from his lips. -Not does this please me.-

Guillermo ran shirtless into the room to find his older brother trembling in the nun's arms. He placed his sibling's hand in his own and began praying. Nish watched the thick muscles of the boy work in coordination to assist in every minor hand movement.

-Nun, you will run the hospital of the bastards because you are the leader of these healers. If one of them is better qualified, decide amongst yourselves. As for supplies, I am donating all the food in that room to you, as well as anything that belonged to the church. If you need more supplies, ask and we will determine a fair price. More donations may follow.-

He knew the nun could hear him but she didn't react to any of his words. She just kept speaking softly to the dying boy. Nish fought the heat rising to the top of his head; he said his six words silently, letting his shoulders fall away from his ears. -As this is the land of the government, I will allow my Vice Mayor to be in control of this situation,- Nish turned to Hercules. The boy looked up, opening his mouth like he was about to say his first words but he froze.

-Vice Mayor Hercules, do you allow the hospital to stay in this building free of rent?-

The stump of a tongue in the back of his throat wiggled like it was trying to get free of the root that attached it to his mouth. Nish kept looking at him blankly until he slightly nodded his head. Nish nodded more emphatically and soon they were mirroring each other. The stab victim stopped his shaking; the nun thanked God with Guillermo and the old women.

-The Vice Mayor has allowed the hospital to stay on the premises free of rent,- Nish shouted to put an end to the chanting. -But will he allow the hospital to share an entrance common with City Hall?- Nish knocked on the doorframe he stood next to. The people in the room looked at him like they were just now aware of the mayor's existence. Nish couldn't fight the blood rising this time; he took a long drink of the warm, flat liquid. Hercules squinted again at his savior. Nish's mouth turned upwards. Hercules moaned loudly, shaking his head.

-A decision has been made. The hospital must run out of the back door. While the Vice Mayor wants the sick and injured to have a roof secure over their heads, he does not want to give the appearance that the hospital is subsidized by the state.- The boy moaned out his approval. Nish turned his attention to the nun. -Keys-, he motioned with his hand. She stared at him with her mouth slightly open. Like she's fucking stupid, he thought. When she'd finally handed them over, the mayor and his second in command exited into the assembly hall. Those left inside the stuffy room could hear the ancient lock of the door move into place and were left with only the light of the candles in the room.

-We need more water fresh,- the nun said to an older woman who nodded silently as she shuffled to the back door. She tried to move the lock but it pushed back with more strength. She tried again, not grunting or making any noise at all, then stopped again. She had braced herself to try a third time when Guillermo laid a hand on her shoulder. She moved out of the way for him to open the door.

-Thank you,- she nodded. He moved the rusty lock and pushed the door open. He wiped the brown residue from his hand but the indention in his skin didn't go anywhere.

-Guillermo, ring the bell for mass.-

The boy stepped out the back door into the minefield of broken glass and wood that would become a city of rattlesnakes seeking refuge from the sun. Running around the front of the church, he saw the boys of the town improving their homes. Two were nearing him with armfuls of what was once the wooden frame of a bed. -What passes, Guillermo?- they smiled, lifting the bundles in their arms in place of waving or shaking hands.

-Mass in half an hour.-

-Okay,- they kept smiling as they walked around to the back of the building. Guillermo reentered the church from the front to climb the two flights of stairs up to the bell tower. When he rang it, the inhabitants of the town froze at its first sounds, their eyes darting to the bell, then to him. In the middle of the freshly cleaned square stood the American and his boy like two oversized ticks on a snow-white dog. The American said something to the child before they disappeared from the middle of the plaza.

The nun walked through the path Guillermo had cleared in the mountains of trash. The old women followed, helping those who could walk and leaving one of their own behind to look after those who couldn't. When the path opened up, the nun saw Guillermo directing people to put their unwanted items on either side of the clearing. He joined the procession as they rounded the side of the church to turn again towards the front steps. The town's boys were waiting in front of the locked doors, confused.

-Guillermo has allowed us to use his land on the river for our worship,- the nun smiled.

The children got in line behind her, thanking Guillermo for his act of kindness. The large group had almost gotten on the short path to the river when a shot cracked through the air.

Everyone's head turned simultaneously like an army making an about face to find the American and his boy down a side street standing over one of the younger children. Nish knelt down to show the bastard how to reload the pistol. The boy beamed, taking aim at the three-legged chair in the middle of the dirt road. Hercules showed the shiny Toledo blade to a stick figure constructed of pieces of broken wood. He swung at the head, the sword embedding itself into his mock enemy. The boys following the nun floated a step down the side street.

-Have hurry, children,- the nun said to the group. They looked back at her before the pistol fired again.

-Who else wants to try?- Nish yelled to the procession. The boys floated towards him even more.

-To the river,- Guillermo pointed. Hercules lopped off the stick man's arm in response.

-Nun, you can go to your worship. Not will the bastards be long,- Nish motioned to the group, who gladly adhered to their new schedule. Soon the side street was filled with boys lining up to shoot the gun or picking up thin pieces of wood to practice their sword fighting. The nun was left standing with her old women, their injured companions and Guillermo. The boy watched the rest of the group intently. The nun noticed his arms make tiny movements as if simulating the slashes and stabs of the children.

She patted him on the shoulder, -You can go. We will be at the river when you are finished.-

He nodded and walked slowly to the group that parted as he neared. He was handed one of the largest fake swords, which he swung to the satisfaction of the other children who cheered him on.

The American paired the bastards off for practice. -The Romans stabbed with their swords, not did they slash, because they knew a cut that was one inch deep could kill their enemy.- Nish demonstrated, the boys' eyes glued on him until he instructed them to practice with their partner.

As night fell, the workers had almost finished setting up the long wooden bar in the three-sided house at the head of the square towards the river. The holes had been cut in the planks for beanbag toss per Nish's orders. He touched his crown of crusted blood, sending a shock to the head of his penis. -Ugly,- he called over a harelipped bastard who had overseen the carpentry. The boy came as Nish finished writing a contract on a piece of paper. -You will receive a chicken a week and the sword best the blacksmith can make when the others come to the village.-

The boy took the paper like he'd never seen anything like it before. Nish patted him on the shoulder, -Bring the agave beer here every night at dusk. You can pay your workers with this,- Nish handed him the paper and pencil. The boy took the writing utensil cautiously, holding it at finger's length.

A couple bastards painted NISH'S BAR in English over the doorway as others brought tables they'd sold to the American for his new business. Nish turned to Hercules, "I know what you're thinking, bars in Mexico are about as necessary as fertility clinics. But I always dreamed of owning a tavern." The boy gave the best thumbs up his mutilated fingers would allow and his savior pulled him close.

Jacobo and the other boys who had been working on their plots of land walked up the path to watch the beanbag toss get christened. Soon, the farmers and workmen were drinking the agave beer, gambling with land deeds or IOU's that Nish or Jacobo had helped to write. The family that had arrived earlier in the day put up a sheet in their newly purchased home so they wouldn't have to see or hear the town's children.

When Nish went for the nightly torture of the Killer, the teen tried to say something to him but Nish poured water in his mouth and he quickly abandoned the attempt to speak. Nish cut off a finger, giving it to the boy guarding the Killer from animals and humans.

-The spring not was it functioning properly,- Nish showed the Killer the pistol's clip as the guard poured alcohol on the fresh wound. The teen screamed loud enough that the newly immigrated family poked their heads out their window. Nish pushed down on the clip; it stayed with his finger as he pulled it out.

-Now, many bullets can be loaded into the pistol,- he explained. The Killer tried to speak again but Nish vomited the liquid contents of his stomach into the sand, then walked back to the bar.

DAY 18

"Goddamn taxes!" the young man stepped directly in front of Nish like he hadn't seen him, throwing a stack of papers on the receptionist's desk. The blood rose to Nish's face as he looked at the back of the man's head; coconuts looked pretty hard, too, he tapped his teeth together.

"Like I don't do enough for this goddamn country," the agent pushed the papers towards the secretary. He wore a pale yellow polo shirt tucked into a belt buckle in the front and left to hang loose everywhere else, making it easier to conceal a holstered firearm at your back, Nish would later learn. Blue jeans, cowboy boots and a pair of sunglasses hanging around his neck made for a different type of 'mobster' than what Nish had been expecting. The young man scratched his head as he addressed the secretary, "Your cousin still do taxes?"

"He still takes money from people for doing their taxes, but he ain't no good at it. I had to pay five hundred to the federal government last year," the middle-aged woman shook her head, the blonde puffball of hair on top of it swaying from side to side. She nudged the papers back towards the agent, "Here you are cutting in front of visitors and cussing like you was raised in a barn." She turned to Nish, "I'm sorry, sir, Mr. Refugio will be right out."

"Sorry about that, brother," the man turned to Nish, then physically stepped back to eye the suit he was wearing. "Boy, that is fancy."

Nish sat down in one of the few chairs in the waiting area. "Thanks, it's from Uruguay," he smiled politely. "They don't call it the Italy of South America for nothing."

The agent nodded gravely, "Uh huh." He picked up his papers and walked past the desk to the open office space beyond. Nish had prepared himself for anything when Jordan said he'd gotten him an interview with Smith Realty. If this was going to be something he did for the next six months, he figured he should make a good first impression with his new colleagues.

After flipping through the hunting catalogs in the magazine rack, he leaned his head back to rest. With the diagnosis still fresh, he hadn't been spending a lot of time sleeping. He was amazed how his mother had taken it. 'Stiff upper lip, the English way,' his grandma had said, but for every tear his mom didn't shed, he cried two.

A wave of laughter spread across the large room past the receptionist's desk. Nish imagined telling a joke and getting that reaction. His new coworkers couldn't have a worse sense of humor than the people at the communications firm, he assured himself.

"Nish Patel," a voice boomed over the laughter, causing all noise to stop. Nish could have sworn that cars outside timidly quieted their engines and birds ducked their heads into their nests. He'd seen the man out of the corner of his eye but figured he was a day laborer or plumber.

"Yes."

"Bill Refugio," the man extended a thick hand. After Nish took it, the man turned abruptly, "Follow me." He led Nish through the main room filled with rows of desks occupied by men as young as their late teens to others who could be their fathers. They walked down a hallway to a spacious office, empty except for a desk and a calendar on the wall with a picture of a deer looking out at Nish over the wrong month. Bill took a seat, motioning for his interviewee to do the same.

After doing so, Nish opened the folder in his hand to take out a piece of paper, "I brought another copy of my resume just in case."

"Same as what you sent over the internet?" Bill made no move to take the paper.

"Yes, sir."

The man reached into the front pocket of his shirt, producing a pair of reading glasses that he placed delicately on his face. They perched there awkwardly; Nish wondered the shame the man must have felt when he'd first put them on. Bill looked at his own copy of the resume.

"You played at Rice?" he raised an eyebrow.

"Yes, sir. Linebacker."

Bill nodded, taking off the glasses to return them to his pocket. "We checked your references, so everything is ready for you to start," he pushed another piece of paper on the desk towards Nish.

Nish picked up his offer letter, skimming for the important parts. Jordan had explained to him the concept of hot and cold teams, the differences in responsibilities and earnings. Most people didn't show up to work their first day and do anything but sit in front of a computer screen and make phone calls. 'Real work,' Nish's high school buddy had said with a look of disgust. It usually took a year to start working out in the field but that was the beauty of having old friends in the DPD, Nish thought. When he'd randomly bumped into Jordan buying beer the same day he'd come back from the doctor's, he thought God must have fated it. His friend was on his way to party with some Smith guys and Nish decided to join him, wanting to kill as many brain cells as possible. It all worked out too easily. But certain people vouching for you was worth a lot. He also didn't doubt that his employment was repayment of some debt owed to corrupt DPD officers.

He signed the letter and was an employee, same as the secretary out front and the Senior Director across the table. His muscles loosened to their natural length; he felt taller, even sitting down.

"Oughtn't to wear a suit on Monday," Bill calmly dug a tissue out of his pocket. After emptying a substantial amount of mucus into it, he folded it twice to tuck it back into his jeans. "But we do dress like gentlemen here: collared shirt, jeans, boots."

"Yes, sir. Of course."

"You have your concealed carry permit?"

Nish nodded.

"You'll be given a signing bonus to cover the amount of a reasonably priced sidearm," Bill continued as if he'd repeated the speech a hundred times. "Due to the events of 9/11 and the dangerous times in which we live, I personally suggest you carry this sidearm on you at all times. You are also eligible to enroll in our 401(k) program, which I will give you information on if you're interested. We offer medical and dental insurance. We do not offer life insurance to support level employees."

Bill stood and extended his hand mechanically. Nish wondered if every time he recited the speech he was reminded of when he'd first put on his glasses. When the man grabbed Nish's hand, all the life flooded his eyes. Bill looked deep into Nish and the younger man looked back at him, nodding professionally. Bill didn't let go; Nish grasped the hand more firmly, narrowing his eyes slightly and feeling his teeth push against each other without him telling them to.

Releasing the new employee's hand, Bill removed the tissue from his pocket to blow another massive wad of snot into the thin paper. Nish discretely wiped his own palm on the back of his pants. After the man had thrown the tissue into the trash, he led the newcomer silently out of the office, past the main room to the front desk. He handed the offer letter to the secretary, then shook Nish's hand quickly one last time. "Monday," he said plainly, then left.

The agent who had been complaining about his taxes walked up. "Looks like it went well."

"I think so," Nish smiled. He had a lot of questions for his new coworkers. He wanted to hear their thoughts on immigration policy, its effects on the economy, how they voted. He knew he'd find some like-minded people, he thought, people objective enough to see the big picture past all the bullshit.

"So what do you think of old Bill?" the young man asked.

"Seemed nice enough."

"Hope he wasn't too nice, they don't call him Billy the Queer for nothing," he turned quickly to the secretary to share a laugh. Nish scratched his mouth.

"Alright then," the agent hit Nish hard on the shoulder. "See you Monday." But the young man wouldn't be there on Monday or any day after that. The old man showed the appropriate amount of concern, everyone else would say, but no more; it was an action that caused Nish to put his plans of self-investment on hold for a while.

After shaking hands with his new colleague, Nish walked out of the entryway, through the armed guard's area and out the front door. No sooner had he done so than his hair stood on end like a cold breeze had struck him even though there was no wind.

"Fuck," he froze. A weight made itself known in his stomach before plummeting downwards. He nervously scratched his head, contemplating if he should go back inside to ask for the 401(k) information or if it would be too awkward after he'd already said goodbye.

"Fuck it," he shrugged. It could wait until Monday.

Little Hercules watched Nish crying naked in front of the dog run. His caretaker hadn't bothered to put on clothes for a second day, prompting some of the younger boys to take his example. The older ones kept the protection on their skin but didn't chastise their little brothers in public. Hercules watched the bastards making deals with the steady stream of newcomers, many of whom went straight to the bar for free water. They stayed there for agave beer, the bastards approaching them with opportunities for land to work and a place to live.

A group of newly recruited boys were drilling with one of the militia's colonels while others drank at the tavern. They made their deals, checking occasionally on the blacksmith's shop next door as the American's first order came closer to completion.

-What passes?- Guillermo said from behind the army's general, who turned his head to find the larger boy staring somberly at him.

-The recruits are coming along well,- Guillermo motioned to the boys swinging their sticks. -The drills were good this morning, we will have twenty to defend the dam as the mayor ordered.-

Hercules nodded, turning back to watch the trainees. Sand had crept into the waxy swirls that reached from his brow to the crown of his head; he gently swept the large burn with his mutilated hand to get it out. He looked back at the second in command and motioned with his hands while he moaned.

Guillermo nodded. -Who should drive?-
Hercules pointed at the trainer.
-Good,- Guillermo left for the American's bar. A naked boy chased
another past Hercules. He watched as the nearby townspeople glanced
at each other, then back at the ground.

-Congratulations,-Jacobo shook the old man's hand. The newcomer's
wife waved at him weakly from a nearby busted folding chair. Jacobo
pointed at the farming equipment, -Ten percent extra, but free for the
first month. With luck, you will be able to buy your own by then,- he
lifted the corners of his mouth.

A bright light danced on the soil around them, finally resting on the
old woman's forehead. Jacobo gritted his teeth as she looked up at him.
The light fell on her cataract eyes, reflecting off the muddy spots as if
the brightness had replaced them in their sockets. The boy turned to
the hills to find the pinpoint of light piercing the rocks and cactus in the
distance. It disappeared. He turned back to the woman who slumped
into her chair to stare at the ground. The boy spit onto the sand before
walking to the path that led back to town.

When he reached the American, the man was throwing beanbags
with some of the soldiers and instructing a nude younger boy to collect
wagers. A dog lie dead at his feet; a group of the town's children
examined the bony corpse like doctors studying an interesting case,
stroking their chins and offering opinions as to whether it should be
eaten or not.

Jacobo tapped the American on his greasy back. The man turned,
his eyes bouncing off Jacobo to land on the boys over the dead animal.
"My mom bought a dog," Nish took a drink of the agave beer in his
pitcher.

Jacobo looked around to see whom the American was talking to.

"When I started playing varsity ball my sophomore year, there was
this mean fucking coach, Coach Johnson." Nish stepped away from
the beanbag game but kept his eyes on the animal. "He coached the
running backs. Racist fuck. Only liked the black players and was always
making comments to me. I used to tell my mom what he said, the
accents he'd put on, and she'd try to comfort me. But I never told my
dad because I knew he would've taken a crowbar to the side of the
ignorant fuck's head. My dad wasn't as tolerant as I am," Nish nodded
gravely. Jacobo checked the shadows to see what time it was.

"One day, Kenny Bosque is telling this joke in the locker room,
something about how the only reason God created black men is
because fat white women need love, too. Coach Johnson hears this and

calls me and Kenny both into his office, even though there was a group of like five or six of us. I look on his desk and there's a picture of him and his wife and not only is she Anglo, she's a fucking whale. I mean, she probably needed one of those special scooters just to get around. Anyway, Coach Johnson goes off, yelling at us about how we're a couple of punk ass kids who grew up rich and had everything handed to us, all that shit. It was a little hard for me to swallow since I usually had to ask my mom to give Kenny a ride home after practice, what with his dad having left and his mom working late some nights. But coach goes into all this sense of entitlement bullshit, calls me," Nish paused. Jacobo tried to interject but the American held up a finger. He spoke through gritted teeth, "He insinuated I smelled like a certain Indian food dish."

Nish spit, his finger pointing at the boy to demand silence. "I went home that night and told my mom. My dad was gone on business, like usual, and I pleaded with her not to tell him when they had their nightly call. I told her to at least wait a week to see if the coach felt sorry for what he'd done; I knew we were going full pads on Tuesday," Nish watched the boys examine the dog to see where the insects had already gotten to and what could still be eaten. "There was this halfback on our team Coach Johnson loved, Gerald Brown. Amazing player, had 1A scouts coming out to tons of games, and a decent guy, too. Anyway, he was blocking on a pass play and I dove for his left knee. It was like tearing a drumstick off a roasted chicken, only louder: the pops, the rips of cartilage and bone and flesh doing things they weren't meant to. Coach Johnson was crushed. The other coaches were pissed but when Johnson yelled at me and said it was intentional, they told him he'd gone too far, blaming a player for doing something like that on purpose. By the time I'd gotten home, one of the parents watching the practice had already called my mom. She didn't say anything about the hit. Next day, she bought the dog."

The boys below had decided to skin the dead canine before cooking it. Nish drank from his pitcher as they hauled it off.

"I saw Gerald last year at a game. He'd gotten some girl pregnant and was trying to carry the baby up the stadium stairs but he still had a little trouble walking after all this time. Coach Johnson died of prostate cancer a few years back. I hope he saw Gerald at every game having to pull himself up the stairs by the railing. And I hope that cancer ate him from the inside out."

One of the nun's old women stopped the boys with the animal carcass. She shooed them away to drag it by its hind legs to the back of the church. Nish looked down at Jacobo.

-Not do I speak English,- the boy raised his hands in exasperation.

Nish lowered the pitcher, pausing for a second before coughing syrupy vomit onto the sand in front of him. Jacobo stepped back as the American leaned forward to dry heave.

-Is coming. From the hills,- Jacobo motioned to the distance. Nish gave a thumbs up, vomiting tortilla and bean mush into the hungry sand that sucked it down as quickly as it could.

-I am good,- he stood to recover, -I am good.- He threw up again.

-Not do you understand me?- Jacobo took another step back. -This is going-

-I enjoy these talks, bastard,- Nish interrupted, spitting out the remnants from his mouth. -Why not do you bring some water?-

Jacobo threw a hand in the air like he was batting a tennis ball in front of him with his palm, then walked towards the path to his land.

-Thank you,- Nish gave another thumbs up. -I will wait right here.-

-Son of a bitch,- Jacobo muttered as two little naked boys ran shoeless down the path in front of him.

Nish sat next to the dried lake of puke, his head in his hands. The crown on his head had grown to rise like a disgusting horn; he revisited his thoughts of ramming people with it as a joke. The thought of their softness yielding to the crusted blood made him crack his neck. Nausea flooded his brain, he heard a knocking. The soup in front of him waiting to be swallowed by the earth was beginning to boil in the sun. It let off a stench he knew he could smell a mile away even if no one else could.

The trucks kicked up plumes of dust that got larger until they were transparent. Hercules watched the new troops bounce away. When they disappeared behind the buildings, he turned to Nish. A boy had come over to help his savior and the man drained his pitcher, then wiped the sand off his ass as he headed to the bar he owned.

Hercules took the conquistador's sword from its new scabbard, walking down the path towards the water. The land on both sides of the river had been sold or leased to farmers, bridges had been quickly constructed for easy travel and transportation of fish and anticipated crops. He walked downstream along the bank, passing newcomers who shot up from their planting with raised makeshift weapons, only to quickly lower their eyes when they saw the general. His steps fell evenly in place, the tracks in the mud he left behind were of equal depth like any other child's. Past the end of the farmland, he paused to gaze out at the mountains. A wind pushed away the stagnant air, causing the needles of furry cactuses across the river to blow in the breeze like a thousand caterpillars moving their legs at once. He let his shoulders fall and cracked his neck. A reflection in the distance caught his eye. A noise came from behind him; he spun around with the sword drawn. Nish slapped it away broadside like it was a pesky fly.

"Good thinking," he drank from his pitcher, "This land will be annexed into the town by the end of the day." Hercules noticed a trickle of blood running down his savior's bare leg. Nish reached for the blade and the boy relinquished it to him.

-Live Free or Die,- Nish read the fresh inscription in Spanish. He smiled, "Where'd you hear that?"

The boy threw his head back to let out a deep mollow into the desert sky.

"Those historical shows I had you watch? Well, I like it," Nish patted the boy's deformed head lovingly, then looked up the river at the immigrant farmers working their land. "There's going to be a lot of new faces around here, which is something Mexicans don't like. They may be constantly coming to the U.S., but they hate immigrants. Mexico deports as many people from Guatemala and Central America every year as we do Mexicans. We need to nip this thing in the bud," he picked his teeth. "Call a meeting for an hour from now, attendance is mandatory."

The townspeople filed into the meeting hall, whispering to their neighbors while their eyes avoided the naked American sitting on the altar. The bastards stood against the walls, joking with each other and comparing the quality of their new weapons fashioned after the conquistador sword. The door to the hospital had been opened so the sick and dying, their numbers dwindling by the day, could hear. The flow of people slowed until the room was almost half full. -Two hundred, more or less,- one of the bastards said to Nish. Hercules jumped onto the altar and roared. The townspeople wilted into their seats.

-Thank you, Vice Mayor Interim,- Nish began. -And many thanks to all of you citizens, the old and the new,- Nish slid off the altar, rubbing his itchy ass on the lip of the stone. -I have called you all here to discuss some issues regarding the town. It pleases me to talk directly, so I start.-

Hercules lifted a map that had been resting on the altar to show the crowd a newer version of the territory. -This is the town,- Nish explained. -The land around it will be annexed tomorrow. The government will own this land and sell it at a discount rate to all who do not already own any. Those who do will pay a higher rate.-

The bastards' attention turned quickly from their swords to the American. The townspeople in the pews muttered to one another.

179

-What is the rate going to be?- a voice from the crowd yelled.

-One half the price.-

The people shook their heads until one stood, -Not do we have no money. This is unfair. Why do the children own everything? Just because they were here before us?- The crowd agreed, yelling out the injustice.

Nish waved his hands to silence them. -Calm yourself, friend, please,- Nish motioned the man back into his seat. The crowd glared at the American, awaiting his answer. -I will say this one time only, if not do you like this town, you can leave whenever you like.-

The crowd moved in their seats like the benches were getting uncomfortably hot. Lips pulled back to reveal rotting teeth. The bastards watched, their fingers tap dancing on the hilts of their swords.

-And go where?- a voice came from the crowd but no one stood up this time. -Not is there water to the south, this town uses it all. And to the north, already there are people with weapons. And now your soldiers go there so it will be yours. Where can we go?-

-Not am I your father,- Nish was getting frustrated. -If I were, I would stink of tequila and the sweat of whores.- He made a mental note to question the newcomer on how heavily armed the people to the north were after the meeting. He'd only seen disparate fires at night but didn't want to be taken off guard. He noticed his penis level with a woman's mouth in front of him. He thought about slapping her across the cheek with it and laughed suddenly.

-Also, not will there be the standards of pricing,- he regained his composure. -In this town, there will exist the market free,- he scanned the crowd. It took a few seconds for the people to register this. When they did, some made noises like they were bloated two-armed, two-legged snakes. Words flew at him like -injustice- and -tyranny-, -long live the people-.

One man rose to his feet to rally the crowd, -Always is it this with the Americans. If a Canadian had taken the town, at least not would we starve to death.-

Nish spit on the floor. -Not do I need advice how to run this town by a Mexican, or a Canadian. Anyone coming from a country where the money has men in uniforms or women in crowns on it, not should they be giving advice on economics.-

The crowd continued to talk openly about their distaste for what the American had said until Hercules jumped nimbly onto the altar to roar at the ceiling again. The crowd silenced, focusing on the mutilated boy.

-Thank you, Vice Mayor Interim,- Nish patted Hercules on the back, then concluded his speech. -Last thing, I would like all men who are available to stay in their seats after the meeting. The town will soon have many people from other places and will grow in size and wealth. We will need a marketplace. Those who wish to help, stay. Payment will be in fish and agave beer. That is all,- Nish waved a hand to dismiss the crowd. After a moment of waiting for something else to happen, they began to get up slowly and walk out the door.

An outburst came from the beanbag game around the side of the bar. Hercules took another drink from his cup, a portion of the clear liquor running out the side of his mouth that wasn't covered by a cheek. He looked upset.

"Don't worry about it, I'm always spilling shit on myself," Nish rubbed the bald spot at the front of the boy's forehead. "There's no use getting down on yourself for things you can't change. Me, I've got a monster that lives in my brain with this mounted .50 caliber machine gun. And when this motherfucker comes out, he's fucking crazy. Always moving, pointing that gun where it naturally falls."

Hercules raised an eyebrow as far as the scar tissue would let him. "You think I'm crazy now?" Nish laughed. "I feel like you're the only person I can talk to sometimes." He rubbed the horn on his head from its base to its tip, pinching along the way to check its hardness. A soldier walked into the tavern from around the corner, throwing what little money he had left onto the bar for a pitcher of agave beer.

"How much is that game making us?" Nish asked his second-in-command.

Hercules moaned as he flashed fingers that made Nish smile. "More than enough to pay for the market's construction. And if they work through the night, that should be built by sunrise. It wouldn't hurt to give them some of the real cash these new townspeople are gambling with. It's good to have hard currency, you can't build a successful economy off speculation and thin air."

-At what hour do we attack tomorrow?- the loser pulled his head out of the pitcher to yell at the full bar.

-Come here, Loser,- Nish pulled a nearby chair over to his table. -I will tell you a story about your ancestors and you will drink from my bottle.- The boy quickly got up to resituate himself at the American's table. The boys from the finished beanbag game came around to the front of the open-air tavern, filling the tables around the mayor as they bragged or cursed their luck.

-I will tell all of you a story, my bastards,- Nish boomed over the crowd to silence them.

-Not am I a bastard,- a new boy nearly rose to his feet but one of the others pulled him down.

-After the independence glorious of Mexico, the nation young had many problems. In the north, the Comanches murdered their citizens. Many families Mexican were slaughtered by the Indians, tortured and killed in manners worse than you could believe. The government had a problem getting their people to move to that area. Their army tried to kill the savages but not were they able to. So the government Mexican invited a group of people to settle the land that they knew could kill Indians, the Americans. The Americans killed the Comanches and were prosperous, so the government Mexican imposed the taxes on them to take their wealth,- Nish took a long drink while some of the boys lit cigarettes. -If there is one thing Americans hate, it is taxes. Especially by a government that not do they consider their own. Not will it surprise you that when the Americans fought a war against Mexico, they won. For this, the Republic of Texas was born.-

Looking over the group, Nish saw the young boys scratch the sand from their hair or give each other questioning looks. He stood, -Like the Americans, you have taken a land that others thought was useless and, through hard work and the opportunism, have turned it into a place of wealth. The government Mexican put the work on the backs of others, then expected to be rewarded, just as others may come to take advantage of what we have created. But will we let them?-

A couple of the boys shook their heads and said -No- like they weren't sure it was the right answer.

-If individuals come in peace, they can share in our prosperity. But will we give armies invading what we have fought for? What your brothers have died for on this very earth?- he yelled to the crowd, shaking his head this time so they would know the answer. They responded with a yell. -No!-

-Like Santa Ana, the dog who came from the City of Mexico, there are others trying to take what is ours. The men who we face tomorrow believe they can take the water that we freed and use it as their own. These same men sat by and watched while your families were killed by the gangsters or died of hunger and thirst. Like the government Mexican, they wanted you to do the work so they could capitalize on your success,- Nish watched as the boys looked to each other, denouncing the name of Santa Ana. A warmth spread through his heart. -This is New Texas, and you are the liberators of this land hungry. If this you believe, no one can stand in your way.-

The bastards let out a battle cry. Someone broke into *The Yellow Rose of Texas* in English that Nish had taught the beanbag players. Others cursed the transparent army to the north. Nish pulled from his jug as

Hercules scratched at the sand in his head swirls and looked at the table like he was trying to figure something out.

The bastard responsible for guarding the Killer stuck a hook just under the skin on the prisoner's thigh along with another a few inches away. He pulled on them gently while using a makeshift scalpel to separate the skin from the muscle underneath.

"My pool should be done right about now," Nish said out loud. The boy looked up at him, smiling in a way that Nish knew he was picking up English. The burnt area where the Killer's testicles had been pulsed under Nish's gaze. He walked away to find the nun.

DAY 19

The first splash of red hung suspended over the mountains; Nish raised the pitcher to his mouth, forcing his throat to pull the alcohol down into him. His brain had unraveled, stretched and dried in the sun until no liquid could moisten it. Like things weren't what they should be, he thought, his brain at the mercy of time to curl back up and reenter his wet skull. He did the one thing he could do, take another drink.

"Nations don't fall by giving their people more liberties, allowing them to govern themselves," he said to Hercules and the boy's lieutenants. "They fall by paranoia, grasping for things out of their reach, putting systems in place that keep a few fat while the rest starve."

The army stood ready in the open area at the top of the square between the church and the newly constructed market. Many of the recently arrived merchants were already in their stalls, preparing their food, clothes, drinks and wares. Some walked amongst the soldiers to sell breakfast to the boys, who all wore shirts with large red numbers painted on them to identify themselves and the unit they belonged to. Eggs mixed with dried donkey meat wrapped in tortillas, goat tamales wrapped in cornhusks, food the bastards readily overpaid for. One of the merchants walked up the stairs of City Hall to where the American and his commanders stood.

When Nish noticed the man approaching, the first thought that flashed through his mind was removing the knife from the belt that hung around his bare waist and stabbing the merchant in his gigantic forehead just to break up the monotony of his plain circular face. Instead, he took a cornhusk, motioning for Hercules to pay the man.

-No sir,- the man waved away the money with a wink.

-Take it,- Nish spat foam onto the steps. -Not are there favors here. You gain that which you earn.- He took a bite into the moist corn meal, juice of the spiced goat exploding into his mouth. He would have found the tamale average in Texas, but he recognized living off beans for a week changes your perspective on food. Hercules stuck the money in the man's face but the merchant stepped back again to decline. The boy withdrew his sword, howling load enough for a monster to invade the dreams of the town's sleeping. The man's eyes became as round as his face; he took the money and backed down the stairs.

"Where are the goats for these things?" Nish asked the lieutenants. The boys furrowed their brows, staring at his lips like they were waiting for the words to come out again slower.

"Goats?" one tipped his head to the side.

"Yes."

The boy pointed upriver.

Nish took another bite, savoring the wet, stringy meat, "Farming goats is the epitome of short-sightedness; they can live anywhere but they destroy the land so nothing can thrive but them." Nish stuffed the last of the tamale into his face, chewing a few times before tipping his head back to let the agave beer splash into his mouth and down his body. When he'd swallowed the mash, he burped loudly. "You've got to figure there are going to be some foreclosures, especially with goat farms. The problem is nothing's going to grow on that land and pretty soon we have plots no one wants to buy. Meanwhile, fucking stray goats are eating other farmers' crops."

He ran his tongue along his teeth to check for remnants of the meat. He looked to the boy, who stared back like a cruelly distorting mirror. "Goat waste that close to a river, being slaughtered upstream of where people get their water, it's no good. We need to create some zoning laws," he shook his head. The boy stood at the ready with the lieutenants trying to pick out words behind him.

"Relocate goat farms along the river, compensate the owners for the move," Nish ordered. "It needs to be done by the end of the day, before they can fuck too much up."

Nish walked down the few steps to relieve his bladder. He tried his best to balance as he raised a foot into the stream. "Protects against athlete's foot," he said over his shoulder as he switched feet. The lieutenants spoke among themselves, trying to decipher the new language.

"When we get back to Dallas, I'll take you to the stadium," Nish wiped a tear away from his eye. "The stars on the outside, the Super Bowl banners hanging from the rafters, the hole in the ceiling. It's magnanimous and beautiful, like God if he were a sports arena."

Hercules lifted a half-hearted thumbs up as he watched the army's formation. The trucks were parked in a line thirty yards apart, looking over the newly acquired land. The new citizens sat in the beds of the pickups, shoving fried tortillas filled with beans into their faces so ravenously they had to chew with their mouths open while they reached for more.

-When did you come to this land?- Nish hoisted himself into the back of his transport. The new boys stared at the giant nude American covered in jelly and sand. One of the younger answered, -Me and my brothers have been here almost a week.-

-There are some of us who lived all our lives here,- another challenged.

Nish turned to him, -Your family owned this land?-

-No, it was owned by the Gonzales,- the boy drank from his glass of agave beer. -The owner, Jesus Gonzales, a man horrible.- He made the motion of spitting but didn't actually do it.

-What happened to this man?- Nish leaned against the tailgate.

-He is dead.-

A smile crept across Nish's face, -You killed him?-

The boy looked at the American like he was trying to read him, then shook his head slowly. The others stopped chewing to watch quietly. Nish shrugged, -Not does it matter. Your lives new start today as citizens of New Texas. You will see the markets, the farms, the ranches, and you will be protected from the tyrants.-

-Thank you,- the boys resumed their eating. Nish knew they were looking at his horn. It had grown to rise out of his skull, threatening to pierce the dehydrated, unraveled brain tissue that had been wrapped around his face in an attempt to suffocate him. He heard the knocking again; he stroked the horn in a calming fashion, admiring the contours of the crusted blood. Never could he have created something like it himself, he thought. He saw one of the boy's cups was empty and refilled it with agave beer.

-This land will be redistributed. Each family will be given a piece, not only to work but to own. There are banks in the town that will give you a line of credit to buy supplies and the rest. I am the owner of one of these, we can talk this over in my tavern.-

He put his arm over the tailgate, tilting his head back to drink from the pitcher and something punched him in the back of the head to fling him forward, his face slamming into the bed of the truck that exploded in red needles in his vision. The horn had been ripped from the top of his head; the noise of soldiers yelling, climbing into the back of the transports and forcing out new citizens coaxed the tiny man from his prison. He screamed from the crown of the wet skull, Nish just happy there was something to keep the little guy's mind off the man underneath him. Arms pulled him into the center of the truck's bed where people and food had been just a second before; people scrambled on top of him, tearing cloth and pressing things on him that put gaps in the thin waterfall of blood that drooled out in front of his eyes. The truck's engine turned on, there was yelling and even more screaming in the distance. Sand and rock crunched under the heavy rubber until Nish gratefully slipped under the blanket of consciousness.

The door opened and closed in such a way that Nish knew his father was home. The electric shock ran through his body. Everything felt hollow, like if someone were to punch him they'd find his skin made of paper mache and his insides empty. He got up from the couch to pour a glass of spiced gin and water, Dave turned off the TV.

"How was work, love?" the voice of Nish's mother came from the entryway. His father handed her his briefcase and suit jacket. "It was alright, mum. What's for dinner?"

"Chicken," Nish's mom walked into the kitchen to pull the bird out of the oven. With the family seated, she laid out the meal of meat, boiled peas and strips of potato fried in vegetable oil. Nish's father served himself, mashing the shapeless peas with the back of his fork. The boys did the same, waiting to eat until after their dad had said the prayer. Their father asked about their day in between bites, starting the nightly competition.

"I made a save in practice," Dave answered.

Their father beamed, rubbing the eldest son's head. "Alright then, boy. That's what you get for keeping a low center of gravity." Nish noticed how his father's speech sunk to his natural lowbrow London accent when talking about soccer.

"You can move quicker side to side, anticipate, strike out with the arms and legs," his dad mimicked the moves in his seat. "It's all about the center of gravity."

Dave was about to elaborate on the save when Nish chimed in, "I had four sacks."

"My athletes!" Mr. Patel gave a thumbs up to both boys. Nish returned the compliment, wondering what movie had first exposed his father to the thumbs up. Whichever one it was, he must have liked it because he hadn't bothered updating his signs of approval in the last couple decades.

"And I asked a girl on a date for the dance next month," Nish kept his hand up. His mother smiled, "Christine Menard?"

Nish nodded at his plate.

"Oh, she's a handsome girl," she opened her eyes wide.

"You don't say girls are handsome, mom. That's weird," Nish lowered his thumb.

Dave laughed, "Don't be upset, I'm sure she's very handsome."

"Who's your date?" Nish turned quickly to his brother. Dave stared angrily at his food, about to respond when their father spoke, "Dave plays the field," he put a hand on his son's shoulder. "No need to tie yourself down. Right, lad?"

Dave forced a laugh. His father continued, "He's going to find his wife in India when we visit there, isn't that right?" Dad sipped his gin and water. Dave nodded, "And Nish is going to marry some blue-eyed girl and eat curry from a restaurant once a year."

Nish felt a piece of chicken wedged between his teeth. He gripped his fork tighter.

"Now boys, be nice. I always liked the blue-eyed birds myself." He leaned over to kiss their mother. When he raised his fist to her later that night, Dave walked out of his room with a cricket bat. After it was over, Dave walked past Nish's door and looked at him like he knew why his brother didn't get up from his homework; not because he was scared but because he was ashamed. And Dave didn't look angry but softened his grip on the bat and went back to bed.

A hot iron was pressed to Nish's face. He opened his eyes, screaming before he was even conscious of it. The nun was over him, -Water,- she held the back of his head with a few strategically placed fingers as she guided his mouth to the pitcher. He looked at her eyes, they could have been staring at a screensaver she'd seen a thousand times before, he thought. Flies stuck to smears of blood on the walls. Underneath, boys wrapped in bandages gazed silently at the red floor or gritted their teeth or pounded their fists against the stone. Nish swallowed as best he could. "This is the shittiest hospital I've ever been in."

The nun let his head down gently to pour water on a rag for his forehead. He intercepted her hand, pulling it close so the woman attached would follow. "Our bodies are mostly water," his eyes lost their focus, bringing on a wave of nausea. "Every human is made up of molecules that make elements. We all have some gold in us. Think if you took every person who died and extracted their gold. You'd be crazy rich." Nish slipped into blackness, the nun let his hand fall to the cot.

Hercules was staring at his savior when he woke up. Nish's eyes took a second to adjust. "Where am I?" An old woman brought over a glass of water but Hercules waved her away, handing Nish his pitcher of agave beer instead. He sat up to inspect it, "What the fuck is that?" The quick movement caught up with him, forcing his eyes closed. The boy gently tilted his savior's head back, pouring the booze into his mouth. Nish choked on the bitter alcohol, coughing violently until it was all out of him. He grabbed the pitcher from the boy to sniff, then raised it to his mouth to drink from until he'd finished half of it.

"I'm thirsty," he swung his legs off the cot onto the floor. Using the boy and old woman for support, he gingerly put weight on the stilts and led them out the door.

Outside, they walked down the path that led through the rotting garbage, around the side and to the front of the church. Nish stared at the desert town in front of him, a post-apocalyptic wasteland some mad man had dreamt up. A slight breeze blew, he realized he wasn't wearing any clothes except for boots. A piece of paper blew into his foot, sticking to a gelatinous goo that covered his body. He pushed the boy and woman away, picking up the paper to find he couldn't understand it. A group of emaciated children neared him. They reminded him of the cars in the junkyard his father would go to some weekends, missing doors or tires or the edges of shattered glass outlining where a windshield should be. They jolted towards him like broken machines. One said something he didn't understand -…everywhere…no,- then more words, then, -also at the dam…dead….rebels…-

It didn't sound like a different language as much as it made Nish wonder if he'd forgotten how to speak. He shook his head, wondering why the boys were talking to him instead of playing soccer or doing homework.

-I am sorry, sir. How are you?- another asked.

"I'm alright," Nish held up the paper. "What is this?"

-A…the rebels. Tomorrow they come. Need to prepare for war.-

Nish cracked his neck, -How many?-

-About twenty. They attacked the unit at the dam. Those who attacked us numbered in the forty.- The red man woke up with a shriek, pointing the .50 caliber down at his host's skull. Nish dug his fingernails into his palm. -How many of us?-

-With the recruits new, and after the battles today, we have sixty, more or less.-

-From where will they attack?- Nish chugged the milky liquid to change the direction of the machine gun. It raised its sight from his head to frantically search for its next target. Hercules pointed at the land past the border of the town, away from the river and mountains. The lieutenants nodded their heads. -Is in the paper, sir. They ask the people of the town to join their cause.-

Nish looked at the flyer again: drawings of stick figures banding together to kill a giant rattlesnake with dollar signs for eyes and a few choice words about the American mayor on it. -Has anyone left?-

-We caught a few of the arrivals more recent trying to leave but we have detained them.-

-Free them, they can choose their fates,- Nish watched the faces of the boys for hints of defiance but found none. A wave of nausea moved over him; he grabbed onto Hercules for support, staggering backwards. When he'd recovered, he let go of the boy. -When all of this is over, we will find tutors for all of you. Boys need to do more than be soldiers.-

The little red man on top of Nish's head screamed at the field in the distance. Nish's eyes had trouble focusing; he staggered backwards too quickly for the boy to grab him, falling on his ass and spilling liquid from his pitcher onto himself. The lieutenants rushed to help him up.

-Tomorrow morning, we will be waiting for them,- he stood with the aid of the bastards, then staggered to the bar for a refill.

DAY 20

Hercules leaned back on one of the sabotaged trucks to watch the light at the base of the hills extinguished before being hit by the rising sun. He dug his teeth into the chicken breast in his hand, pulling the soft meat easily away from the bone.

-Not do I know if we have enough time, sir,- one of the lieutenants jogged up to Hercules. The soldiers trying to change the tires on the truck kept their heads down.

-All of the spares combined would put only one truck into action,- he continued. The general was about to moan out a suggestion when a high-pitched noise came from the desert, followed by a rolling thunder. Hercules motioned for the lieutenant to keep his crew working on the cavalry and to gather the rest of his soldiers. The general strolled easily past the dead machines towards the steps of the church from where Nish emerged, a warlike newborn covered in jelly and naked except for his boots and pistol. The man took one last swig from the bottle of hard agave liquor he'd bought from an immigrant, then sat it on the steps to walk out.

"How many people defected?"

The boy waved away the insignificant number. A tiny piece of the church exploded like the building was spitting out the fragment of stone. "The men all gathered?"

Hercules nodded as the thunder came. Nish ejected the clip from his weapon; he pushed down on the round at the top, it didn't move far so he reinserted the clip and pulled the action back. It rang out as it hit home. The noise hung in the air; Nish imagined some Roman centurion or Aztec warrior preparing for battle. "All this could be avoided if there was just one drop of rain in this fucking place right now," he looked up. The red man had woken up with him and was panting and cracking his neck and gnashing his teeth together. A wave of joy spread through Nish upwards from his feet like it was going to lift him into the cloudless sky. "Alright then."

-No enemy solider has stepped on soil English in almost a millennia. Why is this?- Nish shouted at the boys, lined up by unit and number. He stuck a finger into his teeth to get a loose piece of fish before continuing, -Because they knew they were better than everyone else and it would be a disgrace to their homeland to die at the hands of tyrants. While hundreds of other nations were forming and dissolving, they stayed true to England. Not did they waver. And because of this, an island nation so tiny created the largest empire in the history of the world.-

The boys stood at attention, staring straight ahead at the enemy who made their war cries heard from a hundred yards across the desert. Nish sharpened his rows of teeth against each other. The numbers the scouts had given were exaggerated: fifty boys and a handful of old men weren't much of a problem even without their cavalry, he figured. Without realizing it, he'd dropped to the ground to begin writing in the sand. He'd gotten to the second 'c' in fifty when the high-pitched whistle came from across the football field of cracked earth. The noise was loud and shrill, going straight through his flesh to his backbone. The little man lifted the .50 caliber to take aim.

When Nish didn't get up from his writing, Hercules stepped in front of the troops. He unsheathed his conquistador's sword and howled. The soldiers did the same, saluting their general. Nish motioned to the dog handlers to let the canine unit attack the enemy across the battlefield. The boys undid the ropes holding the dogs back and the animals took off, running after a jackrabbit in the distance. The group of handlers sprinted after them, yelling the dogs' names to no avail as they disappeared into the distance.

"That's not good," Nish picked his teeth.

A loud cry came from across the field as the rebels charged. The bastards watched as they neared; some fidgeted nervously in their stances, others panted in anticipation of shedding the blood of the crazed enemy that came closer by the second, eating cactus and brush and spitting it out behind them. Prayers became audible from the units. Nish removed his pistol, propping up a knee to steady himself. He fired methodically at the rebels waving their machetes as they charged. The first shot had no visible effect, the second dropped a boy, the next two didn't seem to do anything. Nish waited for the enemy to close in before firing any more rounds.

Three long seconds later they were twenty yards away. He squeezed off two more shots, downing an enemy boy so that he rolled to the sand and beat his fists against the ground.

Then the rebels were on them. A child in front of Nish reared back like he was going to throw something. Nish instinctually ducked. A knife slid from the boy's hand and a half second later was sticking out of the chest of Unit 3, #5 directly behind Nish. The bastard dropped his sword, looking down at the hilt of the blade then back up at the American like he was ready to stop playing. Nish moved the pistol to his left hand, grabbing the sword with his right. The enemy soldier took out another knife but by the time he'd lifted it over his head, a bullet had taken out a chunk of his insides. They attacked from both sides. To the left, #1 feigned an overhead strike with his sword, sticking a skinning knife into the enemy's exposed stomach with his other hand. The rebel's organs pushed out like they were trying to escape the crowded cavity. The enemy to Nish's right raised his machete; he swung his sword up to meet it. Despite his strength, he felt the weight of the heavy machete push down on his own blade and he worried for the boys. The rebel prepared to swing again when #12 stabbed the enemy in the stomach. #13 came around the side to stick the enemy in the ribs but the sword only went in a few inches. The injured child froze with his arms out like he was inviting anyone to take a stab at him so Nish did so. His hand pushed against the hilt as he dug the blade deep into the boy; he remembered how much stuff there was inside of people, like hitting a poorly filled sandbag in the child's torso.

#13 pulled out his sword just as a knife caught him under the chin, sticking into the roof of his open mouth and busting a tooth out to protrude from his upper lip. Nish raised the pistol to shoot the old man who had stabbed his bastard. The flash and noise caused #12 to flinch.

"Get the fuck up!" Nish yelled. He quickly remembered his Spanish, -Get up! Take your sword!- #12 pulled his sword from the human pin cushion along with Nish, who stuck his boot against the dying boy's chest for leverage. Out of the corner of his eye he saw someone swing for his leg. He stabbed his sword into the ground to defend himself, then shot the child in the chest.

Nish took in his surroundings, realizing that a small circle had cleared out around him. Behind him, a group of boys from Unit 3 stood poised like they were ready to take on anyone who happened to get past the large, naked American with the gun. The old men amongst the rebels migrated towards Nish. He raised the pistol but the armies were too intermingled for him to risk a shot. Two old men appeared on each side in front of him. One rebel had a cane in his left hand and a machete in his right. He stuck the cane in Nish's face like a boxer using a jab before throwing a powerful punch with his other hand. Nish shot the man in the groin; after the bullet had torn through the soft tissue, the lead embedded itself in the dirt instead of an ally. The old rebel fell; Nish turned to the other man who had just severed the arm of #9 as the bastard had raised his weapon to defend his leader. The boy had a look on his face like he'd just shown up to his own surprise party as he watched the stump drool a lazy red fountain onto the hand still clutching the sword below. The old man swung again, this time at the boy's head. It went through half his neck before getting stuck in his collarbone. Nish stepped towards the man to attack but saw movement out of the corner of his eye; he ducked as a pitchfork embedded itself into the shoulder of #3 behind him. The old man saw Nish coming and unstuck the machete from the child's skeleton to swing. The American blocked the blow, then stabbed at the man's body. The enemy avoided the blade and swung again. This time Nish was just able to block the machete, it slid down his sword until it hit the hilt. He kicked down on the rebel's knee, collapsing his one side. Nish raised his pistol but the old man grabbed his arm. He remembered playing swords with Dave in the backyard, making up the rules as he went along. He lunged at the man's neck and clamped his teeth down. They tore through the tendons and veins to free them from the abusive pressure the head and body had gotten them used to. The skin was salty leather, the man cried out, recoiling as Nish raised the pistol to shoot him in the head. The ground swallowed the offering greedily. Nish remembered loading the tiny piece of lead into the gun; he wondered how many times his pointer finger had curled an inch inwards throughout his life, standing in line at the supermarket or lying asleep.

In the minute the two armies had been fighting, the battle cries had given way to loud grunts and screams and people crying out to Jesus and God and Mary and their moms.

Nish realized he was panting. He looked around to find many of the others doing the same. The opposing side was now heavily outnumbered. They swung their machetes desperately like they knew what was coming. The heavy one-sided blade was too clumsy; the bastards countered with their swords, stabbing with the sharp points to fell the rebels. One enemy child had dropped his sword and was crying, walking around the battlefield like a zombie. Nish put his pistol back in his belt as he walked towards the young boy but Hercules flew from out of Nish's vision, running the child through with so much force that the boy bounced off the hilt of his sword and stood impaled in the middle of the blade. The young rebel stopped crying to look at his killer; Hercules grabbed him by the throat, letting out a noise Nish had never heard before in this world. He pulled the blade out slow like he wanted to savor it. When it was withdrawn, the child fell. Hercules stood over him panting like he was trying to figure out which part he wanted to eat first.

More begging for mercy came from the enemy. Nish grabbed Hercules's arm, pointing at one boy who had dropped his sword to raise his hands in the air. The child reached for the sky like the closer he got to it, the less likely he'd be to get stabbed. Hercules looked back at his savior, Nish patted the holstered pistol. The general stuck a nail between his teeth, digging it in deep. Water rose to his mouth and he spit into the sand that quickly swallowed it up. The color dripped from the conquistador's sword; Nish thought even an artist couldn't have painted it more even and perfect.

The poorer young children from the town came out with slingshots to wait motionlessly on the battlefield for the vultures to end their circling and come down to feast on the pieces of child. Cheering rose from the main group of soldiers. Nish turned away from the captured rifle in his hands to see what was happening. As he neared the circle of boys, he saw Unit 4, #2 get a running start to kick one of the bound POW's in the face. The boy fell to the side while the other prisoners stared at the dirt in front of them, their mouths closed.

"What the fuck?" Nish pushed his way to the center as the army quieted. -What are you doing?-

The soldiers put on the same faces as their captives.

-Not do you treat a prisoner like this,- Nish grabbed the closest POW to cut through the coarse rope binding his hands and feet. The child looked up at the American, his expression unchanged. Nish spoke to the boy loud enough for everyone to hear, -You have an opportunity for a new life in a city that allows you to be that which you want, if you have the ability.- He squatted so his eyes were on the same level as the boy's. -Would you like that?-

The child nodded his head slightly. Nish stood, -Not do you need to say yes. If you want to return to the desert, you can do so a man free,- Nish swept his arm to the side like a game show hostess showing off a new car. The boy's eyes followed his hand as it revealed the wasteland littered with the body parts of old friends. The vultures descended lower while the young children sat perfectly still like guardian angels waiting for the souls to rise out of the dead so they could escort them to heaven.

-I want the city,- the boy muttered.

-Do you see?- Nish smiled to his army, -He has chosen New Texas. These boys are the same as us. No one has a choice of how they are born or that which they do. We now give them an opportunity for a life new. In this situation, they will act the same as you would.- A cool breeze came from the north, blowing away the stink of the dead. He remembered watching the weather on television, those big swirls of white over the blue planet. That's all around us, he thought. It didn't stop at the sky and clouds but enveloped even the room where he was watching TV. When he opened his eyes, one of the boys had their hands up.

-#5,- he called on him.

-Sir, why do we torture the man in the plaza?- he looked confused. The other boys nodded.

Nish stroked his chin like a parody of a man thinking. He hadn't shaved since the morning of the sushi party in San Antonio. He wondered if the smell of the barbecue was embedded somewhere deep in the hairs. His stomach growled, -The Killer had his torture begin before we had established ourselves as a government, before we had the rules and the structures of a society civilized.-

#5 furrowed his brow in contemplation, then shrugged. -Okay.- The other bastards did the same, cutting the POW's free. A younger boy with a slingshot touched Nish's gelatinous, sandy leg to get his attention. The American looked down, -What passes?-

The boy put his head in his tiny hands, refusing to say what was wrong. Nish shrugged, he watched the bastards to make sure all prisoners were cut loose. In the distance, faint clouds of dust showed the nurses were running towards the casualties as fast as their ancient bodies could carry them. The little boy walked around the American to stand in front of him again and resume crying.

-What?-

The boy wiped his nose, -My brother is dead.- He pointed to the mass of corpses. -Not is there no priest here to forgive him so he is going to hell.-

Nish slid the clip out of the pistol to push down on the top round. His finger sank deep into the metal so he reached into his pocket for more ammunition. -Not is this true,- he began reloading. -That is the voodoo. In truth, people are on a path to heaven or hell from their birth; not can this be changed. Someone saying words to you when you die only helps the people ignorant to feel better.-

Hercules called the units to order. The bastards lined up in formation, a few standing around the freed prisoners with their swords drawn. When Nish was finished, he slid the clip back into the pistol. -When you die, you continue to exist the same as you did on Earth. You have your own heaven or hell in a manner.-

Hercules moaned, the lieutenants ordered their units to move out. Nish walked away from the little boy. He brushed past a guard to put his arm around a prisoner.

-Who in this group knows how to play the beanbags?-

The beanbag hit the back of the hole. It hung on the ledge for a second like it was trying to milk the moment for all it was worth, different groups in the crowd pleading with it to drop in or to stay. When it finally fell, the cheers and cries almost matched those of hours earlier on the battlefield. The former enemy who had thrown the beanbag had a bottle of agave liquor thrust into his hand. He took a long drink, then held up the bottle to more cheering. A bastard still in his uniform made a reference to the beanbag champion's former allegiance and people migrated to different sides of the argument, those who won money on the throw being more accepting of their new neighbors, those who lost not sharing in their forgiveness.

Nish grabbed the bottle from the champion to hand to the game's loser, asking if it would shut him up. The crowd laughed and the next player picked up the beanbags. Nish walked around to the front of the bar to breathe in the cool night air. Hercules sat with a glass of agave beer; when he saw his savior, he motioned to Nish if he'd like some.

"No thanks," Nish smiled. "I'm drying out tonight." He cracked his neck, the snapping sound putting him at ease. The stubble on his chin itched. Sand had worked its way in between the hair follicles to harass the skin of his face. He remembered he wanted to shave before he went to bed. It was easy to ignore the itchiness when he was drunk, he recognized, but small things get to you when you're sober.

A pack of homeless children ran through the market with something held high on a stick. When their lap of the town square led them in front of the tavern, Nish stopped them. -What is that?-

A young boy held the stick out to the American to show him the cooked tarantula on the end. The hair had been burned off the spider, its legs curled up around its thorax.

-For what reason do you have this?-

-For to eat,- the boy grinned proudly, running off with his brothers and sisters in tow.

Nish sat at Hercules' table, asking the bartender for a water. "There's a critical mass with these sorts of things. When the rich keep people impoverished for their own sake, they're being shortsighted. The more poor there are, the more of a gap there is, the higher the chance of revolution," Nish flung an arm casually over the back of the chair, "Maybe in the form of large scale policy change, maybe in the form of street crime, or maybe burning down mansions and killing people in the street. But that's why you educate people, give everyone the same chance. There will always be poor but let the poor be the people who deserve it; those who don't offer as valuable a service to society. The stupid and lazy."

Another roar came from the beanbag game around the side of the building. The noise brought a smile to Nish's face. He kicked off his boots to let his toes enjoy the night air. "Unfortunately, the stupid and lazy will always have more babies. If left to their own, these babies would die because the parents can't feed them but it's our responsibility to give every child a chance. And there's the rub," Nish stuck out a finger like the point of his argument had become visible and was sitting on the table. The waiter brought over the water and Nish thanked him.

"You feed and clothe a child but if you don't make sure to finish the job, you're allowing them to grow up and have more babies who don't succeed, and they have more babies. The family tree grows exponentially in comparison to their wealthier counterparts." He remembered Deaf's ancient friend from the diner, "Society destined to chaos."

Hercules shifted in his seat to put his feet under the chair, resting them on the tips of his shoes. Nish saw him as a child for the first time since back in the U.S.

"Before the election, we need to put a few things in place. Incentives for parents above a certain income level to have children," Nish watched the boy for a reaction; Hercules returned his feet to the ground, crossing his arms and nodding.

A group of farmers walked down the side of the square to pull up a table, resting their machetes against their chairs. Nish ordered them a round of agave beer, which they toasted him with. Nish raised his glass of water in return. When he'd taken a drink, he noticed someone sitting behind the men at one of the back tables. The candle on the table had gone out and the giant moon outside the open air tavern couldn't illuminate the child with his head in his hands. When Nish's eyes adjusted, he noticed the boy by his shape. "I'll be right back."

As he neared the child, he could see the deep bruises around his eyes and what looked like a growth under the purple skin of his lip.

-Fatty, what passes?-

-Nothing,- he didn't look over as the American sat next to him.

-That's nice,- Nish winked, pointing at the lip. Fatty turned his head away in shame. Brushing sand from stubble, Nish leaned in, -Listen, the other bastards not do you please them because of your past with the Killer.-

Fatty opened his mouth but Nish held up a hand to silence him. Tears welled in the boy's eyes as he gripped his cup tighter.

-Not does it matter what happens in reality, only what others perceive is happening, understand?-

The boy blinked quickly so the moisture wouldn't roll down his face.

-I am going to make you the policeman,- Nish leaned back with his hands behind his head. Fatty kept his round face pointed at the cup.

-I will announce it tomorrow and give you the rifle we took from the rebels. We need a policeman now, to keep the peace. You understand?-

-Yes,- Fatty's head didn't move even as the American got up from the table to rejoin the general. A band of musicians wandered in front of the bar. Striking their first chord, Nish sipped his cool water.

The rum Jordan had poured into the large soft drink in the movie theater's bathroom caught Nish off guard. He struggled to not cough it all over himself and Rebecca.

"Shit's strong, huh?" Jordan grinned.

"It's not weak," Nish put the straw back in his mouth. Rebecca put her hand out for the cup; he tried not to look at the fingers cluttered with rings from the Middle East, Africa and South Asia, focusing instead on her big blue eyes. When he handed the drink over, she gave her fake smile. Nish hated how she always put it on her face, like someone might take her picture at any second and she wanted to be ready for it. After wincing at the amount of alcohol, she handed it back to him. He took the top off the drink to pour it straight into his mouth.

Jordan whispered something to Liliana who giggled childishly, making Nish even happier there was hardly anyone in the theater. Someone onscreen stabbed another person, prompting yells from the black teenagers down front as if the characters were basing their decisions off audience recommendations.

"Listen to this shit," Jordan pressed his lips together.

Rebecca placed her hand on Nish's to pat it gently. The character in the movie found another victim; the teenagers in front shouted at the screen again. Jordan waited until they were done to mimic them, just as loud but more shrill.

"Oh shit," Nish busted out laughing with Liliana. The teens in front turned quickly, one stood. Nish thought the movie might as well have been paused. Jordan leaned forward to spit dip juice into an empty cup. Nish's date clutched his hand while he ran his tongue over his teeth. He saw the standing teen's eyes look over the group.

The teen said something loudly that Nish didn't understand. Whatever it was, Nish figured his friends must have thought it was pretty funny by their reaction. The teen stuck up his chin like he was looking at the group over an invisible fence. After a few seconds, he nodded and sat down, slapping his friends' hands and saying something about a "cracker ass motherfucker."

Nish let his tongue relax in his mouth. Rebecca was clutching his hand so tightly he had to reach for the cup with his other.

"And there are a lot more of those in Houston," Jordan grinned at Nish, making it a point to be heard.

"I doubt where I'm going." The two laughed, Rebecca finally let go.

"You going to hog that rum and coke?" Jordan put out his hand for the cup.

"Cracker ass motherfucker," Nish shook his head as he handed it over, the two laughing again. He propped his feet on the seat in front of him, allowing the alcohol to do its thing. The warmth spreading across his brain was already allowing him to put an arm around his date. He remembered his father once saying, "No one gets less attractive the more pissed you get. Isn't that right, mum?" His mom blushed in her rocker, "Oh, dad."

DAY 21

The plate of pickled cactus arrived at the table of immigrants dining with Jacobo. He motioned for them to eat his food.

-And one more round,- he smiled at the waitress, a girl of about thirteen who had shown up that morning. The farther the people traveled to get to the town, the more teenagers and young parents there were. Jacobo watched as she walked away, the smile slowly falling from his face until the sound of the men smacking on the wet strips of cactus meat brought it back.

-Gentleman, this is a place of great opportunity,- the boy took a drink of his liquor. -You have been given land for to farm but not do you have nothing of tools, nothing of seed, nothing of help. And more, you come with only the clothes on your backs.- The sides of his mouth dropped to express sympathy. -I know the pain of having the hunger. I want to help.-

Hercules waited while the men signed Jacobo's contracts, after which the newcomers walked back to the markets where their families were waiting for them. Jacobo flagged down the waitress, -The plate of pork fried,- he watched again as she walked away. When he turned back to the table, he was startled to find Hercules standing over him. The American's boy kept his chin tucked into the top of his chest and the butt of his hand on the hilt of his sword; he moved it in a circular motion as if trying to rock it to sleep.

-Mister Vice Mayor Interim, how are you?- Jacobo offered a seat. Hercules looked at the chair like it might be booby-trapped. His hand froze as he sat down.

-Would you like a beer? Some liquor?- Jacobo said just as the girl hurried over with a pitcher for the table. Hercules made her wait while he counted out the money for the drink. Jacobo started to roll his eyes but quickly stopped when Hercules looked at him. After the younger boy was finished paying, Jacobo opened his mouth to speak but his guest turned around in his chair to look at the open area in front of the church. Soldiers and newcomers alike sat on the steps, watching a reenactment of the previous day's battle. One of the actors pointed to

Guillermo, sitting next to an ancient nurse, before delivering a mighty blow that awed the crowd. The people cheered his name when his likeness had finally triumphed over the rebels single-handedly. Hercules looked back across the table at Jacobo.

-I killed two yesterday. Not do I parade around, wanting to be a hero,- Jacobo waved away the scene. -The war is done. If he wants to continue it in his head, is his choice.-

Hercules retrieved a piece of paper from his pocket to place on the table between them. Jacobo's eyes skipped over the drawing to sound out the word beneath, -Election.- He looked back at the boy, confused. Hercules pointed at him. Jacobo took a drink of the strong liquor in his glass before looking at the flyer again.

The artist dipped his brush into the bucket of red paint resting carefully on top of the rickety ladder. Hercules smiled as the giant nipples took shape on the side of the building. He compared his business to the other newly opened brothels on the street, bordering a shantytown that had sprouted like a freshly grown, rotten arm on the bulging body of the city. One of the whorehouses featured a pink clamshell and boasted the name -The Crustacean- while others were more to the point, featuring women in various stages of undress. Hercules turned back to his totally nude woman, larger than any of his competitors' logos, and let a huge grin wipe across his scarred face.

He walked easily to the front of the building where a line of girls stood in the sun. Most had clothes that revealed pieces of their body without meaning to; none seemed to have made any noticeable effort to look more attractive. As he passed through the door, one of his managers, an ex-lieutenant, tapped him on the shoulder, -Sir.- The manager pointed at one of the girls, pulling his eyebrows down. -Too young?-

Something bit Hercules on the back of the neck. He slapped the bug, much larger than usual. His eyes searched the street for its source. A butcher on the corner did business out of a hastily built wooden shack that served as a frame for his mutilations. The old man raised his cleaver high above his head to swing downwards through the neck of a chicken. The bird continued to struggle frantically against the man even as the blood poured from its neck. Hercules pointed at the animal.

The manager lifted the girl's skirt to inspect her well-worn underwear, then motioned her inside with her older sisters.

Nish stumbled from the church to the tavern like his legs were asleep. The sun was high in the sky, the bar populated with people who had come for lunch and then stayed to get drunk. They yelled their greetings to the American who was too preoccupied with the monster drilling into his brain to acknowledge anyone. Laying there like a corpse, he remembered, except for the wetness in his eyes. He shook his head, "I'm a good person."

The crowd cheered him again as if he were saying hello. No more nights like that, he thought, with the red man working on him. That's what he got for letting himself go dry for a day. The next days were always the worst. "You can't forget the basics," he pursed his lips together like he was going to let the tears run down his face again. "You're never better than that," a vision of his position coach spraying spit out of his bulldog mouth. -Liquor,- Nish yelled to whichever waiter wanted the biggest tip. The bartender already had a bottle and a cup in each hand for him.

-And music. Bring me the musicians.-

The crowd cheered again, raising their glasses to their interim mayor.

"Bloody twat," Nish's father spat at the driver of the car. "These frog cunts don't even know what this means," he drunkenly staggered back onto the sidewalk, still pointing at the statue. Nish looked at the man on the horse; he thought the little thing in his hand looked like a baton he was about to pass off until he'd suddenly become frozen in metal.

"What the hell are you doing, boy? Come on then."

Nish kept his arm around his father's shoulder, seemingly out of affection but really more as a precaution in case his dad tried to walk out into traffic again. The sun stole a spot through the hanging curtain of English clouds.

"Beautiful," his dad wiped his face. Nish was embarrassed by the accent. He'd made it a point to only have two beers while watching the game at the pub. A good show of restraint, he thought, since most fifteen year olds don't get to stroll into a bar in America and have pints pushed in front of them.

Petersfield reminded him of a tiny model town that someone had left outside so the grass would grow up in strategic spots. The buildings looked like they were built centuries ago but kept up and presented properly to the pedestrians on the brick and stone side streets. What struck him most were the cars. And going into the supermarkets; the everyday things that make you feel like you're still in the right century but in a parallel universe.

203

When they reached the house, Nish's father opened the door, bowing like a servant as he passed through.

"Hello?" a female voice beckoned them to the living room where the women were having tea. Nish had been surprised to see how the English really did drink tea religiously. He didn't understand what was so appealing about boiled water flavored with dried leaves but he always accepted some when his grandmother offered.

"Hello," Nish took a seat next to his mother, who leaned over to kiss his head.

"How was the game?" she asked.

His father entered the room, "Wonderful, love." He didn't bother changing his accent in the company of his in-laws. Nish winced, turning to his grandmother; he expected the tight bun at the back of her head to explode white hair in all directions.

"Town's just the same as when I used to come here in the service," dad smiled at his mother-in-law.

The older woman leaned an inch towards Nish, raising her nose slightly as if she could smell the alcohol on his breath. "I'm sure you both had a lovely time."

The boy's face turned red. The woman finally looked at Nish's father, "Your son appears to be worse, Arun. Would you be a dear and check to see if he needs anything?" She lifted the sides of her mouth so convincingly that Nish thought she might actually be alright with her daughter being married to the drunk Indian-Briton in the doorway.

"Just a bloody cold, he'll live," Nish's dad turned to walk towards the bedroom where Dave was resting.

"May I have some tea, grandmother?" Nish smiled.

The sides of the woman's mouth dropped back into the downward creases that framed the bottom half of her face. She placed a saucer and teacup in front of him like there was an exact place on the coffee table for them to rest. After she had poured the cup, Nish picked it up to take a sip without waiting for the offer of sugar.

"Travelers setting up outside town," Nish's aunt flipped through the paper. "Rest of the bogtrotters around here can join them for all I'm concerned," she flicked her head towards the window. Nish looked but didn't see anything on the street.

"Every summer," she continued despite no one looking at her. "It's like my shop fills up with them. I catch the urchins trying to rob me blind half the time."

"Everyone's someone's nigger," Nish quoted Verne and looked at the eggs scrambled with dried donkey meat and crumbled goat cheese. He gritted his teeth and closed his eyes as hard as he could, taking a sip of tea. He was careful to replace the delicate cup gently on the saucer.

"They also work at your store, don't they?" mom tried to find a compromise. Her sister responded by stuttering over a syllable. Nish's mom smiled to keep the peace, "There are upsides and downsides to everything. After all, Arun and I are immigrants in the States."

The other two women exchanged glances and chuckled. "That's not the same, darling. You know that," grandmother looked at the coffee table as she spoke. "It's quite different here."

"The Irish," Nish nodded at his grandmother, hoping she'd do the same. She didn't.

"That's whose all in my shop," aunt agreed. "They come over here and make money, then take it back home without giving us anything."

"They work for you," Nish's mom said plainly.

"If it were up to me, I'd pay more to someone actually from this country if it would keep the micks from coming over."

"It is up to you. Simply don't employ them."

Aunt took a sip of her tea. She eyed Nish like he was a stray dog her sister had just brought in. While he'd never been able to visit the family often, he always felt like his aunt was meeting him for the first time.

"Grandmother, weren't you telling me and Dave about how the Irish came over after World War II?" Nish asked.

Aunt nodded, "You're grandmother worked in a hospital in London treating the dying soldiers. She spent nights underground in the tube stations to avoid the Nazi bombings." She looked to Nish's mom, "Arun's from London, he knows. If you had seen that town when he was a lad, you'd think the war was still going on."

"Over forty thousand British civilians killed by those bombings," grandmother interjected. "And the Irish stayed neutral, couldn't even fight the Nazis."

"They help the Germans in both world wars, then they come here for our jobs," aunt shook her head.

Nish's mother sat down her teacup loudly. Nish figured she might as well have thrown it through the window by her sister's reaction to the rude gesture.

"Boy," grandmother never called him by his name. "Go check on your father and David, will you?"

"Yes ma'am," Nish slurped down the last of his tea, immediately regretting his crudeness. He delicately sat the cup down on the saucer to make up for it.

When he left the room, he almost ran into his father waiting around the corner listening to the women's conversation. The man casually swirled a glass of brown liquid with ice in it. "If the Nazis had been knocking on your aunt's door, she probably would have joined them," he grinned at his son. His eyelids drooped from the alcohol, his whole face seemed somehow dirty. Nish felt a string of chicken from the pub in his teeth; he picked at it as he walked to his brother's room. When his aunt came in to check on Dave, she put her hand on the sick boy and Nish almost couldn't tell whose fingers were whose.

A boy walked out from behind one of the hanging cloths, tying the rope that held up his pants.

-How was it?- one of Hercules' managers asked. The customer grinned ear-to-ear, -How good, sir. How good.-

Hercules finished his glass of agave beer, motioning for the girl to get off his lap. He walked to the front door to look across the dirt road at the sign being hoisted over the entrance to Jacobo's brothel. A pair of giant breasts stared out from the top of the building while an open pink vagina surrounded the door the customers lined up in front of. A familiar voice caught his attention; he turned to see Nish standing with his arms crossed in front of a group of immigrants.

-You can stay in your towns. We will pay for the materials: the cloth, the food, the wood for to build,- he swayed backwards, unfolding his arms to regain his balance. When he was sturdy, he reassumed his authoritative stance. -These to us you bring. There are many people here who need these materials and you will get a price very good. Not even do you need to leave your homes to move here.- Nish patted the closest man on the shoulder and tried to lift the sides of his face up.

The man looked at the others in the group around him. A general rumbling of ascent gained momentum until they were all nodding in agreement.

-Excellent,- Nish kept his face the way it had been as he shook hands with each of them.

Jacobo watched from a window of his new building. He finished; the girl rose from her knees, blocking his view of the business transaction.

-Bitch clumsy.- He pulled up his pants to walk out of the room. The girl waited until he was gone to spit the contents of her mouth into his glass of agave beer, where it disappeared into the alcohol's white milkiness.

Nish ambled down the street, taking in the newly colored buildings. Since a couple of painters had opened shop, he'd noticed businesses and homes all over the city seemed to be making use of their services. The result was a flowerbed that had sprung up almost overnight where before there had only been sunburnt adobe and wood. Walking from City Hall to the brothel district, he'd passed the delicious smells of food, fresh wood being opened, burning, rotting, all where there had been nothing. Men and older bastards hovered around the whorehouses in anticipation while only blocks away street preachers surrounded by newcomers railed against the influence of the devil, all where there had been no one. The red man at his crown had slipped back inside the crack in his skull, one of the upsides of a fresh bout of drinking.

Hercules stuck his hand up like a student in class to get his savior's attention. Nish aimed himself towards the boy but was intercepted halfway there.

-Mister Mayor Interim,- Jacobo reached to shake the American's hand. Nish noticed he'd been doing a lot more of that lately. Good practice, he thought.

-What of this election?- Nish took the boy's hand and cut straight to the point. Jacobo stood tongue-tied for a second. Nish laughed, -You will do fine.- He looked past the whorehouses to the new shantytown. -Argentina is a nation of immigrants from all countries of Europe. People who hated each other, of religions different, but they bonded.- He waved a drunken hand towards the sky. -At the end of the century nineteen, they began the Conquest of the Desert. They conquered all of the people indigenous, killing them and moving them to reservations. At the beginning of the century twenty, were one of the countries most powerful in the world.-

A three-legged dog hopped across the sand from a hut to a pile of trash that Nish figured would soon be transformed into another shanty home. He lifted his pistol, training the bead on the animal, then faked pulling the trigger as he made a gunshot noise. -This is the history of many countries. It is the way of the world. People fight and win or lose. Now Argentina is ruined financially. In ten years, is possible that they may be powerful again. The past is the same for the whole world, that which is important is what you do next,- Nish looked up at the boy who smiled politely. The American walked towards Hercules' brothel. Jacobo returned to his own establishment, his face red with frustration until the girl greeted him at the door with his cup of agave beer.

"They look like they're dead but all you've done at that point is either temporarily cut off circulation to their brain or stopped the flow of oxygen. You've got to keep squeezing for a good bit longer if you want to finish it up that way."

Nish nodded. While this wasn't exactly subject matter you take notes on, he figured he could have worse mentors in this line of work than Bill. They stopped at a light, the guns and ammunition store across the street.

"Now what happened to you last week ain't out of the ordinary," Bill spit tobacco juice into his bottle. Nish's face turned red at the mention of the previous week's shootout at the construction site. He figured Allen had told half the office about Nish not being able to squeeze off a single round.

"Don't pay no mind to that, that was the weapon's fault," Bill continued. "That's why I carry a revolver: less machinery. Won't jam on you, doesn't spit out goddamn shells everywhere with your fingerprints on them, and you can conceal a large caliber easily. You can also choose your round, mix it up, not just take whatever's loaded in there for you."

"A lot of the guys said they don't like them because they carry half the shots," Nish said without thinking.

"Fuck that bullshit," Bill spit again even though very little came out. "Boys ain't thinking straight. In a bind, I'll take six rounds from my .44 any day over some automatic. My dumbass daddy carried around a .45 auto and ended up on the boot hill because his weapon jammed on him. Son of bitch got what he deserved."

Nish relaxed in his seat, a smile on his lips.

"Shit hits the fan, you better be wearing a raincoat. And I'm not trusting my life to no goddamn automatic," Bill pulled into the parking lot. "But with free advice, you get what you pay for."

"Revolver sounds like the smart choice."

Bill nodded, "Alright then."

DAY 22

The last raise was added to the pile in the middle of the table, a mix of money, land deeds and IOU's. Nish lowered his cards for all to see, "Straight." Hercules' managers groaned in disbelief as they threw their cards face down on the table.

"Sorry boys," Nish laughed. He put his arms out like he was hugging an invisible obese woman, then let them fall to the table to rake in his winnings. "Last thing I'll teach you for the night is don't outstay your welcome," he tossed a hefty tip to the dealer. He tried to slide his chair back but it caught on a stone; he flailed his arms wildly to balance himself but fell to the ground anyway. The table exploded in laughter, Hercules let out loud howls as he clapped his mutilated hands together. The sleeping bartender sprung to her feet, automatically bringing the bottle of agave liquor to refill the poker players' glasses.

"My dad won my mom's engagement ring in a card game back when he was in the army in England," Nish held onto Hercules for support as the two made their way back to City Hall. "I'm not much of a player but in Dallas the guys have games going all the time." He stopped, keeping one arm on the boy while he opened a stream of urine onto the parched earth. The whole town seemed to be dead asleep. The only noise was the wind, scattering the piss into shotgun pellets. "You'd like the guys in Dallas. You only got to meet John, and he's a great guy, my best friend, but there are a lot of good guys there."

His stream weakened until it pulled back up into his body. He shook his hips from side to side, "When we get back, everything will be cleared up and we'll all hang out. Play some cards," he patted the boy on the head as they began walking again. The sky was crystal clear except for the moon hanging above; it was so large Nish could almost reach up to feel its cratered surface.

Out of the brothel district, they entered the more upscale part of town where restored homes stood at attention on well cleaned streets. Past this, the old center of town. They walked around the side of the plaza to avoid the maze of the empty marketplace. They didn't talk; Nish figured the boy was looking forward to the comfort of bed as much as he was. They had almost reached Nish's tavern when low, unnatural moans stopped them in their tracks. The two instinctively ducked, following the sound to the open area at the top of the square in front of City Hall. There, in plain view, the nun fed the Killer from a bowl.

After a few more spoonfuls, she sat the soup down to take a wet cloth from around her neck to wipe the gangster's face. She dipped the cloth into a lotion she carried, then dabbed it onto freshly opened sections of his body, eliciting another low moan from the teen. She tried to hush him but he didn't seem to understand human things anymore, only base feelings like hunger and pain.

Nish rose from his hiding place, starting toward the nun with Hercules in tow. When she finally heard them over the wind and the Killer's moans, they were less than ten yards away. She dropped the cloth, her eyelids looking like if they peeled back any further, the eyeballs they held in place would drop from their sockets onto the sand.

-Wait, wait,- she stuck her hands in front of her, shaking them quickly back and forth. Nish thought it looked like a dance he'd seen once when he got dragged to a girlfriend's musical in college.

-Only was I giving him food,- she started but Nish shook his head.

-I was very clear on this,- he stood above her. He reached down for the cloth she'd dropped. It smelled of the poultice her old women used on the boys injured in battle. He'd even smeared it on the disappearing scratches on his back and was impressed by the result. -This is the reason that he has been healing so well, nothing of infection in these last days.-

The nun shook her hands for a second longer then stopped moving altogether. She straightened to stand taller, looking Nish in the eye. The booze had cleared from his mind like dissipating clouds, letting a heavy sobriety shine onto the red man's face. He cracked his neck to find the situation warranting his attention. He threw a straight right to her chin, dropping her back down like dead weight.

Hercules took the cloth to stuff into the nun's mouth until it wouldn't take anymore. She tried screaming but the gag had the desired effect. The boy took the belt from his pants to tie her hands behind her back. When she tried to get traction with her feet in the sand, he kicked her hard in the face. Nish picked his teeth, "When you're a kid, you watch cartoons with the good guys and the bad guys. Then one day years later, you wake up and realize that if people were showing your life, the day to day of it, you'd come off on the wrong side of that coin," the gas that had been building up in his stomach escaped. "Thing is, most people don't understand what it's like to really believe something, to carry a thought through to its conclusion and then act on it." He bent over to pick up the nun, slinging her over his back. She squirmed; Nish remembered how much living things move, an uncanny knack for getting free. The red man gnashed his teeth in anticipation.

"It's not that I think people are stupid. They just compromise to protect themselves, their comfort, that of their loved ones. To them, there comes a point where it's not worth believing anymore, so they call those who do 'irrational'." The boy poked at the hollow socket of the teen before following his savior.

They carried her miles into the desert, away from the river and mountains, past the burial mounds of the battlefield. They saw smoke rising from satellite towns in the far distance that had reestablished themselves to sell raw materials to New Texas. The two steered clear of any sign of humanity. When they were far enough, Nish motioned to the boy for the sword.

"Hold her down," Nish unsheathed the blade. It shone as if it were made from a piece of the moon itself. "She's going to kick," Nish emphasized. Hercules gripped the nun's legs tighter.

-Well, we had some times good,- Nish placed his foot on the young woman's chest to keep her down. The moon was getting lower; he figured they didn't have much time before its counterpart painted the sky red. "So the abridged version," he reached down so he could pull the cloth from her mouth. She made frantic noises with her throat.

-Not do you scream,- he placed the tip of the sword at her neck. -Say your prayers and then I will replace it.- This only caused more frantic throat noises and writhing.

-Listen,- Nish poked the tip into her flesh. It pierced the taut skin, juice running down around the bend to the sand. He hadn't meant to stab into her but it got the desired effect as she winced and held herself still. The red man clawed at the air around him, bringing it into him to consume. Nish wiped his eyes.

He bent over again, this time removing the cloth from her mouth. When it was out, she breathed like she'd been underwater for a minute. The muscles of her mouth trembled from being stretched so far and Nish wasn't sure if she would be able to speak. He looked impatiently at the glowing orb falling to the horizon. She tried to close her mouth but it reopened on its own slowly like a bear trap. Her eyes looked all around like the answer to the malfunction was written in the sky or sand or on a cactus. Nish watched her more curiously, letting the man on top of his head dig into him if he wanted. They weren't big on taking gags out in Dallas and the body's reaction fascinated him.

Hercules looked in the distance to find their town awakening, blowing smoke rings into the early morning air. His eyes focused on the first signs of the vendors beginning breakfast, unable to notice the last blinking of the light past the river.

-Please,- the nun pleaded. The boy turned back to his victim to hold her feet tighter.

-Not do we have time for that,- Nish waved his finger. -Your prayers, if you wish.- The nun opened her mouth to make a noise like an insect had just flown into her throat, then closed it to whisper her prayers. Hercules looked out again at the falling moon. When the nun had finished, she opened her eyes, -Please.-

Nish bent down with the cloth. She didn't move but spoke again, this time through clenched teeth, -Retribution comes for all. Not can you wash from your soul that which you have done. The path-

"That's enough," Nish abruptly shoved the cloth back into her mouth. He turned to Hercules, "The fucking melodrama with these people."

The boy shook his head.

"Flip her over," Nish ordered and the boy did so. The nun struggled against him but the boy held her too tight. Her eyes widened like she was going to squeeze them out of her skull, shooting them at her captors, but they didn't go anywhere. Nish looked at the young woman's ass under her habit, his hand grazing over his penis. What if she'd been born in a beach town, he wondered, making drinks in coconuts for tourists and lying out naked in hidden coves. "Hold her tight."

He squatted, grabbing an ankle to let the sword rest on her heel. Then he began sawing off the sole of the nun's foot. He tried to stay close to the bone but had problems with the arch and the coming back down from it. The blade came out. He had to try several times to slip it into the slim meat before the balls of her foot. The actual cutting of the thicker pads under her toes also proved difficult. When the first foot had been shaved clean, an assortment of thin and fat cuts of meat lay next to random chunks on the sand.

Unnatural noises came from the body Nish was performing the makeshift surgery on. The red man vomited his delight into the crack in his host's brain; Nish continued with the other foot. He replicated the process but more efficiently, finishing with only two pieces of meat and a plastic tendon. Just like with running drills, he thought, he always had been a quick learner.

"She's not going anywhere," he stood, handing the sword back to Hercules.

The nun mollowed face down into the sand like a mule trying to scare off a nearing predator. The boy cleaned the blade; Nish wiped off the layer of body grease the blood had splattered on. Wedging his foot between her and the ground, Nish kicked her over so she was facing upwards.

"You think that was bad, wait until tonight," he felt sand in his ass crack and scratched violently, "I'm a saint compared to what's out here." He felt the electric shock run through his body, all the way to the tip of the red man. He closed his eyes to let it take its course. When he opened them again, the boy was standing with the sword in his hand, looking at the desert like it had challenged him to a duel. Nish patted the boy's shoulder as if to comfort him, "Don't worry, the coyotes will eat her up until there's hardly anything left." He turned to walk back towards the town, his own blood seeping out from in between his legs.

Hercules looked down at the young woman, partially choking from the cloth, the source of her guilt. Pools of red formed around her feet faster than even the desert could drink it down. The pieces of meat at their base could have been food she was going to use to feed the condemned. He allowed the sword to float over her throat. The muscles in his hand tightened, his jaw clenched. He breathed more quickly as he focused on the largest vein in her neck straining against the skin that held it prisoner. Then he turned to his savior walking back towards the town. The man frantically scratched the sand out of his hair, stopping to pass gas loud enough for the boy to hear. Hercules flipped the sword in his hand, stabbing it into the ground an inch from the nun's face. He howled to the first beams of red in the morning sky. When he was done, he returned the sword to its scabbard to rejoin his savior on the makeshift trail back to their creation.

The blood seeped from where the boy's gums were being split. He removed the fingernail from between his teeth so he could swab it into his mouth. He ran it along the hard angle of his cut tongue, then over the slick scar tissue. One of his managers appeared beside him in the doorway of the brothel to hand him a glass of water.

-What a night long,- he smiled at his boss. Hercules grunted. The two of them watched the line of boys and men handing coupons to Jacobo's managers at the brothel across the street. A wife or mother would occasionally emerge from the growing crowd of protesters to drag one away but more customers took their places.

-It is said he does this to get more votes in the election nearing,- the manager leaned against the doorway. -I know that the American has told you to support Jacobo, but this,- he lazily waved his hand at the scene, -This is bad for the business.-

Hercules slid the sharp edge of his tongue against his finger. When it had found the hard angle at the end, he looked at his worker and nodded. The manager turned, snapping his fingers at the others sitting at the table in the front room of Hercules' brothel. The group rose and headed for the door.

The group of managers sauntered out of the whorehouse onto the dusty street, their thumbs locked into their belts or their hands dangling by their sides like electric wires waiting for a charge to jolt through them. The people in the line in front of Jacobo's watched them nervously.

-Gentlemen,- Hercules' second-in-command announced, -We have twice the girls at half the price directly across the street. The ladies most beautiful in all of Mexico. And the pussy,- the boy made a fist with his left hand and attempted to drive his right index finger into the middle of it. It finally broke its way in as one of the other managers made a popping noise with his mouth. The crowd broke out in laughter.

-So come, gentleman,- the manager smiled big. -One quarter off that which is on your coupon!-

The men and boys erupted in cheering. Many from the back of the line ran for the door to Hercules' brothel, the owner standing aside to let them enter while another employee collected money. They lined up for their turn at the girls; Hercules watched as the manager herded them, yelling for certain girls upon hearing preferences. Some of the boys were too young to do anything besides brag about the experience afterwards but they showed the same enthusiasm as the adults.

Out of the corner of his eye, Hercules noticed a steady stream of bodies pouring out of Jacobo's and lining up in the middle of the street. His managers also saw this and planted themselves where they stood. A hush fell over the lines of brothel patrons on both sides as the managers of the two houses stared at each other, their fingers soothing the hilts of knives or tapping against clubs.

Jacobo appeared in the doorway of his whorehouse. Hercules stuck his finger back in his mouth as the older boy joined his ranks.

-Hercules, what is this?- he yelled to the boy in the doorway.

-It is business,- his head manager spat onto the sand. -Not do you live in City Hall yet.-

-I have an agreement with the American, his boy knows that.-

-If you want to live for long, silence yourself.-

Jacobo's managers drew their weapons at the insult, prompting the other side to do the same. Hercules drew his sword as he stepped from the door.

-Talk with your man,- Jacobo pointed a long knife at Hercules. -This is for the election. I need to gain the favor of the people.-

-Not do you have our favor with this,- the manager reached behind his back to pull a massive hammer from the belt that held his pants tight. Hercules now stood with his boys across from Jacobo.

-Then go tell the American the next time you lie with him,- one of Jacobo's security raised one side of his lip in a snarling laugh. He was a newcomer to the town with scars crisscrossing his face like his head had been pushed into a fence of razors. Hercules thrust the conquistador's sword through him, it reappeared out of his back. The newcomer's knees trembled like he was about to fall so Hercules quickly extracted the blade to slice through the meat and tubing of his neck. Blood sprayed those nearby so thick that after only a second, eyes and teeth stood out white against dripping red faces.

The lines of boys stared at the collapsed body for a second like it may suddenly rise back to life. A drop of blood falling from the conquistador's sword into the mouth of the waiting sand caught Jacobo's eye. He pointed his blade at Hercules, -This ends.-

A battle cry rose from both sides as the two groups charged at each other. One of Jacobo's security swung his club at Hercules's head but the boy moved nimbly so the heavy weapon swung inches from his ear. Hercules struck the boy in the gut; the blade went halfway into his body before the knots of intestine and muscle proved too thick for the amount of force behind the blade. Hercules retracted the blade just as Jacobo lunged at him. He blocked the older boy's weapon with the cross guard of the sword, then kicked him hard in the chest. Jacobo flew back, colliding with the ground. Hercules jumped forward to stand over the boy. He raised the sword high; when he swung it down, Jacobo backhanded the air in front of him to keep it from slicing his head open. The blade made contact with his arm and cut down along the bone until the top layer of Jacobo's forearm was separated from his body. It flopped to the ground, the older boy screaming at the cut of meat that had been a piece of him just seconds earlier. An explosion from Jacobo's doorway caused the brawlers and onlookers to suddenly freeze.

-What is this?- Nish's penis was still erect and covered in shiny wetness. He looked at the owners of the two brothels, then at the dead body surrounded by a red halo being sucked into the ground. A few yards away, a second, smaller ring grew from another limp body. Several of the boys whimpered as they clutched their wounds.

-Why do you fight?-

The boys looked at the ground like they'd been caught eating cookies before dinner. Hercules pointed to Nish, then to Jacobo's brothel, then threw his hands up as if to ask his savior how the man could betray his whorehouse.

"I had a coupon," Nish picked his teeth with a slick finger. He addressed the boys, -This is New Texas, not is this Mexico. The rich and the powerful not do they receive the treatment special, nor the friends of the politicians. The guilty are the guilty, and are labeled as such after it is proven. That which passed here will be discovered and the accused will be judged and punished if found guilty.-

The boys looked at each other uneasily. One of the stab victims passed out, falling limp to the ground. Nish continued, -In a society civilized, like the United States, the police are charged with maintaining the peace. The same is true here,- Nish turned to look into the dark brothel. Fatty emerged from the doorway in his underwear. With each step he took, ripples went through his body.

-As you know, this is our Chief of Police,- Nish explained. Fatty raised the simple badge in his hand, his breasts jiggling with the movement. The crowd was mesmerized by the circular motion of the oversized dark nipples. Nish waited until they had settled down before attempting to get everyone's attention again. -All of you are witnesses and go to be questioned now. There will be justice.-

Nish and Hercules sipped on their drinks as they watched the artist painting the mural on the side of City Hall. The history of the town formed on the stone: the gangsters of the past, the arrival of the Americans, independence, the war with the traitors, the emergence of commerce, and the growth and prosperity of the town. And through all of it ran a crystal blue streak of a river, standing in great contrast to the reds of blood and browns of starved bodies. A group of children stood back to watch the painting take shape until their mother yelled at them to turn away from such a horrible scene. Nish laughed at the woman, turning to Hercules, "Makes you wonder how things will go when we're out of here."

The boy didn't respond.

"You hear what I said?" Nish waited until the boy met his stare and nodded. Nish smiled. "Some people just don't understand," he motioned to the woman dragging her children away. The waitress sat down a plate of fried pork with tortillas and beans.

-Thank you,- Nish handed the girl money. He stabbed a chunk of the meat with his fork, speaking to Hercules with a full mouth, "It all comes down to the election. Who we have running for office. That

means not killing off the candidate we're backing, you understand?"
He looked at the boy like a parent to a young child. Hercules touched
his stump tongue against the roof of his mouth and moved it back and
forth to draw an invisible line. He nodded. Nish's eyes wandered back
to the story of the town unfolding under -The History of New Texas-.

"The Romans conquered more of the world than most people at
the time even knew existed, and they ruled it wisely with a democracy.
They brought new technology, medicine and justice to savages who
relied on cruel tradition and ritual," Nish rolled up a tortilla to scoop
beans into.

Hercules's fingers traced the hilt of his sword.

"And then Julius Cesar came along and took control of the senate
because he wanted reforms, the poor to have more of a voice and the
powerful to share their wealth. To accomplish this, he turned Rome
into a dictatorship. This began the downfall of the greatest society on
Earth. Rome eventually became weaker than the barbarians they'd so
easily defeated," Nish made sure to get the crumbled white cheese onto
the tortilla before shoving the whole thing into his mouth. His cheeks
distended as he chewed at the mass of food. When he was halfway
done, he took a drink of agave beer that washed the rest down.

"Business is at the heart of a strong society. Competition is the
free market at its finest," Nish took a bite of the pork. The boy lifted
his chin at the point his savior was making. "But like I said, this isn't
fucking Mexico. You can't take away the competition with the business
end of a sword. If someone's guilty, they'll be punished, no matter who
they are. You have to model things for people, especially the ignorant
who aren't used to justice. If you don't, they'll think everything's built
on bullshit."

Nish cut another piece of meat. The boy's fingers stopped tracing
the hilt of the sword as his hand wrapped around it. "The Romans also
thought it was okay to fuck little boys," Nish laughed, then dropped his
fork. He hit the table with both of his elbows so hard the others in the
restaurant stopped their talking to stare at the naked, bloody American
pulling at his hair. He twitched like he was practicing an imaginary
dance in his head. The boy took his hand from the sword to lay it on the
man's shoulder. Nish stopped. He picked up his fork to take another
bite, "Only boys of lower classes, though. Good and bad are shifting
sand, constantly changing. Only you can be constant; shoot a straight
line and see where it lands when it does."

Hercules took a drink of the liquor in front of him. Loud voices
rumbled somewhere in the distance, tripping down the street until Nish
and Hercules could see a mob at the bottom edge of the market. They
looked at each other; Nish imagined some farmer's dog that had come

back from patrolling the desert with blood on its muzzle or gnawing on the nun's habit. He lifted the pistol and ejected the clip. Cursing himself for not reloading the round he'd fired into the sand earlier, he returned the handgun to its resting place before draining his glass. His boy did the same.

-Justice!- the mob passed the marketplace. Some of the vendors chanted along despite having no idea what was happening. The people at the front of the group had their eyes on City Hall; Nish considered ducking into the darkness of the restaurant. When he realized he hadn't moved, he wondered why but didn't do anything about it. His grandmother's face, he remembered. He showed her film of a game from high school that he got five sacks in; he looked down at his weapon, the clumsy automatic, remembering Bill's words.

One of the heads of the mob spotted him in the shade of the tavern with his boy and pointed him out to the group. If he had to do it over again, he'd have carved his initials into the pistol, Nish thought. Even if it wasn't his to begin with, even if he hadn't picked it out clean and fired the first shot through its pristine barrel, it was his more than most things had been in his life. Hercules grabbed the edge of the table like he was going to use it to propel himself into the mob, only twenty yards away now.

"All the kids at your school are so nice," Nish remembered his mother saying after she'd worked at the supplies cart for lunch. They gave her the candy bars for the cart at the beginning of the week and one night Nish found her on the floor with empty wrappers all around her. She was nearly crying, saying how much she hated herself for eating them but she still shoved them into her mouth. "You can't focus on the negative," Nish said to the boy. Hercules had let his hand fall to the hilt of the sword. "Fear, shame, pity, these are things that do nothing but bring you down. Live a good life."

A bound man was spit up from the group, landing feet away from the table. The mob quieted as Nish casually looked at the group's prisoner, -What is this?-

-This,- a man raised his hand to the sun, turning so his people could hear him. -This is a rapist of the children!-

The mob exploded in curses, sucking in onlookers. Relief washed through Nish so quickly he thought his knees might go weak. Instead, he walked to the accused and bent down in front of him as if inspecting the man for visible signs of guilt. While he did this, he wondered how to handle the situation. The lines of pedophilia had become pretty blurred in the town and rape was always subjective.

-Why do you say this?- Nish looked to the leader.

The man stepped closer; he looked like a grizzled, homeless troll whose eyes had been set on fire. Although he stood a foot away from Nish, he yelled loudly enough for everyone to hear him. -This animal touched my three year old daughter,- he pointed at the accused and the mob erupted again. A rusted can flew from the group, hitting the bound man in the side of the face and leaving a dark brown mark.

-Not do you touch him!- Nish yelled to the mob. -He will be taken into the custody of the police and he will be judged. Where is the policeman?- Nish looked towards City Hall where Fatty usually bounced his rubber ball off the steps. There was a rustling in the mob as the obese boy pushed his way towards the front of the group. -I am here.-

-You joined the lynch mob?- Nish picked his teeth.

Fatty looked at the ground.

Shaking his head, Nish motioned the policeman towards him and the boy waddled over obediently. Nish addressed the group, -The accused is now in custody.-

The members of the mob paused for a second. The leader stuck his chin high in the air as if in disdain of the American and his laws. -We demand the justice! This man not should he be free, he should be dead!- The crowd behind him cheered.

Nish looked at the accused and scratched his ass. The bound man flinched; Nish thought of playing baseball, how he shied away from pitches for some reason. No matter how hard he tried, there was a spring inside his brain that caused him to recoil at the last second. As much as his father looked down on the American pastime, he didn't like seeing his son show weakness. At home, Nish would punch himself in the cheekbone and drop his body against the cement stairs that led down to the pool area of the backyard, telling himself a ball couldn't hurt more than that. But at home plate, he continued to shame himself. -Not is he free. We will have a prison built in four hours. Until then, he will be locked in a closet in City Hall. You can guard the door along with the policeman if you want.-

-He raped a toddler!- someone shouted from the center of the group, the rest of them blurted their immediate approval.

Nish dug deep into his ass. -Exactly what passed?-

The leader held up his fist and squeezed like it contained a rotten orange, -He touched my little daughter.-

-Where?-

The leader recoiled in disgust.

-I need actions exact. Not can you prosecute someone with information vague.-

The man's mouth turned in on itself like he'd just tasted something sour. He neared the American, whispering into his ear, -The vagina.-

Nish cracked his neck, -The trial will be tomorrow. But for now, he is in the custody of the police.-

-Kill him!- someone in the mob screamed. Others quickly joined in. -The witnesses should report to the policeman for to give their statements. There will be a trial.-

-We know he is guilty,- the leader cried indignantly.

-Then you will not have a problem with getting a conviction tomorrow,- Nish picked his teeth; the comfort spread from the scarred gum into his brain. -The more horrible the crime a man is accused of, the more people believe he is guilty, regardless of the evidence. Possibly I accuse you of murdering a baby,- Nish spoke calmly to the leader. -I go through the streets dragging you behind me, I hit you when you try to defend yourself.-

-We demand justice,- the leader looked frustrated.

-So you want to throw him into the river tied up? If he drowns, he is innocent; if he flies away, he is a witch. Yes?-

The members of the mob turned to each other, whispering that they hadn't even considered witchcraft could somehow have been at play. Nish spoke loudly over them, -The policeman is locking up the accused. If anyone tries to hurt either of them or stand in the way of the justice, I will shoot them.- He pulled the pistol, his hand floating through targets. It finally settled on a bird picking at pieces of corn next to a merchant's stall. He aimed and squeezed off a round. The explosion from the gun had the intended effect on the animal and the crowd. -Tomorrow at sunrise, the trial.-

He motioned for Fatty to take the man to City Hall. The mob's members grit their teeth at the accused. When he'd entered the old church and their cursing and death threats had died down, they dissipated back into regular townspeople.

The newly built jail house, a shack constructed around a metal pole driven deep into the earth, sat to the side of City Hall, dwarfed by the larger building. Hercules lulled the sword to sleep while he waited for his savior. The sauce from Fatty's chicken taco dripped onto the shirt stretched over his ripe belly. He looked up from his meal to Hercules, -Want some?-

The boy stopped moving the sword; his fingernails tapped on the hilt as if in contemplation.

"Little Hercules," Nish said quietly from behind the boy.

Hercules turned to acknowledge his savior. Fatty stood at attention, still holding the taco. Nish looked at him for a second, then waved him back down to his chair.

"I don't see anyway to get around it," he shook his head in quick, small motions like a character slightly nodding in a movie being watched in fast forward. "It just makes me fucking sick." Hercules shifted his weight from one foot to the other. "There's no way this man will ever get a fair trial in this town. I've been hearing people all over talking and everyone's out for his blood," Nish scratched the sand in his hair. The last time he'd gotten it cut, he'd gone out for chicken fried steak with John afterwards. He turned to Fatty, -You must let him go.-

The jaws of both boys dropped.

-Do it tonight when not is there anyone around, after the moon has reached it height,- Nish used his fingernail to slice into the flesh that connected his earlobe to his head. -You will say he escaped. The jail is new, it is possible. You fell asleep,- Nish nodded in fast forward. -Then you resign.- He grit his teeth, "I'm not going to have the blood of innocent people on my hands. Mob rule, dangerous fucking territory."

Hercules looked at the jail that could become his home depending on the outcome of the witnesses gathered earlier in the day. He spit for both to see.

Nish crossed his arms, "I hate doing this but there's no other way this can go down. It may seem like it would be best for the town to have a trial, them getting what they see as justice, but they don't know," Nish spoke to convince the boy and himself. "It's actually worse, you understand?"

Hercules looked at the man and stuck his finger deep into his teeth. Fatty sat his taco to the side and mimicked him, putting his own chunky digit in his mouth to suck the sauce off. Hercules looked at the prisoner, passed out and discolored plainly enough to see even in the moonlight, then up at the side of the building. Nish joined the group, sticking a finger in his teeth to make a threesome. "You and I are out of here in just a few days, regardless."

Hercules nodded and walked away.

-Not do you fuck this up,- Nish turned to Fatty. The policeman nodded, sucking the last of the taco juice from his finger.

The accused man fell. The needles of a cactus on the ground jumped out at him, sticking to his arm. He pulled himself up to continue stumbling towards the silhouette of the mountains in the distance as fast as his weary legs could take him. Something moved in the sand in his path.

He fell again, this time hitting thorns and rock. He coughed; blood came up from deep inside of him, rattling around where it wasn't supposed to be. He looked up at the sky like the saddest story in the world had been written on its slate in stars. The figure above him extended a hand.

DAY 23

The sun streamed through the window onto Nish's eyelids. He squinted to find the illuminated dust floating against gravity. The silence outside, combined with the buzzing in his head, lured him back into unconsciousness.

Dave clutched grandmother's hand as they neared the corpse. Nish noticed his brother had taken off his bracelet with the Sanskrit their father had given him after his last trip to India. Nish's mom patted him on the back, trying her best to raise the sides of her mouth.

They reached the body at the end of the aisle. "Oh my," grandmother frowned, lifting the handkerchief to her trembling mouth. She and Dave stood over the body for a moment before she sat down in the front pew of the empty church to cry softly. Nish and his mother took their turn. The boy stood on his tiptoes to see into the casket. His grandfather looked like he was wearing makeup or was made of wax like the people in the museum his class had gone to. He noticed the orange pin on the lapel of his suit; he'd asked his grandfather when he was younger if he could wear the old man's long orange ribbons he'd seen in the pictures. His grandfather's face had turned red and he walked silently out of the room. But he was always doing that, Nish thought. He reached his hand out to touch the dead man's face but his mother slapped it down.

"No," she scolded, looking at her son like she was trying to figure something out. They sat in the pew with grandmother and Dave, Nish's father joining them as the church filled up. The preacher said his piece and the casket was closed. The men picked it up to carry the corpse to the hearse. Nish wondered what it would be like to carry the body. Dead weight, he thought and smiled. His father looked down at him and smiled back, patting the boy on the head.

Grandmother held Dave's hand until they had stepped out of the church. Even outside she kept him close as she shook hands with her dead husband's friends and relatives. She introduced Dave to them and they commented on what a nice young man he looked like. Nish stood behind his brother, waiting for an introduction that he occasionally got if grandmother noticed. One man stuck his hands in his pockets when she tried to introduce him to Nish.

"He takes after the father," the man smiled politely to grandmother. She pursed her lips, raising the sides of her mouth. Nish watched the man; he didn't shake hands with anyone. In class, they'd learned about germs, how some people don't shake hands because of them. His teacher had said that in some countries, they bow. Nish imagined a place where everyone was dressed differently like people in movies. He dreamt of traveling the world. That night, he took off his pants to walk through the house, his hairless body exposed and his penis erect. Grandmother's mouth turned into a perfect circle that she quickly hid while his mother scolded him again. Dad just stuck a fingernail between his teeth while he watched his son, removing it only to take sips of his drink.

Little Hercules stood like the rest of the townspeople, silent and staring at the once open area at the top of the square. The naked children with their knife belts, the merchants, the boys at the tavern with their hands frozen around their drinks, the newly pubescent whores on break, all with their mouths open. A young boy on the steps of the church scratched his arm and people looked at him because the movement seemed so out of place, then turned quickly back to the oversized, emaciated wolf with its midget interpreter standing among the mounds of corpses. The bodies were mangled and rotted like the earth had started digesting them before vomiting them back up.

The wolf growled low in its strange speech; the interpreter yelled out his demand again, -The leader of the village.-

Hercules walked slowly to the opening, the hilt of the conquistador sword under his palm. The wolf turned to him on its hind legs, the bundle of sharp sticks wrapped in tanned leather that comprised its body becoming more visible. The eyes of the animal had been eaten out of their sockets by vultures. The boy let out a roar, tapping his finger on the hilt of the sword, slow at first and then gaining momentum. The wolf kept its dead stare.

A woman pushed her way through the people circled around the scene, -He is the Vice Mayor Interim, the boy of the American,- she spat out the last word and several people in the crowd grunted approval of her gesture. The animal raised a claw, the fur burnt from it, to grab its top row of teeth. It lifted until the jaw broke from the rest of its body, its hollow eye sockets looking up to the sun. Its head cracked further backwards until it hung off its own spine to reveal another, slightly more human animal underneath.

-Thanks to God! Much thanks to God!- the woman lifted her legs to step over the corpses. -We have been waiting for you,- she knelt at the wolf's feet. The consistency of the crowd changed, people either moving forward or melting behind those who stepped closer to the priest. Those who neared him filled in the gaps between the bodies left on the ground.

A middle-aged woman with short gray hair that framed her face like a kerchief addressed the figure. -It has been horrible, sir. These bastards, the American and his boy,- she pointed to Hercules. -They have transformed people good into prostitutes and alcoholics.-

-Is true,- a man kneeling between the naked corpses of two boys cried out. -And not can we use the church for to worship. The American has taken it as his home.-

-Is a man without God, the American,- cried another woman. -He tortures that young man,- she pointed to a body partially buried under the corpses, guessing it was the Killer. -And he pays the painters to put pornography on the walls of the buildings for all to see.-

The priest eyed the bodies at his feet, living and dead. He growled something in his strange tongue. -My people,- the tiny interpreter shouted in his childlike voice. -It is a mistake. No man would do things such as this.- The priest lifted his head to the sky; Hercules tapped his teeth at the exposed throat. The wolf closed his eyes to breathe in deeply, then looked back at the group with his exhale and spoke. -You have been through so much,- the interpreter translated the guttural noises. -Allow yourselves to feel the sympathy and the forgiveness for every man. Assume they have acted in the interest best of the people and not of the greed, under the influence of the devil.-

The kneeling looked at their spiritual leader, their fists clenched around pieces of rotting flesh, their teeth grinding, their eyes filled with tears. They screamed to the Virgin of Guadalupe of her kindness for bringing the man of her word. But one man didn't scream out, he pointed at Hercules.

-Not can you forgive some things,- his finger trembled. -Both of my daughters work for that boy, spreading their legs for him to make money,- he choked on his words. -Not can you forgive the treatment of the immigrants to this town. How they use us like slaves. They take our daughters and turn them into prostitutes for their whorehouses, take our sons and turn them into soldiers for their wars.-

-Then leave,- Nish stood at the front door of what was once the church, his naked body covered in grease. The dark skeleton of the priest turned to find the American scratching the mound of pubic hair above his erect penis and drinking agave beer straight from the pitcher. A teenage girl scampered out from behind him, freezing when she saw the mauled flesh and exposed bone of the corpses. She wretched and, trying to hold onto Nish for support, slipped down his greasy arm to fall hard on the stairs. After Nish had helped her back up using his gun strap, he looked to Hercules. "Who's the king of the wild over here?"

The boy moaned his disapproval of the figure. The priest turned to face the American, growling in his foreign tongue. Nish wondered how such a low voice could come from the man's gaunt frame; he must be hollow inside, he nodded his head, the red man taking aim. The interpreter translated in his high whine, -I am a priest traveling, a man simple.-

The wolf towered over the townspeople. Nish figured he was probably six foot three or four, slightly taller than himself and a physical anomaly among the rural Mexicans. His face was long and hairless with skin stretched tight over his jaw and neck so his Adam's apple stuck out a good inch. When he swallowed, Nish's eye was drawn towards the bobbing sphere; it reminded him of the film in science class that showed how the human body worked, all right there on display. The man's wild hair blended with the giant black wolf skin that covered his body. The animal was too large to have come from this starved wasteland, Nish picked his teeth.

"They didn't bury them deep enough, animals got to them," he pointed at the bodies.

Hercules nodded.

"Have some laborers do the job right this time, six feet down. Those little kids are going to have to find something else to eat besides vulture," Nish put his arm around the young whore. "Shit's diseased anyway."

Hercules snapped his fingers at the city workers in the crowd as Nish redistributed the grease on his body, spending an inordinate amount of time on the groin area. The boy motioned for the corpses to be taken to the desert. The workers stayed where they were, glancing at the priest for a sign.

"You want to build a church, feel free," Nish put on the finishing touches. "We've got some of the best carpenters in Mexico." He waited to see if the man spoke English.

The interpreter raised his chin in defiance of the language. The priest growled. -I am appreciative of your hospitality,- the interpreter finished his sentence with a grandiose hand gesture that made Nish think he was about to fly away. Instead, the little man followed his master back into the heart of the crowd standing in front of the path to the river. The hesitant workers whispered amongst each other, finally deciding to start the long task of reburying the corpses.

-The drinks at my bar are half price until the sundown,- Nish announced, expecting more cheering than what he got. He laughed, recognizing some of the men kneeling at the wolf's feet. The priest growled and the translator instructed those on their knees to rise. The woman with the framed face led the group to her land on the river where the priest was already headed.

Jacobo watched the crowd disperse from his table at the tavern. He leaned forward to scrape the strip of fried tortilla across the plate of melted cheese, the bandaged arm in his lap making the simple task much more difficult. When he looked up, the American's boy was standing at his table. Jacobo leaned back calmly to take the knife from his belt and stab it into the table. Leaving his hand on the hilt, he took his time chewing. Hercules took a step forward; Jacobo pulled the blade out of the wood and tried to stand but hit his injured arm against the bottom of the table. He doubled over in pain. Hercules pulled out the chair opposite the older boy to sit down.

-What do you want?- Jacobo asked into his chest, his face red.

Hercules motioned for the waitress to bring him over a glass of agave beer and waited for Jacobo to stop squinting his eyes and grinding his teeth. When the injured boy looked up from his bandages, Hercules put his hands out to show nothing was in them and extended one across the table. The older boy eyed it suspiciously. Hercules ran his tongue on the roof of his mouth, letting the hand fall as he looked around the room. He grunted, pointing at a poster for the election, then at the top of the square. Jacobo leaned forward in contemplation. When he sat back again, the American's boy had laid a handful of heirloom jewelry on the table in front of him and was pointing at the injured arm.

The older boy replaced his knife in its sheath. -A wolf that has more hunger,- he positioned himself in the chair to avoid another embarrassing scene, his arm this time resting on the table. -The past is the past. Like says the American, 'that which is important is that which you do next.' No?- Jacobo extended his good hand and Hercules took it in his.

-Cheese melted?- Jacobo pushed the plate towards the boy as the waitress appeared but Hercules paid for his drink and returned to his own table. As soon as he'd left, Jacobo gritted his teeth in pain and gulped down the last of his liquor.

"You know in Burma, they advertise their virgins in official tourist guides. Girls as young as twelve," Nish put his arms behind his head. The young prostitute rolled off the cot, then squatted over the bowl on the floor. "They send young boys and girls over to Thailand as fast as the Thais and the foreigners can have sex with them. And then, after they're too old to pass as virgins, they're stuck there. Burma won't even take them back since most of them are ethnic minorities. The government shuts the door on them." Nish wiggled his toes, jolts of pleasure running up to his beaming face. He remembered once in college when a girl got up to go to the bathroom after they were finished and he opened a cold beer. He'd felt like a king. "So you see, you got it pretty good," he smiled at the girl. She didn't acknowledge what the American was saying.

-Much thanks,- Nish tipped the female bartender, too young to sell herself yet. He held up the glass of agave liquor. "In a country where they eat nothing but corn, you figure they'd have whiskey." Hercules studied his cards. The bet went to him and he raised. Nish did the same, one other boy stayed in and the rest folded. They revealed their hands.

"Shit!" Nish threw his arms up in mock anger. "Almost had it." He patted Hercules on the back as the boy raked his money from the center of the table. "I'll tell you Herc, this is what it's all about." He smiled at his protégé, then looked at the managers as he rose from the table, -Good. I go to the bar for to prepare the party for Jacobo tonight.-

The smiles dissolved off the faces of the boys. Nish picked up his cup, -You will all be there. We need as many supporters as possible, the election is tomorrow.-

Hercules moaned, still looking at his winnings, and the boys nodded.

-Good.- Nish took a step to find the ground shifting under him. He grabbed the back of the chair for balance, then straightened up and walked out the front door of the brothel.

The mother saw the American emerge from the whorehouse, covered in sand and blood like the dug up corpses from that morning but twice as large and reanimated. She stormed past the children huddled around scraps of food in their lean-to's, past the men and boys being served drinks in line by the girls who had yet to have their first period, up to the doorway of the brothel.

-Your time is over,- she spat at the naked man, moving her hand to the cleaver's hiding spot in the back of her pants.

-Go,- Nish shooed her away like one of the street urchins begging for money.

She wrapped her hand around the handle, -The priest has come to free his people.- She motioned to the doorway behind him.

-Go, bitch crazy,- Nish cracked his neck. The church's bell tower rose in the distance above the homes and stores of town. He squinted; he could have sworn he saw something up there. He felt a pressure in his stomach.

The woman retracted her fist holding the blunt wooden cross, her other hand sliding the cleaver slowly out of its hiding place. Nish pushed her in the chest, "What the fuck you doing punching people? Get the fuck out of here!"

She quickly pulled the knife, raising it above her in head in one swift motion. The moment froze; with her stupid expression and the cleaver in her hand, Nish thought she looked like something out of an old horror movie. He pulled his pistol and shot her in the face. He was impressed with the accuracy, given how quickly he'd done it, and felt a good satisfaction inside. The woman's head jerked back as thousands of red paratroopers were ejected from her skull; they floated downwards slowly to meet the body that had already hit the sand.

At first, the street was more silent than it had been all day: no managers hawking prostitutes, no chanting from the protesters, nothing. Then it was filled with the chaotic noise of cursing and screaming. Hercules and his managers ran out to find Nish holstering his pistol. The man stretched like he'd just woken up. The boy moaned an inquiry but his savior waved away the concern, "Self-defense."

Hercules bounced his hand an inch off his scalded head, looking at the man as if his brain was opening up like the woman's on the ground. One of his managers said something to him but he didn't turn away.

-The people not will this please,- the manager said again.

-It was self-defense,- Nish yawned. -There are witnesses.- He motioned to the men in the street. Some had wandered out of their lines, huddling around the fresh corpse.

-Murderer,- one of them said the word like he was reading it in a book and didn't understand what it meant. He looked to the others for a definition. A couple of them nodded their heads until it became infectious and all those standing around the dead woman were in agreement, -Murderer so barbarous.- They looked to the American, large and naked, as he stared at something past them in the distance.

One of them pointed to yell his accusation, -You murdered this woman,- then raised his head, -Police! Police!- like the more frantic he acted, the faster the law would come.

Nish put a hand to his eyes but still couldn't make it out exactly. He lowered it to wave the men off, -Not am I a murderer. She attacked me, you saw it.-

-I saw you shoot this woman in front of my eyes,- the accuser shot back. Another stepped up, -He must to stand trial.- The others nodded their agreement. -He must to stand trial!- the accuser yelled for the entire street to hear. The more vocal some people were in their agreement, the quicker others melted into the scraps of wood and trash of the shantytown. The protesters, initially frozen by the unfamiliar explosion, came running to find the dead woman's head draining its insides into the sand. They saw the crowd pointing at the American and calling him a murderer and joined in.

Nish dug a fingernail between his teeth as he squared off to the crowd. -She attacked me,- he pointed to where the cleaver had fallen but it had disappeared. -It was self-defense.-

-He must to stand trial,- the accuser stood tall. -It is that which he said yesterday, is the law.-

Nish pulled the fingernail from his teeth to let his hand fall, it hit the pistol on his hip. The accuser shuffled backwards a half step in a way that made Nish think the man didn't realize he had moved at all.

-You are correct,- Nish spoke to the largening crowd in the street. -Is an accusation serious with enough proof to have a trial. The accused should be judged,- he removed the pistol to hand over to Hercules. -I will report to the station of the police,- he walked past the stunned accuser through the suddenly silent crowd all the way to the jail next to City Hall.

"That's why there will never be a black president," dad shooed away the idea. "The blacks may talk like they want that but they don't know what they're saying. You think they want to be held to the same standards as everyone else? As soon as they're equal, they can't bitch and moan anymore, and you know how much they love excuses."

Nish shifted his weight on the couch and kept his eyes on the television. After another sip of gin, his father continued, "Our society doesn't expect as much of blacks as they do of other people. And the truth is, that hurts them more than anything else. And when you play up accomplishments in certain fields, that just stereotypes them."

"How do you mean?" Nish regretting his curiosity getting the better of him; better to just the let the train of thought die out, he thought.

Upon realizing he had an attentive audience, his father became livelier. He put down his drink to crack his knuckles, as if what he was about to say was going to have some sort of physical impact on him that he needed to ready himself for. "You may think you're doing black people a favor by saying they give a lot of cultural contributions but it also gives you an excuse to expect less of them to become doctors and lawyers. And if you don't expect that, then see how willing you are for your tax dollars to go to educating kids in the inner city."

Nish wondered where the dog was. He hadn't heard it since dinner; its tiny collar jingling lightly wherever it pranced. He cracked his own knuckles.

"Whenever there's a 'more than', there's also a 'less than'. That's what racism is." Back in that fucking bedroom with his mom. He remembered when he'd accidentally kicked it so that it flew in the air like in the movies. It was so light that he felt like a giant. "But blacks like their cocks stroked like anyone else. Look at jazz: how many guitars and trumpets and saxophones did they have back in Africa before they were brought over here? It's like if I put a different kind of cheese on a pizza and then said I invented Italian food. But they'll swear to God they were the sole inventors of jazz, blues, anything that's ever involved a black person. Black man lays a brick and suddenly he's an architect."

The dog strutted from around the corner in front of his view. Nish reached out, his stomach growling louder than the animal ever could. His father grabbed his hand and met his gaze like he was going to start suddenly crying. Nish lowered his eyes and beat his other hand into forehead. -It is too tight,- he yelled through the window of the jail shack, rubbing the skin around the restraint on his leg. The bastard looked in the direction of the American punching his own face but acted like the wind must have been talking to him. Nish wasn't sure who had reinstated the obese child but he was going to make sure Hercules, acting interim mayor, dealt with the situation as soon as he finished setting up for Jacobo's party.

A vague sound in the distance distilled into voices singing a religious song. The wolf emerged from the square with a throng of followers. Two of them were carrying a cot with the Killer on it; Nish figured they must have fished him out of the corpses the workers were burying. He could see the boy was still barely alive, his head rolling back and forth in pain. The wolf pointed a claw at City Hall and the two carried the gangster to the hospital.

Nish waved out the window towards the tavern, catching the eye of a patron. The man pointed Hercules in the direction of the jail. "Bring Jacobo over here," Nish shouted over the singing. Hercules moaned to the candidate. The two boys walked to the jail shack, Jacobo losing his balance but catching himself before falling face first into the hard sand. A weight made itself known deep in Nish's stomach; he wondered how the bathroom situation worked in jail.

-Prisoner political,- Jacobo smiled drunkenly. There was a fresh bandage on his arm; Nish figured the pain was too much for him to bear sober.

-Not is this the time for liquor. You need to talk to the people tonight about the dangers of the church, its influence growing. Tell them Guillermo is the pawn of the priest, remind them that the church has taken from them and not given them anything back but shame.-

Fatty picked up his rifle to check out the scene at the shack; Nish spoke more hurriedly, -The bastards original not will they forget how things were before. Tell the landowners of the taxes the church imposes, those with something to lose will lose it.-

-Enough,- Fatty stuck his chest out, the rifle pointed at the ground. -I need to go to the mass of Saturday with the priest, not can there be visitors at this hour.-

-Who put you in charge? You resigned,- Nish gripped the wood of the shack's window.

-The people,- Fatty smiled, putting his arms out as if the air had given him back his old title. -Is a democracy, no?-

-Not is that how it works.- Nish looked to Hercules, "Start the party. Alcohol and free food. Tell the musicians to start playing now."

Fatty frowned at the English. -That is all,- he strained to lift a piece of wood leaning against the base of the shack.

"Start it now," Nish said again to Hercules. "We can't lose-" the wood covered the shack's window. Nish stabbed a fingernail into his teeth and sat in the sand. His blood pulsed around the shackle on his leg. The window opened suddenly, -American,- Fatty shouted into the tiny room. -If you see the nun, tell her we are all down at the river. She will see us.- The wood was replaced, plunging the jail into darkness and making the guard's order even more pointless.

Hercules handed the money to the musician. The procession, with Guillermo and the priest at the front, was moving slowly past the tavern singing a song about the Promised Land. The band members each took their share. -Not is it Christian to let our children starve,- the guitarist looked to others who nodded and lifted their instruments.

DAY 24

"Why do you think they call them World Champions when they've won the Super Bowl, but there are only teams from the U.S. in the league?" John asked.

"Huh," Nish pursed his lips together. "To be honest, I never thought about it before." They swung the gagged man backwards. "One... two...three..." They flung him into the deep grave with the waiting rattlesnakes. The first one struck him in the face.

"Ouch," Nish laughed, dusting off his hands.

Guillermo watched the debate platforms being erected as he took a drink of the cool water from his jug. He'd given as much of it to his older brother as the boy would take but it didn't seem like he was able to keep anything down; Guillermo frowned pensively at the sand until a woman his mother's age interrupted his thoughts.

-Sir,- she held out a wrap. -Burnt milk,- she motioned for the mayoral candidate to take it. He graciously accepted. She watched while he took a bite of the sweet, her mouth open like she was instructing him on what to do.

-How delicious,- he smiled.

She beamed back at him, pointing a hardened finger to the face painted on one of the podiums. -Not is as handsome as in person,- she blushed.

-Thank you. Come to the debate and the election, please. We need the support of everyone.-

-Of course, not would I miss it,- she gave his muscular arm a squeeze and cooed, then turned to walk back to her home.

Something wet hit Guillermo's forehead. He looked up but didn't see a cloud in the sky. -Huh,- he took another bite of the caramel.

The feet of the red man had turned into claws that dug into Nish's skull, locking down into the flesh and bone so he wouldn't slide off.

232

With sobriety stretching his brain so every nook and cranny could have the moisture sucked from it, the man had returned with his talons.

-Water,- Nish yelled for the guard from the dirt floor of the jail shack. -I need water.-

Fatty's faced appeared in the opening, -Water, sir?-

-Not can you hear, Fatty? I need water. Now.-

Fatty disappeared.

After half an hour of yelling, Fatty showed up at the window again. -You need the water? Still?-

-Please,- Nish cradled his head.

Fatty snapped his fingers at the American, who looked up to find the guard holding a cup. Nish stood slowly, balancing himself against the pole he was anchored to.

-Take it,- Fatty pushed the cup forward.

Nish did so carefully. The water was hot, he figured the guard must have let it sit in the sun, but he gulped it down greedily. -Thank you,- he burped.

-Of nothing,- Fatty grabbed it back to return to his post.

Nish rested his hands on the opening, looking out at the one-man platforms with the podiums. -You are taking the job very seriously now. Are here more often than the whorehouse.- He picked the dried blood under his earlobe to reopen the self-inflicted wound. Fatty didn't turn towards him.

-There is breakfast?- Nish felt the red man pull the reins to the side; his head swooned and he fell to his knees to vomit. Just like before school, he thought. Drinking anything but his dad's flavored gin, throwing up in the tight space of the shower and having to carry it in soupy clumps to the toilet because it was too chunky to go down the drain. The heat in his head while he sat in class, at least then he had an air conditioner. He spit the last of the acid into the sand.

-Not would you be able to keep it down anyway,- Fatty chuckled.

-More water. Please.-

-I just gave you water,- the guard leaned back in his chair, propping his hat over his eyes. Nish figured the fat boy had seen old men do it when they were still in the town years ago.

-Where is the nun? Not have I seen her in two days,- Nish watched the boy.

-Not do I know,- Fatty didn't visibly react so Nish continued.

-Did you notice how when the wolf arrived, she disappeared?-

Fatty scratched his neck. The carpenters shouted their approval of the podiums in front of City Hall.

-You are going to hold my hand while I vote?- Nish wanted to rip the skeleton out of the middle of the fat boy and watch the lard and skin puddle around his feet.

-Not will you vote,- the guard didn't open his eyes while he lifted the glass to his lips.

-What?-

-The prisoners not are they allowed to vote.-

-Who said this?-

Fatty was too busy drinking to speak.

-Not do you have the authority to do this!-

-I am a policeman,- he shrugged. Nish wanted to bite into the boy's cheek to look at the layers. Whenever he'd tried to see a good cross section of human, the red always got in the way faster than he could clear it. "Whatever's bad for you is always fun," his father said and Nish agreed. Like life's always out to fuck you. -You resigned.-

-Not did I do it, and I am in charge of the jail. The prisoners not can they vote.-

Nish tried to soothe the red man, -Not have I been convicted of nothing. In the United States, this means I can vote.-

-Not is this the United States,- Fatty smacked his lips together, pretending to sleep. Nish watched him closely: the fat brown nipples, resting on soft mounds of breasts, pressed against the tight shirt. Nish ran his tongue over his teeth to taste a film of vomit and stomach acid coating them.

"Out of place," John moved a full-sized wardrobe to expose the map of the oil fields. It was bolted to the wall in hard plastic. Pointless, Nish thought, considering someone could just take a picture.

"Best if we could just take a picture," John scratched his head.

"Bill said he needs the actual map," Nish restated his orders. The giant started on the bolts. Nish flipped open the hunting knife from the back of his pants, the sharpened blade shone in the office light. He hesitated.

"I got this, man," John kept his eyes on his work.

"Thanks," Nish closed the blade and sat on the ground. His first impulse was to take off his gloves to let his hands breathe but paranoia kept them on. He leaned back against the oak desk. The promise of wings at the bar later that night made him hungry, the thought of getting drunk filled him with a sense of hope. A cool breeze fell over him even though the air conditioning was off. He smiled at the ceiling, "You have any crazy dreams?"

John pulled one of the bolts out of the wall. "I..." the giant hesitated. "Never mind, it's stupid."

"Don't say that. A lot of great ideas were called stupid."

The giant looked at his friend timidly, "I want to own a batter restaurant."

Nish's eyes fell from the ceiling, "What do you mean?"

"A restaurant that serves only batter," John went back to his work to hide the fact he was blushing. "You know, like cornbread batter, cookie batter, brownie batter."

Nish didn't say anything. The giant turned around to face him, "Because when you're cooking something, everyone wants to lick the bowl you're making the batter in. I know I'd rather have cake batter than eat a cake. Granted my momma used to make cakes drier than an eighty-year-old nun in the desert but I seen lots of folks who love batter." His face turned a darker shade of red and he turned to the map again. "Just a thought."

Nish sat rubbing his chin. "That's a fucking awesome idea."

"Really?" John looked back at his partner.

"Of course, I love batter," Nish nodded. The giant grinned ear to ear as he removed the second bolt. Nish ran his gloved hands over the desk; he loved that a thin piece of leather gave him total immunity.

"What about you?" John asked over his shoulder.

Nish opened a drawer, "Dreams?" He closed it, his eyes drifting to the rolodex on the desk's surface. "I always wanted to be a consultant. You know, someone who travels to far away places and gives people advice. An idea guy," Nish flipped through the numbers. "Get taken out to dinner. I figure I could come into a situation, take a look at something and come up with an innovative answer. I do that all the time now," his fingers suddenly stopped moving. "This asshole kept Snake Bait's contact info right on his fucking desk."

Both men looked at each other, then laughed as Nish took the number out. He didn't want to put it in his pocket; if the man who worked in the office was stupid enough to link himself to the guy they'd buried that morning, he figured there were probably plenty of other tracks that would be sniffed out, if it got to that. "Fuck it," he stuck the number in his jeans. He'd burn it later.

Pushing back the man's chair, Nish sat down and stretched. The ceiling looked old. You can really tell how old a place is by the ceilings and the floors, he thought. "You ever notice all midgets look alike?"

"Yep."

"I'm not just saying because they're all short, I mean their facial features," Nish clarified.

"I knew what you meant."

Nish shook his head, "Fucking freaky." The third bolt was out. "Did you know that Peter the Great of Russia had an army of midgets and an army of giants? Of course, back then a giant was anyone six foot or taller."

"Huh."

"It was either Peter or Ivan, fucking Russian history," Nish caught a crack in the ceiling and followed it. "Think of you back then," he laughed, "Scaring the shit out of people."

"We'd be running things alright," John did the same. Nish watched the crack escape from the room into a wall. A noise came from down the hallway. Both men froze. It got louder and Nish leaned forward to vomit again until he couldn't hear anything but the cheering and hisses for a second. Despite all his hopes, an old woman appeared at the door. He grabbed her by the throat, pushing his revolver hard into her skull.

"Fuck!" he yelled into her face. She tried to scream but the noise croaked out through Nish's fingers. "What are you doing here?"

She broke down; when her eyes opened between sobs, Nish could see her looking in two different directions at the same time. Sneaky bitch, he thought. He wished the pistol would turn into a spoon so he could scoop out the walleye. He imagined it rolling on the ground, unable to stop because of the same wobbliness that wouldn't allow it to face straight forward out of her skull.

"Finish taking that thing off," Nish ordered to John.

"I'm just a secretary," the woman bawled. He forced her head down like he was making her touch her toes, then hit her in the back of the head just like Bill had taught him. She fell limp. He scratched his head and when he looked back up there was a plate of food in front of him. He snatched it before anyone else could lay a hand on it.

-Courtesy of your new mayor,- Fatty looked down from the window, then retracted his head, the inside of the cell painted in vomit. Nish shoveled the beans and old, leathery tortilla strips into his mouth. The chants for Guillermo made it hard for him to hear himself chew; he could almost feel the wolf crawling along on all fours in front of the masses.

The fog of unsettled sand sat on the town so thick some people tied kerchiefs around their necks so they wouldn't inhale the dust. The dancing and singing had died down after Guillermo stood on his platform, the priest at his side, and announced there would be a celebration that night. Jacobo cradled his half-arm. He spit into the dust, then walked to Hercules' brothel.

A young girl with a pitcher in her hand noticed him first but didn't know any better than to offer him a drink. The managers jolted upwards, pulling their swords as Hercules watched from his seat at the table.

-Calm yourselves,- Jacobo put his hands up.

-Your blade,- one of the managers motioned with his sword for Jacobo to throw down his weapon.

-Not it do I have,- he looked to Hercules. The boy moaned for his employees to let the older boy pass. The managers lowered their swords hesitantly as Jacobo walked through them to the table where their boss sat dividing money and other forms of payment into different piles.

-Were you at the election?-

Hercules nodded as he continued to sort the day's profits. Jacobo exhaled loudly like he was making a point of being heard. The managers crept back to their seats at the table or the bar, keeping their eyes on the older boy.

-My mother,- Jacobo raised his head towards the ceiling as if in thought. -Before you and the American came, before the Killer, when there were people in this town, I had a mother. An alcoholic. She went to the bar and drank all our money, then had to find the men and drink all their money, also. Was more easy to drink than to raise her children.-

Hercules continued counting, giving out little grunts when he'd finished with a pile and moved on to the next one. Jacobo continued, -Then that priest came to the town, through his man little he told the people of a place in the mountains. A place where he had seen the Virgin of Guadalupe smiling down on him. She told him to bring those who wanted the salvation and there they would find it. My mother gave him the last of that which my family had and she left.-

Hercules finished his counting and looked up at Jacobo, who had now refocused on the ceiling. -Was four years ago. I had a brother and a sister who have died,- his eyes met the stare of Hercules. -My mother was a whore who believed in magic and superstition. She thought she could buy the salvation, and her family she impoverished more than it already was. The priest has returned to bring his paradise Christian to this town. The people here are stupid, they will do what he says as long as he continues to blame others for their poverty. We are the others.-

One of the managers propped his foot on the table to cut his toenails with a small knife. The blade slipped, the red ran down the side of his foot to the wood. Jacobo watched it pool, -And that is only a knife small,- he turned to Hercules. -Imagine what a sword could do.-

Hercules pulled the Toledo blade from its scabbard. He propped his own foot onto the table, then grabbed a large patch of dead skin to slice it off. He shrugged; the managers laughed.

Jacobo sat erect, -So not will you help?-

Hercules looked at the sword in one hand and the dead piece of him in the other.

-You could rid the town of this disease with one strike,- Jacobo leaned in.

-Not can you kill the wolf,- one of the managers spat.

-This I have heard also. But even if it is true, you can kill his translator. No one here understands the language of those indigenous to the mountain. Not could the priest turn people to his side,- Jacobo didn't take his eyes from Hercules. -Or you could watch everything which you have built, everything for which you have shed blood, be destroyed by a tyrant.-

Hercules looked at the wall like he could see through it past the slums and wealthy neighborhood and market all the way to the ballot box in City Hall. His hand gripped the sword tighter. He bit down, the sharp corners of his teeth pressing against one another. His gaze moved to the jail shack holding his savior and he roared in frustration. He flipped the sword in his hand, stabbing it into the ground so quickly Jacobo didn't react until it was almost a foot into the earth. He checked all his parts as Hercules shook his head.

-Fine,- the older boy stood, turning to the managers. -Your boss and the American will be gone in less than a week and you will inherit that which has happened today.-

The eyes of the managers followed him out the door. One spoke up, -Son of a bitch crazy.-

-But he is right about the priest,- another chimed in. -He came to my town years ago and took people with him to the mountains. Never did they return.-

-Is the truth,- some nodded.

-Then what do we have to worry about? He will leave and the crazies will go with him.-

-But he is like the trees large to the south. They grow and when you pull them out, the earth beneath is destroyed, gone with them.-

-Then what do we do?-

The boys took turns stealing glances at the conquistador's sword standing erect in front of their boss until a particularly drunk one burped.

-The Virgin is in those mountains, that part is true.-

They all nodded in agreement, -Of course.-

Hercules stuck a finger in his teeth.

-Throw it,- the supervisor ordered the group of men carrying a tire out of City Hall to toss it onto the growing trash heap.

-Sir, I found a room with food stored,- another worker reported. -Corn meal, beans dried.-

-Good, we will use it for the celebration tonight.- The supervisor turned his attention to the statues of saints and crucifixes being brought out. Another addressed him, -Found these in the basement.-

The supervisor walked over to inspect them more closely. The statues looked to be over a hundred years old but remained in relatively good condition except for a few fresh chips and cracks. -Beautiful,- he closed his eyes as he touched the crucifix.

-Put them up,- Guillermo's voice came from behind the man. The workers jumped to find the new mayor standing with the priest. The sightless wolf's head hung down to obscure the man's face underneath. The tiny interpreter spoke the priest's word, -We will use the church for that which it was built.- The men nodded.

As soon as the first bag of stockpiled food was carried out the front door, Hercules jumped to his feet. Within seconds, he'd left the tavern and was halfway to the church with his managers close behind. He tapped one of the boys nearest him, pointing at the food.

-What are you doing?- the manager yelled at the workers. The men didn't look impressed or scared by the group of pre-pubescent boys yapping at them so no one answered.

-Listen! To you I said something,- the manager focused on the supervisor, a middle-aged man with a bulbous forehead bulging over a tiny face scrunched into the bottom third of his head. The man turned casually, -You bastards need to learn some respect.-

-Fuck you, Ugly. It took us much time to stockpile that food. Is for town emergencies.-

The supervisor laughed, his workers following his lead. -You mean the rich were hording it while the poor starved? The people are dying in the streets of hunger, not is that an emergency?-

Hercules pulled his blade, his managers did the same; the men laughed harder. Hercules drew a line with his tongue on the bottom of his mouth, then opened it to let out a horrible sound. It was like the boy's lungs were trying to expel gravel, but instead of vomit, the deep, unsettling noise came out of his throat. Hercules sheathed his sword.

The smiles fell from the workers' faces as they watched the deformed little boy's body convulse with the dreadful guffaw. Before the supervisor could react, Hercules had pulled a knife from his belt and thrown it deep into the man's foot. At this sight, all the boys joined Hercules in their own laughter.

The workers grabbed what they had at hand for weapons. Hercules stopped his convulsions and roared. Drawing his weapon, he led his boys towards the nearing enemy until a low growl froze their feet in the sand. -Stop yourselves!- the interpreter shouted even though both groups had already done so. -Not do you fight on ground sacred.-

Hercules looked at the source of the order, wrapped in animal skins that blended into his own, rattlesnakes and scavengers and predators woven into the fur; they hung there, waiting for the priest's command to come to life. The boy walked casually to the interpreter. His steps were even and the pace was the same as any other child's. Before anyone else understood what was happening, the point of his blade was positioned to enter the little man's eye socket; the midget puffed out his chest as if ready for the sacrifice. Everyone around was dead silent except for the prisoner in the jail shack.

"Hercules, cut that shit out," Nish yelled. "You're not an animal. This isn't how things are done in a free city," Nish spat what little water he had in his mouth in disgust. "These people look to us as role models, we have to save them from themselves. Everything we've built rests on the head of a needle, now more than ever. Would you ruin that?"

The boy let his own moisture drool out of the opening in his cheek. The wetness spread to his eyes; he replaced the blade with his teeth, gnashing against each other inches away from the interpreter's nose. The growling recommenced.

-You have a friend so intelligent. Give your swords to the police,- the interpreter motioned to Fatty, who had been hiding around the side of the church.

-Are you fucking stupid?- the managers scoffed at the order.

-You are boys young,- Guillermo appeared next to the wolf as if he'd been woven into the fur and had decided to extract himself. -You kill others, you have sex with the prostitutes. You drink the alcohol and smoke. It is obvious this is not right. The crime in this town, the murders, they stop now. Not is it crazy to ask children not to carry weapons.-

-And you?- one of the boys asked.

Guillermo showed his empty scabbard. The boys turned to their boss, who had removed himself from the midget's face and was wiping the drool from his neck and shoulder. He motioned for them to throw their swords to the ground. The managers looked at their blades like they were scared to touch them. Hercules grunted and they did as they were told.

-All are welcome to the celebration,- the interpreter stated matter-of-factly before following the priest into the church.

"So you think Super Bowl next year?" Nish braced himself as the truck bounced along the dirt road. John smiled; Nish thought his friend was happiest and most talkative when football was the topic.

"You bet your ass and two joints of your backbone we'll have another ring by this time next year," the giant slowed the truck to a stop. Nish jumped out of the cab, feeling the small pleasure of his boots on the rocky sand of the road. He breathed the country air: yellow grass and manure. While he'd never admit it to his coworkers, he loved the earthy smell. The whimpering from the bed of the truck brought him back, the tickle of anxiety blooming in his brain.

"Hard thing," he thought about the first time he'd given a light payment. Deaf's truck had rolled by with a shooter eyeing him. "Right there you have to think of what you value. If life isn't up there, including your own, then fuck it."

"If you don't value life, even your own, then fuck it."

Nish didn't like talking around subjects or when his words were coming out of someone's unaccustomed mouth; he dug a fingernail into his cuticle before unlatching the fence for John to drive the truck through. He closed it and jumped into the cab for the final mile. "Yep," John was still smiling, "It ain't easy but you've got to trust that old man. He'll pull it off, just like before."

When the light hit the kennels in the distance, the attack dogs erupted, jumping and biting at their steel fences. John pulled around so the vehicle was facing the exit. The agents got out to pull the tarp off the bed of the truck, exposing the bound old woman. Nish grabbed her feet and pulled her to the edge, where John hoisted her easily onto his shoulder.

Nish led the way past the heavy machinery that he was now able to locate in the dark, "Here's good." John let her down gently as Nish unfolded his hunting knife.

"I've got this," he looked at his partner. The giant met his eyes, then nodded just the right amount of time before turning to walk back to the truck. When Nish heard the truck door shut, he walked to a nearby mesquite tree to cut off twigs, inspecting and discarding them until he found one that was just right. He neared the old woman again, she yelped frantically through the gag.

"Shhh," he placed a finger in front of his lips as he moved the knife to the woman's feet. She closed her eyes as tight as she could. There was a tugging, then the sound of the sharp blade working through toughness and her legs were free. He folded the knife. She looked at him with huge eyes; he wanted to pop the lazy one right out of its socket again. Like a skinless grape, he remembered the haunted houses of his youth. He inspected the dyed blond hair, the chin whiskers that had grown in thick. He imagined biting down on one and ripping it out of her face, root and all. He bet it would leave a hole that would last until the old cunt died.

"You haven't done anything, you were just in the wrong place at the wrong time. You're innocent," he looked into her good eye. "Run and find family as far away as possible, or make a new start for yourself. Either way, you're never seen in Dallas again." He motioned in the opposite direction of the truck, "Go."

She tried to moan something through her gag. He pointed sternly this time, "Get the fuck out of here," and she started off as fast as her frail legs would carry her through the brush.

As Nish walked back around the side of the kennels, the dogs went crazy again ramming their bodies against their cages. He squatted next to the kennel at the end and removed a piece of cloth from his pocket. Balling up the small section of the old woman's dress, he poked it through the crossed steel wires for the dog to sniff. Nish pulled the broken twig from his belt as he sat down. He pushed the heel of his boot hard against the kennel's gate, then pulled the steel pin out that kept it closed, quickly replacing it with the piece of wood that he jammed in awkwardly. He wiped his fingerprints off the steel pin before letting it fall to the ground, then got up to walk back to the truck.

When he climbed into the cab, John didn't act like he'd seen anything out of the ordinary.

"We're good," he hoped John would start the truck immediately. "Alright," the giant granted his wish. No questions, Nish bit his cheek nervously, but John didn't really ask many questions, in general.

"I've never killed an innocent person," Nish lay back on his bed. He never pointed the old woman in the exact direction of the ditch, he didn't let that dog out. She was probably far away from North Texas, cross stitching pillows and playing gin with other crones. And if she wasn't, then fuck it. He wasn't her keeper. You're given a shot, you make your own decisions, then you get what you have coming to you. Nish caught a piece of cheek flesh in his teeth and bit down hard as the death bell tolled. It seemed so loud it might as well have been right next to him. It rang low and everything else in the world stopped. The music of the celebration died, the people stopped their talking and laughing to watch Guillermo emerge from the church behind the priest.

-What passed?- Nish yelled to Fatty but the guard was standing on his tiptoes, craning his neck like he was trying to look over an invisible fence.

-I asked what passed, boy.-

-The brother of Guillermo is dead,- Fatty stayed on his toes, squinting like he was reading something in the distance. -The same as the Killer, God has taken them both to prove a point.-

Nish picked his teeth, -Not do you worry, Fat One. When a tree is cut down, not does it become a bird or a stream, but it stays wood. It is just in a state different. This is the same with the brother of Guillermo. He was a good man.-

Fatty shushed his prisoner as he climbed on top of his chair for a better view.

DAY 25

"Say you have a lemonade stand that makes $100 a week," Nish's dad leaned forward across the restaurant table to lecture his children. His own mother, sitting upright with perfect posture, looked around as if she was embarrassed she had been brought to a Tex-Mex place for the 'night out' during her stay. Nish figured she'd been expecting something fancier since she wore her weird colorful sheets and more diamonds than he'd ever seen anyone have on at once. He was embarrassed, too.

"If there are six people working at the stand, you give them each $10 and you keep the rest to buy supplies and to pay yourself. But," he held up a finger, "Say the workers want to unionize and demand twice as much. You would either have to charge more for lemonade, or start firing people," he looked at both his young sons, who nodded like they'd just been enlightened. "But if you raise prices, people are going to stop buying your lemonade and go to the guy down the street who's selling it cheaper, a guy who doesn't have unionized labor. So then you're out of business."

Nish spooned salsa onto the last of his chicken taco, wishing he'd been allowed to order beef. "What if you don't raise prices?"

"Great question," Nish's dad pointed at his son. Nish knew any question would be well received and that he should ask one before his brother got a chance. Dave had become even more annoying since starting junior high, he needed to know he wasn't that cool.

"If you don't raise prices, you do a couple things: cut down on the price of supplies, or cut your labor force. So when the six people working for you form a union and demand a higher salary, it's not like you can magically grow money to pay everyone; you have to pay half of them twice as much. So in other words, the union has made three people richer, especially considering all they're doing is squeezing lemons and mixing it with sugar, and it's put three people out of work. It doesn't help the working man at all, it makes some wealthy and the rest unemployed," dad leaned back for a second until another thought made him spring forward again, "And don't forget you're having to cut spending on supplies, so your customers are faced with buying an inferior product. Or, again, they can just go down the street and get higher quality lemonade."

"What if--" Dave started but was interrupted by the waiter.

"Any dessert?" he smiled. Nish noticed him trying not to stare at grandmother.

Dad grabbed the plastic dessert/drink specials menu standing upright in the middle of the table. "Don't mind if I do," he smiled at the waiter. Nish shoved the rest of his taco in his mouth so the waiter could clear his plate. He thought grandmother had looked horrified by the amount of food he'd ordered so he wanted to prove he could finish it all.

"We will not need that," grandmother dismissed the man with a wave of her hand and pulled something out of her bag. "I made these last night while you were watching your shows," she opened a plastic container and laid it in the middle of the table. Nish and Dave greedily reached for the sweets, glad they didn't have to wait for dessert. Their enthusiasm died when they looked at what was in their hands.

"Looks like dried poop," Dave said, causing Nish to laugh. Dad slammed his hand into the table, "Boy, don't think I won't take you outside and teach you some manners." He had that look in his eyes, Nish thought, like he had nothing but absolute hatred for whatever was on the other end of his glare. Nish could feel the eyes of people from other tables staring at him and his father and the woman in the weird clothes. He kept his own eyes down on his dessert.

He took a bite, "This is very good, grandmother." He immediately wished he hadn't spoken; maybe the people at the other tables had thought she was just Dave's grandmother and that he was a friend, coming along to the dinner and getting caught in an awkward situation just like the other diners had.

Grandmother straightened her outfit, looking a thousand yards ahead of her like she had for most of dinner. Dave took a bite of the sweet. Before he'd had a chance to chew, he made a noise like there was something delicious in his mouth, "This isn't like the Indian food in the restaurants around here."

"It's not Indian," grandmother snapped at him, turning to him for what seemed like the first time in the whole meal. "It's Sindhi. Does your father not tell you this?"

"Mother, it's not that--" dad started but the old woman continued, "Our family was driven out of our land by the Mohajirs and the British," she shot a glance at Nish's mom, who was looking into her iced tea.

"We were wealthy and influential, and we were pried from our homeland by those animals. But now," she looked like she was about to cry, "We are rich once again."

"I thought the Indian side of our family was from Gurjit," Nish took another bite of his dessert. Grandmother addressed the far wall of the restaurant, "Gujarat."

Dad put his arm around his wife's chair, "But your grandfather was British, son. Grandmother married him soon after she moved to the U.K." He had that steely look in his eye, like he didn't care what anyone else thought. "Isn't that right, mum?"

"Who's family was from Saurashtra," grandmother spoke through a tense mouth as she straightened the necklaces Nish's dad had bought her after he'd made Vice President.

The young girl stared at Hercules' exposed body with her mouth open. He took this as an invitation and grabbed the back of her head like he'd seen the older boys do. He just held her there like he was waiting for something to happen that he had no part in. A noise suddenly came from the front of the brothel. He heard the managers yelling and he reached for his clothes, only to remember his sword wasn't there. The stomping of boots spread quickly through the building until the sheet-door of the owner's room was torn back to reveal a salt and pepper haired man with a club.

-Stop!- he ordered, even though the boy was just lying there. The man paused as if he expected Hercules to speak but the child just looked at him. The man continued awkwardly, -The prostitution is now illegal. This house will be cleared out and the girls will be returned to their families.-

The girl on the bed didn't have a family; she looked to Hercules for directions. The man raised his sword at the boy, -Let her go!-

Hercules motioned for the girl to get off the bed. She gathered her things to leave. The man turned back to Hercules, -Put on your clothes,- but the boy had already begun playing with himself.

Outside, the whores were being escorted into the street. Policemen wearing hastily made badges handed out dresses to the girls. -Not do you need to be taken advantage of,- spoke the Chief of Police, who, with his mustache and body shape, appeared to be a sort of half-man, half-walrus. -You can to have your dignity, be members of a society good and Christian.-

Some of the girls eagerly covered themselves and cried softly into the rough material, others checked their nails like they were waiting for the scene to be over. One of the ex-whores pulled her dress over her strategically cut rags, then went up to a member of Jacobo's security staff to spit in his face. After he'd wiped the spittle away, she slapped him. The police laughed until he slapped her back and she fell to the ground.

-What are you doing?- the Chief pulled his sword.

-She hit me,- the teen responded blankly. -You saw it.-

-Not can you hit a woman,- the Chief looked frustrated that the boy didn't understand this basic idea.

-She hit me,- the boy responded with equal frustration. -In return, I hit her. It is the same.-

-Not is it the same.- The Chief whistled and two officers appeared suddenly on either side of the teen, one holding a rope.

The boy bristled, -This is the sexism.- The muscles in the hands of Jacobo's men tightened like they could feel the heaviness of their natural weapons dangling from their shoulders, swinging in wait. Jacobo stood shirtless in the doorway of his whorehouse, trying to catch the eye of Hercules across the street. When he did, the boy stuck a finger through the hole in his cheek to dig a nail into his teeth. The tiny swaths of blood wrapped themselves around the tooth and glided onto his half-tongue. He spat, then looked back at Jacobo and shook his head.

-This is a law new, also?- Jacobo asked the Chief loud enough for everyone to hear. -The sexism?-

The Chief pointed the sword in the boy's direction, -You are a pimp. The scum of the earth, using others for his own gain,- he spat on the ground. The earth swallowed the saliva immediately.

-These girls were paid for a service, they could leave whenever they wished,- Jacobo scratched his bare chest. -Where there is a demand, there will be one who supplies.-

The Chief whistled again, two more men neared him. The walrus squared off with the older boy, -Not if we arrest all those who supply.-

Jacobo stammered for a second like he'd lost the ability to talk. One of the men grabbed his arm to wrench it behind his back and the words returned, -Not can you do this! Not can you arrest me! To you I have given my whores, not do you have no cause.-

-The intention,- the Chief waved his hand. The men threw Jacobo to the ground to bind him and drag him off to the jail shack with the other boy.

-Oh!- Jacobo winced as he was pushed into the shack with his security guard. -The fucking smell!- He looked up to find the American squatting in the corner.

"The beans are running right through me," Nish picked at his ear. Even in the darkness of the tiny jail, Jacobo could clearly see the smeared red lines running all over the American's body, like his veins were on the outside of his skin. His hair was matted with blood and sand, he bit an invisible bug between his front teeth. Nish jerked his head up like he'd just seen the two of them there, "You have anything to drink?"

-What does he say?- the security guard asked.

Jacobo covered his nose with his shirt, -He asked for a drink.- He turned to Nish, speaking loudly like the American wouldn't be able to understand him otherwise, -Not do we have nothing for to drink.-

-Water, alcohol?- Nish grunted.

The two boys turned away. -Nothing,- Jacobo watched Fatty lock the door through the small window. -Fatty, smells so bad in here. Is there another place we can stay?-

-I am a police now,- the obese boy snapped. -Not can you talk to me like that.-

Jacobo stood dumbfounded for a second, then nodded, -You are right, Fatty, please pardon me.- He stuck his head as far out the window as he could without touching the vomit encrusted inside of the door. -But is there someplace else?-

Fatty finished locking up the shack silently. When he was done, he turned to go back to his post.

-Can you clean it?- Jacobo yelled after him.

-Do I look like a janitor to you?- Fatty yelled over his shoulder.

Jacobo cursed under his breath. -Can I clean it? Have you supplies?-

-Not do I have,- Fatty sat at the guard's post, stretching out in the sun.

Jacobo retracted his head from the opening, the thick darkness of the jail fell over his face. Nish pointed at the boy's security guard, "What's his name?"

-What?-

"His name," Nish stuck a fingernail in a particularly matted area of his hair. He tried to comb his hair with the filthy finger but it got caught; he pulled harder and managed to tangle it more.

-Javier,- Jacobo answered, getting his worker's attention. Nish pulled his finger out of his hair to sniff it.

-Javier, give me your shirt,- Nish ordered.

The brothel worker looked to his boss but Jacobo just shrugged.

-No,- Javier lifted his chin in defiance.

Nish stood up, allowing the juice to run down his legs. He walked over to the teenager until he stood only inches away, looking down at him. -Please.-

Javier looked up at the large American covered in his own blood and shit, then quickly took off the shirt and handed it over. Nish wiped his ass and legs with it, -Thank you.-

-Just like a Texan,- Javier muttered as he retreated to the window area with Jacobo. -Taking that which is ours.-

-What say you, boy?-

-Nothing,- Javier stood next to his boss, lifting his chin again.

-Texas was a part of Mexico for fifteen years. It has been a part of America for more than one hundred and twenty,- Nish folded the shirt to find some clean surface area. He squatted to get deeper in between his legs but his bowels accidentally released in a messy squirt on his hand. -And when it was a part of Mexico, no Mexicans lived there, only the people indigenous.-

-Already you have spoken on that,- Jacobo crossed his arms.

"Then don't let your friend say stupid shit," Nish wiped his hand with the shirt before resuming his cleaning.

Hercules stood outside his closed business, watching the side of the building being painted white. All down the street, government paid workers were covering the illustrations of beautiful naked women who looked nothing like the squat whores inside. The shanty houses that were deemed livable by the church volunteers who had flooded the area were also given a fresh coat. The others were torn down so their inhabitants could be relocated to the homeless shelter in the town's square.

Hercules followed a volunteer, a young woman with a pretty face as long as it was turned to one side and the scars covering her right cheek didn't show. She led two children, barely old enough to walk, towards the center of town. They moved slowly until the volunteer noticed she was being followed; she hurried them along, glancing back over her shoulder at the deformed boy in their footsteps.

They walked past the larger homes, then the preexisting buildings owned by the residents who had shown up earlier, then to the bottom of the square where the market seemed even more lively with Guillermo's officials arguing with merchants about taxes for a welfare program and a school. Staying on the outside of the square, away from the maze of vendors, she led the children past the more established businesses of the blacksmith, the stables, the farm equipment store, and finally to the American's old tavern that had been converted into the homeless shelter. Hercules stopped to watch from a distance as the workers loaded the last of the agave liquor onto a packed cart. He grunted at them, pointing at the cart as if to ask where they were taking it.

-To the desert, to dump,- explained the worker, a young boy that had been in the army for the battle against the traitors. -You should talk to the boss for work, sir,- he dug into his pocket to pull out a wad of paper with ink stamps. -There is much money to be made. This work is completed but there is much more,- he smiled.

Hercules nodded his thanks, running a hand over the top of his scarred head.

The volunteer squeezed the towel in the fresh water, then placed it on the American's skin to wipe off a layer of filth. She looked to be in her twenties; Nish leaned back so his crotch was more exposed. The woman wretched at the stench.

The walls of the jail shack had been torn down to accommodate the growing number of inmates. A dozen boys sat in the open, chained or tied to the metal pole, while workers constructed a larger facility.

"Little Hercules," Nish smiled like an old friend had seen him on his porch and decided to swing by. The boy walked to him, motioning at the tavern and moaning. "I know, it's fucked up." Nish spread his legs so the woman could get the feces that had dried and tangled into his leg hair. "But don't worry, I have a feeling that agave juice is the one thing this desert won't be taking back," he winked. He looked down at the volunteer, "That's it, get up under the hood. I've been shitting myself for days now."

The church bell rang; the world stopped to look at the house of worship as if the building itself was about to make an announcement. The volunteer dropped her towel into the fresh water, turning it brown. She stood to walk towards the church.

"Where the hell are you going?" Nish looked up at her. -Can you at least bring me some lotion for the sun when you return?- She wiped her hands on her dress as she walked up the church steps. He shook his head as he picked up the towel, "I have to do everything myself."

The volunteers, as well as the homeless they were volunteering for, emptied the square until only the merchants were left. Upon realizing there was no one to sell their goods to, they also followed the other townspeople. The prisoners sat alone in the empty square, chained to the pole, grains of sand flocking to their half wet bodies. Nish wiped himself until the last of the merchants was in the church, then motioned to the other inmates. They all jumped to his command, standing on one side of the pole.

-One, two, three,- the group pulled as hard as they could to one side, leaning back so their entire weight was working to loosen the earth's hold on the metal. Nish led them in a continuous circle around the pole as they kept their weight on the chains and ropes that held them. Hercules joined the inmates, pulling on the chains of a boy too young to do any good on his own. Nish saw the metal links lead to the shackle that gripped the young boy's tiny ankle. "You know in certain parts of China, there are still slaves. The snakeheads smuggle folks out of

Fujian same way we do out of Mexico, keep them working until they've paid off their debt. From one slavery to another."

"But they made the choice to take on that debt, same as the Mexicans with us," Bill responded thoughtfully. "Ain't slavery if someone agrees to it."

"Too bad the UN doesn't feel that way about it."

Bill spit the brown juice into his cup. Nish would usually never bring up the hated international body in Bill's presence but he felt they'd gotten to the point they could talk openly, have real discussions. He'd been especially impressed when Bill first quoted some of his favorite historians. There's more to people than you think, his father said.

"It's also different with the Mexicans since half of them are working to add another story to their house. They go back to Mexico and they're living the life."

"But not the folks who come over indentured," Nish cracked his neck so his spinal fluid percolated to the top of his brain. His head tingled with the freshly released liquid.

"They also agreed to it. Everyone makes their choices, that's what the world is. Ain't no free rides. Besides, there's been slavery throughout history. You think some Goth whined about being a slave of Rome? Do Germans still hold that shit against Italians?"

"You also have to think of how slavery was viewed back then," Nish ran a hand along his jaw line. "People didn't really recycle until a decade ago. A hundred years from now, folks will look back on those who didn't recycle and think what monsters they were. And recycling has a much larger effect on the world as a whole than slavery. But tell that to someone now and they'll look at you like you're crazy and keep on throwing their glass and aluminum in the trash while they argue for affirmative action."

"We destroy this earth," Bill nodded. "We might have been made in someone's image but it wasn't God's."

A cool wind choreographed the simultaneous bending of thousands of blades of grass in front of them. The firefighters cleaned their truck as children played little league games. Nish remembered his first time in the Fretz Park pool. His mother had let him go to the lowest diving board and he'd jumped too soon, hitting someone already in the water beneath him.

"That's the problem with history. The more you learn about human kind, the less compassionate you are."

Bill shrugged like he didn't see the downside, causing Nish to reevaluate the statement.

DAY 26

"I heard some asshole say once that he couldn't imagine 'what these people feel who feed on the pain of others'. Fucking ridiculous, like there's a food that has a different flavor from everything else in the world. But the thing is, our taste buds only register certain flavors, so you can predict any taste that's possible, you understand?"

The wood from the shantytown was brought to the jail area where workers had started building a larger structure. The inmates spread out evenly around the pole, a perfect sundial of leathery humanity. The police escorted two more boys to the guard's station where Fatty tried to write their names on a piece of paper along with their crimes.

"You writing down court dates, too?" Nish yelled from the ground. "When's my fucking trial?"

Fatty looked to the policemen, -Not does the fucking American understand that Spanish is spoken in Mexico.- The group laughed.

-Fuck your mother. How is that for Spanish?- Nish grabbed his exposed crotch. Fatty looked to the police who waited for him to retaliate, then picked up the large stick he kept next to his post. He walked close to Nish; the American licked his dry lips as he watched the fat jiggle under the boy's thin shirt. Fatty raised the weapon.

-Stop!-

The boy turned to find Guillermo with his escort. -What are you doing?- the mayor questioned him.

Fatty dropped the makeshift weapon by his side. -Nothing, sir.-

-Not will we have the brutality of the past in our town once again.-

-Yes, sir.-

"That's right, learn to keep your hands to yourself, you fat bitch," Nish tried to spit on the obese boy's leg but only a tiny wad of foam came out. Guillermo inspected the American from afar, making a face like he was trying to hold down his breakfast. -Clean these men. Give them water.-

-Yes, sir,- Fatty fetched his own jug of water while everyone at the top of the square watched. He returned to hand it to the American.

252

"Cheers," Nish grabbed the jug, drinking the entirety of its contents without spilling a drop. The other inmates hissed insults at the American's greed. Nish stood and the others fell silent, staring at him and chewing their own lips. He handed the jug back to Fatty, then put his hands on the ground like he was about to sit down. No sooner had he done this than he came back up with a handful of sand to sling in the fat boy's eyes. The inmates howled with laughter as their guard staggered backwards. The police moved in with their swords drawn.

-Stop!- Guillermo ordered. Everyone did as he said except for the prisoners. -Bring more water for all of them,- the mayor pointed at the police, who sheathed their swords to do as they were told.

Nish sat back down in the sand, -Good thinking,- he said to Guillermo. -I was mayor once, also, you know.-

-Is too much,- the vendor shook her head at the volunteer. A policeman standing around the corner watched closely. The elderly volunteer nodded pensively as if he understood the woman's argument, -I know it may seem like a lot but the children need a school.-

-Why? Some of them are richer than me. Some own all the land.-

-Some are, yes. And we will hold the land for them until they graduate. But the children poor have nothing and deserve an education. Not is this an idea crazy.-

The vendor sucked her teeth. -I will only give ten percent.-

-I understand how you feel but we must make sure the children have a place to learn. All they know how to do is fight wars and drink of the agave. Not do you want a better future for them?- the volunteer reached out his hand to lay it on the vendor's shoulder but the woman took a step away from him. He looked behind him at the policeman, who moved in. -Please, you need to give him the money,- he said like he'd spoken the words a hundred times that day, -Is for the children. They have been living in shacks, prostituting for a living, killing each other. Besides, I have seen how you overcharge.-

-We have all had the hunger,- the vendor muttered.

-Is an order of the mayor,- the policeman sniffed at the air.

-If I overcharge, then people not should they buy from me,- the woman gave him one last look of defiance before reaching behind her stall to produce a wad of the stamped currency, gritting her teeth as she handed it over.

-Too much,- the policeman handed half of it back. She mocked a bow as the two moved to the next stall.

Merchants pulling carts packed with their possessions moved past Hercules's old whorehouse. He watched as they continued down the road out of town and towards the settlements north of the dam. A teenage girl, her belly distended with pregnancy, spit in their trail, -All fucking crooks anyway.-

There was a noise behind him as a policeman came around from the side of the building, both hands on his pants to make sure they were back in place around his waist. -Good,- he shook Hercules' hand and walked towards the town square. The boy went around the side of the building to retrieve his money from the girl.

When the offertory plate made it to John's wife, she put in a ten-dollar bill. The giant did the same, and the children followed with one dollar each. Their son handed the plate to Nish; he looked at the boy staring up at him, then passed the plate on down the aisle. The boy opened his mouth like he was about to ask a question but John tapped him on the shoulder, his finger to his mouth. When they were in line for communion, John whispered to his friend, smiling, "You know, for a guy who talks so much about religion, you don't seem to care much for church."

"You ever notice how they pass around the donation plate just after they make you say the piece about how you haven't lived up to what God wants you to do?" Nish's dad whispered to his son; the boy smiled up like they were sharing a secret. "All this, shaming people into giving money, communion," he waved a finger, "Might as well be Catholic."

John's mouth fell into an exasperated frown.

"You think eating some pita and drinking some discount grape juice has anything to do with whether you're saved or not?"

John lowered his eyebrows, "It's a symbol."

"Exactly. Let them keep that voodoo shit." Nish raised his head to see the latest boys being brought to the jail. He remembered one from the battle against the traitors. He'd been stabbed through the bottom of his face and out through the front of it, making him more recognizable.

-Boy, what passes?- Nish smiled at him. The bastard opened his disfigured mouth to reveal a checkerboard of teeth. He let out a moan.

-How good,- Nish winked at him. He turned to Fatty, -Not will there be any children left to teach.- He laughed but the obese boy didn't turn away from his lunch to join him. The red man screamed at the guard, digging his claws into Nish's scalp as if it were the plump flesh of the child.

A stray dog limped up the stairs of the church like he was checking it out to see if it was acceptable to bring his family to. Nish remembered the stray he'd taken home in fifth grade. He thought it was something people were supposed to do, something people thought was good, but his dad tied the dog up and took off his belt. Every fifteen minutes for three hours he had to knock on his parents' door for his beating. After it was over, his father sat him down with tears in his eyes, saying how it hurt him more than it hurt his son. Nish took the dog out into the alley and beat it with his baseball bat until it looked like it was having a dream about running free. Before he'd started, it was like there was a force field around the animal. But he swung once, then counted his strikes until he reluctantly stopped when he reached the last number.

"Deaf people run around talking too loud because they don't have anything to judge themselves off of, only what they can read off others, you know? But they can't help not being able to hear shit," Nish looked at the boy sitting closest to him, a particularly hard looking one with an eye welded shut by a thick line of scar tissue. The child looked at the American, cracking his neck. The red man smiled back.

-Take care, my son,- the wolf had appeared next to Fatty with a piece of goat in a sauce of its own blood. The boy took the extra food with thanks. The skeleton of the blind animal passed in front of the jail, its dead eyes staring at the sun as it headed to the old bar.

Nish watched from the pole. -In the United States,- he spoke to his congregation, -There are all types of food. There is food in Texas, similar to the food in the north of Mexico but different: the cheese is yellow and soft, the tortillas are made of flour and the beef is from cows fat. Not do you dry it or cook it until it is like leather, it you can eat when it is still red inside. How rich.-

The other prisoners made noises of hunger or their hands drifted to their stomachs with minds of their own. Nish could feel the sun beating down on his skin without the grease to protect him; he covered himself as if he were ashamed of his body.

-There is the barbeque of Texas, also from cow but cooked slowly, for hours and hours, and with a sauce sweet and spicy,- Nish rubbed his mouth.

-I have heard of this,- a boy spoke up. -I have a brother in San Antonio in Texas.- He looked around at the other boys.

Nish nodded, -How good,- then continued. -There are other types of food of the regions different. In the Northeast, eat lobster and soups rich with seafood and cream. Pie of apple so delicious. In the South, barbeque of pig with sauce of vinegar, pie of pecan or pastry of peach over the ice cream,- Nish pinched his fingers together and

255

kissed them. -The food Cajun of Louisiana. In the West, you can eat the bison. You know bison?-

-Yes,- the same boy raised his hand, looking around at the other boys with pride.

-How smart,- Nish figured the child probably didn't know what the animal was but didn't want to embarrass him. -Is like a bull but with more hair. Very strange.- He pretended his head was the animal's, patting his fake hair and horns. The boys' eyes opened wide.

-And the hamburgers with beef American. Can to eat it raw, it is of quality so high. The steaks with the potatoes.- He felt a deeper hunger in him and scratched his head. -There are many breweries, you can to find all types of beer. Whiskey delicious from Tennessee and Kentucky,- Nish used his long fingernail to slice off the scab trying to hold his ear to his head. He surveyed the town with disgust, "In America, there are metal street signs on every corner. Electricity and running water, real football and women taller than four foot six. It's an amazing place."

The talkative boy sat upright, -I am going to the United States.- The other boys looked at their shackles and ropes that fell dead on the desert floor. Nish watched as they nodded their heads; he traced their chains back to the metal obelisk embedded into the earth. A drop of blood tickled him as it broke away from his skin to fall to the sand. "How much have I given this fucking land?" he watched the blood sink. The sand blew over it so no trace was left. "I've fertilized this piece of the Earth pretty well."

He looked north past the dam and the desert to Texas, where the shriveled brown brush spread and grew into gnarled mesquite trees, which dared to stand upright and grow old with moss that reached back down to touch the swampy waters along the gulf. He looked further to Dallas, where the forest and prairie met at its center, travelers getting a final glimpse of the South before entering the West and vice versa. How many body parts had he planted to grow what little the earth had given back?, he wondered. Family trees growing larger and stronger with each national law enacted by a clueless populace. "Just when you think the federal government's out to screw you, they pull something like Operation Rio Grande," the old man showed his teeth just before he let the refrigeration unit drop. The real estate agents watched as Deaf wiped off his hands. There was a cracking like someone had opened an egg in front of a microphone, then the unit hit the ground with a quick thud. The old man stepped back so his new ostrich skin boots wouldn't be touched by the growing pool. When Nish had watched movies as a kid with bad guys who just wanted to hurt others, he'd thought how oversimplified the plots were. But he'd come to see unmitigated greed, the gaining and exercising of power just for its own sake.

"Clean this mess up," Deaf stood upright, cracking his neck loudly. Nish waited until the old man was gone for him to do the same, feeling the satisfaction as he imagined the tiny bones snapping against one another in his body.

"You heard the man," he motioned to his crew. Rusty went to grab the mop, John bent to lift the unit. Nish followed the chains back down to the boys in the sand, dirty and hungry, watched by a guard working on his second plate of food. "This was over before it fucking started."

-Are there many Mexicans in the United States?- the boy addressed the others. He took off his hat and threw it on the ground. "That's bad luck," the man said. The boy didn't understand his words; the man repeated them angrily, pointing down. Nish looked down on the bed at the blue hat with the star on it.

"There's no such thing as luck," he turned to the fat, sweaty Englishman. His father's army buddy wore a gold chain sitting atop a soccer jersey, holding a beer with a look on his face like he wanted to smash it into Nish's skull.

The boy stood up taller. He benched over three hundred now, he reminded himself, he wasn't about to take shit from some limey boozehound. The man gulped down his beer, then burped before turning to walk away. What crude fucking people the Brits are, Nish thought of the visitors. Acting proper until they've had one drink, and then every woman's a 'cunt' and every man's asking for a fight. But somehow they had the audacity to look down on everyone else. He'd never known someone who could puke from drinking while the sun was still up and keep an air of superiority until he'd met his first Englishman, family excluded.

He walked to the living room to see what household items had been broken or desecrated that day. His father's army buddies had only been staying with them for half a week but they'd already marked their territory with a trail of destruction: clothes stripped off and left all over the house, dishes and pint glasses outside by the pool. They'd even gotten his mom's new dog drunk off lager and scotch. But what he disliked most was their habit of passing out wherever they happened to be when the mood hit them. Twice he'd had to kick them out of the way as he headed out to the early morning practice of his summer three-a-days.

"There he is," his dad played up his accent when his friends were in town; Nish clenched his teeth at the noise. The fat one that had been standing at his bedroom door didn't bother greeting him like the others. "This one's got to learn about real football," he smirked.

A bony Englishman with a dead tooth at the front of his mouth pointed at the boy, "Ugly, too." He turned to Nish's dad, "Looks more and more like you everyday, Arun." They all laughed with their mouths wide open and their beers sloshing onto the floor. Nish would have taken offense to the comment except that it was almost noon, which meant that the English had been drinking for long enough that all signs of decency had vanished.

"You should come watch the match with us today, lad," dad's eyes were lit up like a child's. He never called his son 'lad'; Nish put his head down to walk through the living room.

His dad called out to him, "Watch a gentleman's sport. Not like what they have here in the Colonies." They all laughed again.

Nish turned, "The Colonies? Really, dad?"

The Brits put on looks of fake fear like the boy was going to come back at them. He opened his mouth, about to comment on their living in the past, but his father's stupid drunk face smiling at him shut him down. "Jog on," Nish said in a fake accent, sticking his pointer and middle finger up towards himself. The Brits roared with laughter. "Ornery little bugger," one of them said as he walked out.

He passed his brother's room, untouched by his mom since Dave had left for college. After knocking over a picture on the pristine desk, he continued down the hallway to his parents' door. He knocked and heard his mother chirp from the other side, "Come in." He opened it to find her on the bed petting her new dog. It looked up at him and raised an eyebrow.

"Just holing up in here?" Nish sat down on the bed next to her. She nodded but kept looking at the dog.

"Alright, well I'm heading out for afternoon practice," he raised an arm to hug his mother and the animal in her lap uncoiled to strike him hard with its mouth open, its teeth catching Nish's upper lip. It felt more like he'd been punched and less like the dog had bit him in the face; Nish instinctively stuck up his hands like when boxing at the Y. The dog attacked again, this time clamping its jaws around Nish's arm. He threw it to the ground, kicking it hard in the ribs. The animal skid a little ways across the carpet, then scrambled to its feet. It lunged for Nish's throat but he caught it and slammed it to the floor, his hand pressing down on its neck as it struggled helplessly beneath him.

"Stop!" mom screamed. Nish couldn't feel his lip but noticed blood landing on the dog's fur.

"This thing fucking attacked me!"

Nish's mother hit him as hard as she could in the arm, the only time she would ever lay a hand on him, "Stop it! Let him up!" She was crying; Nish looked at her dumbstruck as she tried to beat him. He held the dog by its collar, "Okay mom, I'm sorry." He offered the collar to her. She grabbed it and pulled the dog close, squatting over the animal like she was protecting it.

"Don't ever say that in this house!" she stuck her face into the animal's fur.

"What?"

"The f-word. You never say the f-word in this house!" The dog was barking at him, footsteps running down the hall. Nish's father grabbed his son by the neck, throwing him backwards into the wall. "What happened?" he asked mom.

"I'm sorry mom, I didn't mean to," Nish's face was red. He felt like he was going to cry but the fat Englishman was next to him so he worked to hold the tears back.

"The dog bit me," he explained to his father. "I was just leaning in to hug mom and it attacked me," he blinked quickly. His father's strong hands clutched the boy's face to examine it. He turned to his wife, "That dog's on my last bloody nerve."

Mom looked up from the animal long enough to scream, "Get out!" until all the men had backed out of the room and closed the door.

Outside, the dead-toothed army buddy looked at Nish's face, "It'll be fine." He acted like nothing out of the ordinary had just happened. Even the fat one seemed unaffected by the scene that had just taken place. Nish's dad grabbed the boy's neck again, this time smiling, "Where you going, lad?"

"We have to watch tape and then practice, I should be home in a few hours," he felt like he was watching from outside his body.

His father patted his head. "This one's going to university on scholarship," he beamed at the others. "Not like the older one, costing me a bloody fortune."

Two sides of the jail had been completed, one facing the square and one the church so the majority of people didn't have to see the prisoners. Hercules walked around the side to find Nish crying and the other boys talking to each other or sleeping next to him, like the American was another stray gnawing at himself. The boy stopped. He put a finger between his teeth, then took a step back like that was the last time he'd ever see his savior, tied to a pole in the Mexican desert, starving and without his mind. The other inmates noticed Hercules and the group fell silent. Nish looked up, smiling at the boy like he'd been lost in thought. "Good to see you," he didn't wipe his face but looked around and spoke more quietly. "We ready to go?"

The boy nodded gravely.

"Good, that bullshit cash they're pumping out here won't mean shit in the outside world. We should have more than enough jewelry and pesos to make sure we're not stuck in coffins tomorrow," Nish got nauseous just thinking of the trip. His face turned sour, "Make sure you have your guys get your sword and my gun. If those truckers don't let us pay them, there are other ways to ride in style."

Hercules moaned lightly. Nish looked over at Jacobo, watching them from the other side of the pole. The American nodded and Jacobo looked at the ends of both walls to make sure Fatty wasn't coming, then crawled over.

-Jacobo will ride with us to meet the truck. That which is not taken by the truckers as payment, I will give to him to begin an opposition political to the wolf,- Nish watched Hercules' reaction. The boy's chin raised slightly. -For the survival of the town, we need to have a way to stop the priest.-

Hercules gave a horrible chuckle, lowering his eyes.

-Not are we animals,- Nish spoke through clenched teeth. -This is why I am here in jail, why we do not kill the wolf or his man little, why we let the people vote a mayor ignorant into office. Not will I have our last act here be something that will rot the foundation of what we have built. Without that, we have no legacy. We have nothing.-

Jacobo nodded his head in agreement. Hercules gave another low chuckle, then quickly stood up. Fatty came around the corner to find the three of them, -What are you doing?-

"See you tonight," Nish looked at Hercules. The boy walked away.

-What was that?- the obese guard yelled at the American.

"Nothing Fatty, go back to sleep." The last stragglers of scab from the claw marks on his back flaked off and fell to the sand.

DAY 27

Nish's dad set his glass of spiced gin on the arm of the couch and exhaled. The smell reminded his son of rotten trash, acrid but with something sweet and wrong about it.

"Never let anyone talk to you like that. Be proud of who you are," his father scratched the top of his head. "Especially not these bloody rednecks. These people wave around a flag of a country their ancestors were a part of for four years, a nation that fought a war with the righteous goal of keeping slavery alive. And they got their asses handed to them on the battlefield." He quickly turned to his son like he was going to hit him, "Learn your history, boy."

"Yes, sir," Nish nodded.

His father's hand went back to scratching his head. "Some filthy inbred saying that to you. He needs to learn his history alright. Next time that happens, hit him square in the gob and tell him he's nothing but the scum of the country your family's from. The descendant of criminals."

Nish was only half listening and wasn't sure which country his father was talking about. He figured asking for clarification in the middle of the rant wouldn't be wise.

"In fact, I want to know who this wanker is and I'll smack him."

"It wasn't really like all that, dad," Nish tried to downplay the remark. "And he's a teacher of mine so I don't think hitting him would help." His father's eyes opened comically wide like he couldn't believe what he was hearing. Nish had learned to avoid these conversations and was surprised he'd let himself slip and mention the offhand comment.

"A teacher," Nish's dad chewed on the word before taking a drink to wash it down. "We'll see about that."

One more year, Nish thought.

"Never let someone make you feel less than them, son. That sort of thing can eat you up," dad put a hand on his shoulder. Nish nodded, waiting for his father to remove the hand before saying he had homework to finish. He went into his bedroom to find his brother sitting at his old desk with a drink. "Yours if you like," Dave pointed

261

to the folded Union Jack on the bed. A year of practice squad at Rice had made the neck of Nish's shirt a choker; he pulled down his tie to undo the top button. "You don't want it?"

Dave shot a smug look at his younger brother, "Sure, I'll drape it over my SUV. Dad would've loved that."

Nish had hoped his brother could refrain from his anti-capitalist slights on the day of their father's funeral. "We'll see how much you like that Marxist shit when you're paying inheritance tax," he picked up the British flag and sat on the bed.

"I just need to finish school," Dave leaned back in the chair to place his feet on the desk. "Maybe not even that. A few friends of mine are going to India in the winter and I'm probably going to tag along. May stay there for a while, who knows?" Dave looked at the wall as he took a drink, "Guess you'll be the man of the house."

Nish felt the hit from practice deep in his neck; he jerked his head to one side and there was a crack so loud his brother made a disgusted face.

The night guard's head tipped backwards like he was watching the slowest shooting star in history move across the night sky. When it reached the back of his neck, his muscles jerked forward involuntarily, then began the slow motion fall backwards again. Nish relieved himself as he watched the obese boy. He hadn't felt nerves like this in a long time, he thought. He imagined seeing his mother and John again and the nervous piss escaped from him. He pictured mom after the surgery, her mouth moving again, her eyes looking at him. He figured she might talk a little shaky at first, like she did when she was getting worse, but soon she'd be using her walker, then walking without a limp or anything.

The noise of sand crunching under boots brought him back. He looked up to find Hercules and his handful of managers standing in front of the jail shack, Fatty being led towards him at gunpoint with a key in his hand. The manager escorting the fat boy kicked him to the ground and Nish got a better view of his face: a puffy black and red mask without a nose. After the whimpering guard had undone his shackle, the boy moved onto Jacobo. One of the managers brought Nish his clothes and the man tried not to laugh out loud. His cell phone was still in the pocket. He took the pistol from Hercules' manager, then motioned for all the other prisoners to be set free. -Now, let us wake up the priest and his man little.-

-What is this?- the trucker watched the horses bounce their riders up the path towards him and his son. The man reached under the seat to pull out a sawed off shotgun. Stepping out of the transport, he broke the weapon open to find a shell nestled into each barrel, waiting to be touched off. -Prepare yourself,- he instructed his son, who retrieved the revolver from the passenger's side glove box.

As the horses neared, the trucker made out their ominous riders in the moonlight: boys like incomplete skeletons but more sickening with what little skin and scar tissue they had holding themselves together, a hunched beast riding close to his horse like he was gnawing the back of its neck, and finally the man they'd come to retrieve.

-The army of the dead,- the trucker's son took a step towards his father. He pointed at the figure riding high in the back, -The devil?-

-No,- his father spit, -The American.-

The man they were talking about waved at the truckers like they were old friends. The boy was about to wave back when his father grabbed his hand to pull it back down.

The riders halted their horses in front of the truck, all dismounting except for the beast. As the skeletons neared the man and his son, they lowered their heads like animals inspecting the carcass of a predator. One touched the sword by his side; the driver clicked off the safety of his shotgun.

-Take him for there,- the American ordered. The skeleton henchmen turned away from the man and his son to pull the beast from his horse. Nish motioned for the boys to escort the wolf down the dirt road a ways. A second man, so small that he could have been mistaken for the beast's saddlebag or a large growth on the horse's ass, was thrown to the ground; there was a muted crack like two sticks wrapped in cloth being snapped and the tiny man wailed in pain. The trucker heard one of the boys mutter something to the others and they all laughed. The American turned to the man and his son. The trucker put an arm in front of his boy as the man jolted towards them, moving like his stomach was full of hornets stinging his insides. His hands seemed to be attached to his head, frantically digging through the ball of fuzz for a treasure. When he was within ten yards of the trucker and his son, they both recoiled at the stench. The son put his hands on his knees, wretching.

-Sir,- the American held up a small sack, the first of three in his possession. He blinked his eyes hard like something was in them. -Not will we be riding in the coffins,- he threw the sack at the trucker, who caught it and untied the string to find an assortment of jewelry and pesos inside. The American stepped closer; the man covered his nose while his son hid his face in his shirt.

-Only I ask you to allow us to sit in the bed of the truck. At the border, we will hide. But only then.- Nish motioned to the skeletons laughing at the midget with the broken leg. -Or I can make this decision more easy.-

The trucker held up the bag, -Is good.-

The American winked, then plunged both hands into the tangled mess of hair as he walked back to the boys.

The transporter would have shown up regardless of what was happening in the U.S., Nish thought, trying to not let his hopes get too high that John had smoothed things out with the old man. A foot soldier doesn't know what's happening in the Pentagon, and some Mexican running God knows what around the desert wouldn't have the slightest idea what was happening with a criminal organization in America. Still though, it was a good sign that he was being picked up.

Down the path, Hercules and two other boys stood watch over the wolf. It was on all fours, the parasitic animals clinging to its back and hanging down from its sides. As Nish neared, he swore the eyes of the things turned to him. Two weeks of agave and no pills, he told himself. -Return to the horses,- Nish motioned to Hercules' managers. They nodded and did as they were told. The wolf faced the land below them: the moon lit the river, a twisting line of silver cutting through budding fields to the sparkling town in the distance. And everywhere else, ghost towns and dead earth with ravines where creeks and ponds had been. Like the whole valley had been drained of its life, which was compounded and filtered into the city, Nish thought. He looked to Hercules, who handed him the second sack, then turned to follow his managers.

Nish addressed the vacant stare of the wolf, -I had planned on giving this to Jacobo to start an opposition to your government, but then I realized not is it your government. Not is there a reason the boy mayor can run that town on his own without your influence.- Nish squatted, his jeans making the movement more difficult than it had been when he was naked. -That town is my legacy, how I will live on. Not would I corrupt a mayor, but you are not a mayor,- he threw the bag in front of the wolf. The animal lowered his head as if to sniff at it. -You will move on, away from the town. Not will you ever come back.-

The wolf turned back to the valley with the sparkling city, then spoke in English, "You pay me to ignore those who are dying and those who are killing them. I am a man of God."

"Well, look at you," Nish grinned at the animal's ability to speak his language. His mouth fell suddenly, "We built that town from nothing, the rejects of the desert learning what freedom really is, be smart and live or be stupid and die. And you've done nothing but fuck it up. Not exactly helping the world's overpopulation problem."

The wolf looked back down at the sack. "The stone that the builder refused shall be the head cornerstone." Nish looked up, "What did you say?" His father stared at the frozen eyes and teeth of the animal as he put his hand on his son's shoulder.

"It's not easy, boy, I understand," he looked at his son. Nish thought he saw tears forming in his father's eyes for the first time in his life. "It's not enough," the voice came from the animal's mouth, Nish's breath got away from him.

"It seems like you don't fit anywhere, like there's no one but you," he patted the shoulder, "But you can start your own way," he looked level at him, "But you've got to be strong." The tears came out of Nish. "Alright, dad." His father looked to the animal lying in the alley behind their home. Even in the dark, there was sand visible in its dead eyes; Nish wanted to wash it out and close them. He reached for them and the animal jumped back. Nish lowered his head and stepped closer.

"It was a loud bugger but your mom did love it," Nish's father pulled him in. Nish wasn't sure how it worked after you've already left the house. He looked at his father's belt questioningly. His dad met his gaze, "You can't just carry this one to the park and leave it there. You don't know which parent will get the call from a concerned neighbor," he smiled as best he could, the wetness gathering at the corners of his eyes. He patted his son's head again but Nish recoiled. His dad didn't seemed to notice as he bent down to grab the hind legs of the animal. Nish picked his teeth, unsure of what to do.

"Come on, son," his father pressed his lips together sympathetically. "It's alright. This one will be between you and me." He motioned for the boy to grab the front; Nish's hand plunged into the darkness under the animal's head. It tried to turn away, "You know you cannot do this."

"Don't worry, boy. No one will know," his father soothed him. "It'll be like it never happened. Not everything has to leave a mark." He tried again to smile for his son, his mouth pressed shut like it was in the coffin when he'd snuck a look. With a closed casket, they didn't seem to care much about reconstructing the side of the head but his father's face was the same, like nothing had happened. Fear flashed through the animal's eyes for the first time, he reached downwards to grab its limpness.

Hercules squinted at the ground for the dropped third sack. He'd just found it when he heard the shot. The skeletons turned simultaneously; he moaned for them to watch the trucker and his boy. Hurrying down the path, he found the hybrid beast on its back, motionless. "This is why you always carry a revolver," Nish was on his hands and knees picking through brush. "So you don't leave cartridges behind."

The boy's breath doubled as he approached the wolf. The animal's head had fallen backwards to reveal darkness filling the throat that served as the cap for the priest. The blood drooled out the edges of the wolf's mouth; Hercules' body tightened as if a string had been pulled.

"But I didn't really have a choice," Nish chuckled nervously. "It's not like you turn left at the cactus and there's a guns and ammo store." Hercules breathed in the early morning air until his lungs were full, then he let out a roar so loud that everyone could hear. The trucker and his son, the skeleton army with their hands on their blades, the people in their beds in the valley below roused and looked upwards as if the sky itself had announced its awakening. All noticed but Nish, who finally found the cartridge. He nodded quickly, putting it in his pocket, then walked into the brush to bury the pistol.

The American and the boy emerged from the darkness of the path in silence. The skeletons around the tiny man looked at Hercules. The boy nodded and the translator howled in sorrow. He fell forward to collapse in grief but Hercules caught him by the throat and held him up, unsheathing the conquistador's sword with the other hand to open the man's stomach. A waterfall of sausage and innards fell to the ground; drool leaked out the exposed side of the boy's mouth. When the cascade of intestines had slowed to a red stream, Hercules dropped the midget. Nish nodded to the trucker, -We go.-

The man stood frozen for a second before jumping into action. He and his son climbed into the cab as the American gnawed at something on his hand. The boy stumbled through the dark towards the back of the truck, where Nish was waiting to help him up. The brake lights came on, illuminating the red skeletons that had gathered around the bed of the vehicle.

Jacobo ran to the light to whisper to Nish, -The third sack.- He held out his hand. The American nodded to Hercules, who held it high for all to see, then threw it on the ground past Jacobo. He continued standing as best he could as he unstrapped the conquistador's sword and threw it next to the loot in the middle of the skeletons, then sat down across from Nish. "First thing I'm doing is jumping in that pool," he winked at the boy.

The engine started. Stone and sand crunched under rubber; Hercules watched as the red boys looked away from the truck like it wasn't even there and circled around the objects on the ground, their hands drifting towards their weapons.

DAY 28

Nish pressed the blade against his skin and tugged. The resistance gave way to redness, which came out light and clear. "Fuck," he rinsed the razor. He was almost finished shaving and his face looked like it had been attacked by a wild animal. Hercules completed his two-hour soak, rising from the tub behind him as Nish splashed water on his face.

"Why'd we have to be born handsome instead of rich?" Nish smiled at the boy, who walked naked to the leather couches in Rebecca's living room. Sand stayed behind in the bath, covering the bottom of the tub. Nish's own cleaning had taken twice as long. He'd found sand in places he didn't know he had on his body; he wondered how humans deemed such a place habitable. "Motherfuckers who don't have the sense to move away from that desert deserve what they get," he said to the mirror. But after the cleansing, and a self-inflicted haircut, he felt like he was finally clean.

There was the sound of something breaking in the kitchen, signifying Hercules had decided to make a snack from what little food in the fridge wasn't rotting. When they'd come upon the house, Nish could tell Rebecca was on vacation by the mountain of newspapers in front of her door. The thought of her laying out on some beach, her perfect body barely covered by a bikini, caused Nish's hand to drift to his crotch. As he started masturbating, he felt a few pesky grains of sand that had been hiding in his pubic hair. He threw down the razor in disgust and turned on the shower for another cleansing.

Aisles of all kinds of food: fruit and vegetables and meats, fish from all over the world that had been alive less than a day before and thousands of miles away, and whole meals that were frozen and could be ready to eat in five minutes. Nish dropped to the floor to kiss the spotless tile.

"Fucking doctor's note," he drank from the traveler of whiskey in the parking lot of the pharmacy. "What kind of bullshit is that?" He looked to the boy, picking his teeth as he stared at a few errant hundred-dollar bills that were trying to escape from his savior's pocket. Nish followed his eyes to the money.

"Shit," he stuffed the bills back down. "Thanks, Herc." The pesos and jewelry had fetched a decent amount from the currency exchange and pawnshop but Nish's mind was on the money he'd stashed in the bus station locker before fleeing the country. After arriving in Harlingen the previous day, he'd paid handsomely for him and boy the ride in the back of a pick up just to avoid having to go through the San Antonio bus terminal. He hoped Dave had followed the instructions in the voicemail but his older brother had gone weeks at a time without phone service due to lack of payment. If that were the case, he knew Dave would put their mother's surgery on credit and wait for Nish to pay him. If there was one thing his brother knew how to do, it was finding ways to get what he wanted without spending his own money.

"We need to figure out what's going on," he muttered to himself, thinking about the trap that could be waiting for him if John hadn't yet smoothed things over with the old man. He felt the dead cell phone in his pocket. "Pay phones," he pointed to the sidewalk. The boy had dropped his pants to piss on the nearest car.

After trying John's cell and getting his voicemail, Nish dialed his own number, drinking from the traveler while he waited. Hercules squatted on the ground as he watched him. Nish pressed in his security code and was told he had five messages. The first was a hang up; the second was from John, saying he was heading back to Dallas and for Nish to meet him there; the third sounded like someone rubbing a sweater over the receiver with a high pitched whine in the background; the fourth was the doctor giving his condolences; the last, another hang up. Nish sat the phone back in its place. He ran a hand over his crude haircut, low enough that the open wounds in his scalp were easily visible. He'd discovered abscesses that had formed during his time abroad; the hair had fallen out around them and a couple leaked blood and puss all on their own. Fascinated, he stuck a finger on one of the holes. He could smell the stuff oozing out of him and wondered what it would be like to cook with. "If I had an ingredient no one else did, a monopoly," he chewed his bottom lip. "I'd be rich." His mind jolted back to the money, "Fuck it, we need to hit that bus station. Then we'll know for sure if they're still after us or not," he took a drink from the traveler, then let his hand fall to his side. Hercules pried the bottle from Nish's dead fingers as he stared into the distance. The boy pulled from the traveler before placing it into his own pocket.

They walked to where Nish had parked Rebecca's car, passing a man who looked to Nish like a construction worker on his break sitting on a bench and reading the newspaper. Nish stopped in front of him but he didn't look up. The red man, muffled by alcohol, tried to scream at the worker, just sitting there with his hands around the paper, his face jutting out. Everything about him practically begging to be attacked, Nish thought.

-What hour is it?- Nish asked as he calculated how high to raise his boot to kick the nose flat. The worker kept his eyes on the paper as he shook his head, "This is America, buddy. Learn English."

Nish stepped back. "Sorry," he felt his pocket for the whiskey traveler but came up empty. "First we hit the liquor store, then the bus station," he patted the boy's head absent-mindedly.

"After we get this money, we'll head back to Rebecca's and clean it up. Last thing we need is her coming back from vacation, thinking she's been robbed and calling the cops," Nish pulled from his new traveler, making no attempt to hide the bottle as they walked through the bus station. "Especially when our prints are on everything. If SAPD finds out we're in town before everything's set straight with the old man, that could be hazardous to our health. And we won't spend too long there anyway. We need to be off to Dallas before nightfall."

He felt something fly into his eye. He rubbed it until it was bloodshot and he was seeing the world through a fuzzy lens. "John didn't seem worried but you never know. We've got to be careful." He touched the eye again; it stung him and he quickly retracted his hand. "Got to pay for that pool, too. And the funeral. Always fucking money." He tugged his hair but it was too short to give him any satisfaction so he jammed a knuckle back into the eye.

The two passed into the locker area of the bus station. Nish didn't notice anyone following him or looking up from what they were doing. "The usual assortment of high society types," he chuckled to himself. A homeless man on a nearby bench laughed at something he'd muttered himself and the grin fell from Nish's face.

Removing the key he'd dug up earlier from the nearby park, now happy his brother hadn't followed his instructions, he used it to open the locker. Inside was the backpack with the two bags stuffed inside. Not a drop of blood on them, he noticed, impressed by the tidiness of his past self. Hercules stood on his tiptoes to get a glimpse of the money, drool leaking out through the hole in his cheek. Zipping up the backpack, Nish took it out and closed the locker. After taking one last look around, he winked at the boy, and the two walked quickly out of the station.

"Lunch is on me," Nish smiled at the boy. He was so pleased that he didn't notice the young man sitting against the wall making a call on his cell phone.

The car crept down the alley behind Rebecca's house before stopping at the back gate. "You never know if there are going to be stray animals back here," Nish tried to teach the boy but Hercules had already gotten out to piss on the asphalt. Grabbing the backpack, Nish stepped out and closed the door behind him. "Let's make this quick. We'll clean, grab any food that's still good and then head out." Hercules finished the traveler.

Nish opened the back gate to find the driveway empty, just as they'd left it. The two entered the house through the backdoor. Nish had just opened the bar in the great room to get a glass for his whiskey when he heard footsteps coming closer down a side hallway.

"I'm sorry," Allen stood to the side to let his manager enter the room. Bill raised a plastic bottle to his lips to receive a thick, brown stream of tobacco juice. "As I said, no need to apologize," he looked at the younger man as if it were an order. "That's what we're here for, keep our eyes open."

Nish watched from behind the couch as the two men walked closer. He noticed lines of parallel thin scars brushing the side of Allen's face and ear, new since he'd seen him last; Bill had to tap him on the shoulder to get his attention. Allen turned to find his manager pointing to the cracked back door with his pistol drawn.

"Goddamn you got some eyes, Bill," Allen pulled his own weapon. He moved towards the door slowly, focusing so intently on it that he didn't notice the man hiding behind the sofa he'd just walked past. He readied himself then pushed the door open, aiming his gun at invisible enemies on either side. The pistol fell slowly to his hip as he turned back to his manager, "Maybe we just forgot to close it." The arm holding the weapon was yanked through the opening, which was shut as much as possible to trap the man. Allen yelled out in pain, his crooked arm, now without the pistol, raising his hand to an unseen teacher on the other side of the barrier. Bill spit the brown juice into the bottle one last time as he strode to the door as fast as he could on his shot legs. Nish heard the heavy, off rhythm footsteps nearing him.

"Goddamnit," Allen winced in pain. Bill approached the injured man from the side to get a look at what had done this to him.

"Something got my ass, Bill. I saw it for a split second," he gritted his teeth. "Like a fucking gremlin or some shit." Bill couldn't see anything outside; he took another step closer.

"Get me out of here, man," Allen's mouth moved to produce his last words before his teeth were uprooted and shot out towards Bill along with pieces of his face. Bill stepped back, raising his weapon at the door; Nish pounced on him from behind. He knocked the pistol out of Bill's hand as both men fell to the ground. Nish landed on top with a corkscrew from the bar pointing at his old mentor's neck.

"Just calm down, Bill. I just want to ask you some questions."

Upon realizing who was on top of him, a corner of Bill's mouth rose in a smug expression. "Like you just asked Allen some questions?"

Hercules kicked the young man's body out of the way as he entered the house. Nish watched his mentor's eyes as they registered the sight but Bill reacted as if he saw deformed little boys murder his colleagues everyday.

"Why are you here?" Nish got his attention.

"You look like shit," Bill lifted his head so the corkscrew almost touched his face but Nish held the hand steady. "We're here because you're here. Whole world knows you're back by now," Bill's mouth worked as if he were about to spit but stopped.

The needle tickling Nish's eye acted up again; he tightened his hand around the weapon. "Is John alright?" he couldn't hold back anymore and dug his hand into the red eyeball. Bill pushed the corkscrew to the side, jolting upwards like there was a springboard under him and pushing Nish back. Bill went for his throat but Nish kicked him hard in the chest.

Hercules watched the men grapple on the floor beneath him, the bear of a man looking as if he were about to smother the smaller, then his savior poking a finger in the man's eye to slip out from underneath him. The boy turned towards the corpse. He squatted, running his hands calmly over the body until they found the dead thug's deer knife.

Nish picked up the corkscrew to stab Bill but the bear caught his hand in mid-swing. "What the fuck?" Nish struggled. Bill's hardened strength began turning the corkscrew towards Nish's face until he headbutted his old mentor. The blow stunned Bill for half a second, long enough for Nish to swing the corkscrew into his skull. The metal tool hit the curved bone at an angle and slid off the crown, taking a mess of scalp and hair with it but failing to penetrate.

"Fuck," Nish threw an uppercut but it didn't land square. The bear's scarred, concrete fist smashed into his face and millions of black molecules from each side of his vision grew exponentially until they covered his view.

271

He woke up half a second later with Bill reaching for him, red coloring the side of his head, matting the hair and the better half of his face. Nish kneed his crotch to no avail as his attacker began strangling him. Through the cotton, his eyes found Hercules only feet away, the pistol in this hand.

"Shoot him," Nish's yell came out as a whisper. The boy looked at the side of the revolver to move the safety back and forth like a kid playing with a toy, then looked back at his savior. Nish's finger felt something beside him on the floor. He touched it again, it moved slightly. Bill's eyes followed his victim's arm to the corkscrew; he trapped Nish's elbow against the floor, the full weight of his body now lying directly on top of the younger man. The rough skin of his assailant's throat was inches from Nish's face; he opened his mouth wide like he'd been sharpening his teeth his whole life for this single purpose, and sunk them deep into where the Adam's apple jutted outwards, trying to bite out the juicy lump underneath the brown leather exterior.

Bill recoiled, making a noise Nish had never heard from him before. Nish stabbed the corkscrew through the man's eye into what was behind it. The wad of tobacco fell from Bill's open mouth to hit Nish on the forehead before the bear collapsed onto his killer, dead.

"Fucking nasty," Nish rolled the man off him to wipe his face. "My fucking eyes," he stumbled to the kitchen.

Hercules patted his head as he squatted over the second corpse. The large man's gun lay under the sofa; he retrieved it, sticking it in his pants before joining Nish at the sink.

"Goddamn," Nish held each eye open, awkwardly positioning his head under the faucet. Hercules sat down at the table to pick his teeth. "That was smart, not shooting," Nish pulled his head out of the sink. "Who knows who you would've hit."

The boy pushed his fingernail deeper, letting the blood waft into his mouth.

"There was this one time when Bill and I caught some ghetto bastards trying to do something with company property the old man didn't like. Bill lined them up and pulled their leader to the front. He gave the guy two options: he could either have his hand chopped off by me and we'd call it even, or I'd chop off a thumb of each of his buddies instead. The guy argued at first, saying how things were fucked up, how he'd find us and kill us, all that bullshit. But then he started talking to his guys, trying to rationalize why them losing their thumbs would be better than him losing a whole hand, saying he'd lose too much blood and die versus them just being down a finger. Then they started acting tough," Nish kept his red eyes on the exit for Dallas. "Long story short, I removed three thumbs that day. And let me tell you, without a thumb, you may as well not have a hand. And as much as their leader talked about how he was going to kill us, he was dead within a week and we had nothing to do with it." Nish finished the can of beer and threw it in the back seat as he pulled onto the exit ramp.

DAY 29

"Try starting a company and see what happens. Just going through the incorporation process is painstakingly tedious," Nish guided Rebecca's car down the alley to the driveway behind his house. "But it's not just the fact there are so many details, because I could handle that. It's the fact there are so many tiny ways for the government to discredit the incorporation. If you're funding the company's bank account solely from your personal account, it throws up red flags and the government can hold you personally liable in the event of a lawsuit," Nish thought he saw something dart in front of him and slammed on the brakes; Hercules' head smacked into the dashboard. Nish put his foot back on the gas pedal, "If there aren't meetings held at certain times with certain people in attendance and someone keeping minutes, then the red flags go up again. And the whole reason why you incorporated doesn't mean shit if the government discredits you."

Nish saw the back fence of his house through his good eye. He tried to gently wipe the opaque liquid drooling out of the pus-filled sacks around his other eye but searing pain stabbed at him. He made a claw with his hand to dig his fingernails into the area around the infection. "But don't worry about the system," he chuckled sarcastically. "It manages to stay afloat with the incorporation fees the federal government's gotten out of you. They need to pay the judges and district attorneys somehow. I mean, there's going to be plenty of lawsuits and people going broke now that your business has failed." Nish slammed on the brakes again; this time, Hercules was able to catch himself.

"You see what the fuck I'm saying here?" Nish dug a finger between his teeth. The nail was too short to do anything so he made the claw again as he pulled into his driveway. Hercules stayed in the car while Nish got out, continuing to talk as if the boy was right next to him. Hercules stayed low, checking the rearview mirror again. Nothing. He opened the car door quietly to peek down the side yard to the street that ran in front of the house. Nish disappeared through the gate to his backyard and gave a loud wail. The boy jumped from the car, running to peek through a hole in the wooden fence. The man was on his knees, kissing the tile of the finished pool.

Turning back to the side yard, Hercules stayed close to the house as he crept towards the street. There were cars and trucks with no one in them, nothing directly in front of Nish's home. He ran his hand over the two pistols stuck into the back of his pants.

"You ever fired that thing before?" Nish grinned at the young man holding him at gunpoint in his kitchen. With the minor acne scars under both sides of his mouth and a zit forming between his eyes, Nish figured he was right out of high school. "With all the bad blood out for me, I'm surprised they'd send a new guy."

"Lots of new guys, now," the young man flipped around his tattered baseball hat to get a better shot. "Most of the old are dead or down in San Antone."

"Why?" Nish found it hard to focus while looking at the pimple in between the teen's eyebrows. He wanted to bite it off and suck out all the pus, add it to the collection on his own face.

"You fucked things up, from what I heard. Old man found out just what a dumbass his boy was after y'all created that shit storm, replaced him with the Queer. Only problem was, his boy didn't want to leave office," the teen worked his mouth like he was going to spit but held back. "Been like a goddamn civil war down there. Even spreading up here now, we had two old boys shot in Oak Cliff last week."

"What about John?"

The teen looked at him like he had no idea who he was talking about.

"The other guy with me in San Antonio," Nish bit his cheek.

"I don't know nothing about that."

"Too bad," Nish raised one hand slowly as if to motion to his assassin that he wasn't going to reach for a weapon. With his other hand, he took his wallet out of his pocket.

"Shit," the teen smirked. "You couldn't pay me enough."

"It's not money," Nish looked at him intently. "You see the thing with this wallet," he tossed it in the air to the teen. The gangster's eyes followed it, his hands naturally reaching for it just as Nish's fist connected with his jaw. Nish grabbed for the pistol but the assassin wouldn't give it up easily.

"Fuck," they fell to the ground, wrestling for the weapon. Nish thought how intimate it was, holding someone he hadn't known a minute ago, one of them about to change the other's existence more dramatically than anyone had in their past. He managed to get a hold of the gun and pointed it at the gangster's chest.

"Wait, wait," the teen said like it had gone too far. Nish pulled the trigger; the metal morphed, expanding as it went through the body and taking a decent chunk out the back with it. The teen looked at the gun, then at Nish with his mouth open but didn't say anything. Instead he fell to the tile, trying to breathe air but exhaling blood instead.

"Shit," Nish stepped back from the red pool growing from the gangster's back. He ran to the bathroom, returning with all the towels he had. The teen was coughing blood and staring upwards like he was mesmerized by something on the ceiling. The back doorknob turned, sending Nish scrambling for the gangster's pistol until he saw Hercules enter.

"Nearly gave me a fucking heart attack," he exhaled loudly. "Help me spread these out."

The boy made his way to the fridge to see what was inside.

The men at the loading docks pulled their weapons as the unfamiliar car neared. The window rolled down. "Louie," Nish kept a hand on the wheel and the other on his dead assassin's pistol.

"You're still breathing?" the leader of the group walked towards the vehicle. "House is going crazy. I heard you really started some shit down in San Antonio."

"I do what I can."

Louie put both hands on the roof of the car, lowering his head to speak to the driver. "I've seen a lot of new faces around here."

"You have another one," Nish motioned to the trunk. The thug took his hands off the roof to take a step backwards, like he wanted to physically distance himself from anything associated with the agent in the car. The tiny leader laughed, "You think I'm crazy?"

"I've got good money," Nish reached into the glove box to retrieve a brown paper bag. "Twice what you'd charge."

"And they find out I'm helping you?" Louie stayed where he was.

"I'm not telling them. Doubt he is," he motioned to the trunk again.

Louie moved his lips like he was about to kiss the air. He finally held out his hand for the bag, "Only way you'll get peace is if the old man dies, and that isn't going to be easy. People been trying for two weeks: his son, other motherfuckers from San Antonio trying to make a play. He's a hard man to kill."

"You heard anything from John?" Nish put the bag of money in the thug's hand but didn't let go. Louie shook his head, "Shit's been crazy." He pulled the bag away and opened it to find stacks of money stuffed inside. "I can see why they want to find you so bad."

Nish backed the car up to the dock where the thugs waited to unload the trunk, the tight-shirted Mexican among them. Louie watched as the crew carried the corpse wrapped in the blood-soaked towels, "Should have thrown him in the bathtub."

"I didn't want to get blood on my carpet," Nish gently touched his eye, searing needles struck deep into the socket.

Louie stepped close to the window again. "A lot of people are sick with that greedy ass old man, and this last move with his kid made him even more enemies. You deal with him and you may not even have to run."

Nish wiped the yellow liquid from the top of his cheek before pulling away from the docks.

The tight-shirted Mexican spat on the ground as the agent drove off. -Not will I allow him to escape this time. I will kill him for his disrespect.-

Louie threw the money on the table, "I doubt you'll get the chance."

The prescription rattling in his pocket gave Nish a solace he'd been without for weeks. Hercules followed through the halls of the medical center to the lobby. As a group of doctors left the dining area, one stopped as he saw Nish.

"Mr. Patel."

Nish turned to find his mother's old doctor in the middle of the pack. The man whispered something to his colleagues and they nodded, continuing out of the lobby without him. He approached Nish solemnly.

"Mr. Patel, I thought you might be by," he pressed his lips together.

"Why?" Nish put his hands in his pockets. The pill bottle cooled his fingertips.

"Because of your mother," the doctor's eyebrows pushed lower on his face.

"Oh yeah. I'd like to bury her in a couple days, if that sounds good. I'm not sure how long the body stays fresh or whatever."

The doctor looked around the lobby like he was embarrassed for some reason. "That's being taken care of. I just thought you should know the police should be in touch with you. They would have spoken with you sooner but they haven't been able to reach you."

A pain shot through his eye; he made the claw, trying to dig his short fingernails into his face. "Why would the police want to speak with me?"

"Because of the murder," the doctor looked stunned, like he'd just heard the news for the first time as it came out of his mouth. Nish stepped closer so the two were only inches apart, "What murder?"

"Didn't you get my voicemail?"

"I didn't listen to the whole thing. I figured I got the gist of it when you started off by saying my mom was dead."

"Well, someone disconnected the respirator," the doctor's face went from looking stunned to being annoyed at having to repeat the situation a second time. "I promise you it wasn't hospital staff. We're doing an internal investigation but there's absolutely no evidence there was any wrongdoing on our part."

"That's fine, I believe you," Nish extended his hand for the man to shake. "Thanks for all your help. You were great and I appreciate how you looked after my mom." The doctor stepped back from the pus-covered hand. "No problem," he turned to catch up with his colleagues.

Nish looked to Hercules; the boy was playing with himself with his eyes glued to a nurse walking past. "We need to make a visit to my brother."

The lights were on in the basement apartment but Nish couldn't make out anyone inside through the windows that barely peeked above the ground. He turned off the car's headlights and found himself engulfed in the young darkness. His dead assassin's pistol pressed into his back; he cracked his neck and got out. Hercules waited until he was gone to turn to the back seat where Nish had put the backpack with the money. He opened it, sticking his head in to smell the dollar bills. He inhaled deeply with his eyes closed. The sound of Nish knocking on the door of the duplex jolted him upwards. He zipped up the backpack and got out of the car.

"Will you get that?" Dave yelled from the bathroom.

"I'm already there," his girlfriend stepped over the shoes and sandals strewn across the entryway to open the door. She was met by a large man covered in gashes and bloody holes looking at her through a right eye that was no more than a red slit between two pus-filled balloons dripping their yellow liquid down the side of his face. Behind him stood a miniature burn victim so starved that parts of its body had fallen off in awkwardly angled chunks. She tried to slam the door shut but found a boot stuck in it.

"I'm here to speak with my brother," the voice came from the other side. She threw her shoulder against the door to no avail. Tears of frustration and fear welled in her eyes, "Go away!" she screamed but the boot didn't move. She kicked at the door as the toilet flushed.

"What's going on?" Dave walked out to find her struggling. He froze suddenly, "Fuck." He dropped to the ground to retrieve the baseball bat from under the couch.

"Some guy claiming to be your brother," his girlfriend stomped on the boot jammed in the doorway. "I'm not getting fucking robbed again!"

"Open it," Dave stood ready. She looked back at him like he was crazy. "Do it!" his fingers played with their grip as she jumped backwards. The door didn't move.

"Nish?" the shaky legs of Dave's voice barely carried the name to the front door. It slowly swung open to reveal the man and his creation.

"Wait, so this is really him?" the girlfriend took a step forward like she was trying to be tough.

Nish ran his tongue along his teeth as he inspected her. In his experience, the poorer black people were, the more expensive clothes they wore. If that held true, he figured Dave's girlfriend must have been upper crust: her hair in dreadlocks that fell to a ragged shirt with a picture a unibrowed woman on it, and ratty blue jeans with flip flops.

"So my reputation precedes me," he shot the girl a quick wink with his good eye. She recoiled.

"What the fuck are you doing here?" Dave raised the bat, standing too far away for it to do any good. Nish wiped his face, then rubbed the wet hand on his jeans. "I think you know." By the reaction of Dave and his girlfriend, Nish could tell Hercules had just entered behind him. "I didn't get a chance to see mom before she mysteriously died. I just wanted to make sure my brother was luckier than me."

"Dave didn't take any of your money. And if you want to see your mom then come to the funeral tomorrow. But get the fuck out of here," the girlfriend remembered to lift her chin to look more threatening.

"Why don't you two sit this one out," Nish looked at her like he was giving an order. She looked puzzled until the deformed boy lurched out from behind him. She put up a hand, "Oh no, fuck that," she stumbled backwards, landing on her ass. "Get that fucking thing away from me!"

Dave stepped forward, raising the bat at the boy.

"Calm down, Dave," Nish waved off his brother's melodrama. "They're just going to give us some time to talk."

Dave didn't lower the bat so Nish pulled the pistol from his back. Hercules advanced on the girl. She tried to crawl away but he grabbed a handful of dreadlocks to drag her screaming into the room at the end of the hall. Dave clenched his teeth in frustration as the door closed behind them.

"Don't worry about that," Nish scratched his head with the barrel of the revolver. "Who is she anyway, some socialist cunt you met at a drum circle?"

"She's a fucking intern at City Hall, dick. Her dad's a corporate corruption prosecutor working on taking down big oil. Your little animal harms a hair on her head and it'll cause a state-wide incident," Dave raised the bat, waiting for his pitch.

"You liberals are all the fucking same. You see a foot below the water and think it's the bottom of the ocean," Nish scratched an abscess and it broke open, leaking its contents down his head. He flicked his finger to get the blood and crust from it, splattering his brother's couch.

"You should be glad I didn't let mom see you before she died, what you've become," tears of anger welled up in Dave's eyes.

"Don't say all that cheesy shit," yellow drooled out of Nish's pus-sack. He let it fall down his face to the tip of his chin, forming a long single teardrop. "Did you kill mom?"

Dave slammed down the edge of the bat. "She didn't want to live! She told us both a hundred fucking times, no fucking machines. But you kept her alive in that nightmare."

"I knew you did it," Nish watched him through his good eye. His brother was crying now and Nish wanted to silence him for his weakness.

"You kept her alive so you could justify living your life of crime. Being the errand boy for fucking oil tycoons and slave runners. And you paid for it with filthy money she never would have touched, money I refused to touch."

"I did it because she was our mom and I loved her with all my heart," Nish felt his other eye get wet. Dave let out a sarcastic laugh, "Well that made one of you."

"What the fuck's that supposed to mean?"

"You think she didn't know about the pet cemetery you had going in the park? You think she didn't notice how whenever you had problems with someone at school, they'd magically get beaten up by black kids from up the road?" Dave dropped the bat to point an accusatory finger at Nish. "She might as well have died right after I left for college, being stuck with you and dad."

Nish felt his fingers tighten around the pistol in his hand, "What the fuck are you talking about?"

"Nish, mom thought you were a fucking monster," Dave stepped so close that Nish could smell him; body odor and incense, fucking commie bullshit. Dave reached out, pushing Nish's arm so the gun was pointed at the ground. "After she realized she had a psychopath for a son, she did everything she could to avoid you. But then you got lucky. You had a chance to catch up with her when she couldn't move away anymore. And then you latched onto her, telling her your fucked up thoughts on the world while she's frozen in a hospital bed. She suffered day after day and you were too selfish to care." A noise came from the bedroom and Dave turned his head.

"Do you have any idea what I've done to try to save her?" Nish said low.

"What the fuck's going on back there?" Dave took a step towards the bedroom and Nish hit him as hard as he could in the back of the head with the pistol. Dave stumbled forwards, then turned to look at his brother. He was about to say something but Nish smashed his left eye socket with the butt of the gun. As the beating commenced, Nish couldn't hear what he was yelling or his brother's pleas for him to stop, or what was happening in the bedroom or anywhere else. The pillows around his eye tore open from the movement, bursting their pus and blood onto his victim. Nish pistol-whipped him and said things that he knew were embarrassing when he screamed them out, about how he loved his mom so much and the things he'd planned on them doing together, but he only noted the feeling from a distance like he was checking it off a list. The body beneath him went from being a ripe banana to one turned into mush, battered and soft and discolored. Nish's mouth stopped first, then his arms went limp like they'd been fueled by the words he'd been yelling at the motionless body.

Reentering his own skin, he tucked the pistol into his back. He reached into his pocket to retrieve a wad of money, he figured about $10,000, and dropped it next to his brother. His face was totally wet from the bodily fluids; the smell forced his mouth open and his tongue to venture out for a taste of the concoction. Decent, he thought, but not quite there yet. After another sample, he called for the boy. Two minutes later, Hercules emerged from the silent room.

The stoplight reflected in Nish's good eye, turning it a lighter shade of the crimson slit on the other side of his face. He noticed a line of blood drying to his forearm, "We never should've left Mexico." He tried to open his hands but they wouldn't stretch out all the way. "Fuck it," he shook his head so hard the pus dripping down his face flew off. "I had to. And now I have to finish this shit. But as soon as I do," he turned so quickly to Hercules that the boy's forehead got a shower of the yellow ooze, "As soon as I kill that old motherfucker and find John, this whole country can kiss my ass goodbye. We'll go back to New Texas and live like kings."

Hercules wiped the pus from his face before sticking a finger between his teeth. He dug it deep so the bones split from the gum that held them together and the blood came thicker than it ever had before.

"You have to promise me something, though," Nish grabbed the boy's shoulders with both hands. "If I die tonight at Smith headquarters, you've got to promise me you'll send the money, everything I have, back to those boys." Tears formed in Nish's eyes, "Now that my mom's gone, those little bastards are the only real family I have." He embraced the child, "And you, of course."

The boy felt the man's arms around his back, only inches above the pistols hidden in his pants. While Nish cried, Hercules reached around him to continue picking his teeth with his head on the man's shoulder until the light turned green and people honked their horns at the parked car in the middle of the street.

The gate opened so two trucks could pull out of the parking lot. Nish waited until it had almost closed to slip through, ducking behind the bushes across from Smith Realty. The night guard, a man with the physical prowess and demeanor of a high school gym teacher, came out to check the camera Nish had obstructed. After clearing its view, he returned back inside and Nish made himself comfortable, nestling his six-pack of agave beer in his lap.

The parking lot slowly emptied of its last trucks and cars until there were only four left. Nish recognized Rusty's and figured he'd be driving with someone, probably as the senior man now. One of the trucks was the security guard's, and he assumed the car was owned by the receptionist, the reason why the old man would still be at the office at a quarter of midnight. The last vehicle belonged to Deaf himself. He refused to let anyone drive it, a ridiculous risk for senior management, Nish had always thought. And now it was going to come back to bite him in the ass. He pulled out his would-be assassin's revolver: five bullets for four men. He didn't store the right caliber of bullets for the revolver in his house, and didn't want to risk going to a guns and ammo store as Smith was involved with all the ones he knew. "Be nice to have John right now," he muttered to himself, then finished the last can in the six-pack. He closed the weapon and wondered if it sounded like a Roman's sword hitting its scabbard or an American GI popping in his clip before the transport hit land on some Pacific island. An image of the nun crept silently into his mind. She was standing like the Mexicans' virgin with light emanating from her skin and stilts made of blood. He shook his head; probably the smell of the agave beer, he figured. He pulled on his Smith Realty baseball hat, then pushed the cans aside to walk to the door.

The security guard heard the bell and glanced at the camera for a second, showing a man dressed in jeans, boots, a pullover and an employee cap, before casually buzzing him in. By the time the guard had finished tying his shoe, the man was halfway down the hall with his head still pointed at the ground to hide his face. The guard saw the dark ears coming out the side of the hat, "Shit!" he went for the shotgun by the side of his desk. Nish pulled his pistol and fired once; the bullet tore through the man's shoulder. The guard dropped below the desk as Nish charged, hitting the wood as he fired again. The safety of the shotgun clicked off just as Nish threw himself on top of the desk, ramming his knee into the hard wood. He found the bald man hunched over with the weapon in his hand. He pressed the barrel of the revolver to the guard's back and fired; the man looked up to howl in pain and Nish shot him in the face. The struggling body went suddenly limp like a switch had been flipped.

"Fuck," he stuck the revolver in the back of his pants, the barrel scalding his skin as he grabbed the shotgun. He thought of reevaluating his plan but figured it was best to keep moving, if he didn't have the element of surprise, he didn't have shit. He took the card from the guard's belt to swipe himself into the main office area.

"Hold on now, Nish," Rusty stood at the end of the room with his hands up. "No need to go killing innocent folk."

Nish stopped in his tracks, unable to keep from laughing out loud. Something rustled in the corner behind him and he dropped to the ground, firing the shotgun. The lead ate through a side of the man's chest. As he fell, Nish recognized him as a guy in Payroll and figured the accountant must have gotten a promotion. He turned back around just in time to see Rusty dive behind a desk.

Approaching his old coworker slowly, he shook his head so fresh liquid wouldn't obscure what little vision he had left in the infected eye. He climbed quietly onto one of the desks so his feet wouldn't be exposed, and sat there, the shotgun aimed at Rusty's hiding spot. He figured he could take his time now, he knew the old man wasn't going anywhere just like he knew nobody else had driven his truck to the office that day.

"Okay, wait, wait," Rusty's voice came from under the desk. A 9 mm pointed at the ceiling rose into view, then an open hand. "I'm putting it down, okay?"

Nish aimed the shotgun at where the head would soon be rising.

The voice came back more shaky, "Okay? I'm putting it down." The hand set the pistol on the desktop. "I got no problem with you, Nish. I'm getting up. I'm unarmed now." Rusty rose with a pouty look on his face. "Look, don't shoot my ass, alright? We used to be partners, remember? I used to let you win at beanbags," he raised the corners of his mouth nervously.

"You didn't let me win shit," Nish lowered the shotgun as he stepped down from the desk. He motioned his old coworker away from the pistol and limped to the desk, his knee not moving how it was supposed to anymore. He picked up the handgun to make sure it was ready to fire. "Old man in his office?"

"Yep, he's in there with Maria," Rusty nodded conscientiously. Nish tucked the pistol in the front of his jeans, the back already occupied. Rusty lowered his voice, "Between you and me, I hope you kill that son of a bitch. Dragging us into this fucking shit storm with his boy, making the Queer the head of San Antonio even though the Mexicans hate that shit. He's been making piss poor decisions. Too old for this work."

Nish wiped his face gently on his arm. Rusty continued, "You know he's got metal on that desk, so you better watch out. And a shitload of fire power--"

"I'm going to have to shoot you, Rusty," Nish interrupted. He retrieved the pistol from the back of his jeans.

"What? Why?" Rusty stepped backwards like he was going to make a run for it and try to jump through one of the bulletproof windows. "I'm helping you out, man! Why the fuck would you shoot me?"

"There are weapons hidden all around this office. I need to make sure you don't catch me when I start walking down that hallway, or on the way back," Nish shrugged. "I'm just covering my ass. You remember me teaching you about that."

"I know you did, you taught me so much and that's why I wouldn't ever do anything to you," Rusty spoke as fast as his mouth would let him. "I mean I already gave up my fucking gun, man, and you're like the big brother I never had except for my real big brother but that guy was a fucking douche--"

"This is happening. I won't kill you but I've got to put a hole in you," Nish raised the pistol. Rusty bent over and covered his head, closing his eyes like if he squeezed them tight enough, the bullet might magically bounce off his body. "You know if--"

Nish fired, hitting him in the flesh of his left leg. He screamed out, "Goddamnit you son of bitch motherfucker, you fucking asshole!" and rolled on the ground in pain as Nish checked the hallway and switched weapons.

"Goddamnit, Nish, why the fuck did you do that shit? Goddamn fucking shit!"

"Rusty, I have to shoot you in the other leg now so I know you won't follow me."

"What the fuck are you fucking serious? Shit come on man, come on," he tried cover himself. Nish trained the sight on Rusty's head, "It's either the leg or the brain, you choose."

"Oh fuck, man, fuck," Rusty slowly stuck his leg out as if he were placing it into a bear trap, then pulled it back into his body. "Come on, man, shit. You can't fucking do this."

"You know I will," Nish said matter of factly. Rusty stuck the leg out, yelling like an old warrior running into battle.

With the lights on in the hallway leading to Deaf's office, Nish remembered being a student at his grade school, seeing the place at night for the first time before a choir concert. He thought how exciting it had been as he limped to the CEO's office as quietly as possible. When he reached it, he found the door closed. Standing by its side, he tapped on the doorknob with the shotgun; the door exploded into a million splinters, throwing the weapon from his hand.

"I'll kill her," the old man yelled from inside, followed by a woman's voice, "What? How could--" and then a scream as Nish pulled the 9 mm from the front of his pants. He kicked at the bottom of the door, avoiding the gaping hole in the middle, to swing it open. He waited a second, then snaked the pistol around the doorframe to squeeze off three quick rounds. The wood below where his hand had just been exploded outwards. A second blast from the old man's shotgun peppered the back wall of the waiting room. Nish ducked, snaking his arm around again to shoot twice more. There was a woman's scream that got louder until the secretary burst from the office. Nish grabbed her; she looked at him for a split second, then threw her arms around his neck.

-Oh God mine, thank you, thank you!- she yelled in Spanish. The words barely made it through the cotton stuffed in Nish's ears. "Thank you so much, thank you. You saved me."

Nish put the pistol down on the receptionist's desk behind him to hold her with both arms. She looked at his infected eye and flinched, but continued, "Thank you, Nish, thank you." He began tipping her back into the open doorframe; her expression turned to confusion, and finally to horror. "No, no, wait," then Nish dipped her head low enough and the top of it exploded. He pulled her limpness back up, her mouth hanging down like a retarded person's, he thought. He wondered if her son would end up going to Holland with a grandparent or a foster family. He looked at the scramble in her skull, then dropped the dead body before picking up the pistol on the desk to eject the clip and push down the top bullet to see how many rounds he had left.

Deaf heard the clip slide back into the handgun. He kept the shotgun's sight trained on the door. He could hear footsteps walking away, getting softer and softer, until suddenly there were shots in quick succession like two people firing frantically at each other. They stopped just as abruptly as they had began, then one final shot.

"I got him, boss," Rusty's yell was faint from down the hallway in the main room. The old man didn't move. A few seconds later, "Sir, I got him. You can come out know." Deaf kept the sight trained on the door.

"He was coming around the corner and I killed his ass. Sir?"

"Bring him to me," the old man yelled.

Silent hesitation. "I'm sorry but I can't do that. He shot my legs up something awful."

Deaf ran his finger over the day's stubble on his chin. He stood, the shotgun still aimed at the door, and backed his way to the emergency exit at the corner of his office.

The old man looked through the window to find Rusty sitting in the middle of a dark circle with the gun in his hand, leaning against a desk like he was about to doze off. At the corner of the hallway was the body. He continued to the front door of the headquarters and took out his key.

The reception area was shot up like he'd heard; blood seeped out from the under the security guard's desk to glide across the tile. The old man swiped his card and pushed open the door to the main room cautiously to find a spotty, liquid red carpet had been laid out for him, leading the way from the nearest corner of the office to the corpse in the hallway.

"Shit," Deaf raised the shotgun but Nish was on him, knocking the weapon out of his hand. The old man reached for his knife; Nish grabbed his wrist and tripped him to the ground, making sure to land on top with an elbow in his ribs to break a couple. Deaf sucked his teeth in pain but struggled, pushing the younger man's arms back up until Nish slammed his forehead into the CEO's face. Then he did it again, and again and again until the old man was wearing a mask of blood and his hands and arms had lost their strength.

Nish pried the deer knife from his boss' weak fingers. He opened it and smiled. The blade caught a reflection and he lowered it quickly to Deaf's throat. "I saw this movie once that said every time you kill someone, a piece of your soul dies with them," he watched the old man spit blood from his mouth and blink his eyes so it wouldn't get in. Nish pressed the knife against Deaf's skin; electricity shot through his body up to his leaking eye socket. "But I've been killing motherfuckers for two weeks now and I can't tell any difference." Rusty slumped over in the background and the old man screamed as Nish began cutting off his face.

DAY 30

-One more please,- Nish ordered another coffee to go with his eggs and dried donkey. As the waitress turned away from the table, he grabbed her stubby hand, -Have you any liquor?-

-I am sorry,- she shook her head until Nish produced his wallet bursting with hundred dollar bills. -I will see what I can find.-

The drizzle outside provided a gentle background noise as Nish ate. He admired the décor of the restaurant: posters of famous Mexican crooners, various pieces of clothing from a mariachi's uniform, a mural on the back wall of a tall, muscular Aztec warrior and his black haired beauty standing atop a pyramid to look out at their empire. The waitress waddled back to his table with the coffee; Nish could smell the alcohol before she even sat the cup down in front of him.

-Thanks,- he handed her a hundred dollar bill. She motioned to refuse the large amount but he let it drop on the floor and began talking to himself as he ate; she took the money and left. Nish checked his cell phone again just to make sure he hadn't somehow missed any calls in the last few minutes but there was nothing. His other eye itched; he pressed a fist to his forehead. He hoped it was over, he thought, people had been retired in the past and even those most affected, their closest friends and partners, moved on. It was business, they all said. And everyone hated the old man at the end. He pulled his fist away from his face to scratch it into his fresh eyeball.

Nish closed the door to his home behind him, "Hercules, we need to get ready quick. Funeral's over but the burial's in an hour." There was a rustling from his bedroom, the boy limped out.

"Taking a nap, huh?" Nish pulled a can of the agave beer from the six-pack he'd just bought, walking to the boy the best he could with his injured knee. He held the can out to Hercules, who received a pat on the head for taking it. "I miss this stuff." Nish took a long drink, letting the liquid sit on his tongue before swallowing it down. "I know it's not

288

as good as what we had in New Texas but we won't have to wait long for the real thing," he winked at the boy. Hercules cracked his neck.

"All the booze we can drink, women whenever we want, being able to run things. That's the life," he sighed. "Well, soon enough. But right now we need to get our asses cleaned up and out the door." Nish looked into his room as if he were seeing it for the first time, like something had changed. When people are under less stress, they're more observant of the outside world, he remembered and smiled. He threw his wallet on the bed; Hercules followed it with his eyes, spitting the agave beer back into the can.

As soon as Nish saw the looks on his family's faces, he understood why Hercules had decided to stay home. Judgment from those who only educated themselves with one side of the story, he thought. "If they had any idea what I'd done."

Walking past rows of white foldout chairs sinking into the moist ground, Nish reached the preacher. He whispered something into her ear, mimicking the other attendees who followed him with their eyes. He took his seat in the empty front row, then turned to look at the crowd. Most of the family from England had made it, a couple faces from his childhood, family friends, new babies and young children he'd never seen before. Weird having all these people together, he thought, linked by the extinguishing of a life.

The child behind him coughed; Nish turned to look at him and the boy's eyes widened at the monster's face coming out the top of the black suit. Nish figured he was about six or seven, built sturdy, could probably handle a small sword well. "That's good," Nish muttered to the boy. A tickle came from his less infected eyeball and he dug a knuckle into it.

"I'm sorry we weren't able to see you at the funeral."

Nish spun around to find his aunt standing over him with her family. Upon seeing his face, she decided to leave an empty seat between them as she sat down.

"There was some shit I had to do," he realized how loud he was talking but didn't bother to adjust his volume. "This is the important part, anyway."

"Your busy schedule must run in the family," she adjusted her black gloves.

Nish looked at Dave's empty seat. "Brother always was a lazy fuck."

A quiet wave of murmuring swept over the crowd. Nish realized they'd most likely been in Dallas for a day or two, probably the farthest into the U.S. some had ever traveled. He imagined them all staying at the same motel, meeting up in each other's rooms for drinks before going out to eat barbeque and find some bar with a mechanical bull and take pictures of each other on it. A string of the pus coming from his eye, now the consistency of a thick slime, reached downwards until it dangled just over his mouth. He wiped his face with the sleeve of his suit jacket.

The preacher raised her arms to get everyone's attention before she began speaking. The sturdy little kid squirmed in his chair, catching Nish's attention. He turned around to wink at the kid; the boy's father wrapped a protective arm around his son.

After the short talk, the casket was closed and the attendees placed roses on it while Nish took off his shoes to scratch his feet; wool socks had always itched him, he remembered from his time at the communications firm. He'd sit down in the morning and by lunch he'd have pulled them down around his ankles and scratched the bottoms of his legs until they were white. One of the Brits coughed as if to remind him what he was doing was rude.

"It's just a shell," he continued his work. The body was lowered, the preacher spoke some more and Nish scratched and picked and clawed at various parts of himself until he noticed everyone gathering their things. He stood up to catch the eye of the preacher.

"Oh, yes, one last thing," she motioned for the crowd to stay seated. "A quick announcement before you go. Virginia's son has asked me to inform you all that he would like to--"

"I'm having a pool party tomorrow," Nish interrupted. "A lot of you came a long way for this and it would be wrong if I didn't show you some American hospitality," he brought the sides of his mouth up but it didn't catch on. "Beer, hamburgers, hot dogs, the usual. I know it's not really the season but it's such a beautiful pool." No reaction. "I know my mom would've wanted you all to be there," he nodded his head slowly as he sat back down. He returned to scratching his eye as the aisles cleared. At one point, the preacher put her hand on his shoulder to say something but Nish waved her off as he checked his newly charged cell phone for messages.

The last of the cars pulled away. Nish smiled, thinking how surprised they all must have been when he'd told them about the pool.

Eventually, the cemetery's work crew came to take the chairs. They loaded them onto what looked to Nish like a long golf cart made specifically for that purpose. He tried John's cell phone and left another message. The voicemail lady would cut him off and he'd call back to finish what he was saying, repeating this cycle until the mailbox was full.

Returning the phone to his pocket, he paced slowly through the cemetery as he made a mental list of what he needed to buy for the party. He hadn't expected the large turnout at the funeral, he'd never seen any of the attendees come to see his mom once while she was sick, so he'd need to double what he'd originally planned to get. They can go back to England with a taste for agave, he smiled to himself. He closed his eyes to crack his neck when his foot hit a tombstone.

"George Chambers, 1924-1999, May He Finally Find Peace," he read through the opaque curtain. "At least he had a good run." There was a tapping of metal on rock behind him; he turned to find a pistol aimed at his head. His right eye was completely shut and the left covered in ooze, unable to make out clearly who the person was.

-Devil, not myself do you remember?- her voice trembled. Nish wiped his face to see more clearly but still couldn't recognize the woman.

-By the grace of God, I have found you,- she supported the weapon with her other hand. -I have prayed every night for a month that I would be able to avenge my husband. My prayers were answered when you walked into the hospital yesterday.-

Nish picked at a scab on his head. More hot dogs, he thought. Europeans love sausage.

The woman walked closer as if to make sure she wouldn't miss. -I was visiting my husband when I saw you walk past with that animal foul,- she spat as if the mention of the boy put a taste in her mouth.

-Not can my husband talk correctly. He must go through the rehabilitation for to walk. Is because of you and your friends so cruel.-

The scab came off. Nish brought it in front of his good eye to examine the dried blood with pieces of hair stuck in it. After a thorough inspection, he placed it in his mouth and bit down. The woman cocked back the hammer. Her feet moved in place, getting a firm stance. -Not do you deserve it, but have you any last request?-

Nish ran his hands through his short hair, feeling the scabs and holes oozing their wetness. "Yeah. Seeing as this is America, why don't you speak fucking English." He grinned at himself, then stuck a nail in his teeth. It had grown just long enough to spread the bones apart and he felt a sense of immense satisfaction as he closed his eyes.

Hercules watched from behind the tombstone as the woman spoke to Nish. The boy crept closer using the cover of the graves. When he was ten yards away from her, he clicked his pistol off safety. Nish looked up at the clear grey sky, opening his mouth like an invisible giant was pouring water down his throat.

-For the people good you have tortured and enslaved, for the children without parents, and the parents without children.-

The boy stood upright, tiptoeing closer.

-God, please myself forgive,- she made a cross on her forehead, then steadied the weapon. Nish exhaled the last of the air out of him; the contents of the woman's skull burst forward.

"Fuck," Nish wiped what he suspected to be brain from his face. "You couldn't have come from the side?"

Hercules stood over the corpse. From the smell that came, she hadn't relieved herself since her last meal. Nish cracked his neck again as he walked to the boy. "Don't worry about it. Good job, little man," he winked. "If she'd just gotten on with it instead of bullshitting for half an hour, I'd be a goner." A prayer card lying on a grave caught Nish's eye: the virgin with stilts of blood that disappeared as soon as he'd blinked.

"Fuck it," he wiped his face again, walking past the boy. "Let's get out of here. I'll make some arrangements and the two of us will be in sunny Mexico by the end of the week." Nish smiled at the thought, then went back to his mental checklist for the pool party.

He'd gotten halfway to the parking lot when he realized where he was. "If you want to say goodbye, my mom's grave is right over here," he said over his shoulder to the boy. "If you're into that sort of thing." Hercules followed, not bothering to put the hot barrel of the pistol back into his pants just yet.

DAY 31

Nish leaned over to check his cell phone. No missed calls. People are never on time, he thought. Except for him; you ask him to something and he'd show up early. He touched his newly red eye, the pillows of blood and pus leaving only a tiny window for him to poke his finger to push the needles deeper. Fuck it, he thought, he's not going to be manning the grill until all hours of the night. If they wanted food, they should have shown up when he told them to.

He lowered himself into the pool, his body lighting up with the numbing cold and his teeth clenching involuntarily. It occurred to him that people may have entered through the unlocked front door and not realized to come to the backyard. There were signs all around leading the guests in the direction of his back patio but he guessed people thought he was joking when he said he actually had a pool. He lifted himself halfway out of the water, craning his neck to look into the living room but it was empty.

It would be good to see John again, he cracked open a can of agave beer on the ledge and let half of it drain down his throat. He'd been in the water long enough that it seemed to be the exact same temperature as his own body. He looked over to make sure the gate was unlocked, which it was. Sticking a fingernail in between his teeth, he dug it as deep as it would go. The scarred gum didn't break open so he sliced it with the nail. Blood drooled from his mouth to ribbon into the pristine water, red against white at first, then dissolving until no one would know it was there but him. A leaf danced its way nimbly through the air to land silently on the surface of the water; Nish remembered when he'd drawn a picture of a dinosaur as a kid. He'd thought it was perfect and was running to show his mom while she was rinsing something in the sink. The picture slipped out of his hand and went under the faucet, drenching it. He waited for it to dry but when it had, the paper was harder than it had been before and it looked crumpled from where the water had warped it. He cried and put it under a heavy book for the night, thinking that would get the wrinkles out, but it looked the same in the morning. He tried ironing it but it just warped the paper even

293

more and he realized you can't undo what you've done. You can't unsee what you've seen, you can't unfeel what you've felt and you can't bring people back to life. He watched the leaf as the water ate at it, finally pulling it under. He looked down into the still liquid to watch it sink and realized no one was coming.

LaVergne, TN USA
18 October 2010
201274LV00001B/48/P